S[...]
THERE'S SO MUCH ST[...]
MAKE OUT THE WO[...]
SHE HEARD IT. SHE[...]

Hello?

She is certain, in this moment, that her life will never be the same again. That something incredible—something impossible—just happened.

Hello.

It's just a word. She clutches the receiver hard against her ear, shock waves echoing through her brain along with the two syllables she couldn't possibly have heard just now. But she did.

She knows she did, dammit. She heard it.

Yes, it's just a word. A word everyone says when they pick up the phone. But nobody—*nobody*—says it quite like *he* does.

PRAISE FOR WENDY MARKHAM'S
THE NINE-MONTH PLAN

"A wonderfully touching romance with a good sense of humor."

—*Romantic Times*

"Touches upon the simplest of pleasures, the purest of joys, and the most complicated of human emotions."

—*Heartstrings*

"A winner! . . . loved these two people."

—*Romance Reviews*

Please turn to the back of this book for a preview of Wendy Markham's upcoming novel, *Bride Needs Groom.*

Also by Wendy Markham

The Nine Month Plan
Once Upon A Blind Date

Hello, It's Me

Wendy Markham

WARNER
FOREVER

NEW YORK   BOSTON

Cover design by Diane Luger
Cover illustration by Andrew Condron
Book design by Giorgetta Bell McRee

Warner Books

Time Warner Book Group
1271 Avenue of the Americas
New York, NY 10020
Visit our Web site at www.twbookmark.com

Printed in the United States of America

First Paperback Printing: March 2005

10 9 8 7 6 5 4 3 2 1

*This book is dedicated to
the 9/11 widows and widowers,
in solemn memory of
their lost loved ones.*

*And, with love and gratitude,
to Mark, Morgan, and Brody.*

Hello,
It's Me

Prologue

Hey, you've reached Andre. You know what to do. Wait for the beep and don't forget to leave your number."

Clutching the phone between her shoulder and her ear, Annie Harlowe dabs some hot glue onto the straw wreath frame she's working on. This seashell wreath was a brilliant idea, if she does think so herself. Tomorrow, she'll take the kids back down to the bay beach with bigger buckets and get—

Beep.

"Hey, babe, it's your lovely wife." Annie plops a sun-bleached oyster shell into the glue. "Where the heck are you? I made dinner and I'm waiting for you, so get your butt home before I eat without you. I fed the kids already. We were on the beach all day and I'm starving to death. Love you."

Her stomach punctuating the good-bye with a ferocious rumble, she disconnects the call and sets the cordless phone aside.

The rice and seafood dish she concocted earlier is probably drying out in the oven. She made up the recipe herself, as she often does, based on ingredients she happens to have on hand. Sometimes, the results are disastrous; other times, sheer brilliance. This risotto-ish paella-ish concoction will most likely fall somewhere in between—although given her appetite, the hot glue would probably taste delicious right about now.

Shouldn't Andre be home by this time? What time *is* it, anyway?

Annie never knows, and usually doesn't care. She hasn't owned a watch in years, and the only clocks in the house are on the microwave in the kitchen and the nightstand upstairs.

Too lazy to leave the screen porch with its view of the dunes and the Atlantic, she glances at the sky. The sun set a while ago, and it's getting dark.

Today is the longest day of the year, isn't it? The summer solstice. Or was that yesterday? Or tomorrow?

Annie frowns, as uncertain of the date as she is the time. Sometime in mid-June, that's for sure. She meant to buy a calendar back in March when she saw them on clearance in White's, but it slipped her mind. Boring, organizational things always seem to slip her mind.

Oh, well.

It's safe to say that it's past eight o'clock, summer solstice or not.

Andre should have been home a while ago. He called after he got in from fishing earlier and said he was stopping by the beach for a swim before heading home. That should have taken him an hour, maybe a little longer at the most.

Annie shrugs off a chill that has nothing to do with the ocean breeze and the fact that she's wearing only a bikini top and shorts. Her husband has been known to lose track of everything while he's in the water.

What if . . .

Nah.

Annie reminds herself never to watch *Jaws* again, even if the only other viewing options at three A.M. are decades-old sitcom reruns and infomercials.

Shaking her dark curls, she turns up the radio again, having muted the volume before making her call.

She smiles, hearing the opening chords of an old Todd Rundgren song. She and Andre saw him in concert a few summers ago, when she was pregnant with Trixie. She likes to tease Andre about his affinity for seventies pop music, everything from Rundgren to Barry Manilow to disco.

"Hello, it's me . . ." Annie sings along with Todd.

She selects another shell, this time the delicately sculpted interior of a whelk. She squints at her masterpiece, deciding where it should go, then squirts more hot glue onto the wreath frame.

"Mommy?"

She looks up to see Milo standing in the doorway in his pajamas, his tattered blue blanket trailing from one hand. His green eyes, the same translucent sea-glass shade as Annie's, blink sleepily above freckled sun-pink cheeks. He's always wiped out after a day at the beach, poor guy. She shouldn't have promised him that he could stay up until Daddy gets home.

"Can you fix my cape?" he asks, hiding a yawn behind his little hand.

"Sure. C'mere." Annie quickly plunks the whelk into the rapidly setting dab of glue, then turns to help her son.

"Why don't you go up to bed, buddy?"

"I want to see Daddy. I have to tell him about my tooth."

Annie smiles, tucking one edge of the blanket into the back of his pajama top at the nape of his neck. Milo lost his first tooth today. He almost swallowed it, but Annie saw bright red blood against the white flesh of the apple he was munching and realized what had happened. The tooth was safely rescued from his mouth and is already under his pillow, waiting for the tooth fairy.

"Okay, you can wait up," Annie promises, finishing with the blanket and bending to kiss his tousled, sunstreaked brown hair.

"Thanks, Mommy. Is my cape back on?"

"Yup. You're all set, Superman."

"I'm Batman," he protests.

"Oh, right. I almost forgot."

Annie grins, watching him "fly" out of the room, arms straight out in front of him, "cape" flapping behind. Milo has been one superhero or another on a daily basis for a few months now, ever since Andre rented the *Spider-Man* DVD and let him stay up late to watch it.

"Isn't this too scary for a five-year-old?" Annie had asked, poking her head into the living room to find father and son cuddled on the couch, munching popcorn, riveted by the action scene on television.

"Nah, he's fine."

He *was* fine. Milo, unlike Trixie, doesn't have nightmares.

His younger sister has been waking up screaming on a regular basis pretty much all of her three years. When she was an infant, the pediatrician told Annie and Andre she was probably just hungry, or collicky, or teething. But when she failed to outgrow it, he informed them that it was night terrors.

"She'll probably grow out of it," Dr. Blythe promised.

So far, she hasn't.

Night terrors. Poor Trixie, Annie thinks, perusing the array of shells scattered across the table. At least by day, her daughter is as happy-go-lucky as the rest of the family.

Yup, life is good. Married to her college sweetheart almost ten years, living in a seaside town where they both make a living doing what they love, with a boy and a girl and a roof over their heads. A leaky one, but nothing's perfect. Annie figures her life is about as close as you get to that.

In spite of—or perhaps, because of—her contentment, she can never quite shake the sense that it could all be snatched away in a heartbeat.

Especially now, with Andre late and no word. Knowing she's a worrier, he always calls to check in when he's been delayed.

Well, maybe he stopped by their spot for a while. Did he have the metal detector in the truck when he left this morning?

Probably. He keeps it close at hand these days, certain he's closing in on the treasure he's spent years searching for on a lonely, rugged stretch of coast called Copper Beach, not far from here.

"You're searching for buried treasure?" Annie asked incredulously when he first told her. A more logical woman might have dismissed him as a loony tune, but not Annie. She was captivated by Andre's tale of a ship that wrecked off the coast a hundred and fifty years ago, carrying a fortune in gold. According to Andre's grandfather, one of the sailors managed to haul a chest full of doubloons off the sinking ship and rowed it to shore. He buried it in a secluded spot near a stand of copper beech trees—hence the contemporary name for the place—but died before he could ever retrieve it.

Even Annie, gullible as she tended to be, had to ask, "What proof do you have that this ever even happened?"

"My grandfather told me," Andre replied, "and his grandfather told him."

For Andre, that's proof enough. The Harlowe family goes back many generations to the seafaring days of eastern Long Island. They're as much a part of this place as the boulders, tide pools, and surf.

Whenever Andre has spare time, he's out there on the beach, combing the sand and rocky crevices and roots of the trees with his metal detector. Sometimes Annie and the kids go with him. They like to fantasize about what they'll do when Daddy finds the treasure.

"Money can't buy the most important things in life," Annie always feels obligated to caution.

"No, but it can buy time. Time, and freedom," Andre likes to say. "Time and freedom to be together, babe. There's nothing more important than that."

True. It seems as though their entire relationship has been about craving togetherness.

If they had more money, Andre wouldn't have to leave the house in the wee hours of the morning to head out to sea on his commercial fishing boat, usually just as Annie is crawling into bed after a long night of working on the handicrafts she sells at boutiques.

"Why can't you come to bed early and get up early with me?" Andre likes to ask, though he knows her reply by heart.

"Because I'm not a morning person. I do my best work at night."

When Andre's feeling romantic—which he typically is—he'll reply to that with a quirked eyebrow and a suggestive, "Oh, yeah? So do I."

Annie exhales through a puffed out lower lip, blowing the sticky tendrils of hair from her forehead. It's muggy for June, and for this time of night. Time to put the air-conditioning units in the bedroom windows. She'll have to remember to have Andre drag them out of storage this weekend. She hates to hit him with a lengthy to-do list every time he turns around, but there's always so much to keep up with around the house.

There's something money can buy, she thinks, shaking her head. A handyman. And a maid.

"Come on, Andre, where are you?" she mutters, poking through the pile of shells.

Suddenly, it occurs to her that he might have found the treasure. Maybe that's why he's so late. Maybe he's loading doubloons into the truck bed.

Annie grins, picturing her husband tossing shiny gold coins gleefully into the air.

Nah. Too far-fetched, even for her wild imagination. People don't actually find pirate treasure on Long Island in this day and age.

As she strains for the familiar noise of tires crunching on gravel that announces the arrival of Andre's truck in the driveway, Annie's ears capture instead an unsettling sound.

At first it's more faint than the crashing surf in the distance, but it quickly grows louder, closer.

A siren.

Annie stands with a razor clamshell poised in her hand, head cocked, listening.

The siren passes, and she pictures the ambulance racing along the highway a few blocks from the house, headed east. It can't go far. There are only a couple of miles and relatively few houses between here and the spot where the tip of Long Island's South Fork gives way to the Atlantic.

A couple of miles, a few houses, and the stretch of coast where Andre likes to surf. And Copper Beach.

Annie's heart races.

Something's wrong. She can feel it.

Calm down, babe, she can hear her husband saying. *Don't let your imagination carry you away.*

I can't help it, Annie retorts, using the back of her wrist to shove a black curl away from her face. *Imagination is my forte.*

She frequently says that to Andre, and he always grins and agrees. Imagination *is* her forte. Her best friend—and occasionally, her worst enemy.

When she was pregnant, every abdominal twinge was the start of a miscarriage. When one of the kids got their first case of the sniffles, it was a potentially deadly respiratory infection.

It's not like she can chalk up all her worries to a common case of novice maternal anxiety. If anything, her imagination has grown more vivid over the years. Whenever their old house creaks in the night, she's certain it's a ghost or a serial killer on the prowl; if a mosquito bites her, she's convinced it's carrying West Nile disease.

It's almost enough to make her wish for the uncreative psyche that ran in her family until she came along.

Almost.

When you come right down to it, Annie wouldn't trade her unconventional life for the lives of her staid and stable nine-to-five Upper East Side dwelling older brothers, or her widowed, remarried father, now retired to a microcosm of golf and bridge in Boca Raton.

She'll take a weathered three-bedroom Montauk cottage, a treasure hunter/fisherman husband, a superhero son, and a night-terror–plagued daughter over anything the rest of her family has. Give her flexible self-employment and freedom any day, even if it comes with a vivid imagination and a tendency to imagine all sorts of unlikely scenarios.

Like Andre being eaten by a great white shark while swimming.

Annie should never have doused her clams with so much hot sauce at dinner last night. A wicked case of heartburn led to wee hour channel surfing, which led to *Jaws*, which led to her being deathly afraid for her husband's safety now.

Which, of course, is ridiculous.

Andre is at home on—and in—the sea. He grew up out here; grew up sailing, swimming, surfing. He's fine.

Of course he's fine.

He'll be home soon, Annie promises herself, ignoring the chill creeping along her spine as she goes back to her hot glue and her shells.

Part One

June

Chapter
1

Hey, you've reached Andre. You know what to do. Wait for the beep and don't forget to leave your number."

Clutching the phone between her shoulder and her ear, Annie pipes another stripe of red icing along a rectangular sugar cookie, wondering how many stripes an American flag has, anyway.

Not that it matters. There aren't fifty white dabs of icing on the square of blue to the left of the stripe. Who cares whether a flag cookie is historically accurate, as long as it tastes good?

Beep.

Annie sets down the tube of icing and presses a button to disconnect the call.

Someday, maybe she'll leave a message, just for the hell of it. Even though Andre's phone, its battery long dead, is lying useless in a drawer, along with the other personal effects the hospital handed her that awful day.

Or maybe someday, she'll stop calling Andre's cell phone just to hear the sound of his voice. Yes, someday, she'll stop paying the bill just so she can do that.

After all, it's not as though she can afford it. She can't afford much of anything these days. The Widow Harlowe is in dire straits, reduced to decorating cookies for some wealthy Hamptonite's Flag Day soiree tomorrow night, just to earn enough cash to keep her kids in Fritos and Lunchables.

She's lucky, she supposes, that her friend Merlin's catering business has taken off so quickly. With the summer season about to kick into full swing, she can probably count on enough cookie-decorating gigs to carry them through the summer.

Then what?

Come September, the rich New Yorkers will flee back to the city, leaving the eastern end of Long Island to the hardy natives once again.

As much as she cherishes warm days in the sun and surf, Annie has always preferred the off-season. She may not have grown up here as Andre did, but she learned early on to resent the "outsiders" who clog the roads and restaurants and beaches from Memorial Day to Labor Day.

Now, she resents that they've become her livelihood.

Hell, what—and who—doesn't she resent at this point?

The summer people, the bill collectors who call incessantly, even her friends—especially those who are happily attached.

The Widow Harlowe can't help but notice that the world is one big Noah's Ark, made up of twosomes, which leaves her . . .

Alone.

You're all alone, Annie.

A tear drops into the icing stripe, bleeding red across the white buttercream background.

Annie is instantly reminded of Milo losing his tooth in the apple the day her world turned upside down.

The day that began as happily as the endless string of others before it, and concluded with sirens and a uniformed policeman at her door.

And now . . .

Well, now she's all alone.

Everything happens for a reason, Annie.

Andre said those words frequently—usually, whenever she was complaining about something that hadn't gone the way it was supposed to.

Everything happens for a reason.

Yeah. Right.

What reason could there possibly be for this? For Andre dying, for Annie being left alone to—

Thud.

Annie looks up at the water-stained kitchen ceiling.

Okay, not quite alone.

In fact, never alone. Never, ever alone.

Being with her children 24-7 has taken some getting used to. She still isn't accustomed to not having a minute to herself during the day; nary a reprieve from her maternal watch.

Andre always liked to take Milo and Trixie off on adventures, leaving Annie with time to herself. She hasn't had that in almost a year now, but was too caught up in her grief to realize how much she craved relaxing solitude until recently.

"What are you doing up there, Milo?" she calls, even as she wonders whether the teardrop will make this cookie taste salty. She can always toss it aside . . . but then she won't have a full sixteen dozen, and Merlin—or his snooty client—are sure to notice.

Not that she's even met the man who's throwing the Flag Day shindig. But it's safe to assume that anyone with a waterfront estate in Southampton is snooty.

"I'm practicing, Mommy," Milo shouts down the stairs.

Practicing. Of course.

"Just be careful, okay?" she calls wearily, wiping her eyes on the hem of the violet-sprigged vintage apron she's wearing.

She pipes another, slightly jagged red stripe on the slightly soggy cookie and concludes somewhat illogically that it'll serve the snooty Southamptonite right to taste the tears of the Widow Harlowe.

Thud.

"Be careful, Milo!" she calls again.

"I will, Mommy," comes the reply. "That time I almost did it."

Sure he did.

He almost flew.

That, after all, is what he's been trying to do for months. Blanket/cape tucked in at his neck, arms outstretched, he attempts to take off on a daily—all right, an hourly—basis. His mission: to fly up to heaven so that he can tell his dad about his lost tooth and his new superhero action figures and his first year of elementary school and everything else Andre has missed in the dozen months since he died.

Annie hasn't the heart to tell her son that his mission is futile. How can she, when she herself spends every day longing for one last chance to tell her husband that she loves him?

With a trembling hand, she pipes another strip of red frosting, this one more wobbly than the last, on the cookie. Oh, hell. It looks like a zigzag, not a stripe.

Annie tosses aside the icing tube and reaches again for the phone.

She dials the familiar number and waits as it rings once . . .

He's not going to answer. You know that. Even when he was alive and remembered to turn on his cell phone, he never picked it up on the first ring.

Twice . . .

Usually, he didn't even grab it on the second. Remember how you used to picture him fumbling around, looking for it in his pocket, or the glove compartment, or at the bottom of his beach bag or tackle box?

Three times . . .

He's not going to answer it. Not ever again. Why do you keep doing this to yourself, Annie? Fifty bucks a month just so that you can hear his voice?

Four . . .

There's a click, and then the inevitable:

"Hey, you've reached Andre. You know what to do . . ."

She waits for the beep. This time, when she hears it, she doesn't hang up.

This time, heedless of the tears streaming down her face and plopping like raindrops onto the half-finished flag, Annie leaves a message.

"No, Andre," she wails, "you're wrong. I don't. I don't know what to do. I need you so badly . . ."

Unable to force another word past the aching lump in her throat, Annie hangs up and stares bleakly into space.

Raising a crystal flute to his mouth, Thomas Brannock IV takes a sip of champagne. It's odd, he thinks, to be drinking champagne when the afternoon sunlight is still beaming through the tall paned windows of his dining room. Happy hour is a few hours away. But then, this isn't pleasure; it's business. These days, what isn't?

"What do you think? Too dry?" the stereotypically buff, good-looking, and effeminate caterer asks, hovering at his elbow.

"Too fruity," Thom pronounces, biting back the urge to add, "No offense." He sets the flute on the freshly polished surface of the eight-foot table that once graced his grandmother's Newport dining room. "Can I try the other one again?"

"Of course."

The caterer—Marvin? Myron?—flits back to the first bottle and pours sparkling amber liquid into a clean flute.

"Keep your menu in mind."

Thom nods, sipping the champagne. What is the menu again? By the time he's finished selecting the beverages that will be served, will he even remember? Or care? Did he ever care in the first place?

"Dry enough?" Marvin or Myron asks.

It isn't, but Thom declares it just right. If he doesn't stop now, he won't be able to focus on his work. And when one is at the helm of a major financial institution and in the midst of yet another corporate takeover bid, one cannot afford not to focus.

"You're working again tonight?" Joyce pouted earlier

when he informed her that he couldn't join her for dinner after all. "I thought you were on vacation."

Vacation.

Yeah, right.

He might be spending as many long weekends as he can at his sprawling seven-bedroom summer house complete with tennis court, pool, and private beach, but he doesn't really use the amenities. His mind is rarely far from his Wall Street office.

He watches the caterer make a note on a clipboard, then look up with a brisk smile. "We'll do the red wine next."

"Actually, Marvin—"

"It's Merlin."

Oops.

"Actually, Merlin, I'll leave that up to you."

"But—"

"I'm sure you'll choose the right wine."

"But—"

"If you'll excuse me, I'd better get back to work," Thom says in his best class-dismissed tone, pushing back his chair.

I could have been a teacher in another life, he thinks, watching as Merlin takes his cue and begins clearing away the wineglasses and bottles.

A teacher.

Sure.

That would have gone over well with Mother. About as well as Thom's sister Susan's temporary engagement to an actor a few years ago.

An Oscar nomination and a Beverly Hills mansion

meant little to Mother. What counted more than anything, as far as she was—and is—concerned, is breeding.

Susan's former fiancé didn't have it.

The man she eventually married does.

And so, Thom thinks with a twinge of resentment, does Joyce.

Like him, she grew up on Park Avenue and in Southampton. Like him, she went to all the right schools, rubbed shoulders with all the right people. Like him, she's attractive and intelligent.

Unlike him, she's thinking that it's time to settle down.

As far as Thom is concerned, his whole life has been settled down. He can't help longing to . . . well, *unsettle*.

"I'll just need to go over a few more details with you, and then I'll be out of your hair," Merlin announces, breaking into Thom's errant thought pattern.

Which is for the best, of course. There's little time for daydreaming when you're in the midst of putting together a multibillion-dollar corporate takeover bid to acquire a New England–based seafood packaging company *and* hosting a political fund-raiser for two hundred of your—make that your mother's and sister's—closest friends.

With a sigh, Thom dutifully shifts his attention from fantasies about unsettling to Myron and his clipboard.

The next morning, Annie is sitting on the porch swing with Trixie, a bag of cheese crackers, and a dog-eared copy of *Green Eggs and Ham* on her lap when she hears the rain-dampened gravel crunching at the foot of the driveway.

For a moment—the most fleeting and exhilarating of moments—she thinks, Andre's home.

Then the familiar, bittersweet sound of crunching gravel gives way to the sight of a vehicle that isn't Andre's truck. No, it's Merlin's latest ridiculously extravagant purchase: a cherry red 1956 Mercedes convertible 220S.

What that cost him, Annie thinks ruefully, would probably provide a few years' college tuition for one of her kids.

Stop resenting Merlin's money, she chides herself.

His money *and* his newfound domestic bliss with Jonathan, a Sag Harbor antiques dealer he met in January.

A lifelong friendship shouldn't be tainted by the fact that Merlin is living happily ever after while Annie has become the Widow Harlowe, as Merlin himself dubbed her after one too many margaritas at a Cinco de Mayo bash last month.

Merlin's black sense of humor, along with his checkbook, have buoyed her through this stormy year. She has no right to resent his good fortune.

"It's Uncle Merlin, Mommy!" Trixie shouts, leaping from Annie's lap. "Hey, Milo! Come outside! Uncle Merlin's here!"

Setting the book aside, relieved to have this morning's third round of *Green Eggs and Ham* curtailed, Annie rises and brushes the Goldfish crumbs from her faded cutoffs. Belatedly, she realizes that the porch floor will be covered with bugs again in no time. She had to hose it off last night after she found the remains of a grape Popsicle hosting the entire ant population of Montauk less than a foot from the screen door.

The house is falling apart inside and out. It's hard to believe that she and Andre ever pulled up in front of this nondescript two-story cedar-shingled bungalow and proclaimed it their dream home. What were they thinking? They'd have been better off in a condo or a townhouse, like her brothers said. Especially now that Annie alone is responsible for the upkeep of antique plumbing and wiring and a huge yard she actually once, in her misguided new homeowner's bliss, considered an asset.

The grass needs mowing, the shrubs need pruning, the beds need weeding, and she really should move the snowblower back into the shed. It's been sitting under a tree since she abandoned it there in the middle of last February's single significant snowstorm, after realizing she had no clue how to use it. That, like lawn mowing, was Andre's department.

Not that he ever got much practice. Splurging on that snowblower as a holiday gift for him one year was wishful thinking on Annie's part. Since childhood, she had longed for a white Christmas to rival Dickens's London, but it never happened. Not once. At least, not way out here on Long Island.

Snow rarely fell on Montauk that early in the season, and it never stuck. The big storms, if they came, were reserved for February; March, even, when crystalline drifts had been known to blanket crocus blooms and emerging daffodil spires.

"I'll get my white Christmas sooner or later," she used to tell Andre. "You'll see."

"Only if we get rich enough to buy a snowmaking machine," was always his reply.

"Are we going for a Serengeti motif now?" Merlin

calls, stepping out of his car in Gucci loafers and wading gingerly through the puddles by the car, then the over-grown grass on the lawn. "Should I be keeping an eye out for roaming zebra? Or their droppings?"

"Bite me," Annie retorts to the man who is more of an uncle to her children than her two married older brothers ever have been.

"How about I loan you my gardener instead?"

"If I could afford a gardener, I'd trade him in for a maid."

Annie stoops to pick up a small plastic army guy; the kind that kills one's bare foot if one steps on it while blindly feeling one's way to the bathroom in the middle of the night. She's done that enough times to have de-clared all army guys "outside toys." She probably would have been better off banning them to the garbage while Milo was busy with his flight training in another room.

"I'll loan you my gardener *and* my maid," Merlin offers.

Descending the porch steps, Annie laughs and says, "No, thanks."

"Come on, Annie. I'm serious."

"I know you are, but—"

"Let me do something nice for you."

"Merlin—"

He reaches into his pocket and pulls out a platinum credit card. "Here, if you won't let me loan you Enzio and Louella, take this and go shopping. It'll get your mind off your troubles. My treat. For your birthday."

"My birthday was in April."

He shrugs. "I never got you a present."

"You gave me a Prada bag."

"Oh, that." Merlin dismisses her with a wave of his hand. "It was a knockoff."

"Yeah, right."

About as much a knockoff as Merlin's Dolce & Gabbana silk shirt. It's a creamy shade of yellow that offsets Merlin's salon-manufactured golden hair and the expensive spray-on tan he gets weekly at a place in Amagansett. It's becoming more and more difficult for Annie to remember that this tawny, buff boy toy was once a pasty, dark-haired misfit in husky-sized dungarees.

"Go ahead, Vivian," Merlin urges. "Take the card. Go shopping."

Vivian. Annie rolls her eyes, recognizing the reference to Julia Roberts's character in *Pretty Woman,* a movie she and Merlin watched together at least a dozen times back in high school.

"Vivian?" she echoes with a laugh. "And I suppose that makes you Richard Gere?"

"Only in my dreams, cupcake," he says as she forces the credit card back into his hand.

"Thanks, but no thanks, sweetie. Even a shopping spree won't cure my problems these days."

"Never underestimate the power of retail, Annie." Merlin looks down, where Trixie is tugging his sleeve. "What's up, gumdrop?"

"Uncle Merlin! My name's not Gumdrop!"

"Oops, sorry . . . Jujube."

Trixie screams with laughter.

Annie struggles to fight off a pang of regret as she watches Merlin scoop her daughter into his arms and swing her playfully overhead.

Andre used to do that.

Does Trixie even remember?

Annie's youngest child's memory of her father is fading with every day that passes. Unlike Milo, Trixie rarely mentions Andre now, and when she does, it's in the abstract, rather than a concrete memory.

Behind Annie the screen door groans and bangs. She turns to see Milo stepping out of the house, cape fluttering around his bare legs.

"Milo, where are your shorts? And your underpants," she adds, catching a flash of exposed white skin as he bends to pick up a glass jar from the step.

"In the laundry."

"Did you have an accident again?"

"No, I just got tired of wearing pants," Milo says with a shrug.

"But Milo, you can't go around naked from the waist down."

"Why not?"

Why not. Why not? Annie's too weary to figure out why not.

Milo has moved on to a new topic anyway, hollering, "Uncle Merlin, look what I found!"

"What is it?" Merlin asks, after setting Trixie on her feet and kissing Annie on the cheek.

"A poisonous tarantula. See?"

Merlin peers through the glass at the innocuous daddy longlegs lounging on a bed of grass. "Wow. That's cool, Milo."

"Yeah. I'm saving it to show my dad."

Merlin catches Annie's eye. She shakes her head.

Normally, she'd gently remind Milo that his dad isn't coming home again, but that would only lead into a discussion about Milo's upcoming mission to visit him in heaven. This morning, she's just not up for that. Annie wouldn't be *up* at all if it weren't for Trixie's latest night terrors startling her out of a bone-weary sleep at dawn.

"Come on," Annie says, "let's get out of the rain."

"It's only sprinkling, Mommy," Trixie says.

"But it's going to rain harder any second now, with lightning and thunder," Merlin announces, herding both children toward the house.

"How do you know, Uncle Merlin?"

"I'm magical, remember?"

"You're also addicted to the Weather Channel," Annie points out, knowing him too well.

"Only when I've got an outdoor shindig scheduled. Which is just about every day in season."

Annie shakes her head. "Is it supposed to rain all day?"

"Nope, just this morning. Then clearing for my big event later, thank goodness."

"Great, because the cookies are good to go," Annie says, leading the way up the steps and into the house.

The screen door groans loudly as she opens it, reminding her that Andre always meant to spray some WD-40 into the hinges. She really should get to that—if only so that she'll be subjected to one less memory of her husband.

"Duck," she reminds Merlin out of habit, and he lowers his towering head to fit through the doorway.

While house-hunting, Annie and Andre noticed that there are two kinds of old houses: those with towering ceilings, and those with impossibly low ceilings. Theirs falls into the latter category—not that it's an issue for anyone other than the towering six-foot-five Merlin.

"I so hope you appreciate the fact that I was decorating your grand old flags until one in the morning," she tells him.

"I always appreciate you, honeybun. And they're fabulous," Merlin proclaims, peering at the plastic-wrapped trays that line the kitchen countertop.

"I want one." Milo reaches for the nearest cookie.

Annie stops his hand before he can touch it. "No! I told you, sweetie, those are for the snooty people."

Merlin laughs. "They're not that snooty."

"Yeah, right." Annie hands him the invoice she made up this morning, hoping he'll pay her now. He often does, but last week he had to wait a few days for payroll to take care of it.

To her relief, Merlin reaches into his pocket and takes out his checkbook.

"What's today?" he asks, Montblanc pen poised above the dateline.

"June fourteenth," Annie tells him. "Milo, go put your shorts back on."

"I don't like shorts."

"I want to put shorts on," announces Trixie, who insisted on donning a party dress less than twenty minutes ago and is now decked out in pink organza and Mary Janes.

Annie sighs. "Fine. And Milo, if you don't want to wear shorts, put jeans on. *Now*."

"Underwear, too," Merlin advises, as Milo sulks out of the room. "Interesting kid. Think he'll grow up to be a flasher?"

"Lord, I hope not."

He turns back to his checkbook. "I can't believe *you* know the date. What's up with that?"

She shrugs. "It's Flag Day."

"Says the woman who's usually clueless about which day Independence Day falls on." Merlin finishes filling out the check and hands it to her with a flourish.

"July fourth," Annie says, sticking out her tongue.

"I'm impressed."

She would have been, too, prewidowhood.

That she's acutely aware of the calendar now is testimony to the approaching anniversary of Andre's death — which did, indeed, occur on the summer solstice.

June twenty-first.

Ironically, for Annie, the longest day of the year will forever feel like the longest day of the year.

Even more ironically, it wasn't a shark, or a riptide, or any of the other things Annie used to fear that took Andre's life.

No, her daredevil husband was felled by the most horrifically natural and random of causes: a blood clot in his lung.

Looking back, Annie can't recall a single warning sign. If Andre wasn't feeling good in the days or weeks before he keeled over on the beach, he kept it to himself.

It wouldn't be the first time.

He learned early on in their relationship that if he mentioned a symptom—any symptom—to Annie, she blew it out of proportion. Andre didn't like doctors and he didn't like tests. She had to schedule appointments for him behind his back, and force him to keep them. If she had known he was having trouble breathing, or had the slightest pain in his chest, she'd have dragged him to the ER. Then the blood clot would have been diagnosed, and Andre would have been saved.

You can't keep thinking like that, Annie reminds herself. *It's not your fault that he died. If anything, it's his fault.*

Damn him. Damn him for not taking better care of himself. Damn him for brushing off her frequent worries as hypochondria. Damn him for not thinking they needed life insurance at their ages. Damn him for leaving her alone.

This, Annie realizes, as the surge of fury toward her dead husband ebbs within her, must be the anger phase her psychiatrist friend Erika keeps warning her about. Oh, well, it's about damned time Annie feels something other than profound, overwhelming, mind-numbing grief.

"Listen," Merlin is saying, as Annie tucks the check into her back pocket and wonders whether the bank is open till noon or one, "how desperate are you for money?"

"About as desperate as you were for a date last New Year's Eve. Does that answer your question?"

Merlin pats her arm, smiling the benevolent smile of one who is confident of never again finding oneself dateless on New Year's Eve.

"Can you get a sitter tonight?" he asks Annie.

"No."

"Oh, come on, Annie. Yes, you can."

"You act as though all I have to do is snap my fingers and Mary Poppins will appear. It's not that easy, Merlin. And anyway, why do I need a sitter?"

"Because I need an extra waitress for the Flag Day fund-raiser tonight."

"No way," Annie says promptly. She may be broke, but she draws the line at waitressing.

"Come on, Annie. I'll pay you double."

She shakes her head.

"In cash."

She hesitates only briefly, then says, "Nope."

"Why not?"

"Because."

"Because . . . ?"

Because I can't bear the thought of leaving Milo and Trixie at night. What if he falls out of bed trying to fly? What if she wakes up screaming and I'm not there?

"Because . . . ?" Merlin prods.

Because I can't bear the thought of waiting hand and foot on a bunch of snobs. I can't stomach watching them barely touch meals that cost more than a year's worth of my mortgage. I can't—

"Annie?"

"Just because," she says churlishly.

"You need the money. And I can find you a sitter if you can't. I bet Erika would do it."

Erika Bauer is Annie's closest female friend, and she adores Milo and Trixie. But she's in Florida at a conference, and Annie tells Merlin as much.

He shrugs, unfazed. "I know for a fact that Jonathan's niece is available and—"

"Then let her waitress for you."

"She's only fifteen. That's too young to waitress."

"Too young to babysit, too."

"Oh, come on. You and Andre used to have your

neighbor's daughter watch the kids when you went out to dinner Friday nights. She couldn't have been more than thirteen."

She wasn't.

Annie closes her eyes briefly, staving off memories of their weekly tradition.

My dinner with Andre, she used to call it. Funny how they never even rented that movie. They always meant to, but . . .

But.

"I can't help you out, Merlin," Annie says tersely. "Sorry. You'll have to find someone else."

Find someone else.

Again, a memory rushes at her like the incoming tide, nearly knocking her off her feet.

"If anything ever happens to me, I want you to find someone else," Annie told Andre once when she was worried about some imagined fatal illness or other.

"Oh, don't worry. I've already got her lined up," he said, eyes twinkling. "The second you fall into that coma, I'm outa here."

"I'm serious, Andre."

"Yeah, well, you'd better not find anybody else, babe."

She laughed.

"Hey, I'm serious, too," he said, eyes still twinkling. "If I'm ever in a coma, I expect you to visit me every day and sit by my bed and hold my hand. You promised to stay by my side forever, remember?"

"I remember."

Their wedding: barefoot on the beach on a warm May sunrise as Merlin sang a cappella, "All I Ask of You" from *Phantom of the Opera*. Neither of them was particularly fond of traditional wedding vows.

"Talk about depressing," Andre said. "Who wants to discuss the potential for sickness and death on the happiest day of their lives?"

Not Andre. Not Annie. For them, the future held only happiness.

Instead of pledging to love each other in sickness and in health, till death do us part, they recited vows they had written themselves, vows that were as blissfully unconventional as they were.

Andre promised to keep his cold feet on his side of the bed, to never grow a beard, as Annie loathed facial hair, to stay by her side forever, and to tell her that he loved her every day.

Annie promised to laugh at all his bad puns, to never paint her nails when he was in the room because he hated the smell of polish, to stay by his side forever, and to tell him that she loved him every day.

"So if I'm in a coma, you'll stay by my side, and if I'm dead, you'd better not abandon me, Annie. You need to bring flowers to my grave and sit there talking to me for at least four hours a day. That'll keep you busy so you won't be tempted to date."

Rolling her eyes at the ludicrous notion of ever "dating" again, Annie pointed out, "I thought you wanted to be cremated and scattered in the Caribbean."

Their honeymoon: a five-day cruise to the Virgin Islands that depleted their newly established joint bank account but yielded three bulging photo albums filled with glorious memories.

"Does that mean I don't get a gravestone?"

She shook her head, laughing.

"Not even a memorial plaque somewhere? Listen, I need a stone or something. Where else are you going to brood and plant flowers?"

"Annie?"

She looks up, startled by Merlin's voice and his touch on her shoulder.

"Are you okay?"

She realizes tears are trickling down her cheeks.

"I'm fine," she lies, brushing them away, remembering something. "It's just . . . I'm one cookie short of sixteen dozen."

"I know, but I love you anyway."

"You counted?"

"Counted what?"

"The cookies. I'm one short—"

"Oh! You meant literally." He chuckles. "I thought you were acknowledging that you're a little nutty."

"I am not nutty!" she protests indignantly.

"Sure you are. But in an adorable way. Anyway, you were saying . . . ?"

"I'm one cookie short. I cut the recipe too close and I had exactly enough . . . but then I had to throw one away," she says, gesturing at the trays. "I, uh, dropped it. Facedown."

"It's okay. I'm sure Thom won't notice."

Annie is sure that he will, but he'll just have to live without the soggy, tear-stained flag.

Just as she has to live without Andre.

Okay, it's not the same thing.

If she were prone to smiling these days, she'd be

amused by the ludicrous comparison of a snooty cookie-counting Southamptonite to the Widow Harlowe.

But Annie isn't prone to smiling. She's prone to tears.

She sniffles and Merlin removes a neatly folded white linen handkerchief from the pocket of his khakis and passes it to her. "Here," he says. "Blow."

She raises the handkerchief to her nose.

"Better?" he asks.

"No." She leans against him as he pulls her close. At barely five feet tall, she finds her chin in the vicinity of his navel.

When Andre hugged her, she could put her head on his shoulder. He was only a few inches taller than Annie. They fit together perfectly, in every way. Oh, Lord. How is she going to make it through another day, another hour, another minute without him?

"When is it going to get easier?" she asks Merlin, closing her eyes against the terrible ache.

"I wish I knew, Twinkie. But it will. I promise."

"How do you know?"

"I know everything, remember?"

She laughs. So does he. Once upon a time, when she was Annie Grimes of suburban Commack and Merlin was literally, though never figuratively, the boy next door, she used to tease him about being a bossy know-it-all.

He captures her left hand in his and raises it to look at her fourth finger. "You haven't taken it off yet."

She flinches and lifts her chin stubbornly, glad he can't also see Andre's gold band dangling on a chain inside the collar of her T-shirt. "I'm not going to take it off, Merlin."

"Annie—"

"In my heart, I'll always be married to him. I'm not taking it off." Never mind the fact that the ring keeps sliding dangerously close to her second knuckle, thanks to all the weight she lost. She should really have it made a size smaller.

Yeah. As if there's money to spare for that.

Merlin shakes his head. "Wearing a ring a year later is just . . . look, Annie, sooner or later you might meet someone else. You might want to—"

"No way, Merlin. Andre made me promise that if something happened to him, I'd never replace him."

"He did not."

"He did so."

"If he said that he was teasing. Andre wouldn't want you to be alone."

"I'm not alone. I have the kids."

Merlin looks as though he's going to say something else, but just shrugs and drops her hand. After a moment he asks, "So how about bailing me out tonight?"

Annie thinks about the stack of unpaid bills on her desk and the check in her pocket, which won't cover half of them.

It's tempting. Really tempting. Not just the money, but the idea of getting a sitter and leaving the house, alone. Even if it is just to wait on snooty Thom and his rich friends.

"Annie? Come on, what do you say?"

She says, "No, thanks."

Then she stands in the doorway flanked by her children as Merlin drives away through the rain in his fancy car.

"Can we have lunch now, Mommy?" Trixie asks when the sound of crunching gravel has faded.

"Sure."

She makes them sandwiches using the last of the peanut butter and adds that item to the lengthy grocery list stuck to the refrigerator.

Then, feeling vaguely guilty, she allows the kids to eat in front of the television, something Andre always forbade. As a single parent, Annie finds herself relying on the good old electronic babysitter more and more frequently now that school is out for the summer. In fact, it's pretty much turned on all day, every day. It's the only way she can buy herself a few moments' solitude.

Back when Andre was alive, she kept the radio on most of the time. She always loved a house that was filled with music. But the radio on the kitchen windowsill has been silent for almost a year now.

Her appetite having vanished permanently when Andre did, Annie skips lunch. Again.

Instead, she sits at the kitchen table, listening to the raindrops on the roof, sipping this morning's cold coffee, and flipping through the stack of bills she hasn't a prayer of paying in their entirety.

The trick, Annie realizes, after the third flip-through, is to prioritize. She sets aside the mortgage statement, the electric bill, the health insurance bill. Merlin's check and the money left in her account will cover these, and leave enough for groceries if she buys generic brands.

Okay, so far so good. A little caffeine goes a long way.

She nukes the remainder of this morning's coffee for good measure, and while she's waiting in front of the microwave, she again goes through the bills still left in her hand. If she doesn't pay the minimum on the Visa card soon, they'll cut her off. And Andre's cell phone is past due. She can't let that lapse.

Can't you?

It makes no sense to keep paying it, just so that she can hear his voice every now and then and pretend he's still there, somewhere, on his way home.

It makes no sense, and yet she can't seem to help herself. Try as she might, she can't let go of the foolish fantasy that someday, she'll dial the number and he'll answer and she'll realize that this whole thing has been a bad dream.

A night terror.

Rubbing her exhausted eyes, Annie sinks into her chair again. She sets aside the pile of bills and sips some coffee. It tastes acrid, but she needs the caffeine to make it through the day.

She lowers her head to the table for a few blessed moments, fighting off sleep, wishing she could crawl back into bed.

Yawning, she forces her eyes open and stands up, looking around the cluttered kitchen.

Her gaze falls on the telephone.

Instinctively, she reaches for it and begins to dial. Just this once, she promises herself. One last time. Then she'll have the line disconnected and throw away the bill.

One ring . . .

This time, of course, she'll hang up at the beep. She should never have left a message yesterday. Milo overheard her talking and thought she had reached Andre.

Two rings . . .

She had to explain to her son that she was talking to

herself, not to Daddy. He wanted to know why she was holding the phone if she was talking to herself, a question she found impossible to answer.

Waiting for the inevitable third ring, Annie reaches for the cell phone bill. This really is ridiculous. It's time. Time to get rid of the indulgent expense. Time to let go.

Then, as she's about to rip the invoice in half . . .

"Hello?" her dead husband's voice says in her ear.

Chapter
2

God, how I hate these things," Thom tells his older sister, Susan, as they stand on the flagstone terrace surveying the clusters of white tables and chairs being arranged on the lawn below.

"You hate rental chairs and tables?"

"No, I hate occasions that call for rental chairs and tables."

He sighs and gazes out at the slate blue Atlantic that lies beneath the still overcast sky just beyond his property. As soon as the thunderstorm that came through earlier rumbled off to the east, the island's Saturday morning sailors took to the sea.

How he longs to be aboard one of those cutters skimming the storm-churned waves, rather than out here overseeing a few final details for tonight's fund-raiser.

"Oh, come on. It'll be fun," Susan says, laying a manicured, bejeweled hand on his arm.

"No, it won't. It'll be incredibly dull. These things always are."

Susan looks at him, the expression in her wide-set blue eyes her only means of conveying her concern.

Thom's sister, like Joyce and Mother and just about every female in their circle, has resorted to regular Botox injections to erase the slightest facial indication that their teenaged years have passed. Apparently, the inability to truly smile or frown is a fair trade-off for the absence of wrinkles.

"You're in a terrible mood today, Tommy," Susan observes. "What's wrong?"

"I wish I were out there all by myself sailing," he says promptly, looking wistfully again at the white triangles on the horizon.

Susan reaches up to pat her motionless blond coif, as though it might have been mussed by the mere thought of skimming the open sea on a boat after a thunderstorm.

Thom smirks, thinking a hurricane couldn't budge his sister's well-gelled and thoroughly sprayed hair. There was a time when her style was as footloose as her outlook.

Now both her mane and her spirit have been smothered into submission.

When did she become Mother?

Thom mentally answers his own question promptly:

Susan became Mother the moment she agreed not to marry the Oscar-winning actor she adored.

Thom, however, refuses to become Mother. Or Father, for that matter.

With his long, lean build, distinct cleft chin, and bold eyebrows that form straight slashes above piercing dark blue eyes, he might bear a startling physical resemblance to the late scion of the Brannock family. But fortunately, that, and a passion for his work, are about all he has in common with Thomas III—and all he wants to have in common with him.

Father was a no-nonsense corporate raider by day; a gallivanting rogue by night. On some level, Thom once pitied him, being married to manipulative Mother in a socially and economically suitable match that was reportedly arranged by their parents with all the romance of a corporate merger.

Thomas III led a life that was driven by others' expectations, in both business and family matters. Who wouldn't feel sorry for him?

On another level, Thom grew to despise his father for keeping a mistress—perhaps many—behind Mother's back. On the surface, Thomas III might have played by the rules, conforming to others' expectations and marrying the prim beauty handpicked for him by his parents. But he indulged an untamed rebellious streak until the day he died.

Now that Thom is a man, sharing boardrooms and barrooms with colleagues of his late father, he's found himself privy to bawdy paternal escapades that he'd rather not know about. He never lets on to his father's peers that he finds his father's behavior reprehensible. Nor does he like to admit to himself that he might possess a shred of, if not tolerance, then at least empathy.

"Sailing alone when there are whitecaps is risky," Susan comments, interrupting his thoughts.

"The best things in life are risky."

"That's a ridiculous statement."

Thom shrugs. He finds himself doing that a lot these days. Especially with Susan. And with Joyce.

Yes, Joyce frequently inspires shrugs, eye rolls, and

shudders on his part, but he tends to suppress them whenever he can. When he can't, she seems to think he's merely teasing. She has no idea that he disagrees with just about everything she says and does.

At least, he doesn't *think* she realizes it. Maybe she does, and simply pretends things are hunky-dory so that . . .

Well, why would she do that?

Because she doesn't want to make waves? Because she's afraid that if she does, he won't marry her?

Marriage to Joyce. Now there's a stomach-churning thought.

Marrying Joyce would be to Thom what marrying Mother was to his father.

He really should break up with her sooner than later. The longer he dates her, the more convinced she'll be that they have a future.

Which they don't.

No matter what Mother chooses to believe.

The trouble is, dating Joyce is easier than not dating anybody. Because when he's not dating anybody, Mother has a way of parading eligible women past him as though he's a judge at the Miss Blue Blood America Pageant.

"I'm trying, Tommy, but I really can't think of one worthwhile thing in life that's risky," Susan presses on.

"You mean, besides sailing?"

"I don't think sailing is worthwhile."

"You used to."

If he closed his eyes and let time slip away, he would see her as a carefree teenager, wind in her sun-streaked blond hair, a broad grin crinkling her sunburnt, freckled face as she handily hoisted the sail on one of their father's boats.

But that was before she was diagnosed with the heart condition that threatened her life. It's been under control for years, thanks to medication, but Susan will never be the same devil-may-care girl she once was.

"Well I was just a kid back then," she echoes Thom's thoughts aloud. "Kids are supposed to be reckless. I'm an adult now, Tommy, and so are you."

"Yeah, well, I think you need to learn how to live a little."

"Live a little? I'm not dead, brother dear. I'm married."

Thom fights the urge to tell her that in her case, it sometimes seems like the same thing.

Instead, he says, "Sushi."

"Sushi?" She looks around. "What are you talking about?"

"Some people think eating raw fish is risky." Some people, including Joyce, who is hard-pressed to find anything she can order in Japanese restaurants, Thom's favorite places to eat out.

Sushi is raw and she doesn't do raw. Tempura is deep-fried and she doesn't do deep-fried. Noodles are carbs and she doesn't do carbs. She doesn't do red meat or shellfish, either. While perusing restaurant menus, she likes to tell him about all the reasons she doesn't do any of the above. Dining with Joyce is about as much fun as a medical seminar.

"Eating raw fish *is* risky," Susan informs Thom. "You can get food poisoning. Not to mention, it's disgusting." He's certain that if she could wrinkle her nose, she would.

"I happen to like it. Yup. Sushi is one of the best things in life."

"Sushi? Sailing? That's the best you can do?"

"Bungee jumping. Hostile corporate takeovers. Rare hamburgers. Climbing Mount Everest. Driving fast. Swimming with sharks. Rocketing to—"

"Okay, I get it."

"—Mars," he concludes, utterly unfazed by the utterly unfazed expression on his sister's face.

"So those are the best things in life?" she asks.

"I can come up with more."

She shakes her head, holding up a hand. "No! I get it. I just don't happen to agree. You don't have to risk your neck to do something meaningful. There's something to be said for stability."

Thom would shrug, but he's sick of shrugging. He's beginning to think talking to Susan is a waste of breath when it comes to philosophical discussions about life. She was once his greatest ally, but she's become one of *them* and not just because of her heart condition. He hasn't seen a glimmer of her former self in years. Not since Christmas in Aspen, right before she got married, when he unexpectedly hit her square in the face with a snowball he'd been aiming at a tree.

The next thing he knew, his big sister was instinctively scooping and throwing in retaliation. The two of them romped in the falling snow for a good five minutes until, breathless and ruddy-cheeked, they were caught in the act by an incredulous Wade.

Susan's then fiancé wasn't amused when she attempted to draw him into the fray with a perfectly aimed snowball.

Thom will never forget the look on Wade's face, or his own guilt when Wade reminded his fiancée that physical exertion could trigger her heart condition, or his sinking feeling as he watched his sister's smile fade and her embarrassed attempt to quickly brush the white from her hair and wool dress coat.

In no time, it seemed, Susan was once again draped in white . . . only then, it was silk and lace, and she wasn't giddy with exhilaration the way she had been during the snowball fight . . . or the way a bride should be on her wedding day.

It was as though Susan had slipped into an alternate universe, leaving behind her kid brother—and the promising spark her life had once held.

She had traded all that for Wade and a last name that's abbreviated on the NASDAQ and emblazoned on more than one old stone building in Manhattan.

Stability.

That's what Wade represents, all right.

It's what everyone seems to crave these days.

Everyone but Thom.

Yes, he really should break up with Joyce, before she gets the wrong idea.

"What's the matter?" Susan asks.

He looks up to see her watching him, blue eyes still full of concern. With her head turned at this angle in the slender beam of sunlight that's slipped through a hole in the western sky, he can see the faint hint of freckles beneath the layer of pancake makeup on her nose.

"Nothing's the matter," he lies. "Why?"

"You sighed."

"I did?" Oops. "I was just thinking about Joyce."

The tight skin around his sister's mouth attempts to curve into a semismile. "She's lovely."

"Yes."

He doesn't explain to his sister that his sigh wasn't the kind of sigh one sighs when one is appreciating loveliness.

Susan, after all, adores Joyce.

Mother adores Joyce.

Susan and Mother assume Thom also adores Joyce.

That's part of the reason he's been avoiding the breakup. It's going to be messy. Nobody is expecting it. Least of all, Joyce. For all she knows, he's been out shopping for engagement rings in his nonexistent spare time.

Which reminds him . . .

"I've got some business to take care of before the party," he tells Susan, his thoughts already flitting ahead to the conference call he needs to make and the report he needs to finalize to prepare for the Saltwater Treasures takeover bid.

"You're starting to sound just like Wade. All work and no play."

"Mmm."

"The party will be a success. The weather is supposed to clear up. And the grounds look lovely. Not a violet in sight." The smile Susan's face is incapable of producing is evident in her voice as she gestures at the acres of impeccable lawn below them.

Thom can't help chuckling. Violets are the bane of Mother's existence every June. He remembers her instructing the gardener to pluck by hand every offensive purple blossom that dared to mar the green landscape at home. Thom and Susan secretly thought they were pretty, but never dared pick a bouquet of the miniature blooms Mother considered weeds.

Thom strides toward the house, grateful for the one thing in his life about which he can feel passionate: his work. If it weren't for that . . .

Well, what else would he have that matters?

Nothing.

Absolutely nothing.

Money, art, real estate, cars . . .

None of it is worthwhile. None of it inspires him.

Thank God, Thom thinks as he steps into the air-conditioned mausoleum that is his summer home, for work.

Static.

There's so much static, Annie can barely make out the word. But it was there. She heard it. She knows she heard it.

Hello?

She is certain, in this moment, that her life will never be the same again. That something incredible—something impossible— just happened.

Hello?

It's just a word. She clutches the receiver hard against her ear, shock waves echoing through her brain along with the two syllables she couldn't possibly have heard just now. But she did.

She knows she did, dammit. She heard it.

Yes, it's just a word. A word everyone says when they pick up the phone. But nobody—*nobody*—says it quite like he does.

Hello?

"Andre!" she shrieks when she finds her voice at last, at the precise moment her legs give way against a fierce tide of panic. She sags against the counter, shivering, noting somewhere in the back of her mind that a wintry draft has permeated the kitchen.

"Where are you? Andre? Andre!"

Static.

"Mommy?"

She looks up at the sound of Milo's voice, sees him and Trixie standing in the doorway. Somehow she processes the image through a mental maelstrom and realizes that her children are frightened.

"It's okay," she manages to say, "it's okay. I'm just talking to . . . to . . ."

"Daddy?" Milo asks solemnly.

"No!"

"You said Andre. That's Daddy's name."

"That's because I'm . . . I'm talking *about* Daddy. Go back and watch your shows, sweetie. Go. Take Trixie."

Miraculously, they go.

She staggers with the phone through the screen porch and to the backdoor, slips out into the rain, wailing her husband's name.

The connection is terrible, the static deafening. And yet, she can just make out Andre's voice, coming from a great distance, coming from . . .

No. This can't be happening. This is impossible. Andre is dead. She saw him, dead. Touched his cold hand.

Cold.

She shudders, trying to keep that atrocious memory at

bay, but it drifts in like a stiff breeze off the water, prickling the skin at the back of her neck.

They let her see him in the morgue. He was lying on a table, covered in a sheet, eyes closed.

She always heard that the dead were cold, but she never realized the term was literal. Not until she grasped her husband's eerily solid, icy hand, the one with the familiar scar on the knuckle. He'd gotten it from a fish hook years ago.

She'd held that hand countless times; now only the scar was familiar.

How could he have been so cold? He died in the heat of summer, nothing was cold on that awful day. Nothing but his hand.

Intellectually, she knows that the weather is warm again today. Hot, even, out here in the sun. And yet . . .

She's shivering. She's chilled to the bone.

"Annie . . ."

She sinks to the back step, her body quaking.

It's him. His voice. Despite the static, despite the fact that it can't possibly be him, it is. It's him.

A sob escapes her along with his name. "Andre. Please. I need you. Andre . . ."

Static.

He's speaking, but she can't make out what he's saying.

She listens helplessly, straining to decipher the snatches of sound.

Only two words are clear.

"Kids."

"Love."

Oh, God. This can't be happening. She tells herself it can't be happening. She rakes a hand through her hair, shakes her head, tries to snap out of this . . . this . . . dream. Or nightmare. Or hallucination. Or whatever it is.

She closes her eyes, knowing she'll wake up any second. She'll be in her bed. *Their* bed . . .

She opens her eyes.

She's still collapsed on her back steps, the static is still in her ear, an inexplicable iciness still surrounds her—or perhaps radiates from her—and there's *still* no sane explanation for what she's hearing.

"I love you, Andre," she says plaintively.

Static. A jumble of faint, incoherent words. And then . . .

" . . . love . . ."

It's barely audible. She can't discern the phrases that come before or after, but that doesn't matter. She knows what he's saying.

He loves her.

She feels him here. All around her. Inside her. Feels him in a way she hasn't in months.

A slow warmth has begun to infuse the strange chill.

"We need you, Andre," she begs. "Please. I don't know what to do without you . . . please tell me what to do . . ."

A garbled rush of sound, but in its midst, she again picks out a word.

" . . . job . . ."

Annie pounces on it. "What about a job? Andre, what? I can't hear you. Please . . . please tell me what to do."

" . . . Merlin . . ."

Her breath catches in her throat. That was clearer. Still staticky, but unmistakable.

"What about Merlin?"

"... job ... tonight ... go ..."

Three words, buried in a garbled jumble of others.

"I don't know what you're saying, Andre," she says plaintively. "Please ... I can't hear you."

"... love ..."

"I love you, Andre. I love you. I love you."

"... love ..."

Again.

He's telling her he loves her.

Salty tears stream into her mouth.

"I love you." She says it over and over, until the static gives way to abrupt silence, and the connection is broken.

Chapter

3

Just south of the quaint rows of shops in Southampton lies a residential neighborhood into which Annie has never before had occasion to wander.

Tonight, as a warm June ocean breeze stirs her curls through the open car window, she isn't wandering, but driving with a purpose.

The purpose, ostensibly, being to earn enough cash to keep her family afloat a little longer.

But there's another reason she's here.

Because your dead husband told you to come? her inner voice scoffs as she consults the scribbled directions on the seat beside her, then makes yet another turn down yet another leafy seaside street lined with mansions partially hidden beyond dense green walls of privet.

You and your imagination, Annie.

Obviously, her forte has gotten way out of hand.

In fact, if Erika weren't at that conference in Florida, Annie probably would have called her this afternoon to ask which stage of grief entails delusory telephone conversations with one's late spouse.

Of course the call wasn't real.

Annie was certain of that moments after the imaginary call supposedly ended.

It was almost as though she came to from a fainting spell, finding herself huddled on the back steps clutching the phone.

As the afternoon wore on, she grew positive that in her bone-weary state, she had fallen asleep for a few minutes.

Standing up? In the kitchen? In broad daylight?

If only the scoffing inner voice would pick a side and stay on it.

One minute, she's doing her best to convince herself that the call wasn't real; the next, to convince herself that it must have been.

In any case, here she is, on her way to a catering job that, if nothing else, will result in money she desperately needs.

If nothing else. Yeah.

What else are you expecting, Annie?

Are you thinking Andre's ghost will reveal itself to you at the snooty mansion?

Maybe.

Maybe, even if the paranormal telephone conversation was a dream or a hallucination, this was her subconsciousness's way of sending her on a meaningful mission.

The meaningful mission being an actual glimpse of her dead husband.

And cash.

"You're losing it, chick," she mutters aloud. "You really are. You need to get a grip."

Annie sighs, thrumming the fingertips of her left hand on the outside of the car door.

Driving with the window down in all but the stormiest weather is one of her quirkier habits. At least, Andre always thought so. But Annie isn't a big fan of climate control, preferring fresh air and the wind in her hair.

She checks the directions again, glances at a street sign, turns another corner, and reaches for the radio dial. Music is what she needs. Something to take her mind off what happened today.

Or rather, what *didn't* happen.

". . . Think of me . . . you know that I'd be with you if I could . . ."

Annie reflexively hits the brakes so hard the tires screech.

Todd Rundgren is singing on the radio.

And the warm June breeze has gone arctic.

"Andre?" she whispers, her suddenly icy fingers clenching the steering wheel. She turns her head slowly, almost expecting to find her husband sitting beside her in the passenger's seat.

It's empty.

Of course it is.

The song is a coincidence.

They play it all the time on this station.

Still . . .

Everything happens for a reason, Annie.

Maybe this is why he wanted her to come tonight. So that she would be in the car, listening to the radio, hearing this song at this moment. Maybe the song is a message from him. His way of reaching out from beyond the grave. His way of telling her that the phone call was real; she didn't imagine it.

Listening intently to the lyrics, Annie shivers.

She didn't imagine the phone call, and she isn't imagining the cold. It's almost as if . . .

No. Glancing at the dashboard, she sees that the car's air conditioner hasn't suddenly kicked on. The window is still down, the early evening sun still perched well above the horizon.

Annie has read her share of ghost stories, seen her share of supernatural movies. Enough, certainly, to be aware that haunted places are supposed to be unnaturally cold.

"Andre . . . are you here?" she asks the empty passenger's seat.

No response.

Yet she can feel him, just as she did earlier.

Overcome by an aura of utter well-being and the bizarre realization that she is no longer alone, Annie reaches a trembling hand toward the empty seat, almost expecting to encounter . . . something.

There is nothing. Nothing tangible, anyway.

"You're here, aren't you? You're with me?"

She listens intently, hearing nothing but Todd Rundgren singing on the radio.

Then an abrupt blast of sound nearly sends Annie bolting from the car.

Gasping, she turns to see an SUV behind her. Its impatient driver honks again, gesturing for her to drive on.

Her right foot automatically shifts from the brake pedal to the gas.

The chill is gone, and so, all at once, is the comforting presence.

But he was here.

It wasn't her imagination.

Or was it?

Tears pool in her eyes, nearly blinding her as she coasts to a STOP sign. She wipes them on the sleeve of her white blouse, belatedly grateful she didn't have time to put on mascara.

Maybe it *was* her imagination. She sniffles.

You want so badly to believe that he isn't gone . . .

Badly enough for her errant thoughts to conjure the voice of the man she loved, the ghost of the man she once loved.

No . . .

The man you love, *Annie.*

Present tense.

If I'm dead, you'd better not abandon me, Annie.

It was such an innocent, teasing thing for him to say at the time. Neither of them ever imagined it would happen so soon.

Well, it has. He's dead.

But perhaps he hasn't abandoned her after all. The phone call, the song on the radio . . .

He's still with her. She believes it, right here, right now, deep in her heart, though the precious little comfort it brings does little to fill the yawning chasm he left there.

"I won't abandon you, Andre. Not ever. I promise," she whispers.

Coasting to the next STOP sign, Annie fights the impulse to turn the car around and head back home. Why should she go through with it now that the evening's true purpose has been revealed to her?

Why, indeed.

She still needs the cash. That hasn't changed. And the kids are fine. They seemed content to be spending the evening with Jonathan's adorable and energetic teenage niece.

Who knows? It might do Annie some good to be out of the house, away from them for a few hours. Even if she's merely going to be waiting on Merlin's snooty client and his snooty friends.

So far, the soiree is going exactly as expected.

Which isn't particularly a good thing, as far as Thom is concerned.

The guests are staid, familiar, resplendent in their required red, white, and blue dress. The food is divine, the backdrop breathtaking—the latter two elements courtesy of Merlin's magic. Thom's sloping seaside lawn has been transformed into a fairyland awash with thousands of candles and twinkly white lights draped in white canvas canopies: Merlin's trademark, or so he claims.

The sun has disappeared beneath the sea and in the distance, Thom can hear the waves breaking as the tide comes in. He'd give anything to be out on the beach right now. Instead, he's holding court beside a bower of fragrant white roses with Joyce at his side, in the midst of mind-numbing small talk with a Republican congresswoman and her stodgy husband.

"We've said that countless times ourselves, haven't we, darling?" Joyce asks Thom, laughing at something the congresswoman apparently just said.

"We certainly have," Thom replies, feigning both comprehension and amusement.

"We'll need to do something about it then, shall we?"

"Oh, we'll leave it up to the experts," Joyce tells the congresswoman. "Won't we, Thom?"

"Absolutely," he agrees jovially, as though he has a clue what they're talking about.

Joyce slips her hand into his. Her skin is surprisingly cool on such a warm night; her fingers resting delicately—almost limply—in his. She holds hands the way she dances, he notes, doing his best to fight his disdain. She'll make the first move, but then as soon as he touches her, she seems to wilt. It's almost as though she's confused ladylike reserve with spiritless indifference.

As the conversation meanders onward, he finds himself wondering again why Joyce chose a flowing white dress to wear this evening. An elegant blue or vibrant red would have been far more flattering against her porcelain skin and flaxen hair. In white, she looks almost wraith-like.

Earlier, when she stepped out of her chauffeured town car and he paid her the obligatory compliment on her appearance, she smiled and informed him that she felt "positively bridal."

What was that supposed to mean?

The comment has been troubling Thom all evening.

It's definitely time to put an end to this so-called relationship, even if it means opening himself up to Mother's matchmaking once again.

Yes, first thing tomorrow, he's got to tell Joyce he's had a change of heart.

Or perhaps he shouldn't say *that*.

Is it worse to imply that he was once in love with her and fell out of it? Or worse to admit the truth: that he never cared for her at all?

"Penny for your thoughts," Joyce says, and he realizes that their companions have drifted away.

She's watching him through narrowed slate-gray eyes, her tone light-hearted, her expression anything but.

"Only a penny?" he volleys expertly. "My thoughts are worth at least a dollar in today's market."

"Oh, what the hell. I'll give you two dollars." She chuckles, a mostly mirthless, practiced emission of staccato sounds he's grown to loathe.

"Really. You must have high expectations, big spender."

Thom marvels at the fact that he can stand here flirting with the woman whose future he's about to shatter. That's one of the things that bothers him most about himself: his ability to mask his true feelings so easily, to carry on the social charade with the smooth proficiency of a reality dating show contestant.

"One question before I pay up," Joyce croons, leaning close enough for his nostrils to be inundated with the strong, spicy scent of her perfume. "Are those expensive thoughts about me?"

"Guess." He flashes an evasive grin and excuses himself, saying he has to check something with the caterer.

"Don't be long," Joyce instructs as he turns toward the house.

"I won't be."

Again, he notices the sound of the surf in the darkness beyond the party's glowing lights, and wishes he could escape to the beach instead of the house. But a host can't very well disappear in the wrong direction in the midst of several hundred guests. People would notice. People would talk.

Who the hell cares what people think? Thom asks

himself, stepping through the nearest set of French doors into the cool interior of the house.

Not me. Not anymore.

Yes, first thing tomorrow, he'll break it off with Joyce. Then, for good measure, he'll inform his mother that he has no interest in meeting other eligible women.

As if that will stop her. Thom shakes his head, thinking the only thing that could throw Mother off his bachelor trail would be if he were safely engaged . . . or uninterested in women, period.

He smiles, wondering if magical Merlin would be opposed to posing as his new love interest. He discards that idea promptly, thinking that under the best of circumstances, he would never manage to convince anyone that flamboyant Merlin is his type.

No, he thinks, rounding a corner toward the kitchen, his type would be more like—

"Oh, I'm sorry!"

"Sorry!"

Thom takes a step back from the woman he just slammed into, not accustomed to displaced strangers wandering the corridors of his house.

The first thing he notices is that she looks as though she's seen a ghost.

The next thing he notices is that she's beautiful.

Not the way Joyce and Susan and yes, even Mother, are beautiful. No, they work at it.

This pint-sized woman is a natural beauty, with sun-kissed cheeks, pale green eyes unenhanced by makeup, skin that's a healthy, freckled tan against her white blouse, and a halo of dark curls determined to escape the simple ponytail at the nape of her neck.

"Can I help you find something?" she asks pleasantly, seeming to recover from her scare.

Thom, who is also unaccustomed to being shown around his own home, smiles at her. "Oh, I wasn't lost. I was just on my way to the kitchen."

"It's that way." She points in the opposite direction; the direction in which she was heading. That is, the *wrong* direction.

"Technically, you might eventually get there going that way," he tells her, "but you can get there much faster going this way."

"How do you—"

"Because I live here," he informs her, and watches her face tint an attractive shade of pink.

For a moment, he's certain she's going to apologize or, at the very least, become even more flustered.

But a swift transformation takes place.

This woman, who is so obviously a hired member of the catering staff, doesn't appear particularly intimidated by an unexpected tête-à-tête with the lord of this manor. In fact, if anything, she seems almost . . . perturbed?

"Can I help *you* find anything?" he asks politely, feeling oddly as though *he's* invading *her* privacy.

"I was actually headed for the . . ."

"The kitchen?"

"Yes," she admits reluctantly, and mutters, "This place is huge. I thought I was going the right way."

"Follow me." He starts walking, then stops, realizing she hasn't budged. "Coming?"

"Yes," she says reluctantly, and he gets the distinct sense this is a woman who isn't particularly interested in playing Follow the Leader.

Nor is she interested in conversation.

Normally he isn't, either. Not that he's opposed to exchanging pleasantries with the hired help. In fact, on a night like this, given the choice, he'd much rather chat with the hired help than invited guests.

Still, he has no idea why, exactly, he finds himself asking her name as they walk along the corridor toward the back of the house.

"Anne," is the straightforward reply, delivered sans the slightest turn of the head.

"With an 'e,' or without?"

"With."

"Oh. Well, I'm Thom. With an 'h.'"

Silence.

"The 'h' comes after the 't,'" he points out helpfully.

Silence, still.

He forges on, Lord help him, as haplessly as an adolescent on a first date. "It comes after the 't' and before the—"

"'O,'" she cuts in. "I know."

"I wasn't sure you . . ."

"What?" she asks when he trails off. "Knew how to spell 'Tom'? Or 'Thom'?"

"You don't pronounce the 'h,'" he tells her, before realizing that she knows damn well you don't pronounce the "h." She's doing it to irk him.

So why the hell isn't he irked? Why is he feeling infinitely more intrigued than irked?

If Joyce were half as mettlesome as this woman, he might be inclined to keep her around for a while. Certainly, he would never be bored.

He slides the invitingly pertinent Anne a sidelong glance in an attempt to catch her eye.

She promptly turns her head to examine a French Impressionist painting in an ornate gilt frame.

"That's beautiful," she murmurs, almost to herself.

"Yes."

"I love the muted colors of the landscape."

"Mmm." He smiles to himself, admiring her coy attempt to appear fascinated by the artwork. Women do this sort of thing all the time.

Anne steps closer to the wall, peers at the canvas, and exclaims, "Look at what he's done with the brush strokes in this corner. The way he's used the texture to convey the subtlest change in light . . . it's genius."

Oh.

Perhaps she really *is* more interested in the oil painting than she is in Thom.

"It's a Renoir, isn't it?" she concludes, wearing a smug smile, glancing up at him at last.

"Yes." He can't help but be impressed that she recognized the artist—and that her smile reaches her eyes, wrinkling the corners. No frozen face muscles for her.

"I knew it!" She turns her attention appreciatively back to the Renoir.

"I'm surprised. It's one of his lesser-known works."

"Not if you know art."

"Which you obviously do. Are you an artist?"

"I majored in it." She frowns at him. "Surprised I went to college?"

"No, but I'm surprised you were an art major. Since you're so proficient at spelling and all. I thought you probably majored in that."

"You thought I majored in spelling?"

"Relax. It was a joke. Forget it. It wasn't funny."

To his shock, she laughs. "Actually, it *was* funny."

He gapes at her. "Who are you, and what have you done with Anne?"

She laughs again.

He can't help comparing the spontaneous, merry ripple that spills from her lips to Joyce's subpar imitation of genuine amusement.

For some reason, he finds himself glancing down at Anne's hand. Specifically, her left hand. More specifically, the fourth finger of her left hand.

Pleased to see that it's bare, Thom isn't quite sure what to do with that information, other than file it away for future reference.

Yes, in case he feels compelled to date a waitress/art major in the near future.

Wouldn't *that* get Mother's goat? It would be almost as tantalizing as introducing Merlin around as his latest love interest.

Too bad he can't just get Anne's number and take her to dinner, preferably at Mother's country club.

But no, he can't do that.

Or rather, he won't do it.

Not because he's too good for Anne. Rather, just the opposite.

He would never stoop so low as to involve this spunky yet sincere female in an elaborate ruse to piss off his mother.

He'll have to come up with some other tactic to put a kibosh on her matchmaking.

But for now, they've reached the end of the road: the

kitchen, bustling with a dozen other waiters and waitresses dressed identically to Anne, in white shirts and navy pants with red cummerbunds.

"Here we are," Thom says, wondering what she'd look like in something more flattering. Say, a flowing white dress . . .

Stop that, he scolds himself immediately on the heels of that bizarre thought. Women in white dresses are off limits to him, even as fantasies.

"Thank you for the escort," Anne says politely. "Enjoy your party."

"Oh, I won't."

She half smiles, and again he admires the way it crinkles the edges of her eyes. "Pardon?"

He grins and leans in conspiratorially to say, "That wasn't a joke. I hate parties like this."

"Then why are you having it?"

"Good question." He's willing to bet there's very little that this woman does on other people's terms.

Lucky, lucky her.

"Nice meeting you," he says, stretching out his hand.

"You, too." She looks taken aback.

He can feel the curious stares of other workers on them as he shakes her hand, careful not to let his fingers linger as long as he wants to. Her hand is warm, her grip firm.

Again, he finds himself comparing her touch to Joyce's lackluster grasp.

Ironic, isn't it, that this is the first woman toward whom he's felt the slightest spark of attraction in ages?

Looking down into Anne's wide-set, celery-colored eyes, he curses the fates that make it inappropriate for him to say anything other than, "Well, good night" before slipping back to his party.

Joyce is waiting patiently for him, of course.

He has the feeling that she'll wait patiently for him for as long as he lets her.

He could probably string her along for years, feigning a relationship that has a future.

Tomorrow, he tells himself again. Tomorrow, he'll set himself free.

"Well, Annie?" Merlin asks, as they walk through the darkness toward their cars parked in a secluded lot a short distance from the Brannock estate. "What did you think?"

"About what?"

"The job. It wasn't as bad as you expected it to be, was it." It isn't a question. She caught him watching her a few times tonight, wearing a little smile as if he were pleasantly surprised to see that she wasn't downright miserable.

"No," she admits, patting her pocketful of cash. "It wasn't *that* bad."

The snooty people weren't rudely cold, as she expected. They were merely coolly detached, which was fine with her. They treated her as though she were invisible.

Everyone, that is, but the evening's host, Thom-with-an-'h'-Brannock. He was different. Perhaps just because he was the host. Or perhaps because they literally bumped into each other head-on, while her interaction with the others involved politely passing hors d'oeuvres and champagne.

In any case, Thom Brannock wasn't cold. He was, in fact, almost . . . well, warm.

In addition to being warm, he also happened to be pretty hot. Not that she had any interest in noticing that the man had more than his share of sex appeal.

But it was a hard thing to miss. Especially since all the women in the kitchen were chattering about how "hot" he was. Hotter than hot, one waitress called him. Another kept referring to him—behind his back, of course—as Big Blue, a reference to his eyes and not, as Annie initially assumed, to an affiliation with the tech industry.

Never before has she seen eyes that unusual shade, a deep, dusky navy that reminds Annie of ripe blueberries.

Still, more than Thom's eyes or his overall good looks, Annie was taken aback by his casual friendliness.

When she found out who he was, she was all set to resent him. But for some reason, she didn't.

No, she almost *liked* the guy. And when he said goodbye in the kitchen on his way back to his party, she almost found herself feeling sorry for him.

Which was odd. Why would she, a destitute widow with two young children, pity a millionaire or billionaire or whatever he is?

Because there was an odd aura of isolation about him, that's why. He was surrounded by the trappings of wealth and the fabulous people who are drawn to the trappings of wealth, yet he seemed utterly alone.

And loneliness is something to which Annie can reluctantly relate now that Andre is gone.

Thom Brannock isn't married.

She's fairly certain of that. If he were married, he wouldn't seem so alone.

Or maybe he would. Maybe he and his wife lead separate lives. Lots of couples do. Her brothers and their wives, for example.

But if Thom were married, his wife would have more likely been the one working with Merlin on the party arrangements. That's the way it works with Annie's sisters-in-law.

Then again, you never know. Maybe Thom Brannock and his wife, if he has one, are the exception to the rule among the socially elite Hamptonites.

So is he married, or isn't he?

There's only one way to find out . . . and find out, Annie must. She doesn't know why, but she has to know.

"Is he married?"

Merlin looks around at the dark seascape, as though expecting to spot the "he" in question lurking in the dunes. "Is who married?"

"Sorry . . . I meant the guy who hosted the party."

Somehow, she can't bring herself to say his name, though she'll never forget it. Thom with an "h."

But saying it aloud, especially to Merlin, might make it seem as though she's interested in the man. Which she isn't.

She's just curious about his marital status because . . . well, who the hell knows why she's curious? She's curious about a lot of things. Like . . . like . . .

Well, right now, she can only think of one thing in particular, but that's because it's well after midnight and it's almost the longest day of the year.

"His name is Thom, and no, he's not married."

"Oh."

For a moment, there isn't a sound but the waves crashing in the distance and their footsteps on the grassy path. Just when Annie is convinced the subject has been dropped, Merlin asks, "Why did you want to know, Annie?"

"I just wondered."

"Because you're—"

"No, not because I'm interested in him. So don't get any ideas," Annie warns.

It's a dark night; she can't see the look in Merlin's eyes but she can feel him watching her, just the way she could feel Thom watching her earlier when she feigned fascination with the Renoir.

Not that she isn't a fan of the late French Impressionist. She studied his work in college, comprehensively enough to recognize the obscure painting in Thom Brannock's possession.

Thank goodness for that; art history was a welcome distraction from her unexpected, unwelcome, and inappropriate attraction to the master of the house.

"Did you meet Mr. Brannock?" Merlin asks.

"Just for a second. I ran into him when I got lost. He helped me find my way back to the kitchen."

"Can you imagine having a house so enormous people could get lost in it?"

"I can't imagine having a house big enough that you can sneeze without everyone in it immediately saying gesundheit," Annie tells Merlin wistfully.

"Maybe you should sell it and move."

"No."

"But Annie, you can find something bigger and in better shape and more affordable someplace else."

"I can't sell the house, Merlin. It's my home. Andre and I planned on living there forever."

She waits for Merlin to point out that Andre is no longer living, period.

But he's silent.

Again, Annie thinks about the strange telephone call earlier, and the odd feeling that came over her in the car on the way here.

She opens her mouth to tell Merlin about it, but she's too late. He's already speaking, telling her about another catering job he has lined up for late next week, a golf luncheon in Bridgehampton.

"Do you think you can line up a sitter for a few hours and help me out, Annie?"

She shrugs, feeling the weight of the cash in her pocket. "Maybe. I'll let you know. But don't think this is going to be a regular thing, Merlin. I still have my business."

"I know you do." He pauses. "Has your stuff been selling any better now that the summer people are trickling back?"

"Dribs and drabs. I'm sure it'll pick up," she adds without much conviction.

Back when Annie wasn't the head of her household, it was a hell of a lot easier to ignore the fact it takes more than a hot glue gun and a whimsical flair to make a living. Yes, she earned a nice supplemental income and the enthusiasm of local shop and gallery owners. But that's no longer enough.

"I'll see if I can get a sitter for next Thursday," she reluctantly tells Merlin, as they cover the last few steps toward their cars.

"Good. Let me know."

They jangle their keys, aim their remotes, simultaneously unlock their doors.

Annie yawns. "Good night. I'll talk to you tomorrow. And thanks."

Merlin's hand rests briefly on her arm. "You're doing great, Annie."

"Waitressing?"

"Surviving."

Emotion swells her throat so that she doesn't dare respond.

She sinks into the driver's seat, closes the door, and resists the urge to rest her head against the steering wheel. She can feel Merlin watching her; she doesn't want him to see how damned weary she is, or how close to tears.

Survival? Is that what this is? Funny, it doesn't feel like survival. Just the opposite, in fact. It feels to her as though a little more of the old Annie dies every day.

Merlin waves at her.

She forces a smile and waves back, pretending everything is just terrific. "See you," she calls.

"See you," he mouths back, before getting into his car and driving off, heading home to Jonathan.

She reaches down to turn the key in the ignition, remembering how comforted she felt earlier, when she was so certain Andre was here with her.

She tells herself that if that was real, that if he's truly out there, somewhere, he'll send her another message.

A song.

When the radio comes on, she'll hear that song again. "Hello, It's Me."

Or is that asking too much?

Is she being too specific?

Do ghosts take requests?

A choked little laugh escapes Annie, seeming to echo in the decidedly empty car.

All right, it doesn't have to be that particular song again. It can be any song. Any song with meaning will do.

She'll hear it, and she'll know that he's there. She won't be alone anymore.

She takes a deep breath, steeling herself for disappointment, even as she acknowledges that she's not asking too much now.

Just send me a song with meaning, Andre. That's all. Then I'll know you're really with me.

But will she?

Odds are, when you turn on the radio, a song is going to be playing, and if you search hard enough, you're going to be able to find meaning in it somehow.

So maybe she just wants so desperately to believe . . .

What, Annie? What do you want to believe? In ghosts? Is that it?

Yes. And that she didn't imagine the phone call earlier today. That the Todd Rundgren song confirmed that it was real. That Andre was still with her, is with her now, will always be with her.

Here goes.

She turns the key.

In the fleeting instant before the engine turns over, she knows. She knows it isn't going to happen. Not now. She doesn't feel him now.

". . . another hot one tomorrow, with temperatures in the low nineties inland and ten degrees cooler at the shore. And now, here's an old one from Long Island's own Billy Joel."

Annie reaches for the radio knob and turns it abruptly to the left, cutting off the opening strains of "Uptown Girl."

Grim-faced, the Widow Harlowe drives home in solitary silence.

Chapter
4

Thom had every intention of breaking up with Joyce first thing that sunny Sunday morning.

Or at least, first thing after he's read the Sunday *Times* while enjoying his usual two cups of black coffee and a couple of leftover cookies from last night's party.

Sitting on the terrace, the warm breeze rustling his newspaper and the leafy boughs overhead, listening to the surf and the distant hum of a seaplane, Thom contentedly nibbles the crumbly, red-frosting-piped corner of another cookie. The opening line of a poem Mother used to recite floats into his head as lazily as the single billowing white cloud that drifts against this morning's dazzling cerulean sky.

"What is so rare as a day in June?"

Finding a heap of iced sugar cookies on a platter on one's polished granite countertop, that's what.

Normally, Thom has fruit and yogurt for breakfast. But today, when he broke off a star-spangled edge of a buttery, cleverly frosted flag while waiting for the percolator to do its thing, he was a goner.

If James Russell Lowell had tasted these cookies, he'd have amended his famous poem to include them, Thom decides, flipping a page of the Sunday *New York Times Magazine*.

Cookies.

Yes, there's another item he should add to his list of risky but worthwhile pleasures.

All cookies, but these in particular.

They're so decadent and delicious that before one knows it, one has eaten two. Or six.

One might lose count.

If Thom woke to find these cookies in his kitchen every morning, it wouldn't be long before he'd be struggling to button his chinos.

Hence, the potential for peril.

But this morning, Thom isn't in the mood to think about peril.

Nor is he in the mood to think about Joyce, or breakups.

Not yet.

He turns another page, takes another bite, sips more of his coffee, and sets the mug on the edge of the paper so that it won't blow away.

He's wondering why his coffee tastes so darned bitter this morning when a shadow falls over the table.

"Mr. Brannock?"

He looks up to see Norma, his weekend housekeeper, towering above him. Big blond Norma towers above Thom even when he's standing, but she's particularly formidable from this vantage point, all but blocking out the sun.

"What's the problem, Norma?" he asks, because taci-
turn Norma only interrupts him when she has one.

"I found this."

Something glints in the palm of her outstretched hand.
He takes it from her.

"It's a wedding ring," he informs her—which is, of
course, quite obvious.

If she were Anne from last night, she might roll her
eyes or volley a wise-ass comeback, but she's Norma, so
she merely nods and says, "Yes, it is."

Anne from last night. Now there's a woman more rare
than a day in June. More rare than a snowstorm in June,
Thom muses, nibbling another sugary crumb of cookie
and turning the gold band over in his hand.

"Where did you find this?" he asks Norma, even as he
busies himself coming up with a more suitable name for
the green-eyed waitress he'll never see again.

"Anne" is simply too staid. She doesn't look like an
Anne. And certainly not an Anne with an "e," which is
precisely how all the Southampton and Park Avenue
Annes he's ever known spell their names.

This particular Anne looks—all right, *looked,* since
she isn't here and he'll never see her again—like someone whose name should be more upbeat and breezy.

Breezy as this day in June, for that matter, which leads
him to wonder what she's doing on this breezy June day.

It's perfect weather for sailing.

He glances at the ubiquitous white triangles on the
horizon and finds it all too easy to picture Anne on a boat,
wind stirring her curls, sun kissing her cheeks . . .

"Mr. Brannock?"

Oh. Right. Norma.

Norma whose blond bun is as tight as her lips, which are growing more taut by the second as she waits for him to respond to whatever it is she's waiting for him to respond to.

Oh. Right. The ring.

He weighs it in his open palm, noting that it's fairly lightweight. Too lightweight to belong to him—if he owned a gold wedding band, which, thank goodness, he does not. Anyway, it's too small to be a man's ring.

"Where did you find it, Norma?"

"On the floor in the butler's pantry."

If the ring's lack of heft didn't rule out the party guests as possible owners of the ring, the fact that it was found in the butler's pantry would. The first floor powder room is as far off the domestic beaten path as any woman in his mother's and sister's social circle would venture.

Feeling a bit like Angela Lansbury in that old detective show Father liked to watch, Thom deduces that the wedding band must belong to a member of the household staff, or perhaps to the caterer's waitstaff.

He tilts it to see whether anybody's initials are inscribed. Something is written there, but it takes a few different angles to make out the scrolled engraving.

ONE LOVE, ONE LIFETIME.

Thom recognizes the lyrics, but can't quite place them.

He slips the ring thoughtfully into the pocket of his chinos.

"I'll take care of this, Norma," he assures the hovering behemoth.

"All right."

Thom is certain that she's imagining him hocking the ring and treating himself to a round of golf with the profits. Little does she realize that the ring is virtually worthless in the grand scheme of things. Thom's things, anyway.

But it means something to somebody, and he's going to see that it's returned to the former bride.

Again, Anne wafts into his thoughts.

She worked in the kitchen, and most likely in the butler's pantry as well.

But she wasn't wearing a wedding ring.

Maybe because this belongs to her, and it had already fallen off.

Thom's heart beats a little faster at the thought of seeing her again . . .

To hand over her wedding ring?

His nostrils curl in disdain. What the heck is wrong with him today?

And why does his heart beat just as quickly when he tells himself that the ring most definitely does not belong to Anne because she most definitely isn't married?

Her marital status is of no concern to him.

His only concern, this fine, rare June morning, is Joyce's marital status.

More specifically, seeing that Joyce maintains her current single one.

But he'll have to get to the breakup a little later.

For the moment, Thom is a man with a mission.

Patting the ring in his pocket, he grabs another cookie and heads inside for the phone.

"One love, one lifetime."

The words slam into Annie like a hurtled barbell.

"Say you'll share with me one love, one lifetime . . ."

The lyrics are from "All I Ask of You," sung by Merlin at her wedding . . . and permanently engraved into her wedding ring.

A ring that is currently missing from her finger.

She didn't even notice.

How could she not have noticed?

"Yes," she tells Merlin, clutching the phone hard against her ear in her disconcertingly bare hand. "Of course it's my ring. Do you have it?"

"No."

"I thought you said—"

"Thom Brannock has it. His maid found it. He's going to drop by with it this afternoon."

"*He* is? Or his maid is?"

"He said he would."

What is there to say other than "Oh"?

But Annie has plenty to think about. Which is why, upon hanging up the telephone, she remains rooted to the kitchen floor, brain careening.

That she could have lost her wedding ring and not realized it is disconcerting.

That she's about to come face to face with Thom Brannock again is even more so.

"Mommy? I want more toast."

She looks up to see Milo standing on a kitchen chair, trying to reach the open loaf of bread beside the toaster on the crumb-covered counter.

"Sit down, Milo," Annie says sharply, hurrying over to steady the chair.

"But I want more toast."

"Is that how you ask?"

"Please."

She shakes her head and automatically says, "Start over," as she runs the tip of her left thumb over the vacant base of her left ring finger.

"May I please have more toast?" Milo intones.

"Yes."

Annie deposits the heels of the loaf into the toaster, pushes the lever, and wonders how much a jeweler will charge to resize a ring.

Too much.

She'll have to run out and buy a ring guard . . .

How much do those cost?

Well, she can always wind yarn around the inside on the bottom, the way she did in high school when Colin Albertson gave her his class ring to wear.

The toast pops up, and Annie spreads it with the last of the butter.

"Thank you, Mommy," Milo says politely as she places it in front of him.

"You're welcome." She plants a kiss on his head. "So you really had fun last night with Carly?"

"Yup. Except she wouldn't let me practice crash landings. She said it was too dangerous and I might break my head or a vase or something."

Score one for Carly.

"When is she coming again, Mommy?"

"I don't know. Maybe sometime."

"When?" Milo presses.

"Next time I need a sitter."

"When will that be?"

"I don't know, Milo. Soon."

It isn't a lie, exactly. Everything is relative. Next winter could be considered soon. It all depends on how you look at it.

"How soon?"

Annie clenches her teeth, wishing desperately that Andre were here to come to her rescue.

Back in the old days, he would swoop in to expertly divert Milo's line of questioning. He'd say something like, "Look out the window! Is that a swarm of locusts heading in our direction?" Or the Green Goblin? Or a runaway train . . .?

Then, after Milo had searched long enough for Annie to extract herself, Andre would say, "Oh, wait . . . I guess it's just a mosquito." Or a plant. Or a Matchbox car.

The little everyday things. That's what she misses most.

Oh, who is she kidding? She misses the little everyday things, and the medium-sized things, and the big things. She misses every damned thing about having a husband, about having a daddy for her children.

"How soon, Mommy?" Milo asks again.

"Just . . . soon," she snaps. "Okay?"

She can tell by her son's expression that it isn't okay, but mercifully, Milo falls silent, at least for the time being.

On her way back to the counter, Annie reaches over to pick up a stray crust that somehow landed three feet from the table, and notices that the wooden floor could be cleaner. In fact, it's downright grungy.

She should mop.

Straightening and glancing around the kitchen, she tries to see it the way a visitor might. Say, Thom Brannock.

Dirty dishes are piled in the sink; clean ones are heaped in the drying rack beside it. The counters are littered with breakfast makings, yesterday's newspaper, unclipped coupon fliers, and a scattering of unpaid bills. Small fingerprints smudge the windows, the lower section of screen on the backdoor has been pushed out again, her vintage apron collection is spilling out of a half-opened drawer, and several pieces of curling crayon artwork have dropped off the front of the refrigerator.

Good Lord. Annie should do more than mop.

She should move.

Milo announces, "Mommy, I can't eat this toast."

"Why not?"

"Because it's the ends. I don't like the ends."

"That was all that was left of the loaf, sweetie," she says guiltily. "We'll go shopping later and get more bread."

Butter, too.

And milk, and eggs, and cereal, and everything else they've run out of again.

"Can we get ice cream, too?"

No, she thinks. There isn't money in the budget for ice cream.

"Yes," she says. She'll have to scrimp somewhere else. Her little boy wants ice cream.

"Yummy! Can we get chocolate chip?"

"Sure."

"Can we go now?"

"No."

"When?"

"Soon, sweetie."

"When is soon?"

Lord help her. Lord help them all.

Somehow, Annie swallows her frustration. This time. "Milo, go pick up the Legos that are all over the floor by the front door, will you?"

"But—"

"Milo, I need your help. Please."

Perhaps sensing the weary despair in her tone, he scuttles out of the room.

"Thank you," Annie whispers to the ceiling, or God, or Andre.

Then she turns on the water and reaches for the detergent, prepared to tackle the dirty dishes.

She isn't going anywhere until the house is presentable . . . and her wedding ring is back on her finger where it belongs, courtesy of Thom Brannock.

Driving along Montauk Highway with an old Bruce Springsteen CD blasting, the top of his BMW convertible down, golden sunshine and warm wind in his face, Thom feels almost carefree.

Never mind that he should be heading west, toward Joyce's summer home, instead of east, toward Anne's . . . well, presumably year-round home.

Thom could easily have instructed a member of the household staff to deliver the ring to its owner . . . or he could have left its retrieval up to her.

Instead, here he is, playing messenger . . . and procrastinating what he's supposed to be doing today. Namely, breaking up with Joyce.

If only he could extract himself from their relationship as easily as he fell into it.

If only the wedding ring he found belonged to somebody other than Anne.

Annie, he corrects himself with a grin, remembering the caterer's response when he read the ring's inscription over the telephone. Merlin was distracted when he called, busy with a client on the other line, but he paused long enough to say, "Oh, that's Annie's ring."

Right. Thom just knew it.

Not that the wedding ring belonged to the green-eyed brunette he met last night, but that her name couldn't possibly be simply Anne.

Annie.

Funny how one letter can make such a huge difference.

Annie suits her.

Anne does not.

It's a damned shame she's married, Thom thinks, braking for a traffic light in the heart of bustling Montauk. Married and, according to the rushed Merlin, so anxious to have her ring back that she wouldn't want to wait for an overnight delivery. According to Merlin, nothing would do but that Thom arrange to get the ring back to her immediately.

It was a presumptuous and hurried request.

So why didn't Thom refuse? Why did he assure the presumptuous and hurried Merlin that he would personally bring the ring back to its owner?

It was almost as though his vocal chords were momentarily taken over by a stranger. An oddly agreeable stranger.

Thom doesn't have time for this.

He doesn't have time for much of anything these days.

Yet here he is, miles from home and work and Joyce, to whom he's supposed to be saying farewell forever.

Foot on the brake, he watches a T-shirt–clad family of five strolling leisurely across the road in front of his car. The mother is pushing a chubby baby in an umbrella stroller; the dad has one child on his shoulders and another clinging tightly to his hand.

They're laughing. All five of them.

For some unearthly reason, Thom wonders what it would be like to be that laughing dad. He supposes he'll never know. He can't remember his own father ever wearing a T-shirt, holding his hand, or strolling anywhere, not even on a Sunday afternoon in summertime.

He wonders wistfully if Annie and her husband have children; if they spend Sunday afternoons together; if they laugh together.

Yes, too bad she's married.

Or perhaps, too bad he isn't.

The light changes.

Thom drives on.

If Annie weren't married . . .

You wouldn't be here, he reminds himself. *You wouldn't be seeing her again.*

Irony of ironies, the only reason he's seeing her again is that she *is* married.

Really, it's a shame. Because on a day like today, Thom might just be tempted to kiss a pretty waitress.

What the hell are you thinking? he asks himself promptly. *What the hell are you doing?*

It must be all those dangerous cookies. The spike in his blood sugar is making him feel irresponsible. Reckless, even.

The shops, restaurants and hotels of Montauk quickly fall away as Thom drives east, along the highway's increasingly sandy shoulder, past thickening clusters of trees and brush and scattered homes set back from the road.

He has never had occasion to travel this far out on the island—not by car, anyway. He's sailed around the tip and up toward the coastal islands off New England in the past, although he hasn't had the time or ambition to do even that in a long, long while.

But today, of all days, for whatever reason, venturing into uncharted territory seems to suit Thomas Brannock IV just fine.

Chapter
5

"Mommy! A guy is here!" Trixie yells from the living room.

Oh, no. Already?

"I'm coming," Annie calls, straightening from a futile attempt to vanquish a sticky spill from the kitchen floor with a damp sponge.

She should have mopped.

She *would* have mopped . . . if she weren't so busy de-cluttering and vacuuming and dusting and washing and drying and putting away and folding and scrubbing and—

Why doesn't the house look clean? She's just spent an exhausting hour and a half trying to make it presentable. Now Thom Brannock is here and all he'll see is dirt and cobwebs and clutter.

Oh, well.

Who cares what he thinks?

What matters is that he's returned her wedding ring.

Dropping the sponge into the empty sink, Annie juts out her lower lip in an attempt to instantly blow-dry and style the bangs that are plastered with sweat to her forehead. She must look like a wreck. She had planned to change out of the ancient denim cutoffs and circa 1994 cropped white tank top she threw on after her shower this morning.

This skimpy outfit may have been suitable for today's designated project—gluing beach glass to painted wooden frames—and it may have been suitable for the cleaning marathon she just completed, but it's hardly suitable for a tête-à-tête with a good-looking Southamptonite.

Not that it matters. Thom Brannock is here to hand over her lost ring, which will take all of two seconds. He's not here to take note of what Annie is—or isn't—wearing.

"Mommy!" Trixie calls. "The guy is knocking on the door!"

Annie scurries into the living room, stepping over a laundry basket heaped with clean laundry she took out of the dryer. Or is it dirty laundry she meant to put into the washer?

"Hello?"

The male voice coming through the screen isn't quite as deep and intimidating as she recalls. Or maybe it just seems that way because the sound has less room to reverberate in her hovel the way it did in his granite and marble palace.

In any case, Annie finds herself relaxing just a bit as she sidesteps the Legos Milo was supposed to pick up and gets a first glimpse of the visitor—a.k.a., The Guy—on her porch.

Thom Brannock is wearing khaki slacks, loafers that

are identical to Merlin's Gucci ones, and a coral-colored shirt with a familiar miniature polo rider logo below his left shoulder. His dark hair, so neatly combed to one side last night, looks a little spiky today, and his cheeks appear to be sunburnt.

He looks almost like a regular person.

He *is* a regular person, Annie reminds herself. A regular person who's hotter than hot and worth more than a small Caribbean nation, with eyes the same hue of the Caribbean at dusk . . .

But a regular person nonetheless.

"Hi." She opens the screen door, which squeaks loudly.

Andre. WD-40.

Memories.

Dammit.

"Hi." Thom Brannock smiles.

"Did you have any trouble finding us? Sometimes Merlin doesn't give the best directions."

"He didn't. I plugged your address into the Internet and came up with the specifics."

"That was smart," says Annie, who is certain she's the only person on the planet who has never been on-line. She and Andre could never afford a computer. But she isn't about to admit that to Mr. Ralph Gucci Lauren.

His hands are in his pockets, his legs casually straddled. He doesn't appear to be in any hurry to hand over the ring and be on his way.

"Um . . . do you want to come in?" she asks, certain he'll say that he doesn't.

Praying he'll say that he doesn't.

"Sure."

Terrific.

Annie takes a step back, kicking a hunk of Lego out of the way as she does so.

"Watch your step," she tells her visitor as he steps over the threshold, bringing with him the misty citrus scent of expensive cologne. "My son has the place booby-trapped."

"How old is your son?"

"He's six," Trixie pipes up, materializing at Annie's elbow. "I'm four. I'm going to kindergarten in September. Mommy is thirty."

"Is that so." Thom grins at Annie. "You might want to break her of that habit in the next few years."

"What habit?" Trixie asks.

Annie watches Thom crouch beside her daughter and gently push her dark hair back from her ear to whisper into it, "A woman never admits her age . . . or another woman's age."

"Yeah, only I'm not a woman," Trixie informs him. "I'm a girl. And my brother is a boy."

Thom laughs.

"And Mommy is a woman," Trixie continues. "And Daddy was a guy."

Thom's smile fades.

"Was?" He straightens to his full height, which is considerable, and looks down at Annie.

She nods, unable to speak. These days, she never knows when an unexpected wave of emotion is going to render her mute.

"Daddy died a long time ago," Trixie tells Thom.

"How long ago?"

The question is directed at Annie, but she can't seem to force sound past the lump in her throat.

She thinks she'd be used to it by now. It's been a year since she became a widow. Most of the time, she's acutely aware that she's a widow.

But the thing is, she's used to being around people who are also acutely aware that she's a widow. People who respectfully sidestep questions and comments and painful reminders.

In any case, Annie seems to have taken a giant step backward in the grieving process upon hearing her daughter utter the words "Daddy died."

"I'm sorry." Thom shakes his head. "I didn't know."

She nods mutely, wanting to tell him that it's all right. Not that it is; nothing is all right, nothing will ever be all right again.

She can't speak, anyway. It's all she can do to contain the tears that are pooling in her eyes.

"Who are you?" Trixie asks.

"I'm . . ." Thom falters, looking to Annie for an explanation.

It takes her a moment to find one, and another to find her voice.

"He's dropping something off for me," she tells her daughter.

"What is it?"

"Just something that I lost."

"What is it?" Trixie persists.

"Jewelry."

"Which kind of jewelry?"

"Trixie—"

"Where did you lose it?"

"Go find Milo," Annie orders her daughter, having had her fill of Trixie for the moment. "He was supposed to pick up his Legos."

"But—"

"Go."

Trixie goes. But not without casting a curious backward glance at Thom Brannock, who smiles at her and gives a little wave.

"Cute kid," he tells Annie, cutting off the apology she was about to offer.

She isn't certain what, exactly, she was going to apologize about. But she's pretty sure that men like Thom Brannock aren't accustomed to playing Twenty Questions with four-year-olds.

"Thank you," she says, for lack of anything else.

"She looks like you."

Annie nods. It's true. Trixie does resemble her. So does Milo. That neither of the kids looks anything like their father is a cruel twist of fate, as far as Annie is concerned.

Then again, maybe it would be harder to see Andre every time she glances at her children. It's bad enough to occasionally glimpse his personality in them, or spot one of his many quirks, or hear a distinct vocal inflection she thought was his alone.

Didn't she watch her own father visibly flinch whenever he looked at her in those grim months after after Mom died?

"You look more like her than she did, in the end," he often said, sounding a little hoarse.

Poor Dad.

Poor me.

Annie isn't sure which is more torturous: watching a loved one fade slowly and painfully with every passing day, or waking up one morning to find them gone without warning. One thing is certain: She'll never make the mistake her father did and remarry.

Not that Annie has anything against the stepmother who joined the family rather abruptly after Dad met her on a cruise a few years ago. It's just that Carolyn isn't Mom. And what she *is*—a quietly pleasant middle-aged woman—simply isn't enough. Not for any of them. Even Dad. The spark went out of Larry Grimes's eyes when his wife died, and clearly, nothing can ever bring it back. Not even the companionship of a woman who shares his love of golf and cards—something, ironically, Annie's mother did not.

Obviously, it takes more than shared interests to create sparks.

At least he isn't alone, Annie tells herself frequently, shuddering at the memories of what she mistakenly assumed were the darkest days of her life. Dad alone was even worse than Dad at Mom's deathbed for weeks on end. He was just . . . *lost*. Little boy lost. Utterly bereft— the way Annie feels without Andre.

"So you have two children?" Thom asks, glancing around the cluttered living room.

"Yes. But it looks like I have ten, doesn't it?" Annie tries to see the place through his eyes, noticing the heaps of primary-colored plastic toys, the television tuned to cartoons, the furniture and rugs that are already askew.

"Do you want something to drink?" Annie offers her visitor belatedly, then wonders what she'll do if he says yes. It's not as though she has an iced pitcher of lemonade or chilled Perrier and lime wedges at the ready.

"That would be nice."

Damn.

"What can I get you?" Annie asks. "Coffee? Juice box?"

He laughs.

So, after a moment, does she. But she says, "Trust me, I'm not kidding."

"Well, that's fine. I've had enough coffee today, so I'll take juice."

"Juice box."

"Juice box," he amends with a grin, and Annie feels an odd flicker of something she has no business feeling.

"Scary Cherry Berry or One Bad Apple?" Annie calls from her kitchen as Thom walks over to the couch.

It takes him a moment to realize she must be talking about juice box flavors.

He calls back, "Surprise me."

Surprise me.

Yes. Annie Harlowe already has done just that.

She isn't married after all.

A loud thump sounds overhead, so violent it shakes the glass in the Victorian light fixture above the front door. Thom looks up, wondering if something happened to one of the kids.

But their mother, opening and closing the refrigerator in the next room, isn't rushing frantically to the scene, meaning she obviously isn't concerned that bodily harm has come to her offspring.

Thom decides not to be, either, and goes back to pondering Annie's startling marital status.

So the wedding ring in his pocket—the ring she so desperately wants back on her finger—was placed there by her *late* husband. Annie is single.

Well, not exactly. She's widowed.

Yes. And widows are single.

And the fact that Annie is single changes everything.

Now you can fall in love with her.

Thom blinks.

That particular thought seems to have come out of nowhere . . .

Kind of like his earlier response to Merlin's request that he get the ring back to Annie pronto.

"What is *with* you today?" he mutters to himself, sinking onto the couch . . .

. . . and bolting up again with a yelp.

"Are you all right?" Annie appears in the doorway, clearly alarmed that bodily harm might have come to her visitor.

"I'm fine. I just sat on . . . something." Thom gingerly examines the cushion for whatever it was that bit his posterior, and retrieves only an innocuous-looking, inanimate piece of olive-green plastic.

"Milo!" Annie shouts, rolling her eyes skyward.

There's another jarring thump overhead.

"Are your kids all right?" Thom asks, trying not to blatantly admire the patch of tanned midriff and navel visible where the hem of her white tank top fails to meet the waistband of her tattered shorts. In that getup, with bare feet and her dark hair falling in loose waves down her back, she's Daisy Duke come to life; an adolescent boy's fantasy.

Except that Thom isn't an adolescent boy. He's a grown man with a thousand and one important things to accomplish today, none of which involve belly buttons.

And that, he thinks illogically, shifting his attention to Annie's face, is a real shame.

"The kids are fine," she informs him. "Milo's just . . . um, he's fine." She raises her voice again, bellowing, "Milo! Get down here and pick up your Legos and your army guys!"

Army guy?

Thom examines the object in his hand and sees that it does, indeed, appear to be an army guy. He wonders why he never got to play with army guys when he was little as he hands it over to Annie. Then he turns to examine the cushion, wondering if he dares lower himself again.

"Careful." Annie leans past him to give the couch a quick sweep with her hand. He finds himself inhaling her distinct scent; one that makes him think of springtime and firelight.

She pats the cushion, apparently deeming it safe for immediate occupancy. "Okay, you're good. Have a seat."

He does, without incident, and glances at the television, where an animated, buck-toothed yellow sponge in boxy Bermuda shorts and a tie is laughing maniacally. Mesmerized by the bizarre sight, he looks away only when footsteps suddenly pound down the stairs.

A child leaps into the room, the pillowcase that's tucked into the back collar of his T-shirt billowing behind him.

"Pick up your toys, Superman," Annie says, heading

back to the kitchen with a toss of a gloriously unkempt mane that's downright begging somebody's fingers to comb through it.

"I'm not Superman. I'm Batman."

"Pick up your toys, Batman."

"Who're you?" Milo asks, parking himself in front of the sofa and narrowing a pair of eyes that are precisely the shade of his sister's and his mother's.

"I'm Spider-Man," Thom responds, quite cleverly if he does say so himself. He sticks out his hand. "Very pleased to meet you there, Batman."

"You're not Spider-Man."

"How can you tell?"

"You don't look like Spider-Man. Spider-Man would never wear pink."

"This isn't pink," Thom protests, looking down at his shirt.

"It looks pink."

"Well, it isn't. It's Nantucket Red."

"Spider-Man doesn't wear 'tucket red, either. He wears spiderweb red."

"You're right. He does . . . but only when he's—I'm fighting crime. I'm not fighting crime today."

"Why not?"

"Slow crime day."

Annie's son seems to be weighing the likelihood that Thom is telling the truth.

"What do you wear on a fast crime day?" he demands.

"I wear my official Spider-Man uniform in blue and web red, of course."

"It's not a uniform."

Thom tries again. "A leotard?"

"No!" Milo recoils with the horror of a boy who has a younger sister and knows all too well what a leotard is. "Spider-Man isn't a girl. He's a man and he wears a *costume.*"

"Curses. Foiled again."

The little boy's jaw drops. "You're a bad guy in disguise, aren't you?"

"Nope."

"But bad guys say 'Curses, foiled again.'"

"Well, I'm a good guy."

"But not a superhero."

"No," Thom agrees, "not a superhero."

"Well, I'm a superhero," says Batman. "And I have superpowers."

"Like what?"

"Like I can fly. Almost. Sometimes I crash-land."

Which would explain the thumping overhead. Thom forces back a smile.

"As soon as I get better at it, I'm going to fly up to heaven and see my daddy," Milo goes on, and Thom instantly finds himself struggling against unexpected tears instead.

The thing is . . . Thom never cries.

Ever.

He didn't cry when he broke his leg falling out of a tree when he was nine and he didn't cry when his sister got married and he didn't cry when his own father died.

So why is he on the verge of tears because this little boy's father died?

It's the word "daddy" that gets to him, Thom realizes. First when the little girl said it, and now when the little boy did.

His own father was Father. Never Daddy. Perhaps if Thomas Brannock III had been Daddy, Thom might have cried when he lost him.

"When I find Daddy, I'm going to bring him back with me," Milo informs Thom.

"Good for you." Thom probably shouldn't encourage the kid, but he can't quite bring himself to dash his hopes, either.

"Yeah. It stinks around here without him. And if my daddy was here he could find the treasure at Copper Beach."

"Treasure?"

"Yeah, somebody lost it near Copper Beach a hundred years ago and my daddy was trying to find it. I was helping him."

"Oh. Well that's . . ."

Heartbreaking. That's what it is. Thom swallows hard.

"And if my daddy was here," Milo goes on dreamily, "my sister would stop having nightmares all the time and my mom wouldn't be so tired all the time, or sad, and she'd stop crying and Daddy could help her do stuff and he could help me do stuff and I'd fine'ly learn how to tie my shoes."

Thom responds to this fresh trail of tearjerkers with a lame, "You don't know how to tie your shoes?"

"Dad was s'posed to teach me." Milo shakes his head. "And I can't ride a bike, either. Or shoot bows and arrows."

"Well, I can probably take care of the shoe thing right now. Got a pair of sneakers with laces?"

"Yeah! I'll be right back!" Milo dashes toward the stairs, cape flapping.

Shaking his head, Thom surveys the army guy, hastily

tossed onto the floor, and the Legos strewn in the entryway.

The last thing Annie would ever expect to see in her living room is a billionaire tycoon crawling around picking up Legos and watching *SpongeBob SquarePants* on television out of the corner of his eye.

But that is precisely the sight that greets her when she returns from the kitchen with a juice box for him and a cup of coffee for her.

"What are you doing?" she asks, stopping short in horror.

"Picking up Legos."

"I can see that, but . . . why?"

"Because they're there," he says affably, dumping a handful of plastic bricks into a nearby tub that holds the rest of them.

"But you don't have to— Milo!" she calls. "Get down here! Where are you?"

"He's finding his sneakers," Thom says helpfully, and gestures. "Is that my juice box?"

"Oh. Yes." She hands it over and waits for a reaction, fairly certain the man has never seen, much less ingested, a juice box before.

"Snazzy Black Razzy," he reads from the label.

"I was all out of cherry and apple."

"That's okay. I'm a big fan of Snazzy Black Razzy."

Sure he is. Just like she's a big fan of Krug Grande Cuvée, the champagne served at his party last night. She never heard of it until she found herself pouring it, and she's willing to bet he never heard of Snazzy Black Razzy until now.

Still, he's looking it over with interest . . . or so she thinks, until she realizes he's more likely trying to figure out what to do with it.

"Here," she says, gesturing for him to return it to her. She pries the plastic-encased straw from the side of the carton, slips it from its wrapper, and pokes it through the hole in the top of the box.

"Huh. Learn something new every day." He takes it back, sips, and smiles. "Thanks."

"You're welcome." She raises her coffee to her lips.

The beverage is lukewarm and so bitterly potent, thanks to six hours on the burner, that even her liberal addition of milk and sugar can't mask the taste.

Still, it's caffeine, and God knows she needs it to get through yet another long day. She didn't sleep well. She kept dreaming that the phone was ringing, that Andre was on the other end, that every time she picked it up, the line went dead.

"What's the matter? Too strong?"

She looks up to find Thom watching her.

"The coffee? No, it's fine." Annie wonders how to go about politely getting her ring back and hustling him out of here. He seems to be in no hurry to rush home and resume polishing his silver and gold or whatever it is men like him do with their spare time.

"Do you want me to turn off the television?" he asks.

"No, that's all right. I usually just leave it on."

"For how long?"

All day, every day doesn't seem like an acceptable reply, so she says, "A while. It keeps the kids occupied while I'm busy with other things."

"Your son is charming," Thom informs her, giving the

cushion another quick once-over before sitting on the couch.

"Oh, he's charming, all right."

"He says he can fly but he can't tie his shoes, so I offered to teach him."

"To fly?"

He smirks. "To tie his shoes. I'm afraid my wings are in the shop this weekend."

"Well, that's a shame."

"Yeah. It's such a pain to walk everywhere."

"Or drive," she adds, having glimpsed the shiny BMW convertible in her driveway. "Listen, I know you probably think I'm a lousy mother for not teaching him how to tie his shoes, but—"

"I don't think that."

Maybe he doesn't, but she does.

She goes on wearily, needing to explain to him—or maybe mostly to herself, "My husband had a lot more patience than I do. He was trying to teach Milo how to tie his laces when . . . well, he never got around to it."

He never got around to a lot of things.

She follows Thom's gaze to the mantel, with its large collection of framed photos of Andre, the variably-sized rectangles scattered as randomly as gravestones in an ancient cemetery.

"So Milo's still wearing Velcro sneakers," she rushes on, looking at the floor, "and I keep promising to teach him to tie—I even bought him regular sneakers with laces before school ended, so he'd be ready. But I haven't had a chance. I've been . . . busy."

"Yeah, well . . . I know how that goes."

"You do?"

"The being busy thing," he says with a laugh. "It seems like I never have time to do anything these days."

Really. Then why the heck is he sitting on her couch slurping a juice box?

Annie takes another sip of her coffee, wishing the caffeine would hurry and do its thing. She's absolutely and thoroughly exhausted. She'd love to sink into the recliner opposite the couch, but she's afraid that if she sits down, Thom will never take his cue and leave.

Why do you want him out of here so badly, Annie?

It isn't just because she's anxious to have her ring back, or because the house is a mess, or because she has other things to do, like go out and buy chocolate chip ice cream.

No, it's mostly because his presence makes her nervous. And the thing about it that makes her nervous is, ironically, that he doesn't seem . . . well, out of place.

You would expect a man like Thom Brannock to stick out here like antique English bone china in a Tupperware cabinet, but he doesn't. He seems oddly comfortable.

Which makes Annie decidedly *un*comfortable.

She can't go getting used to having dashing billionaire tycoons dropping in for midafternoon juice boxes, because life isn't like that. Her life, anyway.

Her life is about unpaid bills and untied shoelaces. Stray army guys and scattered Legos and kids who ask too many questions and think they can fly.

Meanwhile, his life is about . . . well, what is it about, exactly?

She decides it can't hurt to ask him. The worst that can happen is that he'll think she's rude and leave.

"What is it that keeps you so busy, Mr. Brannock?"

"Don't call me that. It's Thom, remember? With—"

"An 'h.' Got it. What is it that you do, Thom?" She lifts her mug to her lips again.

"I'm in finance," is the reply, which could mean any number of things . . . none of which she is likely to understand.

Before she can think of an intelligent question to ask about finance, he looks around and says, "This is a great old house."

Annie nearly snorts coffee through her nose.

"This great old house is falling apart," she tells him, just in case he hasn't noticed the sagging steps and worn moldings and uneven hardwood floors.

"I think it has character."

Annie smiles. She can't help herself. She wants to hate this man, but she likes him . . . and not just because he likes her house.

"Your place has character, too."

"My house has about as much character as the guests at my party do."

She raises an eyebrow.

"Don't look so surprised, Annie. I don't have any illusions about where I live or who lives around me."

"Then why do you do it?"

"What?"

"Live there? Surround yourself with . . . those people?"

"They're the only people I know, and it's the only summer house I own."

"Sell it and buy a new one," she says with a shrug. "Or an old one. A great old house with character."

"All right. Is this place for sale?"

She laughs. "Sorry. It isn't. You'll have to find some other great old house with character."

"Are you serious? You wouldn't sell this house to me for . . . say . . . half a million bucks?"

Is he offering?

It doesn't matter. She isn't taking.

"Nope."

"A million?"

"Uh-uh."

"Really."

"Really."

She figures he isn't serious, and figures he doesn't know that she *is*.

She isn't about to explain to Thom Brannock about Andre and memories and this house being her only link to her husband.

All right, not her *only* link. There are the kids, of course. And her wedding ring, if he would just give it to her. And the cell phone she keeps hooked up so that she can hear Andre's voice on his outgoing message . . .

And imagine that he's answering calls in person.

Now that twenty-four hours—and all those vivid dreams—have elapsed since the phantom phone call, Annie is positive she imagined it.

As soon as Erika gets back from Florida, she's going to ask her about grief counseling after all. Maybe it will help.

Or maybe the therapist Erika refers her to will conclude that she's lost her mind and belongs in an institution.

"Why would you want this house, anyway?" Annie asks, turning her attention back to Thom.

He laughs. "Maybe because you just told me that I can't have it. That's what I do, you know."

"Buy old houses?"

"No, I acquire corporations."

"You're a corporate raider? You mean, like hostile takeovers?"

"Only when it's absolutely necessary." He shrugs. "What can I say? I happen to like a challenge."

Overhead thump.

Footsteps on the stairs.

Annie closes her eyes wearily. Her son's endless energy can be so . . . exhausting. She reluctantly allows herself to drop into the chair, promising herself that she'll get up in a moment.

"Hey, I found 'em, Mr. . . . what's your name?" Milo bounds into the living room again and slides to a sock-footed halt in front of the couch, sneakers in hand.

"My name is Thom."

"Just Thom?"

"Just Thom."

"With an 'h,' " Annie can't resist adding, prying open her heavy eyelids to gauge Thom's reaction.

He grins at her as Milo says, "But Thom starts with a 't,' not an 'h.' "

"Hey, you're right. Smart kid."

Annie returns Thom's smile through a yawn.

"Sit down," he tells her son, patting the couch beside him. "First thing you're going to do is take the laces and make an 'x' . . ."

Annie yawns again.

Her eyes are burning.

If only it were evening. If she were able to crawl into

bed now, she suspects she might actually be able to sleep straight through until morning.

Then again, that rarely happens anymore. In fact, it never does. Sooner or later, a nightmare always wakes her . . . or Trixie's night terrors do.

The Widow Harlowe—who before she became the Widow Harlowe was the sort of person who invariably climbed into bed, closed her eyes, and fell promptly into a sound sleep—is convinced that she is doomed to live the remainder of her life without ever again experiencing REM.

"No, not like that. Do it this way," Thom Brannock is telling Milo.

His voice seems oddly far away, Annie notices, just before it fades altogether.

Chapter 6

Annie is dreaming.

Dreaming of classical music and a mouth-watering aroma and Andre's gentle hand stroking her forehead.

No.

It isn't a dream.

As her senses awaken, she realizes she really is hearing music, smelling food, feeling somebody's fingertips . . .

But not Andre's.

Andre is dead, she recalls, with the jarring awareness that strikes her every time she returns to consciousness after a restful reprieve from her own harsh reality.

Andre is dead.

Her eyes snap open to take in the scene.

She isn't in bed.

She's in a recliner in the living room. But it can't be her living room because the television is off and the stereo is on and it's playing classical music. This can't even be her house, because it smells like food—real food, not food from a can or a box or a pouch, not that her tragically bare cupboards can possibly contain even cans, boxes, or pouches.

Okay, so it's her imagination again, carrying her and her growling stomach away.

"Annie?"

Andre isn't saying her name. Andre isn't standing over her. No, it's . . .

Thom Brannock?

Annie bolts out of the chair. "What are you . . . ?"

He laughs. "Yup, I'm still here."

"You fell asleep, Mommy!"

Trixie is standing beside Thom, looking gleeful. She's wearing a bibbed white apron with red rickrack, circa 1940. Her hair is pulled back in a bread bag twist tie and a substance that looks like ketchup is smeared beside her mouth.

"Mommy, we made dinner for you!"

Annie shifts her gaze to Milo, whose pillowcase cape is now tucked into the front of his shirt and splashed with crimson stains.

"What time is it?" she asks, dazed, looking around the room and realizing that the light is different. Different, as in fading quickly.

"It's dinnertime! Let's go eat!" Trixie giggles and dashes toward the kitchen with Milo on her heels.

"Dinnertime?" Annie echoes incredulously.

"Actually, it's almost seven," Thom says, checking his watch.

"Oh, cripes. I can't believe I did this." She zings an accusatory glare at him, needing to blame . . . somebody. Somebody other than herself. She's sick of blaming herself for everything. She demands of Thom Brannock, "Why did you let me do this? I can't just . . . sleep."

"Why not? You were tired."

"But . . . I have children!"

"No kidding. That's probably why you were so tired. They have a lot of energy, don't they."

Somewhere in the midst of her groggy dismay, Annie notes that his pinkish-red shirt is dotted with pinker, redder splatters, that he currently smells more of frying onions than cologne, that his hair is spikier than it was earlier, as though he's been raking his fingers through it.

"You've been watching my kids?" she asks, shaking her head in a futile effort to clear it. Nothing makes sense.

"Yup."

Thom Brannock looks pleased with himself.

Well, bully for him.

Annie has never been more disappointed in *herself*. What kind of mother just . . . goes to sleep? Entrusts her children to the care of a complete stranger and . . . goes to sleep?

A lousy mother.

That's what kind.

A lousy, incompetent mother.

Annie definitely isn't a survivor. She sucks at survival. The house could have burned down while she was lying here catching a few "z"s. Somebody could have been hurt, or killed.

Tears spring to her eyes.

"Annie?" Thom touches her arm.

She jerks reflexively out of his grasp.

"Annie, don't," he says softly, his hand finding her again and holding her steady this time so that she can't slip away. "Don't be upset with yourself. You're overwhelmed."

She opens her mouth to protest, and to her horror, a sob escapes.

"It's okay."

She stops fighting his grasp.

No, his . . . embrace?

Yes.

Embrace, because, somehow, impossible though it is, he seems to be . . . hugging her?

Yes.

This total stranger—this billionaire tycoon total stranger—is hugging her.

Comforting her.

This, Annie thinks, should not be comforting. This should, in fact, be the most *un*comfortable moment of her life.

She must be delirious, because she seems to have decided that she fits very naturally into Thom's arms, a place she has absolutely no business being. Ever.

But he's right. She *is* overwhelmed.

Awash in self-pity, she allows herself to lean against his broad chest, the way she used to do with Andre.

He even touches her hair the way Andre always did, tenderly weaving his fingers through the tangle of waves.

She looks up to tell him that she's sorry, that he can leave now, but the unexpectedly provocative look in his dark blue eyes robs her of speech, of breath.

He's going to kiss me, she thinks frantically, and realizes, even more frantically, that she wants him to.

She can hear his ragged breathing, feel it stirring the wisps of hair that have fallen around her face. Something flutters to life in the pit of her stomach, sending gossamer quivers along dormant pathways into places that long ago ceased to exist for her.

His mouth is inches from hers.

He really is going to kiss her.

This is all wrong, and this is so right, and it doesn't matter whether it's wrong or right because Annie wants it to happen. More than that, it's *meant* to happen.

Everything happens for a reason, Annie.

Deep inside her, restraint takes flight, leaving in its wake only urgent, aching need.

She closes her eyes and Thom's lips brush hers lightly; too lightly, pulling back all too soon.

Frustrated, she opens her eyes and sees his tentative gaze. Touched by his cautious uncertainty, Annie allows the last of her own to fall away like a thick woolen coat on the first warm day of spring.

"It's okay," she whispers and tiptoes up to meet him this time, welcoming the exquisite pressure of his mouth against hers.

He kisses her hungrily, or perhaps she kisses him hungrily; she can no longer discern where her own desire gives way to his. Boundaries have been crossed and inhibitions shed; there is nothing but here, and him, and . . .

And then something clatters in the kitchen, severing the ethereal bond in a shattering instant.

With a gasp Annie springs away, clasping her mouth as though she's been branded there.

"Mommy! Milo dropped the pot lid and made a mess!" Trixie calls.

"Don't touch the stove!" Annie hurries toward the

back of the house, half afraid that Thom won't follow her, and half afraid that he will.

In the kitchen, she finds Milo picking up the lid and Trixie setting the table. Kettles simmer away on the stove, emitting fragrant tendrils of steam.

"What's going on?" she asks, dazed at the sight and scent of it all.

"We made pasta!" Milo informs her, climbing on a chair and stirring.

"With what?" She plucks him off the chair, pulls it away from the stove, and removes the saucy wooden spoon from his saucier hand. "That's dangerous. You could fall or get burned, Milo."

"I was being careful," he says, and adds, "We made it with tomatoes and onions and noodles."

"And chicken," Trixie reminds her brother, as Annie peers into one bubbling pot, and then another.

"Where did you get all this stuff?"

"We didn't. Thom did," Milo tells Annie.

"He left you alone to go shopping?" asks Annie, who left them alone to go to sleep and is consequently feeling guiltier by the minute.

"No, I had the stuff delivered," Thom's voice says in the doorway behind her.

She turns to see him watching her.

"You had tomatoes and onions delivered?"

"And pasta and chicken."

That must have cost a fortune, she thinks, even as she reminds herself that he has one.

"Thank you," she says aloud. "You didn't have to—"

"I know. I wanted to, Annie. I don't do anything unless I want to."

Judging by the look in his eye, he's talking about more than arranging grocery delivery.

But something inside of her refuses to accept anything he's offering.

"Let me repay you," she says, going for the Prada bag—courtesy of Merlin—that she keeps on a hook by the door. Ironically, all that's in it is her old nylon wallet, and all that's in that is the cash she earned waiting on Thom and his fancy friends last night.

Of course, the money is already ear-marked for other expenses. But she'll come up with more somehow. She'll borrow it from Merlin, or she'll work that luncheon he mentioned later this week.

Suddenly, it seems very important that she not allow Thom Brannock to do her any favors.

"Stop," he says, crossing the kitchen and putting his hand on her purse before she can open it. "I don't want your money. The only way you can repay me is to let me stay for dinner."

"But—"

"Come on," he cajoles, a twinkle lighting his blue gaze. "After all this hard work, the least you can do is let me sample my own cooking."

"All right," she agrees helplessly, and glances at her beaming children.

"Can you come for dinner again tomorrow night, too?" Milo asks Thom, who shrugs and looks uncomfortable.

He begins, "I don't think—"

Annie cuts him off with a brisk, "No, Milo, he can't."

To Thom, she says in a low voice, "Never say 'I don't think' to a kid. All kids know that where there's an 'I don't think,' there's a way."

"Gotcha," he says with a wink—a disappointed wink, she can't help thinking. Almost as if he was hoping to be invited back for dinner again tomorrow night. Which, of course, is utterly ridiculous . . . no matter what just happened between them in the living room.

"Guess what, Mommy? I made place cards," Trixie announces. "And I used a purple crayon because Thom's favorite color is purple. And we made Pasta à la Trixie!"

"And Chicken Milo," her son puts in. "Thom knew the recipes. He didn't even need a cookbook. And I never even heard of Chicken Milo until now."

"Neither did I." Annie laughs.

"I'm not sure it's any good," Thom tells her in a whisper as the kids finish setting the table. "I've never cooked before."

"You haven't?"

"No, but I used to watch our housekeeper do it when I was a kid. I always wanted to try it. How hard can it be?"

Annie shakes her head, speechless.

It's all so surreal. Why is this man living out his domestic fantasies in her kitchen?

Never mind that. Why is he kissing her in her living room?

The next thing you know, he'll be moving up the stairs to the—

No.

Her bedroom is off-limits.

And so, for that matter, is her consideration of the skills Thom might be tempted to put to use there.

*   *   *

The meal is over, the dishes are done, the kitchen spotless once again.

All right, it was far from spotless when Thom saw it in the first place. But now it really is clean, thanks to the hour he and Annie spent in here chatting and tidying while the children watched television in the next room.

The conversation flowed as easily between the two of them as it did among all four during the meal.

It's almost, Thom can't help thinking, as though he's stepped onto a movie set, expertly playing the role of a suburban dad. He can practically see himself settling into an easy chair in front of the television with his feet up, dozing off to sleep.

The strange thing is that he longs to do just that.

Ever since he saw that family crossing the street in front of his car earlier . . .

No, it goes back even further than that.

He's been off-kilter ever since he woke up this morning. It all started with those cookies. One indulgence led to another, and another, and the next thing he knew, he was setting aside his productive plans for the day in order to play nursemaid and personal chef to a widow and her fatherless children.

And kissing her. Don't forget that, Thom.

Yes, kissing Annie was the mother of all indulgences. Her lips were sweeter than iced sugar cookies, and he wouldn't have stopped at just one if the children hadn't interrupted when they did.

Thank goodness they did.

It's time he nipped this homey little fantasy in the bud.

"I have to get home, Annie," he says reluctantly, looking around with wistful satisfaction at the sparkling sink, counters and appliances. He's a novice, but he must admit, there's something to be said for good, old-fashioned cleaning.

Just as there's something to be said for a good, old-fashioned kitchen without all the bells and whistles that come with his. Sure, there are scratches in the porcelain sink and worn spots on the floor in front of it, fraying dish towels and yellowed recipes spilling out of a file box.

But this place is as real and down-to-earth as its mistress; its battle scars as undisguised as the crinkly lines around her eyes when she smiles.

Annie's home is lived in; Thom's home is not.

Home, however, is where Thom belongs, and Annie isn't protesting.

He wishes she would.

Not that he'd stay if she asked him.

Still . . . why doesn't she ask him?

Maybe things would be different if the meal he'd prepared for her had actually tasted good, he thinks ruefully. Unfortunately, cooking isn't as easy as it looks, and food doesn't always taste as good as it smells.

But Annie didn't complain about the flavorless pasta or rubbery chicken, and neither did the children. He got the impression that they either have impeccable manners or were having such a good time chatting that they failed to notice his lack of culinary talent.

"I'm sorry," she says now, tucking strands of hair behind her ears, only to have them spring loose again the moment she moves her head. "You probably never counted on staying here more than five minutes."

If that long, he thinks, feeling the weight of her wedding ring in his pocket.

He removes it, holds it out to her. "I guess I should give you this, since it's the reason I came."

"My ring."

"Yes."

She just stares at it for a moment, before taking it from him. She slips it onto her finger, a gesture so melancholy, so *wrong,* that it's all Thom can do not to tell her to take it off again, because she isn't married. She doesn't belong to . . .

To somebody else.

But she doesn't belong to you, either.

Thom finds himself resenting the man whose shoes he unwittingly stepped into for a few precious hours. Resenting him, and pitying the poor soul because he couldn't stay here forever.

Well, neither can you.

"I have to go," he says again, as if repeating it will make the option more appealing.

"I know." She's staring down at her ring now, obviously having retreated to some other realm, well beyond his reach.

"Maybe I'll call you sometime," he suggests. "Just . . . you know. To check in on you. And see how Milo is doing with the shoe-tying."

"Did you teach him?" she asks, looking up.

"I tried. He doesn't really get it, though."

"No. He never did. Andre tried, too."

Andre.

Her husband.

The man who had everything . . . until his luck ran out.

Thom wants to ask her what happened to him, but he doesn't dare. Maybe he'll never know.

Why does it matter? It's none of his business, really.

"Good night, Annie," he says, heading for the door.

She makes a move to follow him, but he can tell that she doesn't really want to.

"You stay," he says. "I'll say good-bye to the kids."

"All right. Thanks again."

"You're welcome. See you."

But he won't.

As much as he wants to, he won't.

And that, Thom tells himself as he walks out of her house, out of her life, is that.

Chapter
7

Thank goodness you're back! I have never been so glad to see anyone in my entire life."

"Talk about a warm welcome..." Ebony-haired, ebony-complected Erika Bauer steps onto the porch and hugs Annie. She has to bend over to do so, being a full head taller.

Annie, in yesterday's shorts and a rumpled T-shirt, with dabs of dried hot glue in her hair and on her hands, returns her former college roommate's embrace a bit gingerly, feeling as though she's going to leave smudges all over Erika's fresh-from-a-day-in-the-office pristine white linen pantsuit. And her friend's tidy cornrows are a blatant reminder that Annie hasn't combed her hair since last night's quick bedtime shower.

Well, that's par for the course of their decade-old friendship these days.

Erika is an upscale, childless, city-dwelling professional with a full-time psychiatric practice. Annie is a single mom with two kids to support and a fixer-upper that's pretty much falling down around her.

"I missed you. It seems like you've been gone forever."

"It does," Erika agrees. "What's new around here?"

"Not a darned thing," Annie lies.

"Working on a new project?" Erika gestures at the array of rocks and seashells scattered on newspapers all over the porch floor, gleaned from an afternoon beachcombing outing with the kids.

"Yes. I'm making paperweights," Annie says halfheartedly. She's had more inspired ideas, that's for sure. But none in the past year. No wonder the gallery owners she's been trying to reach haven't returned her calls.

"How's business?"

"Don't ask." Reaching toward the bedraggled flowers in a terra-cotta planter that Merlin brought her on Memorial Day, Annie quickly deadheads a couple of faded pink blossoms and makes a mental note to water them later.

"That bad?"

"Kind of."

"Well, it's not even the season yet. City people will be swarming the Hamptons in about two seconds. It'll pick up."

Not to the tune of thousands of dollars, Annie thinks grimly. That's basically what she needs to bring in if she's going to keep her tiny household in groceries and utilities.

Aloud, she says to Erika, "Come on inside so I can keep an eye on the kids while we catch up."

"Where are they?"

"Eating chocolate chip ice cream for dessert in the kitchen. You want some? There might be a teaspoonful left in the carton." Annie stifles a yawn behind her hand.

"No, thanks."

"How about a glass of wine?" Annie offers, remembering that she has a bottle of white chilling in the fridge, courtesy of Merlin's last visit. He doesn't like to arrive empty-handed.

"No, thanks," Erika says again. "But you go ahead. Maybe you can use a drink."

"A drink would probably knock me out right now."

Erika nods. "You look as wilted as those pansies, Annie."

"They're petunias," she informs the botanically challenged Erika. "And I'm just tired. Trixie was up a few times last night, as usual."

Erika doesn't seem satisfied with that explanation. "Are you really okay?"

"Sure. I'm fine." Yeah. Sure she's fine.

"No, you aren't. Of course you aren't. Stupid question, huh?"

"Erika—"

"No, really, I'm sorry. Sometimes I forget."

"It's okay," Annie says, wishing that she could.

How merciful it would be if the Widow Harlowe could just forget, even for a moment.

"The anniversary is in a few days," she tells Erika. "I guess it's just harder than usual because of that."

"Milestones are difficult. This one in particular."

"I know, and I thought I was ready to face it. But I guess I'm not. Not that it matters. It's coming, either way. The longest day of the year." She sighs . . . then starts as a sudden gust stirs the windchimes hanging from a rafter above the porch and flaps the edges of the rock-weighted newspapers at her feet.

"Breezy this evening, isn't it?" Erika shivers a little. "It feels good, though. Especially after the heat in Florida. And at least it's not raining. It rained every day down there."

"Come on inside." Annie opens the screen door with a deafening creak.

WD-40. Andre, she thinks wearily.

"Oh, hey, here, I brought you something." Erika hands over the gift-wrapped box and shopping bag she's been holding.

"What is it?" Annie moves aside so that her friend can step past her into the house. The door groans closed.

WD-40. Andre.

"It's just something I bought in Florida. I saw it and thought of you. And in the bag is some stuff I got for the kids at Disney World."

"I thought you were there on business."

"I was. But the conference was in Orlando and so is Disney, so . . ."

"So Aunt Erika decided to make a pit stop and spoil the children. You shouldn't have. They love you even when you don't shower them with gifts."

"Does Trixie still love Pooh Bear?"

"Yup." Annie sits beside Erika on the couch.

"And Milo hasn't outgrown Buzz Lightyear yet?"

"Nope. Erika, I mean it, you really shouldn't have—"

"Relax. It's just T-shirts and beach towels."

"Well, I'll call them in to see when they're done with their ice cream," Annie says, needing to savor the few precious moments of childfree time with her friend.

"Open your box, Annie."

Protesting, she nonetheless rips into the seashell-stamped parchment paper.

How long has it been since somebody got her an unexpected present?

Andre used to do it all the time. Nothing fancy; just CDs and books and an occasional trinket. But he always wrapped them. He said presents were more fun when they came in pretty packaging, and when they came for no occasion at all.

Shoving aside the sharp pang of regret irrevocably soldered to her marital memories, Annie lifts the lid on the plain white box. Inside, in a nest of tissue, is a delicate heart-shaped wooden picture frame with intricate scrollwork.

"The guy who hand-carves those frames was selling them at a street fair and I thought of you," Erika says, leaning over Annie's shoulder to look at it. "Plus, he was so fine I had to have a reason to flirt with him."

Annie laughs. "Oh, sure, use me as an excuse to hit on some unsuspecting street artist. Did he ask you out?"

"No, but at least I got this great frame out of it. I thought you'd like it."

"I love it."

But what am I going to do with it? Annie wonders, swallowing past a rising lump in her throat. A year ago, had somebody presented her with a heart-shaped frame, she would have popped in a recent photo of herself and Andre.

Now what?

She doesn't even have current pictures of the kids. Her fancy Nikon—the one Andre bought her after she dropped their camera into the Caribbean taking pictures of dolphins on their honeymoon cruise—has sat, un-touched, on her closet shelf for a year now, presumably with a half-shot roll of film inside. She can't bring herself to finish shooting it, or to have the pictures developed. Maybe someday she'll be able to face the last captured images of family life before everything fell apart.

But not yet. Not for a long time.

Turning the new picture frame over and over, telling Erika how much she loves it, Annie silently reminds her-self that she can always put in an old snapshot of Andre alone.

But the mantel and her bureau top have already turned into virtual shrines to her husband. Maybe it isn't healthy to keep doing that.

"I'm an idiot."

Startled, Annie looks up at Erika. "What?"

"I said I'm an idiot. Why did I get you that frame? I'm sorry, Annie."

"What are you talking about?"

"It made you think of Andre, right? I can tell by the look on your face."

"Everything makes me think of Andre, Erika. It's no big deal. I love the frame and it's perfect for a picture of the kids." *As soon as I can get my life together and take one,* she adds silently.

Why does it have to be so hard?

Damn Thom Brannock and his kisses.

Okay, maybe not everything is his fault, but his barg-ing in here the other day and kissing her did nothing to expedite her grief process. If anything, she now has the added burden of guilt.

She hasn't kissed anybody but Andre since . . .

Well, since kissing somebody meant you were a couple and you wound up wearing their class ring entwined with yarn.

Then again, is this so different?

One kiss from her high school sweetheart, and Annie was envisioning a future as Mrs. Colin Albertson.

One kiss from Thom Brannock, and for a split second, Annie almost believed she might fall in love again . . . and, even more preposterously, that a man like Thom might fall in love with her.

"Annie, something's different. What's going on with you?"

Startled out of her reverie, Annie looks up to see her friend watching her. Erika's Hershey chocolate–colored eyes seem to see right inside of her. There's no use trying to hide anything, she realizes.

She blurts, "I kissed somebody."

Wishing she could take the incriminating statement back the second it's out, Annie braces herself for shocked reproach.

"*What?*" Erika looks shocked, all right . . . shocked, and delighted. "Who is he?"

"He's . . . nobody."

Nobody who happens to be a major somebody—at least, in the Hamptons and Manhattan.

Annie rushes on, before Erika can insert another question, "It was a huge mistake and it's never going to happen **again**, so it isn't a big deal, not to him, anyway, but it is to me because . . . well, not because I'm interested in him but because . . ."

"Because you feel guilty."

"Of course I feel guilty," she says in a near whisper,

lest her children, chattering and giggling over ice cream in the kitchen, overhear. "Andre hasn't even been gone a year, and here I am . . ."

"Living? Living without him?" Erika touches her arm gently. "What else are you supposed to do, Annie?"

"Not *this*. Not kiss somebody else. I'm not ready."

"Okay. Maybe you're not. But someday—"

"No, Erika. I won't be ready someday. Not ever."

Who, Annie wonders, *am I trying to convince? Erika? Or myself?*

"I know you think that now," Erika tells her in a soothing tone, "but—"

"You don't understand," Annie interrupts with a tear-choked laugh. "It isn't just what I think. It's . . ."

"What is it, Annie? What's holding you back?"

"It's . . . it's Andre. He told me that if anything ever happened to him, I'd better not find somebody else."

"Oh, Annie, that's not—"

"Erika, he really said it."

"But he didn't mean it. People say things."

"He meant it."

"Are you sure you're not just using Andre as an excuse? Some kind of twisted rationalization for your reluctance to get involved with somebody new?"

Annie just shakes her head, running her thumb along the inside of her wedding band, wound with yarn that, irony of ironies, obliterates the engraving.

One love, one lifetime.

Andre Harlowe was the love of her life.

Thom Brannock could never take his place . . . even if he wanted to. Which he doesn't.

Why *would* he?

Why would New York's most eligible bachelor take on the likes of Annie Harlowe when he could have any baggage-free, blue-blooded beauty his heart desires?

The wind abruptly jangles the chimes outside the front door again.

Annie flinches.

"Hey, what else is going on?" Erika asks softly, squeezing her wrist.

"What do you mean?"

"You're jumpy. And you're exhausted. Even more than usual."

Annie nods. These last few days have been brutal. When she isn't reliving the forbidden kiss with Thom Brannock and longing for another, she's obsessing over the phantom phone call: one minute certain that it really happened, the next, absolutely positive that it didn't.

She has to tell somebody, she realizes, before she drives herself crazy speculating.

But what if Erika decides she's gone off the deep end?

"I need to talk to you about something, Erika. But it's kind of . . . out there."

"Okay," says Erika, with a seasoned psychiatrist's open-minded patience—or perhaps, with the open-minded patience of a loyal friend who is no stranger to Annie's capricious past.

"Do you believe that when a person dies," she begins, treading cautiously, "that they're really . . . dead?"

Caressing her chin and wearing the intent expression Annie considers her the-doctor-is-in face, Erika asks, "What do you mean by that?"

"I mean . . . do you believe in ghosts, Erika?"

She waits for her friend to burst out laughing, or shake

her head sadly, or whip out her cell phone and speed dial the loony bin.

But Erika simply says, "I'm not sure. If you had asked me a few years ago, I would have definitely said no. Remember back in college when everyone in our suite got into Ouija boards that one semester? I thought you were all nutty."

"You thought everything we did was nutty."

"Wearing shorts to class in a January blizzard wasn't nutty? Going through the Burger King drive-thru backwards for kicks wasn't nutty?"

Annie can't help laughing . . . or fiercely pining for that era of uncomplicated amusement and constant companionship. Back then, her personal motto was "If it feels good, do it."

That motto, of course, is ancient history now.

"Maybe we were a little nutty," she admits to Erika, always the voice of reason, even in the old days.

"A little nutty?"

"Extremely nutty," Annie concedes. "But what you're saying is that you've totally changed your mind about Ouija boards and ghosts?"

"Not totally. But a colleague of mine in Manhattan, whom I completely respect, by the way, has done some fascinating research on parapsychological communication, and now . . ."

"Now you believe?"

"I wouldn't go that far. It's just that now I'm not so sure," Erika concedes. "Dr. Leaver is writing a book based on his findings, but when I saw him last weekend at the conference he mentioned that he's been ridiculed for it. Not everyone in our profession is willing to accept parapsychology as a science."

"Including you?"

"I'm not ridiculing him, but I'm not exactly jumping on the bandwagon, either." Erika shrugs. "So what's going on, Annie?"

"You'll probably never believe me if I tell you. *I* don't even believe me, really."

"Try me."

Annie remains silent, daunted by the prospect of vocalizing the improbable event and wishing she could figure out a way to back out of what she started.

"Did you see Andre's ghost?"

"No!" Annie says quickly, as though Erika has accused her of diving naked off the Throgs Neck Bridge into the East River. "I think I might have talked to Andre's ghost, though," she admits after a moment.

Once again, Erika defies her expectations by taking her seriously—or at least, appearing to. For all Annie knows, she's mentally plotting imminent institutionalization as she asks a bit too nonchalantly, "What did Andre's ghost say, Annie?"

"I don't know, exactly."

"You don't know?"

"I couldn't hear very well."

Erika waits, clearly expecting elaboration.

"There was a lot of static," Annie says reluctantly.

"Static?"

Might as well spill the whole bizarre tale, Annie decides. "Okay, Erika, the thing is . . . it was over the telephone and I'd swear I imagined the whole thing, but there's a part of me that thinks it might really have happened because I absolutely *know* I heard the song on the radio that night, and I couldn't have imagined everything that happened to me that day, could I?"

"Song on the radio?" Erika frowns. "You need to start back at the beginning, Annie. I think you've lost me."

"Along with my mind?"

Erika grins. "Just tell me what happened, Annie."

Seated across a cozy candlelit restaurant table from Joyce, Thom masks his misery behind a pleasantly attentive expression.

The prospect of breaking up with her in a public place five days behind schedule is bad enough, but he can't seem to find a polite way to interrupt her long-winded account of last night's charity auction, which he was supposed to attend with her.

Thanks to an extended meeting to discuss another potential corporate takeover target, he had to miss the auction, as well as a scheduled dinner with Joyce the night before that when a shareholders' meeting waylaid him. And on Monday, she was the one who canceled their plans to have dinner at his apartment. She said she had a headache, but she didn't sound very convincing. Thom found himself wondering if she actually had a premonition that he was about to break up with her.

Then again, she shows no indication tonight that she anticipates the bombshell he's about to drop. She's nibbling her endive and watercress, sipping her Vernaccia di San Gimignano, and delivering a convoluted monologue to rival David Letterman's, minus the dry wit and willing, captivated audience.

As Joyce prattles on about authentic Chippendale

chairs and Mitzi Longenbacker's manicure, Thom finds himself wishing he were anywhere other than in this charming East Side bistro with this svelte blond beauty.

Okay, he might as well admit it: He'd prefer to find himself in a shabby cottage out east with a widowed waitress.

But acknowledging, even merely to himself, that he can't seem to get Annie Harlowe off his mind doesn't solve the problem at hand.

Thom extracts a petal-thin sliver of beef carpaccio from its bed of chicory and crumbled Gorgonzola, pops it into his mouth, and washes it down with Brunello di Montalcino, nodding as though he's listening intently to Joyce while wondering whether to dump her during the main course or prolong the agony—and eventual ecstacy—until dessert.

If he dumps her during the main course, he can probably rule out dessert; something she never orders anyway, and he shouldn't necessarily allow himself this evening.

After he left Annie's house on Sunday night, he went home and polished off the rest of the caterer's sugar cookies.

His newly developed sweet tooth unsated, he returned to Manhattan, with its Belgian chocolatiers and Italian pastry shops and a delightful little spot called Dylan's Candy Bar, which Thom passed every day on his way home and never noticed until now.

Wandering amidst the dazzling displays of cellophane-wrapped stickiness, Thom found himself fantasizing about bringing Milo and Trixie here for a shopping spree.

It would never happen. Of course it wouldn't.

He would have to be content filling a small plastic box

with bulk Mary Janes and Laffy Taffy, then toting it home to his lonely penthouse and munching in thoughtful solitude. He couldn't help comparing his silent and spotless—all right, sterile—apartment with the chaotic household he encountered Sunday in Montauk.

It wasn't the favorable comparison he might have expected. His priceless ancient Chinese pottery wouldn't last an hour with Milo's constant take-offs and landings, and Trixie would undoubtedly be frightened of his collection of medieval armor and the moose head mounted over the fireplace in the den, courtesy of an inheritance from his paternal taxidermy fetishist.

Yes, and both children would surely leave a trail of crumbs on the white carpets, smudges on the ivory upholstery, fingerprints all over the custom-made curved, blue-tinted floor-to-ceiling windowpanes overlooking the roof garden and terrace. Heck, if the kids decided to play catch indoors, the way they did after dinner Sunday night before their mother put a kibosh on it, they might even break a custom-made glass pane or two, which at a couple hundred grand apiece would cost a small fortune to replace.

Not that Thom doesn't have a small fortune to squander. Or a large one, for that matter.

The Harlowes' bare cupboards, worn clothing, and threadbare home didn't escape his attention. In fact, for the past few days, whenever he isn't stressing about Joyce or work, he's daydreaming about what he—and his money—can do for the underprivileged trio.

Not to mention what he—and his raging libido—can do for the unwillingly celibate Annie.

Okay, obviously Thom's sweet tooth isn't the only

thing left frustratingly unsated in the wake of Sunday's fleeting indulgences. Obviously, he's developed a . . . a crush.

A crush on a waitress.

Isn't that convenient?

It takes little more than pop psychology 101 to figure that one out, Thom thinks wryly as one waiter clears away appetizers, another refills water goblets, and Joyce yammers on without missing a beat.

Nothing like a grown man exhibiting good old-fashioned adolescent rebellion against his overbearing mother.

Nothing like a seasoned corporate raider setting his sights on the one acquisition that's well beyond his reach.

Well, he's one step ahead of his unsuitably infatuated inner self. He understands exactly why he thinks he has feelings for Annie Harlowe, and knows precisely what he should do about them.

Absolutely nothing.

By the time Annie reaches the part about hearing "Hello, It's Me," in the car on her way to Thom Brannock's estate, she's been interrupted several times by the children.

Naturally, once they've discovered Auntie Erika's presence—and presents—Milo and Trixie begin an annoying ritual of popping in and out of the room to climb on her lap and leave chocolate fingerprints on her white linen suit and model their new T-shirts and beg to go to the beach with their new towels.

Finally, Annie banishes them to their rooms—but not

before Auntie Erika promises to play Don't Break the Ice with Milo and make some braids in Trixie's hair.

Left alone with her friend again at last, Annie decides to leave out the details about losing her wedding ring and Thom Brannock dropping by to return it. No need to go *there*. At least, not aloud.

Never mind that he's haunting her thoughts as effectively as Andre's ghost.

Annie simply concludes her account with a matter-of-fact, "I think that if I didn't imagine it, and it really was Andre's voice I heard, he was trying to send me a message."

"The message being . . ." Erika assumes a low-pitched, phantom monotone, droning, "Take the catering job, Annie."

"Hey! I wasn't kidding around," she protests, but she can't help chuckling. It does seem vaguely . . . absurd.

"Don't get me wrong, Annie. I mean, I understand what you're getting at, but you have to admit that it seems kind of . . ."

"What? Out there?"

"A little." Erika smiles.

"Well, don't say I didn't warn you. So what's the verdict? You don't think my husband is popping up from beyond the grave to prod me to get off my butt and earn some extra bucks?"

"Well, I guess stranger things can happen . . ."

"Yeah, especially in my famous imagination," Annie says ruefully.

"You don't think you imagined it, Annie."

"No. I don't. And I think that what Andre was trying to tell me is that he's not really gone. That he's still here, with me and the kids. He made me take that catering job so that I would get into the car and turn on the radio, because I never play it in the house anymore. And he knew I would hear that particular song, and that I'd connect it to him, and the phone call . . ."

Catching sight of Erika's dubious expression, Annie says, "Listen, I know it's far-fetched. I know you probably think I'm crazy. I guess I even think I'm a little crazy."

"You're not crazy, Annie."

"Is that an official diagnosis?"

Erika laughs.

Annie, lost in thought again, does not. "Maybe I just really need it to be true," she muses. "You know, that Andre still exists somewhere, on some level. Maybe I need to know that so desperately that my subconscious made up the whole phone call thing."

"Maybe," Erika agrees, and Annie's heart plummets.

She wants Erika to tell her that it really happened, dammit. That it can happen again. That if she dials Andre's cell phone right now, he'll pick up on the other end and talk to her.

All right . . . if that's what you believe, why haven't you dialed the number since last Saturday?

She knows only too well why she hasn't.

Because as long as she holds off on actually dialing Andre's number again, she can almost convince herself that it's possible he might answer.

The second she calls and gets nothing but his voice mail, she'll know it wasn't real.

So in other words, Annie, you prefer indefinitely de-

luding yourself over returning to your daily habit of dialing a dead man's cell phone?

She shakes her head. Either way, she's a potential institutionalizee.

Picturing herself in a straitjacket and locked up in an asylum, Annie finds herself almost enamored of the idea. Pure solitude, no clutter, no decisions about what she can possibly find to wear each day, free meals . . .

"Why are you laughing?" Erika asks.

"Who knows? I really think this single-parenting thing is getting to me. Maybe I need a vacation."

Yeah. To, say, a lush tropical beach resort in the Virgin Islands. Or a cushy padded cell.

"Leave the kids with me and get away for a few days," Erika offers promptly, not for the first time.

"I can't possibly do that," Annie protests, not for the first time.

"Why not?"

Because fatherless children need their mother 24-7, and because she doesn't have the money for a vacation, and because of a thousand other reasons she frequently enumerates for Erika whenever her well-meaning friend urges her to get away.

This time, in lieu of presenting her itemized "Thanks But No Thanks" list, Annie simply assures Erika, "Look, I'm really fine."

"I know you are. But maybe you should see somebody."

An image of hotter-than-hot Thom Brannock bursts before Annie, igniting a flash fire somewhere inside of her.

"I already told you," she protests, squirming, "I'm definitely not interested in dating."

Erika laughs. "I meant that you should see a therapist. I can give you some names—"

"What about your friend?"

"Which friend?"

"The one who's writing the book."

"You want to talk to Dr. Leaver?"

Do I? Annie asks herself, feeling as caught off-guard as Erika appears to be.

She answers her own question, and Erika's, aloud with a noncommittal, "I don't know. Maybe."

Erika shrugs. "I'll ask him if he's willing to see you, but . . . Annie, I'm not sure he has answers to the questions you'd want to ask him."

"I just . . . never mind. You're right. I shouldn't talk to him. That wouldn't help anyway. I can't think of anything that will, at this point."

Other than waking up to discover that the past year has all been a bad dream.

"Therapy will help you to heal, Annie. And time. And maybe . . . falling in love again. Someday," Erika says quickly, seeing Annie open her mouth to protest. "Not right away. But someday, I know you will be ready to date again, and when you are, you'll find someone."

Annie closes her eyes wearily . . . and once again, Thom Brannock's handsome face is emblazoned against her eyelids.

"No," she says firmly, snapping them open again. "I won't find someone. Nobody can replace Andre."

"You aren't married, Annie. You don't have to feel

guilty. It isn't as though you're cheating on your husband."

"It feels that way to me."

Erika is silent for a moment. Then she reaches into her pocket and pulls out her cell phone.

Terrific. Time to speed dial the loony bin.

But Erika says, "Here," and thrusts the phone into Annie's hand.

"What?"

"Call him."

"Erika, I don't even know his number."

It's Erika's turn to say, "What?"

"Thom. I don't know his number, and anyway, I can't just—"

"Annie, I don't know who Thom is . . . although I have a pretty good idea." Her cool fingers graze Annie's bare arm, and her voice is gentle as she says, "What I meant was, call Andre."

"But—"

"If you call and you get his voice mail like you used to, you'll be able to move on . . . at least, from wondering whether he's out there somewhere. And if you call and he answers . . ."

"Then what?"

Erika shrugs. "Then you can tell him whatever it is that you need to say to him. Go ahead, Annie. Call."

She stares down at the phone in her hand. "I'm afraid."

"Do you want me to go into the other room?"

"No. Stay here. If he answers, you can hear for yourself."

Erika nods.

But, looking into her friend's dark eyes, Annie can see that she doesn't believe it. Any of it.

It happened, Annie thinks with sudden, savage conviction. *And I'm going to prove it.*

She dials the familiar number swiftly.

Hits SEND.

Holds her breath as the line rings once . . . twice . . . three times.

"Hey—"

For a split second, hearing her husband's voice, Annie believes that he's speaking to her.

"—you've reached Andre. You know what to—"

Stricken, Annie hangs up.

"Voice mail?" Erika asks quietly.

Too upset to speak, Annie merely nods.

She doesn't know what she was expecting. Of course it was his voice mail. Of course he's not out there, answering his phone from some other dimension. That's as ridiculous as . . . as . . .

As Milo thinking he can fly up to heaven.

As Annie thinking a billionaire tycoon might fall in love with her.

Tears sting Annie's eyes. She looks at the worn spot in the rug, at the peeling paint on the wall, at the crack in the windowpane . . . anywhere other than at Erika, in whose eyes she's certain she'll see pity.

Pity for the poor, hallucinating Widow Harlowe, who conjures telephone calls from her dead husband because she can't accept the fact that he's gone forever . . .

And who pretends that Thom Brannock is going to be back any second to sweep her off her feet.

I can't help it, her own voice echoes back to her from long ago and far away. *Imagination is my forte.*

Finance is Thom's forte.

Women—more specifically, conducting nonplatonic, non-professional relationships with women—are most certainly not his forte.

Which is why, try as he might, he can't get Annie Harlowe off his mind. The darned woman has persistently flitted into and out of his head all the way through the palate-cleansing mango sorbet and his main course of veal medallions with wild mushrooms and artichoke hearts. Every time he seems to have banished her from his thoughts, she pops up again with all the persistence of Mother's violets.

Somehow, Thom can't entirely convince himself that his feelings for Annie Harlowe are mere rebellion on his part, courtesy of Thomas Brannock III's gene pool.

Nor can he figure out exactly how to break the news to Joyce that she will never be anything more to him than a mere social companion.

Nonetheless, now that the main course has been cleared away, he really must proceed with the breakup agenda.

Joyce doesn't order dessert, but she does order a cup of herbal tea.

"What about you, darling?" she asks Thom, as the waiter hovers overhead. "Are you going to have some tea?"

"No, but I will have baked Alaska, and a cup of coffee."

"Decaf?" the waiter asks.

"Caf," Thom replies, secretly enjoying the way

Joyce's pale eyebrows disappear beneath a paler sheath of bangs.

"Should you be having caffeine so late at night?" she asks Thom, who bristles as much at the question as at the air of would-be wifely concern that delivers it.

"A little caffeine never killed anyone, Joyce."

"That's true, I suppose . . ."

The waiter delivers a small plate lined with tea bags.

Thom watches Joyce peruse them before selecting one and carefully reading the paper label.

"It's definitely tea," Thom can't resist saying.

"Oh, I know that. But I wanted to make sure there's no caffeine."

"Didn't you order herbal?"

"Yes, but some herbal teas contain caffeine."

Why does he react to such an innocuous comment the way he would to Styrofoam squeaking against Styrofoam?

Because this relationship has dragged on long enough, that's why. Health-conscious, philanthropic, polite and drop-dead gorgeous Joyce is getting on his nerves, dammit.

Especially when his dessert arrives and she shakes her head sadly, saying, "Baked Alaska? Darling, that's loaded with calories and fat and carbohydrates."

"All of my favorite ingredients," Thom replies affably, deciding not to wait until after dessert to deliver marriage-minded Joyce to her unwed doom. He has no idea what he's going to say, but if he waits until he can mentally conjure and rehearse a script, they'll be here into the wee hours.

Baked Alaska, he concludes as the waiter departs, is a dish best served cold . . . and so is a breakup speech.

Without further ado, he plunges into both, blurting around a spoonful of iced silken sweetness, "I think we should probably break up."

"Pardon?"

He watches Joyce lower her teacup and stare.

"I said . . ." Hunting for a more delicate way to put it, he reluctantly sets down his spoon and comes up with only, "I think we should probably break up . . . soon."

Brilliance, Brannock. Absolute brilliance.

"Or tonight," he amends, cursing the injections that have rendered Joyce expressionless.

She rests her teacup carefully in its saucer. Then she says, "I agree," so readily that it's a wonder he doesn't fall face-first into his baked Alaska.

"You . . . agree?"

"I was just trying to figure out how to tell you the same thing."

"You . . . were?"

"I thought you'd be upset if I ended things. I'm so relieved."

"You're . . . relieved."

She must be lying to protect her fragile ego, he tells himself.

Yet, when he looks into her eyes, he's fairly certain that he sees genuine relief.

"I guess I just don't see this going anywhere," she tells him. "We don't have much of anything in common, really."

"No," he agrees, "we don't."

Although, on the surface, they appear to have everything in common. Far more, certainly, than he has in common with Annie Harlowe.

Annie, again.

Thom dips his spoon into his dessert again and shovels a hunk of meringue-covered ice cream into his mouth, swallowing so quickly a numbing pain radiates up from his neck.

"Head freeze?" Joyce asks, watching him wince.

"Yes."

"You shouldn't eat so fast."

"No, I shouldn't."

And Joyce shouldn't nag him. But that, he supposes, is just her nature, and not the wifely concern he assumed.

Perhaps he should be insulted that she isn't any more in love with him than he is with her.

Who knows? Maybe tomorrow, he'll wake up with second thoughts. Maybe once she's out of his life for good, Thom will want her back in it. Maybe . . .

Nah.

Watching Joyce watching him devour the remainder of his baked Alaska, Thom realizes that she'd be wrinkling her surgically enhanced nose if she were physically capable.

He also realizes there's only one woman he'll wake up longing to hold once again.

And now there's no reason why I can't.

Thoughtfully, he savors the last taste of his rapidly melting chocolate ice cream—and the first of his newfound freedom.

Chapter
8

Late Thursday afternoon, climbing out of her car in the driveway after the golf luncheon in Bridgehampton, Annie finds herself several hundred dollars richer, and utterly exhausted.

But it's a nice kind of exhaustion for a change. Much different from the emotional, spiritual kind caused by sleepless nights and overwhelming grief.

This is the purely physical exhaustion that comes from hustling a hundred folding chairs from the caterer's van to the lawn and back again; countless full trays from kitchen to table and back again.

Annie's face hurts from smiling and her shoulders ache from lifting and her throat is sore from saying repeatedly, above the live jazz band, "Would you prefer the herb-roasted chicken with lemon and capers or the grilled red peppers and baby eggplant on a bed of fresh farfalle Florentine?"

In fact, merely saying "fresh farfalle Florentine" over and over all afternoon without tripping over her own tongue was feat enough to keep Annie's mind suitably far from her troubles . . . the disturbing kiss with Thom Brannock being the least of them.

The accountant just sent an overdue bill for his tax preparation services, which Annie mistakenly assumed she had paid back in April. Meanwhile, Trixie has already outgrown her new summer sneakers, the washing machine is on its last leg, and the car just made a disconcerting rattling sound all the way down Route 27.

Fingering the folded bills in her pocket, Annie concludes that after she pays the babysitter, she might have enough left to pay the accountant . . . but not for shoes, much less a mechanic or a new appliance.

Trixie can probably make do with just her sandals for another few weeks. At least she can't outgrow those as easily as sneakers. And with any luck, the washer will last until sweater weather and the car will make it through the summer without anything falling off or exploding.

Mounting the steps to the porch, Annie stops to pinch a couple more spent blossoms off the leggy, flaccid pink petunia plant. She still hasn't watered the poor thing.

I'll get to it later, Annie silently promises the wilted flowers, grateful that water, at least, is free.

"Carly? Kids?" she calls, opening the screen door with a squeaky reminder of better days.

"We're in here, Mrs. Harlowe."

Wincing as much at the memory of her husband as at the sound of her married name, Annie allows the door to swing closed behind her with a satisfying bang.

The house appears neater than it was when she left this morning; no sign of the dry cereal that was scattered on the coffee table or the maze of wooden train track that wound around the carpet.

God bless Carly, Annie thinks, kicking off her sneakers and wriggling her bare toes before venturing into the kitchen.

She finds her children and Carly seated at the table with construction paper, scissors, markers, and glue sticks. The kitchen, too, has been cleaned, with no sign of the mixing bowl and baking sheets Annie left in the sink after making cookies this morning.

"Guys, look who's home," Carly says.

"We're making collages, Mommy!" Trixie exclaims, jumping up to hug Annie. "Carly says mine is the best."

"She did not," Milo pipes up. "She just said it was good. She said mine was spectacular."

"Well, she said mine was speck-ular, too."

"They're both spectacular," Annie and Carly assure the children in perfect unison.

Annie shoots a grateful glance at the perky redheaded babysitter, who smiles and says, "Hey, I didn't realize you were an artist, Mrs. Harlowe. Uncle Jonathan never mentioned it. Milo and Trixie were telling me that you sell stuff at boutiques in town and in the Hamptons."

"I do . . . only lately, there hasn't been much demand for seashell art and driftwood sculpture," Annie admits to the girl, as her thoughts once again dart to her mounting household expenses.

"Well, now that the summer people are coming out again, I bet business will pick up."

"I hope so." Speaking of which . . . "Did I get any phone calls while I was gone, Carly?"

Devonne Cambridge, proprietress of the Harborside Emporium in Sag Harbor, still hasn't returned Annie's call about bringing in more sea-glass mobiles before the end of the week.

"Actually, somebody did call . . . I wrote down the message on the pad of paper by the phone in the other room," Carly informs her with precocious efficiency.

Annie opens the fridge in search of something to quench her thirst. "Was her name Devonne Cambridge?"

"Actually, it was a he, and his name was Thom. Thom with an 'h.' "

Annie turns her head so quickly she hits it on the refrigerator door.

"Oh, my gosh, Mrs. Harlowe . . . are you okay?"

"I'm fine." She rubs the sore spot above her ear. "Did you say his name was Thom with an 'h'?"

"That's what he told me. He didn't say why he was calling, but he left a phone number and he wanted to know what time you'd be back. I told him late afternoon."

Frowning, Annie closes the refrigerator door, her thirst forgotten as an unsettling hunger seeps in to replace it.

She tells herself that Thom is probably only calling her because . . . because . . .

All right, she can't think of a solitary logical reason he might call.

Sure, you can. Use your brain for a change, and not your imagination.

Okay . . .

Maybe Thom needs to hire a waitress for some event.

Or he really does want to buy her house for a million dollars.

Or maybe she inadvertently lost some other piece of jewelry at his house and he wants to return it.

Yeah, right.

As if she even *owns* another piece of jewelry that would be worth the effort.

Okay, so maybe he called because he's . . . interested.

In Annie.

That scenario is about as likely as . . .

As snow on Christmas, Annie?

The inner voice sounds suspiciously like Andre's.

That could happen, she reminds herself—and Andre—with her usual stubborn persistence.

All right, then Thom calling because he's interested in Annie is about as likely as Annie suddenly finding out that the faux-fancy cubic zirconia earrings she once bought on clearance at Target are authentic one-carat diamonds.

In other words—it ain't happening.

Brain, Annie. Use your brain. Common sense is in order. Surely you have some.

All right, so why *did* Thom Brannock call?

There's only one way to find out, Annie tells herself, sensibly—and reluctantly—heading into the next room.

There's nothing quite like rush-hour traffic on the Long Island Expressway in June, Thom thinks, tapping the steering wheel impatiently as he brakes to a standstill once again.

All right, there *is* one thing like it: The parking lot at the Meadowlands when the Giants are playing at home. In other words, a sea of cars that aren't going anywhere in the foreseeable future.

Apparently, everyone and their brother—not to mention their brother's broker, personal trainer, and private chef—is en route from Manhattan to the Hamptons to usher in the first official weekend of summer a whole day ahead of schedule. It used to be that just Friday nights were insanely busy, but now the weekend seems to start on Thursday and end on Monday.

Thom, who usually opts to make the trip late Friday nights in a chauffeured limousine and passes the time conducting business from the backseat, finds himself relishing the opportunity to drive out alone on a Thursday . . . even if the actual driving consists mainly of inching forward between bouts of brake lights.

What matters most is that Thom is now a man in control of his own destiny.

And his destiny . . . which he may not reach until tomorrow, at this rate . . . involves a certain brown-haired widow, whom he called this afternoon on a whim. Not that he regrets it. No, not one bit.

As though triggered by the thought of Annie, his cell phone rings shrilly.

Reaching into his pocket to answer it, Thom wonders if it can possibly be her returning his call.

No.

It would be too coincidental for her to call him at precisely the moment he was thinking about her. So coincidental that he'd have no choice but to take it as some cosmic sign that he should . . .

Well, that's out of the question. Settling down with a ready-made family is out of the question.

"Thom Brannock."

"Hi. This is Annie Harlowe."

His heart stops.

It's her. Annie Harlowe. Head of the ready-made family he doesn't want. Really, he doesn't. Still . . .

What are the odds that it would be her?

Pretty high, he reminds himself, considering that he left her a message to call him at this number.

Well, what are the odds that she would call at the precise moment she was on his mind?

Pretty high, considering that he's spent almost every waking moment thinking about her lately, when he should be thinking about what will happen if Saltwater Treasures rejects his takeover bid.

Nonetheless, he chooses to take this phone call from Annie as a cosmic sign.

"So how are you?"

"I'm fine," Annie says in the pleasantly detached tone one might use with a doctor's receptionist. "How are you?"

"I'm fine."

"That's great."

"My babysitter said you called," Annie says tentatively.

"I did. I called."

She's silent.

Waiting, he realizes, for him to tell her *why* he called.

Suddenly, he isn't entirely sure of the reason.

He's been so busy obsessing about Annie and yearning to connect with her again that he never managed to plan exactly what he would do when and if it actually happened.

"I was wondering if you were free for dinner," he blurts.

"Tonight?"

Tonight?

Well, why not tonight?

"Yes," he says like a child who's just been offered a three-day Park Hopper to Disney. "I'm on my way out to Southampton for the weekend."

"On a Thursday?"

"I'm working from home tomorrow."

"You mean, home in the city?"

"I mean, home in Southampton."

"Oh."

"Anyway, I thought I could pick you up later and we could go to—"

"I can't," she interrupts.

"You can't?"

"The kids. I don't have a sitter."

"I thought a sitter answered the phone when I called this afternoon."

"She did, but . . ."

"But . . . she's gone?" he prods when she trails off.

"No, she's still here, but she's leaving."

"Well, maybe she can stay."

"I don't think she can."

Hmm. Where there's an "I don't think," there's a way, Thom reminds himself.

"Don't you want to check with her, at least?"

"I don't think she can," Annie repeats so firmly that it's clearly out of the question.

Either she's not interested in seeing Thom, or . . .

Or what?

Clearly, she's not interested in—

Then it hits him. Sitters cost money.

Relieved at an explanation that involves something other than Annie not wanting to see him, he wracks his brain for an alternative.

He can offer to pay the sitter . . .

But something tells him Annie might not take kindly to that.

He hears himself offering, "We can bring the kids with us."

They can?

Sure they can.

Kids are allowed in restaurants.

Aren't they?

What is he getting himself into?

He should probably cut his losses and when she turns down the perfunctory offer to include the kids, as any sensible woman would, he'll just wish her well and hang up.

"Oh, Thom, I don't know," Annie says . . . and he's a goner.

It's that simple. Hearing his name on her lips is all it takes. Never has he heard that single syllable spoken quite that way.

"The kids aren't really used to going to restaurants," she goes on.

Resisting the urge to beg her to say his name again, Thom attempts to vanquish the image of Trixie shattering fine china and Milo flying from table to table in his pillowcase cape.

Aloud, he says, "I'm sure they'd be fine."

"Well, maybe if it wasn't a fancy place . . ."

"What do they like to eat?"

"Chicken nuggets."

"Great. Okay. So we'll go to a kid-friendly place that serves chicken nuggets."

Silence.

Then Annie asks, "You know kid-friendly places?"

Nope.

"Of course I know kid-friendly places," he says, as though she's asked whether he's certain he is, indeed, a man.

He's a man, all right. A red-blooded man with one thing on his mind. And it isn't chicken nuggets.

"I'll pick you up at eight-thirty," he says, after checking the clock on the dashboard.

Normally, Montauk would only be an hour from this spot, but he figures with the traffic, he'd better allow extra time.

"All right."

"You don't sound very enthused, Annie."

"I guess I'm wondering why you want to come all the way out here and take the three of us to dinner."

Truth be told, a part of him is wondering the same thing.

Frankly, he has no idea what's come over him lately.

But he honestly suspects that it's more than a subconscious desire to rebel against his mother and his sister and the trappings of their world. That it's more than spring fever, more than good old-fashioned lust, more than a sympathetic need to help destitute Annie and her charming children.

The only thing Thom knows for sure is that for the first time in his life, he's going with the flow. And it feels good.

To Annie, he says simply, "I like you. And I like your kids. Does that make sense?"

She laughs. "Not really. But we'll be ready at eight-thirty anyway."

*   *   *

Suddenly, a loud rapping infiltrates Annie's dream . . . a sensual dream about Thom Brannock, featuring languid kisses warmer and sweeter than sugared molasses cookies fresh from the oven.

She bolts out of bed . . . only to find that she isn't in bed after all. Nor is she naked, as she was in the dream. She is—or *was*—on the couch, in her living room, fully clothed . . . and alone.

No, not alone.

But not with Thom.

Dazed—and yes, disappointed—Annie looks around and sees the kids sprawled on the floor facing the television, also fully clothed . . . and still sound asleep beneath the blanket she tossed over them earlier. The *Rescue Heroes* video they were watching earlier has been replaced by a meteorologist and a weather map of the tristate area. It can't be that late . . . can it?

Annie peers at the curved wooden antique clock nesting in the Andre photo gallery on the mantel.

Yes, it's past ten . . . and there's that loud banging sound again.

As always, Annie's instinctive reaction is extreme. Is the roof caving in overhead? Are they under machine gun fire? Is a crazed killer trying to break in?

In the next moment, those wild visions give way to the levelheaded realization that the banging is actually knocking, and it's coming from the front door.

Okay, somebody's at the door. Crazed killers tend not to knock first, so . . .

Once again, icicles of dread pierce Annie's heart.

Flashback: that warm evening last June, sirens in the distance, a knock on the door . . .

No. That's over. Andre is gone, and the children are here, safe and sound, and . . .

Thom.

He was supposed to be here a few hours ago.

It all comes back to Annie as she hurries toward the door, her sleepy legs wobbling from both the abrupt movement and the wave of panic that's sweeping toward her.

No, Annie. Don't think that way. He's fine.

Her imagination is already up and running, though, far ahead of the still-groggy rest of her. Terrible scenarios race through her mind: carjackings, accidents, heart attacks . . .

But if something had happened to him on the road, the police wouldn't come to your door, anyway. You're not Thom Brannock's next of kin. You're nothing to him.

Still . . .

She can't bear the thought of losing him.

Losing him? You don't even have *him, Annie.*

She has no right to worry about him the way a wife would worry about a late husband, but . . .

But she can't help it.

She backtracks mentally as she fumbles with the lock on the heavy inner door. Thom called from the road at nine to say that he was stuck in traffic. Annie gave her famished children microwaved pasta and put on a video to quell the questions about when Thom was going to get there.

Secretly as disappointed as the kids, if not more so, Annie waited for Thom to call back and say he wasn't coming after all, but he never did.

Or maybe he did, and she was so sound asleep she
didn't hear the phone ring.

In any case, she opens the door and there he is, standing in the glow of the porch light.

"I'm so sorry, Annie," is the first thing he says.

She just nods, swallowing hard over an unexpected
tide of emotion. Her instinct is to hug him.

"The traffic was a nightmare all the way out," he goes
on, reaching for the screen door handle as she slips the
hook from its latch. "And my cell phone battery died so I
couldn't even call you back to tell you where I was. I left
my charger in Manhattan."

He opens the screen door.

The loud squeaking sound stops Annie cold.

WD-40. Andre.

The tide of emotion that had been sweeping through
her stops short at the wall that has gone up in a flash, pro-
tecting her from . . .

Him.

From him, and the risk of loss that goes hand in hand
with loving somebody.

"I thought it would be a good idea to just come straight
out instead of stopping at home to call you."

"Oh." The word gives way to the steady chirping of
crickets and the distant crashing of waves.

He hesitates in the doorway, waiting for her to invite
him to cross the threshold.

But she won't let herself. She can't. She can't do that.
She can't do . . . any of this. Not again.

"Annie . . ." He bends down to look into her eyes, lifting her chin with his hand.

"What?" she asks guardedly.

"Are you okay?"

She nods, her heart pounding at the thrilling sensation of his fingertips on her face.

Why did he have to touch her?

She was doing fine until he touched her. Now the wall is crumbling and she's powerless to stop it.

"Can I come in?" Thom asks softly.

What is there to say, other than, "Sure?"

All right, there's a lot to say. Stuff like, "No" and "Get lost."

But Annie is too weary—and all right, too attracted to the man—to resist him.

She takes a step back and gestures for him to come in . . . only to watch him spin on his heel and head down the steps.

"Where are you going?" she asks, dismayed, wondering if she's so out of it that instead of "Sure," she accidentally said, "Get lost."

"I have some stuff in the car," he calls over his shoulder, disappearing into the darkness beyond the porch steps.

Annie watches the moth ballet around the bulb in the porch ceiling and does her best to ignore the fluttering of wings in her stomach.

There's something about a man in a suit . . .

Well, there is now, anyway. Annie, who was never drawn to corporate types and never once saw her own husband wear a tie, not even on their wedding day, suddenly finds herself fantasizing about the power Thom Brannock must yield in the boardroom . . . and the bedroom.

Stop it! Nothing is going to happen between us, she tells herself firmly.

After all, it's not as though she's alone with him. The kids are right here, and . . .

And even if they weren't, nothing is going to happen. Period. She'll erect a steely core of willpower around the most vulnerable part of her soul. She'll be totally prepared to resist him if he tries to kiss her again.

Thom reappears with two big paper bags balanced on either hip. He must have left his suit jacket in the car, and the sleeves of his white dress shirt are rolled up as though he's about to get to work.

Doing what? Annie wonders, and she asks him what's in the bags.

"Food. I promised you dinner."

"Yes, but at a restaurant." She holds the door open for him, wincing when it squeaks.

He steps past her, into the house, saying, "Well, the restaurants are still open, but I figured it was too late for the kids."

She watches him start striding toward the kitchen, then stop short when he spots Milo and Trixie sleeping on the rug.

"I'm sorry, Annie."

"It's okay."

"I promised them chicken nuggets."

"I fed them. And really, it's okay. You couldn't help it."

"I know, but . . ." He shakes his head. "Do you want me to carry them up to their beds?"

No. She doesn't want him to carry them up to their beds.

For one thing, that would leave her alone with Thom.

For another, that's something only a daddy should do, and Thom isn't their daddy. He never will be. Not their daddy, and not their . . .

Stepfather.

Okay, there. Annie admitted to herself that somewhere in the back of her frighteningly creative mind, she may have entertained a fantasy about marrying Thom Brannock and living happily ever after.

So? She's also fantasized about winning Powerball and becoming a famous sculptor and finding Andre's lost treasure of Copper Beach.

She doesn't expect any of those things to actually happen. It's just harmless fun to dream about them.

But it isn't harmless fun to dream about marrying Thom Brannock. It's . . . stupid. That's what it is.

Stupid to think that a man like him can come along and make all her problems disappear.

Stupid to get her children's hopes up about dinner out in a restaurant, then shatter their expectations with canned pasta.

It wasn't just the restaurant dinner they were anticipating so eagerly, Annie reminds herself. It was seeing Thom again.

Trixie insisted on wearing a purple sundress just for him, and Milo, so hungry for a masculine role model, wore his sneakers with laces in case Thom had time for another tying lesson after dinner.

"Just let me put these bags in the kitchen, and I'll carry them up," Thom says softly.

"No!"

Halfway out of the room, he looks back, startled by Annie's sharp tone. "Why not?"

"They can sleep there."

"On the floor?" He looks as incredulous as she feels.

What kind of mother leaves her children sleeping on the hard floor?

"I'll get them upstairs myself," she says before he can reproach her.

"You can't carry them. They're too heavy."

Annie, whose back still aches from lugging trays and chairs all afternoon, shakes her head. "No, they aren't. I do it all the time."

They're my children, she wants to tell him. *My children, and my responsibility. I don't need your help. Or your groceries. Or your sympathy.*

All he has to do is utter the slightest protest, or reach toward one of the children, and she'll let him have it. All that and more.

But he doesn't.

To his credit—and Annie's dismay—he simply shrugs and proceeds to the kitchen, where she can hear him rattling bags and opening and closing the refrigerator.

Stifling a grunt of pain, she tosses the blanket aside and begins lugging her slumbering children up to their beds. Only when they're safely tucked in for the night and she's descending the stairs does Annie realize that she is now, quite disconcertingly, alone with Thom Brannock.

Chapter
9

"What? You didn't think I was going to subject you to my cooking again, did you?" Thom asks with a laugh, spotting Annie's relieved expression as she stands in the kitchen doorway.

"I . . . I guess I wasn't sure what you were doing down here," she admits, taking in the table set for two and the array of plastic supermarket containers filled with cold salads and sliced roast chicken.

"Well, I wasn't cooking, that's for sure. I think we both discovered the other night that I'm probably not going to be getting my own program on the Food Network anytime in the near future."

"I thought the kids did all the cooking."

"Oh, that's right. I can blame it on them."

Annie cracks a smile at last, and Thom admires the faint network of lines around her eyes. No Botox for her.

Is that why you're here? he asks himself, as he slices a loaf of sourdough bread at the cluttered countertop. *Because she's the opposite of Joyce?*

Not to mention . . . Mother.

There are times when he's certain that it is, and times when he's certain that it's more than that. Much more.

Like right now, glancing up out of the corner of his eyes to see her sneaking a Greek olive from its container on the table. She pops it into her mouth and reaches promptly for another.

Okay, so she probably isn't the type to scold him for ordering baked Alaska. So she has a healthy appetite . . .

For olives, he reminds himself sternly, furtively watching her lick a drop of oil from her fingertip.

Just because a woman likes . . . *olives* . . . doesn't mean she has a healthy appetite for . . . other things.

"Sorry," she says a little sheepishly, catching him looking at her. "I couldn't resist. I'm starved."

For dinner, *Thom. She's starved for dinner.*

"Well then, let's eat." He plunks the bread, still on its cutting board, unceremoniously in the middle of the table, thankful he resisted the urge to hunt down candles and light them while she was upstairs.

There's nothing, he tells himself as he pulls out her chair for her, the least bit romantic about a midnight supper at a rickety kitchen table.

Except that there is.

As they eat, an air of intimacy settles over the room.

Dinner for two is dinner for two, no matter how you look at it. There may not be champagne or candlelight, but there's a good bottle of chilled pinot grigio Annie pulls from the back of the fridge, and the overhead lighting is dim thanks to a couple of burned out bulbs.

And . . . she's wearing makeup. That's why her large green eyes seem larger and greener than usual. Makeup, and a dress, and jewelry.

Not designer silk or sequins with dazzling diamonds at her ears and wrists and throat.

No, Annie has on a flirty reddish-orange sundress that bares her sun-coppered shoulders and legs. Her earrings are big gold hoops and she has a stack of slender gold bangles on one arm. Add to that her sleep-tousled glossy spirals, and she could be a free-spirited gypsy.

"I forgot to tell you how nice you look tonight," Thom says, and watches her blush beyond the rim of her wineglass.

"Thank you."

"All dressed up with no place to go. I'll make it up to you. How about if we go out to dinner tomorrow night?"

She shakes her head promptly. "You're making it up to me right now."

"But the kids are missing out."

"They'll be okay."

"I know, but I had my heart set on treating them to chicken nuggets."

She laughs. "You did not. You probably don't even know what a chicken nugget is."

"Sure, I do. It's a small . . . nugget . . . of chicken."

She laughs again, shaking her head, and Thom notes that the faint lines around her eyes are surely as much a result of grief as they are of laughter. This woman has endured a brutal loss. No wonder she's skittish when it comes to . . . well, just about everything he says and does.

Or maybe she just isn't interested, he silently informs his ego as he pokes his fork halfheartedly into a heap of pasta salad.

But she certainly seemed interested when he kissed

her the other night. Granted, she did eventually pull away—but not before she kissed him back. Not before he was able to sense that her pent-up passion was on par with his own.

"Aren't you hungry?" Annie's innocent question cuts into his libidinous thoughts, and he finds himself tempted to tell her just how hungry he is.

But he doesn't dare.

"Maybe it's just too late to eat very much," he says benignly, noting that she's polished off everything on her plate, and had seconds.

"It's never too late to eat . . . at least, not for me. Do you want some coffee?"

"Decaf?" he can't help asking.

She frowns. "I don't even keep decaf in the house."

"It's okay. I don't drink it, either. I'll have regular."

"Do you want dessert, too? I made cookies this morning."

He laughs. He can't help it. If she were consciously trying to be the anti-Joyce, she couldn't accomplish it more effectively.

"What's so funny?" Annie asks.

Ignoring the question, he tells her that he would love to sample her . . . cookies.

Keep your mind on cookies, Thom. What could be more wholesome than homemade cookies?

"They're molasses," she's saying. "Milo's favorite, so I try to make them every week, even though it's hard to heat up the kitchen at this time of year."

Somehow, Thom manages not to suggest that he and Annie heat up the kitchen together.

He clears the dishes while she rummages through the

cupboards and starts the coffeemaker. She chatters about her children while he pretends that he isn't imagining what it would be like to sweep her into his arms and carry her up the stairs to her bedroom.

The next thing he knows, they're back in the living room, waiting for the coffee to finish brewing, and he's devouring the most sinfully delicious molasses cookie he's ever tasted.

"I can't believe this is homemade," he tells Annie, wishing she wouldn't sit on the opposite end of the couch as though she's afraid he's going to sink his teeth into her neck.

"Is there any other kind?" she asks with a smile. "It's my mom's old recipe."

"Does she live nearby?"

"My mom?" Her expression clouds over. "No, she died not long after I got out of college."

"I'm sorry."

"It's been a long time, so . . ." She looks down at her hands in her lap.

"What about your dad?" he feels compelled to ask. "Is he . . . around?"

To his relief, she looks up and nods. "He's living in Florida with my stepmother. They'll probably be up to visit in August."

"That's nice."

"Yeah. I don't really see them as much as . . . well, it would be nice to see more of my dad, especially now that . . ."

"I know. Do you have any other family?" Thom asks, needing her to tell him that there's at least somebody in her life that she can lean on, so that he can . . .

Well, so that he can't wish he could be that person.

"I've got two older brothers, both married, both in Manhattan. But I don't really see them, either."

"Why not?"

"They're just really busy. One is a CEO and the other is an account executive. They travel all the time, and my oldest brother has a couple of kids. Both my nephews are in college, so . . ."

"So basically, your family isn't around much."

"Not unless you count Merlin."

"The caterer?"

"Yes. He's like family. And so is my friend Erika. She's always there for me. What about you?"

"What about me?"

"Your family?"

"Oh! I thought you meant . . ."

"What?"

That I'm always there for you, like Erika is. Or that you want me to be.

"Never mind," he mutters, embarrassed. What is *wrong* with him? He's managed to mentally insinuate himself into the life of a virtual stranger. Except that Annie doesn't feel like a stranger. She feels like . . .

Well, never mind that.

He steers his mind back to her question. His family. Hardly his favorite subject.

"My mother and sister were at the party last Saturday, actually. Maybe you met them."

"Not formally," she says with a wry smile. "But I might have passed them a canapé or two."

He can't help laughing. "What did you think?"

"Of your mother and sister? I don't know which ones they were."

The ones who didn't give you the time of day.

But that pretty much describes the entire guest list, he thinks ruefully.

"No, I meant what did you think of the party?"

"Well, it was definitely A-list," she says. "I think I saw a Trump in the crowd. And I thought all the flowers were beautiful."

He isn't going to let her off. "What else did you think?"

"It was just a nice party," Annie says, in such a stiff, fake tone that he raises an eyebrow at her.

"Come on, Annie."

"What? Didn't you have a good time?"

"I've been to wakes where the dead guy had more fun than I did at that party."

Okay, why did he have to go and bring up wakes and dead guys to a woman who just lost her husband? Mortified, he shoves a molasses cookie into his mouth whole—mainly, so that there won't be room for his foot.

To his surprise, though, she grins and says, "Well, next time, you should tell Merlin to serve something with a little more pizzazz."

"Like?"

"I don't know . . . frozen margaritas."

"Unfortunately," he says, swallowing the rest of his cookie, "the only frozen thing allowed at A-list parties are the women's facial muscles."

She laughs. "I can't believe you said that."

"Why? You didn't notice?"

"Oh, I noticed. I just . . ."

"Thought I didn't?"

She shrugs. "I thought you . . ."

"Were one of them?"

"No!" Annie's black curls bob furiously. "I mean, I know that you *are* one of them, but you're different. At least, you seem different. Oh, Lord, I can't believe I'm saying this. I wonder if the coffee's ready?" She makes a move to get up.

"Wait, Annie."

"What?"

"Talk to me. Or just . . . listen to me. I want you to know where I'm coming from."

Where, he wonders, did *that* come from? And where *is* he coming from? He has no idea what he even wants to tell her. He only knows that he can't let her go. Not to the kitchen. Not . . . anywhere. Not yet.

"No, I know where you're coming from. You already told me. You like a challenge. You want whatever you can't have."

"That's not true," he protests.

"You said it yourself."

"All right, it is true. In business. Maybe even most of the time, in life," he says, seeing the doubt in her eyes. "But not now. Not with you. Just sit down, Annie, and listen to what I have to say. Please. This is different for me."

"All right," she says, settling back on the couch, safely keeping her distance. She looks almost amused, yet still wary. "So tell me, then. Where are you coming from, Thom?"

He touches his chest. "From here. I'm coming from the heart, Annie."

Okay, somehow, that doesn't sound as corny as he

might have anticipated, had he bothered to weigh his words.

It doesn't sound corny at all. And she's looking at him as though . . . well, as though she wouldn't be opposed to sliding a little closer to him.

Encouraged, he goes on, "I really like you. And the kids, too. All week, I haven't been able to stop thinking about you, or . . . caring about what happens to you."

"But why? Don't you have a billion-dollar empire to run or something?"

"Oh, that? It practically runs itself."

"Yeah, right." She returns his smile. "This is crazy, Thom."

There it is again.

And then, all at once, his name isn't all that's on her lips.

One unexpected kiss from Thom, and Annie is a goner.

In the instant his heated mouth brushes against her own, her so-called steely core of willpower is transformed into a puddle of molten desire.

She sinks back into the cushions, pulling him with her, cupping his face in her hands as he deepens the kiss. He tastes of molasses and wine; his tongue playing a delicious game of hide-and-seek with hers.

He breaks off to lift his head and look questioning into her eyes. She kisses him again in response, and that kiss rapidly melts into another, and another.

"I can't do this," she murmurs helplessly against his lips, and she isn't merely talking about kissing him. The length of his body is pressed against hers; that she can feel how much he wants her merely fuels the fire inside of her.

"I'm sorry." He lifts his head and looks down at her, panting. "I didn't mean to . . ."

"I know."

She shifts her hips and succeeds only in bringing the hard evidence of his need even closer to the most vulnerable part of her.

He groans. "Annie . . ."

"I'm sorry," she whispers, squirming. The movement sends luscious quivers through her, a reminder of what could happen between them . . . if only she'd let it. But she can't, because . . . because . . .

Why can't she, again?

If it feels good, do it.

With another groan, Thom rakes his hand through his hair and looks away, his breathing tortured.

"Thom, I didn't mean to—"

"I know," he says, and props himself on his elbows, gingerly lifting himself away from her.

Her body protests, her hands jerking up to pull him close again as if guided by an invisible puppeteer.

"Annie, you don't know what you're doing to me," he says with a ragged moan, and allows his weight to sink against her once again.

But she does know.

She knows, and she can't deny a giddy recklessness at her own potency. She weaves her fingers into his hair and fervently pulls his mouth back down to hers, pouring everything she feels for him into a soul-searing kiss.

"If we don't stop now, Annie . . ."

"It's okay," she says softly. "We don't have to stop."

"But you said—"

"I know. I changed my mind."

"You . . . what? Are you sure?"

"Positive."

He kisses her neck, caresses the length of her waist gently. "Are you absolutely sure you're sure?"

"Absolutely," she says with utter conviction. "But just . . . not here. The kids might—"

"I know." He stands and pulls her to her feet. "Does your bedroom door lock?"

She shakes her head quickly. "Not there, either," she says simply, grateful when he doesn't press her for a reason.

Of course he knows why and must sense, also, that she doesn't want to dwell on it.

Thrusting a shard of Andre from her thoughts before it can shatter the mood, Annie darts a glance around the room, seeking inspiration.

Finding it quickly, she says, "Come on," tugging him along toward the backdoor, stopping only to swoop down and grab the blanket she discarded earlier.

"Where are we going?"

"Outside."

The night is velvety warm, scented with the sea and the riot of wildflowers that are growing rampant in Annie's unkempt planters and garden beds. There's just a sliver of moon in the vast starlit sky that arches overhead like one of Merlin's trademark canopies.

Annie leads Thom down the steps and into the yard, the overgrown grass cool and moist beneath her bare feet. She stops in a secluded corner beside the untamed, early-blooming honeysuckle hedge and spreads the blanket on the ground.

She looks up to see him gazing down at her, almost in wonder.

Annie smiles and pats the blanket.

"I can't believe this is happening." He kneels beside her, facing her. "Are you sure, Annie?"

"Why do you keep asking me that?"

"Because I wouldn't want you to have regrets . . ."

"I won't."

She wants to tell him that she isn't sure what this means; that she can't think of anything that might happen beyond this moment or anything that came before. She wants to tell him that she can't make any promises.

But Thom isn't asking for promises, Annie realizes as she rests her arms on his shoulders and presses a gentle kiss to his lips. He isn't asking for anything he isn't willing to give himself.

This isn't about the future, or the past. This is about the present; for once, Annie will allow that to be the only thing that matters.

With a sigh of pleasure, she loses herself in the here and now, tumbling backward with him on the blanket, stretching her body languidly alongside his, kissing with the torrid conviction of two teenagers who haven't a care in the world.

"Still okay?" he lifts his head to ask after a while.

"Still okay." She smiles.

Thom reaches out and brushes her hair back from the base of her neck with the back of his hand. Then he leans over and nuzzles her in precisely that spot, burrowing into the tender crevice just above her collarbone.

Delicate tremors burst inside of her, and Annie buries her face in his hair, the brisk scent of his shampoo blending intoxicatingly with the heady fragrance of honeysuckle in the air.

"Are you okay?" he asks.

"Yes."

"Is this okay?" He slips a finger beneath the narrow strap of her sundress and pushes it off her shoulder.

"Yes."

"This?" He slips the other strap off her other shoulder and carefully tugs the bodice down to her waist.

"Yes."

He lowers his head and she gasps at the sudden, shocking sensation of his wet mouth on her bare breast.

"Okay?"

Barely able to speak, Annie manages a strangled-sounding "Yes." She grasps his hair, holding his head fast against her, certain that she'll die if he stops.

But he goes on, and on, until at last Annie pulls his face up so that she can kiss him again; kiss him endlessly, swept along on a tide of emotion.

I could love this man, she thinks illogically, with at least the vague presence of mind to be grateful the words remain stranded in her throat with an unanticipated flood of yearning.

No. She can't love this man. She can't love anybody but Andre. Andre, who died a year ago . . .

Don't think about tomorrow, Annie. There's just tonight.

Needing more, she reaches for the front of his shirt and releases first one button, then another, and another. Finally it falls away, joined momentarily by his T-shirt, his trousers, his boxers, her dress, and her panties.

With that, it's almost as though Annie has glided into her own dream: lying naked in Thom's arms, feeling his warm breath mingling with wisp of night breeze to stir her hair, feeling him moving over her and then inside of her.

There's only tonight. This is all you have, Annie. Be in the moment.

She wills time to stand still, but the stars continue to twinkle overhead and the waves crash rhythmically in the distance, and the earth is presumably still turning, and all too soon, she knows, it will be over.

Then, of course, it is; Thom has collapsed against her, breathing hard, murmuring her name.

Holding him close, Annie gazes at the sky with tears in her eyes, knowing that nothing in her world will ever be the same; that in a matter of hours the shortest night of the year will give way to the longest day.

Chapter
10

"Good morning, cream puff," Merlin calls from his car window, pulling to a stop at the top of the gravel driveway.

Annie reluctantly lowers her coffee mug and pushes herself wearily off the porch swing, where she was sorting dried flowers for a new batch of wreaths.

She normally welcomes Merlin's morning pop-ins, but today, of all days, she'd rather be alone. Of course today, of all days, he's particularly inclined to check in on her.

She meets her old friend at the base of the porch steps, where he plants a kiss on her cheek and a shopping bag from Neiman Marcus at her feet.

"What's this?" she asks, looking down.

"Just a little something from your fairy godfather."

"Thanks," Annie says with a laugh. "Can I open it?"

"Go ahead. Where are my precious little Swee-TARTS?"

"Still sleeping, thank goodness." Peering into the bag, Annie sees billowing white cotton.

"Merlin . . . did you shop for me?"

"I shopped for you, Vivian," he says gleefully, leaning his chin on her shoulder to see into the bag. "It's just a little something to say thanks for helping me out this past week."

"A little something? Merlin, this is a Hanro nightgown!" She pulls it out of the bag with a gasp. It's the most elegant sleepwear she's ever seen, made of luxurious georgette and embroidered in delicate lace.

"You like?"

"I love, but Merlin . . . what are you doing? You know I usually just sleep in T-shirts and boxers."

"I know." He wrinkles his nose. "I thought you could use something pretty to wear to bed."

She narrows her eyes at him, wondering if he knows about Thom.

But he couldn't possibly, unless he's psychic. It happened mere hours ago.

And anyway, Annie has no intention of ever actually sleeping next to Thom . . . or, for that matter, sleeping *with* him ever again.

He tiptoed away into the darkness long before dawn, at her insistence. The last thing she wanted was for one of the children to wake in the night and find that she was missing . . . or that he was there.

Sure enough, moments after Thom left—with a last lingering kiss and a promise to call her this afternoon—Trixie erupted in blood-curdling shrieks.

It took Annie close to an hour to settle her back down, at which point she finally collapsed into her own undisturbed sheets.

But sleep refused to come, thanks to the madly spinning carousel that had taken over her brain in the wake of

Thom's departure. Her body was dead tired, but her thoughts were alive with the giddy memory of their love-making.

Guilt waited until dawn before stealing over her like an unexpected late frost in the garden, snuffing out the fragile shoots of hope that had foolishly taken root within her.

Now, gazing at Merlin through bleary eyes that feel as though they've been scrubbed with a loofah, Annie is nothing but exhausted. Yawning loudly, she weighs the odds that she'll be able to squeeze in a nap at some point this afternoon.

"I don't suppose," Merlin says pointedly, draping an arm around her shoulder, "that I can bribe you with the robe that matches that nightgown?"

A nightgown that costs almost as much as a new washing machine, Annie thinks wryly.

"Bribe me to do what?" she asks aloud.

"Work at another event this weekend. My waitresses are dropping like *Survivor* castoffs, and I'm shorthanded again."

"What, are you killing them off?"

"No, they're just too young and stupid to hold down a job. It's hard to find responsible help, Annie, let alone classy help like you."

"Flattery and nightgowns will get you nowhere, Merlin."

"I was planning to throw in quite a bit of cash, too."

"Well, that's tempting . . . but I can't."

"Please, Annie. It's for the Corringtons," he adds significantly.

"What is the Corringtons?"

"Not what *is,* who *are.*" He begins rattling off credentials that include bloodline, résumé, and real-estate holdings to rival . . . well, the Brannocks.

Annie cuts in to say, "You couldn't convince me to work a wedding today, Merlin, if it was the second coming of Princess Diana and she'd agreed to walk down the aisle and give Prince Charles another shot."

"No, I didn't mean today," he says hastily. "Do you think I don't know it's the anniversary of Andre's death, Annie?"

She swallows painfully. Will she ever get used to hearing the words "Andre" and "death" spoken together?

"But what about tomorrow?" Merlin asks gently. "You need the money. I need you. It's a Sunday afternoon wedding that should go pretty late. And Carly said she'd babysit."

"You asked her without checking with me first?"

"I was trying to make everything easier for you, Annie. I know that this is a tough weekend. Tougher than usual. I'm worried about you."

Annie sighs. She desperately needs cash; no doubt about that. But another long day spent waiting on hordes of upscale summer people is enough to make her want to turn Merlin's offer down flat.

"I'll think about it," she says instead, realizing she doesn't have the luxury of saying an outright "no" to potential income.

"Great! You'll think about it." He pauses. "For how long?"

"Just give me a few hours to clear the cobwebs out of my brain, and I'll call you on your cell and let you know,

Merlin." Yawning again, she takes another sip of her coffee. "I need a refill. Do you want some?"

"No thanks. I have to get home. Jonathan and I are playing tennis in a half hour if it doesn't rain."

They both look up at the clouds that are rapidly moving in from the water to obliterate the patch of blue.

"Is it supposed to rain?" Annie asks, thinking a storm might suit the bleak mood of the day.

"Yes, but just a quick thunderstorm, then it's going to clear up," Merlin tells her with the authority of the closet Weather Channel addict he is.

"Well, I'm off." He kisses her on the cheek, then lifts her left hand and examines it. "I see you've got your wedding ring back."

"Mmm-hmm. Thom brought it over last week."

"Thom?" Merlin echoes with a knowing look. "Rather intimate with Mr. Brannock, are we?"

Annie can feel her cheeks growing warmer than the coffee that's left in the bottom of her cup. "No, we are not intimate with Mr. Brannock," she lies, feigning outrage.

"But we are on a first-name basis."

Annie shrugs. "It doesn't mean I'm sleeping with him."

"Sleeping with him!"

Oops.

"Annie, you're sleeping with Thom Brannock?"

"I just said that I *wasn't*."

Merlin gazes at her.

"Shut up, Merlin."

"I didn't say anything."

"You didn't have to."

Merlin continues to examine her face thoughtfully for

a few moments, then shakes his head. "I know you too well."

That, he does. But she'll admit nothing. Her relationship with Thom Brannock—if that's the right term for what happened between them—is none of his business. One word of acknowledgement, and Merlin would dub himself matchmaker and begin catering a wedding extravaganza.

"You don't know me as well as you think, Merlin."

"Whatever you say, sugar pie. I'll talk to you later."

She watches him pull out of the driveway, speeding off to his tennis date with Jonathan.

Lucky Merlin, she thinks wistfully, with his blissfully uncomplicated love life.

Not that he doesn't deserve it, after all the strife of adolescence and lovelorn adulthood, when he had every right to be jealous of Annie's easy romance with Andre— and blatantly admitted that he was.

A raindrop lands on Annie's arm.

Now it's his turn to live happily ever after, she tells herself, slowly walking back up the steps onto the porch, aware of a sudden chill permeating the warm summer morning. *And my turn to look on with envy.*

She pulls the screen door open with a loud squeak.

Suddenly, Annie misses her husband so profoundly that it's all she can do to keep her legs from buckling beneath her.

She forces them to carry her to the kitchen, where, shivering in the sudden iciness that seems to fill the air, she shakily refills her coffee cup, stirs in milk and too much sugar with a wobbly hand.

Then, as though it were her intention all along, rather

than sudden inspiration, she reaches for the telephone and begins dialing.

"Thom? Are you even listening?"

"Hmm?" He looks up from his black coffee to see his mother scowling at him across an arrangement of elegant white roses and greens.

No, he wasn't listening.

No, he doesn't care about Bitsy Worth's new Irish wolfhound whose pedigree is as sterling as Bitsy's.

Mustering appropriate contrition, he says, "I'm sorry, Mother," and spoons a bit of hollandaise sauce onto the last of his English muffin.

Lillian Merriweather Brannock arches pencil-enhanced eyebrow at her son, but says nothing.

"I'm just beat this morning. I've been working too hard this week," he offers as an excuse.

With a trace of the Boston-bred accent that transforms her "ar"s into "ah"s, she informs him, "Hard work is good for you."

What fun. Thom nods. "I know, and I'm not complaining. Just explaining."

That line never worked on Thomas Brannock III, but Mother's gaze softens a bit as she passes the basket of toasted English muffins to her only son, urging him to take another.

The elegant brick terrace adjacent to Lillian's formal dining room is bathed in sunlight this morning, the sea an inviting aqua backdrop in the distance.

"I'm so glad you convinced me that our brunch should be al fresco this morning. 'What is so rare as a day in

June'?" Mother quotes aloud, and Thom can't help
smiling.

"Oh, I can think of a few things."

"Would you care to elaborate?"

"Not at the moment."

As he savors another mouthful of Eggs Benedict,
Thom wonders if Annie and the children would enjoy
sailing later this afternoon. It's been too long since he
was out on the ocean. He has some business dealings to
address back at home after brunch, but he promised
Annie he'd call her as soon as he's available.

She smiled and kissed him again, and mentioned that
she'd be home all day.

Leaving her last night—or rather, in the wee hours
this morning—went against every instinct Thom pos-
sessed. If he'd had his way, the two of them would have
fallen asleep in each other's arms beneath the blooming
honeysuckle, then awakened to make love again as the
sun streaked the horizon pink and orange.

"What are you smiling about?"

Startled, he glances up to see his mother watching him
shrewdly over the rim of her china teacup.

"I met someone," he hears himself say . . . then braces
for the inevitable barrage of questions.

He doesn't have to wait long.

"Who is she?"

Knowing his mother isn't merely asking for a name,
but a pedigree to rival those of Bitsy Worth and her new
show hound, he says briefly, "You don't know her."

"What about Joyce?"

"That's over."

To his surprise, his mother nods. "I'm sorry to hear

that. But I can't say it wasn't obvious last Saturday night at the party that neither of you had any intention of taking it any further."

Again, Thom is taken aback that Joyce was apparently not as interested in him as he assumed. Is he that clueless when it comes to women?

"I only hope neither of you has any regrets in the future," his mother goes on. "Women like Joyce are few and far between, Thom."

No. Women like Annie are few and far between. His world is crawling with women like Joyce.

"But . . ." Lillian offers a what-are-you-going-to-do maternal sigh and busies herself brushing stray crumbs of toasted muffin from her linen place mat. "What's done is done. Tell me about this person you met."

"Her name is Anne . . . *ie*." Might as well put it right out there from the start. "Annie Harlowe."

"Is she an actress?"

"An *actress*?"

"There was an actress by the name of Harlow in those old black-and-white films your father liked to watch. I just wondered . . ."

Thom grins. "I doubt that it's her, Mother. She doesn't look a day over thirty."

Lillian has the grace to crack an almost-smile. "I didn't think that it was her, silly. I only thought there might be a connection."

Or that I might have followed in my big sister's footsteps and fallen in love with one of those pesky theater people?

Aloud, Thom merely says, "No, Mother. She isn't an actress. She's . . ."

An artist?

A waitress?

What more is there to say?

Certainly nothing that will convince his mother that she's the woman of his dreams.

He settles on, "She has a place in Montauk."

"Montauk?" Lillian considers this, then nods her semi-approval.

Apparently, as the boundaries of socially acceptable Long Island real estate expand eastward of Southampton, Montauk is moving up in the world.

Next question: "Where does she live in the city?"

Ah-ha. Here we go.

A brazen seagull swoops low over the terrace to steal a discarded crumb of muffin from the brick at Mother's feet. Watching the bird swoop off into the bright blue sky with his prize, Thom suddenly relishes the thought of telling Lillian Merriweather Brannock exactly who Annie is . . . and *isn't.*

"She doesn't live in the city at all," he informs Lillian almost jubilantly. "She's in Montauk year-round."

He waits for Lillian to react as though he's just informed her that Annie is a high-priced call girl.

Though her eyebrows attempt to edge another fraction of an inch closer to her preternaturally unwrinkled forehead, Mother says merely, "I see."

"She has two children," Thom can't resist saying, certain that to Mother, it's the equivalent of amending high-priced call girl to common street hooker.

"She's divorced?"

"Widowed."

"That's a shame."

"Mmm."

What is going on, here? Is it possible that he merely imagined years of matriarchal interference in his love life? Or is Mother playing some outlandish little game?

That, Thom tells himself, would be utterly out of character. Mother doesn't play games.

No, that was Father's department.

And perhaps, his own.

What are you doing? Thom asks himself uncomfortably. *Why do you crave Mother's disapproval?*

It isn't that he craves it so much as that he anticipates it, he tells himself.

Yet an unsettling air of doubt settles over him. Doubt about the true motivation for his all-consuming attraction to Annie.

In the broad light of day on Mother's terrace, it's almost possible to wonder whether he really is falling in love, or if he's merely infatuated with a woman of whom his mother would never approve.

"How, exactly, did you meet a widowed mother of two in Montauk?" Lillian wants to know.

Here goes. Time to pull out the big guns and watch her fire back. If she doesn't . . . well, Thom wouldn't be surprised if the blue sky abruptly gave way to storm clouds.

In other words, Mother's reaction to this bombshell is as predictable as the next five minutes' weather.

"Annie was a waitress at the party last Saturday night, Mother."

Lillian Merriweather Brannock—of the Back Bay Merriweathers and the Park Avenue Brannocks—slowly shakes her salon-coiffed head.

Shakes her head!

The response is so unexpectedly—and perhaps yes, disappointingly—prosaic that Thom can't help darting a glance at the sky for thunderbolts as he asks, "You're not upset?"

"That you're dating a waitress? Of course I'm upset."

"Then why aren't you berating me? Or at least trying to throw some eligible Vanderbilt heiress my way?"

"Because that has never worked in the past," Mother informs him. "And because, as your sister pointed out to me just the other day, the worst thing I can do at this point is try to steer you in the right direction. I'll only succeed in driving you away."

"Susan said that?" he asks, thinking back to last week's conversation about sushi and swimming with sharks.

Mother nods. "She thinks you're feeling restless. She mentioned that you might need to sow your wild oats before you're ready to settle down."

"Sow my wild oats?" Thom makes a face.

Is that what he was doing last night with Annie?

"It seems most men have a need for it. If not before marriage, then afterward," Mother adds, somewhat remorsefully.

So.

She's worried that he'll end up like Thomas III, with a proper wife and a bevy of mistresses.

What is there to say to that?

"Don't worry about me, Mother." He stands and plants a kiss on her surgically plumped cheek. "I'm not even thinking about marriage at this point."

"I hope not, if your . . . *Annie* . . . has two children to raise and put through college."

The implication is clear enough to send a cascade of ire through Thom.

"Annie isn't looking for a benefactor, Mother."

"I'm glad to hear that."

Clearly, she doesn't believe it.

And now, thanks to her, neither does he. Not entirely.

Is it remotely possible that Annie is using him?

Perhaps even more discomfiting: Is *he* using *her*?

It's him.

Again.

Andre.

"Annie . . ."

The voice that calls her name is as static-ridden as before, but this time, Annie doesn't waste a moment questioning the presence. She knows her husband is there, somewhere; perhaps she can't hear him clearly, but she can *feel* him.

"Andre, I'm here." Her voice wavers; she takes a deep breath to steady herself, determined not to let the looming current of hysteria sweep her away. "Andre, please help me. I need you."

Again, a blast of sound; incomprehensible words rushing past her like a Long Island Railroad express bypassing her stop.

"Please, Andre . . . I can't hear you."

Nearly sobbing in frustration, Annie paces the drafty kitchen, barely aware of the chill or the ache of goose bumps rising on her bare arms.

"Tell me how to do this alone, Andre," she pleads, somehow mustering the presence of mind to keep her voice low. If the children wake up, it will be over. She doesn't know how she knows that, but she knows.

". . . Annie . . ."

Her name is bookended between two unintelligible phrases, filling her with plaintive desperation.

She gazes helplessly out the rain-spattered window. A bolt of lightning reaches down from the overcast sky.

"I can't hear what you're saying, Andre."

More static. Nothing but static.

What is he trying to tell her?

Is it something about . . . Thom?

Annie closes her eyes, tipping her forehead against the glass in defeated desperation. "I'm sorry, Andre. If that's what you . . . I'm sorry."

Does she even mean it? she wonders, vaguely aware of footsteps overhead.

Is she truly sorry for what happened with Thom? If she were given the opportunity to do it all over again, would she really turn her back on him?

Torn between her loyalty to her late husband and the promise of a new love, Annie is filled with anguish. God help her, she can no longer cope with the turmoil her life has become.

"I'm going under," she whispers into thin air, talking more to herself than anyone else. "I just can't do this alone anymore."

Static.

And then . . .

". . . copper . . ."

"Copper?" Annie pounces on the interference-riddled word like a drowning sailor seizing a lifeline. "What about copper, Andre? Copper Beach?"

Garbled noise.

"You want me to look for the treasure on Copper Beach? Andre—"

"Mommy?" Floorboards are creaking overhead, their daughter's distant voice calling for her.

"Andre, don't go," she begs, hearing Trixie's bare feet beginning to descend the stairs.

The phone beeps twice.

"Andre?"

Nothing.

"Andre!"

Nothing.

Annie looks down at the digital display on the receiver.

CALL LOST.

Chapter

11

Dropping the shovel and metal detector, Annie runs her fingertips over the heart-encased initials carved into the thick trunk of the old copper beech tree.

A. H. + A. H.

She smiles faintly, clearly remembering the day Andre carved the letters there, along with the word "Forever," added below as an afterthought.

"Who's A.H.?" she asked with a frown.

"Andre Harlowe."

"No, I mean the other A.H.?"

"That's you."

"My initials are A.G.," she pointed out.

"They are? Then we'll have to do something about that, won't we?" He was already sinking onto one knee in the grass, reaching into his pocket for the diamond engagement ring . . .

"Bet you can't catch me!" Milo shouts, racing off down the beach with Trixie at his heels, his ever-present cape flapping behind him. Both children swing plastic buckets in their small hands, ready to collect whatever treasures the sand and water yield today.

Tears sting Annie's eyes as she watches them, wishing their daddy could see them now.

Maybe he can.

"Andre?" Casting a dubious glance at the heavens, Annie whispers, "Are you there?"

Her words are lost in the rushing surf and the screeching of a carefree seagull that swoops low overhead. The bird skids to a landing on a rock outcropping at the water's edge. It hops a little closer, almost seeming to eye her reprovingly.

Of course Andre isn't there, Annie silently tells herself—all right, and the bird—feeling more ridiculous, and more desolate, with every passing moment.

Andre is dead.

How many times does she have to hear those words, even just in her own head, to believe them?

Andre is dead, and you're all alone.

All alone on Copper Beach, aside from the mangy gull and the children in the distance.

All alone in the world, save for a few precious moments last night in another man's arms.

Another man.

Annie shakes her head, Erika's voice echoing within.

You aren't married, Annie. You don't have to feel guilty. It isn't as though you're cheating on your husband.

Blindly watching as the feathered interloper scavenges for food in the rock's crevices, Annie wonders where Thom is right now.

Why didn't he call her? He promised he would.

Why, long after the morning thunderstorms had once

again given way to sunshine, did she feel compelled to linger in the house? She stayed inside until this late in the afternoon, working on her shell sculptures, alternately praying the phone would ring and hoping that it wouldn't?

He promised.

Well, maybe something came up.

Or maybe he's trying to reach her at home right this very moment, wondering why she isn't answering.

Maybe he's worried about her. She did say she'd be home all day.

Well, too bad. You changed your mind and went out. And you don't owe Thom Brannock anything.

Especially today.

Today, of all days, should be only about Andre.

Her thoughts drift back to the impossible conversation she had this morning with her dead husband. It seemed so real . . .

It was real, Annie tells herself. *That's why you're out here right now, planning to comb the beach for the lost gold until you find it. Admit it.*

Oh, God. Is she truly losing her mind?

The call seemed so real . . .

But then, so did the rush of emotion she felt for Thom last night.

That, Annie tells herself firmly, was as much a figment of her imagination as today's phone call to Andre.

Wasn't it?

With a sigh, she turns back to the grove of trees at the edge of the beach, the site of her engagement a lifetime ago . . . and her late husband's fruitless search for buried treasure.

Does she dare to believe that a chest filled with gold doubloons lies somewhere in the rocky, sandy soil, there for the taking?

Annie reaches for the discarded shovel and metal detector, wondering what she's supposed to do next.

The least Andre could do was mark the spot with a bold, heaven-sent "x", she thinks wryly.

Should she dig in the sand, or under the trees? Why didn't she pay more attention all those years that she came out here with Andre?

She glances up at the sound of a gleeful shout to see Trixie turning an imperfect cartwheel, her long ponytail trailing in the sand. Milo's sandals have gone missing and he's splashing along, barefoot, at the water's edge.

With a wistful smile, Annie allows herself to dream about what a windfall of pirate gold would do for them. New shoes. Ice cream. College.

Is that so much to ask? Any of it?

An irritatingly reasonable voice butts in.

You don't need a treasure chest in order to provide those things, Annie. You can work harder, or get a real job, or sell the house . . .

No. She can't sell the house—she *won't*. And she can't get a real job: nine-to-five in some office, away from her children.

Other people do it.

Why are you so determined to be different?

Because I lost my husband, dammit.

Other people lose their husbands. They carry on.

I'm carrying on, too, Annie tells herself stubbornly, willing pessimism to take flight with the seagull that in an abrupt fluttering of feathers has taken to the sky once again.

Andre wouldn't want her to sell the house, or get a real job. Andre would want her to cling to her dreams, to *their* dreams. He would want her to live life on her own terms, just the way they planned. He would want her to look for that treasure, just like he said.

Or did he?

She wants so badly to believe that she heard his voice today.

Because if Andre could find a way back to her, he would. If it were possible for him to communicate with her from beyond the grave, he would.

Annie is positive about that.

A.H. + A.H.

FOREVER.

With a sob, she turns her back abruptly on the tree, throwing the shovel and metal detector aside once again.

"Mommy!" Milo beckons from the water's edge. "I found a starfish!"

You were wrong, Andre. Nothing lasts forever.

"Mommy! Come see the starfish!"

Annie kicks off her sandals and carries them in one hand, walking down to where Milo and Trixie are crouched over a shallow tide pool.

This is the hardest day you'll ever have, Annie.

From here on in, she promises herself, it will all be downhill.

Or is it uphill?

Why does it sound like a challenge no matter how it's phrased?

"Look at him, Mommy," Trixie says, pointing to the

living starfish that lies in a few inches of water several
feet from the lapping waves.

"He's beached," Milo says sadly. "Can I pick him up
and put him back into the ocean?"

"No, don't touch him, sweetie. You might hurt him."

"But he's stuck." Trixie's voice is little-girl plaintive.

"Yeah, Mom, he wants to go swim out to sea."

"When the tide comes in, it'll take him back out,"
Annie tells her worried children. "Why don't you both
see if you can find some pretty shells for me?"

"I want to find Daddy's treasure instead," Milo says,
racing away with his bucket and shovel.

"Me, too! Wait for me!" Trixie cries.

"Hey, Batman," Annie calls after her son. "Wait for
your sister."

He turns around with a scowl. "I'm Green Lantern,
remember?"

"Sorry, Green Lantern. I forgot. Wait for your sister.
She can be Wonder Woman."

"I don't want to be Wonder Woman!" is Trixie's inevitable protest. "I want to be Barbie."

"Green Lantern doesn't hang around with Barbie,"
Milo protests in disgust. "She's not even in the Justice
League."

Annie sighs. "Milo, please."

"I'm the Green Lantern!"

"Well, I have a mission for you, Green Lantern. You,
too, Barbie. Go see if you can find that lost chest of
gold."

With that, they're off down the beach, in search of
Daddy's treasure.

Facing the sea, Annie closes her eyes wearily, the sand hot between her toes and the salt wind cool in her face.

She's so damned tired of whirling around and around on a carousel of endless grief.

So damned tired of longing for the impossible.

Dwelling on the phone calls to Andre that most likely never happened; yearning for another from Thom that will probably never come.

When she opens her eyes again, she finds herself gazing at a distant white triangle skimming along on the water.

What she wouldn't give to be out there on the waves, sailing away to . . .

Where, Annie? Where could you possibly go?

Andre is gone, he isn't coming back. There's no escape from that reality, just as there's no escape from the responsibilities that anchor her firmly here in her solitary life.

Lucky you, she wistfully tells both the sailor at the helm of the distant sailboat and the seagull that soars toward the horizon.

Then, shaking her head, she looks down, her gaze falling once again on the stranded starfish, waiting helplessly for the tide to come in.

With a deft hand on the tiller, Thom navigates the custom-built cutter away from the wind, bringing her around parallel to the distant shoreline. A smattering of dark rooftops jut from clumps of green foliage in the distance, marking the last populated area before the tip of the island.

Easing the sails all the way out, Thom launches the boat into an exhilarating run along the whitecaps toward Montauk's famed lighthouse.

It's no accident that he's chosen to head out east this afternoon instead of following his usual southwestern route along the barrier island.

Annie's out there somewhere, Thom thinks, wishing in one instant that he had thought to bring a pair of binoculars on board; loathing himself for that unsettling thought in the next.

Yeah, sure. What is he going to do? Spy on her house from out here, with the stretch of sea to provide a safe buffer between them?

He should have called her, at least.

Why didn't he call her?

Because he isn't man enough. Because he doesn't know what to say. Because he doesn't know how he feels.

Yes, you do. Who are you kidding? You're crazy about her.

All right, so he knows *how* he feels—he just isn't sure *why* he feels it.

And questioning his motives is the wisest thing he can do right now, for his own sake and for Annie's. The last thing he wants is to come to terms with the possibility that he's subconsciously been using her. But if that's the case, he can nip it in the bud before somebody gets hurt.

Namely, Annie.

Or, God forbid, her children.

And you think the kids aren't still waiting for the chicken nuggets you promised them?

You think Annie isn't expecting the call you promised her?

They'll all be hurt when you let them down. That's a given.

The sails are flapping in the breeze, Thom realizes. He glances up at the blue and red telltales tied to the shrouds and mainstay.

The wind has shifted.

He quickly trims the sails, expertly turning into a broad reach, then a beam reach, just the way his father taught him decades ago.

"Harness the energy," Thomas Brannock III would bark, watching his son struggling to control the rig. "Timing is everything. Keep her in position, or you'll capsize."

Tempting as it sometimes was to do just that, tossing his unrelenting father into the waves, Thom always managed to stay on course. But he could hardly wait for the day he'd be skilled enough to be alone out here on the whitecaps, fully in command.

Well, here he is. Fully in command, with nobody to answer to. Nobody to tell him how to harness the energy, to stay on course, to keep from capsizing.

Nobody around for what seems like miles other than Thom, and a seagull that swoops low over the boat, squawking loudly. It splashes into the sea nearby, ostensibly diving for fish.

All at once, alone is the last place Thom wants to be.

Keeping the tiller steady with one hand, he reaches into his pocket with the other and pulls out his cell phone.

He flips it open eagerly . . . then frowns when he sees the words NO SERVICE flashing in the display.

He turns the phone off.

Then on again.

Still no service.

"What the . . . ?" Shaking his head in frustration, he turns it off once more, then on again with an almost frantic jab of his finger.

NO SERVICE.

Thom curses so loudly that the gull bobbing on the water beside the boat flutters its wings, startled.

He tosses the phone aside and it lands with a clatter at his feet. So much for calling Annie. It wasn't meant to be.

The gull gazes up at him with one unblinking beady eye, almost as if he is challenging him.

Suddenly, nothing matters more to Thom than hearing Annie's voice.

He's made calls to shore many times in the past, although never from this far out on the island.

There must be service nearby.

He'll just keep sailing until he finds a spot where his telephone can make a connection.

The phone is ringing as Annie herds the children in the door after a futile few hours spent on Copper Beach.

"Telephone, Mommy!" Trixie announces unnecessarily.

"I hear it, sweetie." The moth ballet swiftly reclaims the stage in Annie's stomach, and it's all she can do to keep from racing toward the nearest receiver.

It won't be him, she tells herself, forcing her legs to merely saunter across the living room.

Still, when she reaches the phone, she finds herself snatching it up with a breathlessly hopeful, "Hello?"

"Hi. Are you all right?"

"Erika." Annie exhales heavily. "I'm fine. Why?"

"Because today is—"

"You don't have to remind me!"

"I'm sorry."

"It's okay." Annie runs a troubled hand through her hair, wincing when it snags in the wind-blown tangle of curls. "I didn't mean to snap at you, Erika. I just . . ."

I just hoped you'd be somebody else, that's all.

She doesn't dare say it. Not unless she wants Erika on her case about dating again.

"You don't have to apologize to me, Annie. Listen, I'm on my way out so I don't have time to chat, but I just wanted to let you know that I talked to Dr. Leaver this morning and he said you should call him."

"Dr. Leaver?"

"I told you about him the other day . . . ?"

"Oh!" Annie shrugs. "I don't think I need to call him after all. I'm fine."

After a pause, Erika says, obviously weighing her words carefully, "I'll give you the number anyway, Annie. Just in case. Do you have a pen and paper handy?"

"Did you forget who you're talking to?" Annie asks ruefully, gazing around at the cluttered room. "I'll just get the number from you next—"

"Go hunt down a pen and paper, Annie," Erika says in the same no-nonsense tone Annie uses with her children when their options are severely limited.

It takes Annie a few minutes to locate a working pen and a scrap of paper that isn't already scribbled on. She reluctantly takes down the number Erika rattles off, then slips it under a magnet on the fridge.

"You should call him, Annie."

"I will."

But she won't.

"Have fun tonight," she tells Erika as she wanders back to the living room. Her friend, she remembers, has a date with somebody new, a stockbroker she met through one of those Internet dating services she's resorted to using.

"I'll try."

"What's wrong?"

"It's just so much work," her friend says wearily. "Getting to know somebody new, asking and answering all those first-date questions . . . who needs the stress?"

"Not me," Annie quips.

"Don't let me discourage you. I've been doing this without a break for years, Annie. The fun has kind of worn off. It'll be different for you, when you're ready to start dating again."

"Careful, Milo, don't fall," Annie warns her son, who has climbed onto the couch but is nowhere near on the verge of falling.

He tells her so, loudly.

But at least Annie's succeeded in changing the course of the conversation, as Erika asks how the kids are doing, and whether they'd be interested in coming into the city the week after next to see the latest comic-strip-turned-feature film opening next weekend.

"I'd invite them to see it this Saturday, but it'll be hard to get in opening weekend."

"Yes, and if it works out with this guy tonight you want to make sure you're free next weekend."

Erika laughs. "You know me too well."

"So am I invited on this outing, too?" Annie asks.

"Not to the movie. You can drop the kids with me and then go off and do something on your own."

"You're kidding, right?"

"Nope. If you're around, how can I possibly spoil my godchildren with too many Sno-Caps and Jujubes?"

"What am I supposed to do with myself while you're all at the movies?"

"That's up to you," Erika says breezily. "Let's make it a week from Wednesday, and you can all spend the night. I'll make sure I'm free on Thursday morning. We'll go to breakfast."

"Erika—"

"Put it in your calendar, Annie. A week from this Wednesday. You can meet me at my office. My last Wednesday appointment always ends at four."

"But—"

"Gotta run, Annie. Mr. Wonderful might be waiting."

"Good luck." Annie hangs up with a shake of her head, envying Erika's freedom to dash out the door unencumbered, even if it is merely for an evening of stiff conversation with a total stranger who may or may not turn out to be a jerk.

Funny how Annie's conversations with Thom lack that first-date awkwardness. Not that they've ever even had an official "date."

Or ever will.

"Where did Auntie Erika invite us and not you?" asks Trixie the expert eavesdropper, darting at Annie's feet as she crosses the room to replace the phone in its cradle.

"A movie."

"Are we going?"

"Only if you're good," Annie says with a smile.

She knows what Erika's up to. Her friend, whose taste runs to independent films and imported caviar, is about as interested in Jujubes and G-rated blockbusters about super heroes as she is in staying single for the rest of her life. Her intent is to give Annie some time to herself . . .

And I'll take it, Annie thinks. If nothing else, she can lounge around alone in Erika's one-bedroom apartment eating popcorn and watching HBO. Bliss.

Too bad it's almost two weeks away.

But maybe it's just as well.

Today, she has other things to think about.

Then again, today, the day she's been dreading for so long, is winding down. Soon it will be over, another milestone behind her.

"Where are you going, Mommy?" Trixie asks as she heads for the backdoor with the receiver.

"I'll be right back, sweetheart. I just have to make one more call."

"Can't you call from inside the house?"

"No," Annie says simply. "I can't."

Outside, she sits on the back step, the telephone in her trembling hand.

Dusk is just beginning to fall; the world around her still and hushed the way it always seems to be at this time of day in summer. The air is heavy with humidity and the scent of the sea and everything blooming all around her—perennials and weeds alike.

Annie inhales deeply, exhales heavily, slaps a buzzing mosquito away from her ear. She looks up at the darkening sky, where a pale moon is barely visible beyond the leafy branches overhead.

Where are you, Andre? Are you up there? Are you right here beside me?

Why don't I feel you?

I should feel you now, today, of all days.

If you're going to make contact with me, it should be now.

Holding her breath, she dials the phone.

This time, it's going to happen.

She knows it.

She can sense it.

It's as if the entire earth is holding its breath, waiting for her to connect with Andre once again.

"Hey, you've reached Andre. You know what to do. Wait for the beep and don't forget to—"

Annie presses the TALK button in utter despair, disconnecting the call.

She's a misguided fool, a grief-stricken wife, a pathetic, lonely widow. Andre is gone; he's been gone for a year now.

It's time to move on, time to let go, time to forget.

So why can't I?

"Mommy?" Trixie calls from somewhere inside the house. "I'm hungry."

Yes. Her children are hungry. Her children have needs. It's her job to take care of them. Alone.

Milo and Trixie are Andre's legacy; they're all she has left of him. They'll have to be enough.

Wiping tears from her cheeks, Annie steels herself for the lonely night ahead, the lonely lifetime ahead.

Back in the house, she returns to the living room, where her children are waiting.

Then, about to return the phone to its cradle, Annie notices that the answering machine's red light is blinking.

*   *   *

She never called him back.

Should Thom be surprised?

Probably not . . . but he can't help it.

Painstakingly inching his way back toward Manhattan's distant skyline in Sunday night traffic, he tells himself firmly that he's leaving Annie behind, both literally and figuratively.

He wasn't even planning to call Annie on Friday.

Not only did he call her, but he left an effusive message about what a wonderful time he'd had the night before. The entire time he was talking, he was wondering whether she was there, listening, screening his call.

Maybe she was.

Maybe she wasn't.

In any case, she didn't call back.

So what?

He's a busy man. He doesn't have time to play games with a fickle female, and that, he concludes, is precisely what he was doing the other night.

All right, his feelings for her felt authentic at the time.

But that's because he's hardly a relationship connoisseur.

He'd surely be able to recognize a forged Renoir, a Rolex knockoff, a lesser champagne trying to pass itself off as Cristal . . .

But when it comes to love, Thom is far from an expert.

Not that love is what he assumed he was feeling in the first place. No, but he did think it was something.

Something real, some life-altering emotion he'd never before experienced.

Well, he won't be fooled again.

Not that he'll have the chance.

Annie didn't call him back Friday night, or Saturday, and she didn't call him back today.

He jumped every time the phone rang, and it was always business.

As it should be.

As it very likely is now, when his cell phone rings as the car creeps toward the Midtown Tunnel just ahead.

But it isn't business.

It's Annie.

"I got your message," she says hurriedly, "and I'm sorry it took me so long to call back. It just hasn't been a good weekend around here."

"It's okay."

Do not be elated just to hear her voice, you idiot.

"I figured you'd be back in the city by now ... are you?" she asks, sounding almost hopeful.

Okay, so he gets it. She waited to call until it was too late to possibly get together. She doesn't want to see him any more than he wants to see her ...

Except that he does.

So badly that if a U-turn were possible here, he'd be making one. But he's boxed in by other cars, and suddenly, every time the brake lights in front of him go off, the car ahead seems to be moving entire yards forward at a time, rather than a few inches.

"I'm not back in the city yet," he tells Annie hurriedly, knowing the cell phone signal will die the minute he ventures into the tunnel. "Why? Did you want to get together?"

"Tonight?" she sounds surprised ... and promisingly hesitant.

Behind him, a horn blares.

Oh. The car ahead has moved forward again, and Thom has momentarily failed to catch up to its bumper.

Releasing his foot from the brake, he scowls at the impatient driver behind him, and reluctantly edges closer yet to the mouth of the tunnel.

"Where are you?" Annie asks. "Are you driving?"

Yes. Away from you. Forever.

"I'm in the car," he admits. "But if you want to try to get together tonight, I can turn around . . ."

"How far away are you?"

"Not far," he lies.

She's silent for a moment.

He's forced to move closer to the tunnel again.

"No," she says abruptly. "I can't. I was just, um, returning your call."

"How about next weekend?" he asks eagerly, too eagerly, even as he wonders what the hell he's doing. "Dinner Saturday night, Annie. Okay? You and the kids."

"I—"

"Don't say you're busy. Just say you'll come."

"I don't know . . ."

He brakes again, poised on the threshold of the tunnel, holding his breath.

Road rage erupts behind him, the angry driver honking loudly and repeatedly. Others take it up, a chorus of blaring car horns.

But Thom isn't budging until Annie agrees to see him again.

"Come on, Annie, say yes."

Silence.

On the phone, at least. Now drivers are shouting expletives out their windows. In another moment or two, somebody's probably going to start shooting at him.

"Yes."

"Yes?" he echoes, not sure he heard her correctly.

"Yes."

Relief courses through him.

"Okay," he says quickly, "it's a date. I'll call you during the week to confirm it. Okay?"

"Okay."

"I have to go now, Annie . . ."

Before they open fire.

And before I say something stupid, like "I love you."

"All right. Bye."

"Bye."

With that, he allows the tunnel, and a ridiculously intense sense of well-being, to swallow him up at last.

Chapter

12

So that's a chicken nugget," Thom muses the following Saturday night, as the waitress sets two plates in front of two beaming children.

"Not really." Milo pops one into his mouth. "It's a fake one."

"A fake one?" he asks, amused by the notion of knock-off nuggets. Obviously, Milo is a connoisseur.

"Well actually," the boy says, "they call them chicken tenders here so they're not really fake." Seeing the look his mother shoots him, he adds hastily, "But they taste like chicken nuggets."

"Please don't talk with your mouth full, Milo."

"Sorry, Mom."

"Do you want to try one?" Trixie asks Thom shyly.

His heart melts, same as it did when he laid eyes on her mother half an hour ago. Annie is dazzling tonight in a simple white sheath and sandals, her hair caught back in a filmy white scarf.

"I'd love to try one," he tells Trixie, who is nearly as

lovely as her mother in a daisy-sprigged sundress, her long hair in a single braid.

"You need to dip that into some ketchup," Milo advises as Thom accepts the golden fried morsel from Trixie's fork. "A lot of it. Like, tons."

Thom nods at the waitress. "You heard the man. We'll need tons of ketchup as soon as possible, please."

"Coming right up, sir," she smilingly says mostly to Milo, and vanishes toward the kitchen.

"I'm surprised they even have ketchup in a place like this," Annie tells him.

"Yeah, and I'm surprised they have chicken nuggets in a place like this," Trixie pipes up.

"Chicken tenders. And I'm not surprised," Milo says confidently. "Thom promised."

"It's Mr. Brannock." Annie moves her son's precariously placed water goblet away from his elbow.

"Thom is fine."

Daddy would be better.

Thom blinks. Where on earth did *that* thought come from?

For Pete's sake. What the heck is he doing?

You don't know what you're doing. That's the whole point. You're clueless about this stuff, remember?

What if he's wrong about Annie, the way he was wrong about Joyce?

Maybe Annie isn't really interested in him after all. Maybe she's the kind of woman who . . .

No. There's no question about what kind of woman Annie is. She's not the one who might have ulterior motives here.

He is.

Still uncomfortably uncertain about the nature of his feelings for her, Thom told himself that if she didn't call back last Sunday night, it might be for the best. Then there would be no risk of anybody getting hurt . . .

Other than him, of course. Because if Annie didn't call back, he would have been devastated.

But she did call. And when she did, he spontaneously asked her out to dinner, and here they are.

To hell with motives, his or hers, whatever they might be. He's going to enjoy this evening with Annie and her children, ketchup and all.

On that note, the waitress arrives with a white porcelain ramekin on a doily-enhanced saucer.

"What's that?" Milo asks, standing on his tiptoes to peer at it with suspicion.

"It's ketchup," Annie tells him. "Sit down."

"Why is it in a fancy bowl?"

"Because this is a fancy restaurant," Trixie tells her brother, who is already dunking a hunk of chicken into the ketchup.

"Milo! Use the spoon to put some on your plate!"

"Oops. Sorry, Mom."

"You were s'posed to use your good manners tonight, remember?" Trixie says worriedly. "Otherwise Mr.— Thom—will be sorry he took us to a fancy restaurant."

"Sorry," Milo says again, looking so embarrassed that Thom pointedly dunks his own chicken nugget directly into the bowl.

Milo shoots him a grateful smile, and Annie hides her own behind her cloth napkin.

"How do you like it?" Trixie asks anxiously.

"Delicious," Thom pronounces. "Almost makes me wish I'd ordered this instead of the filet mignon."

The children, of course, are delighted to hear that, and eager to share more of their nuggets.

"No, you guys go ahead and eat them. I'll order my own next time."

Milo pounces on that. "You're going to take us out to dinner again?"

"Sure." Thom looks over at Annie. Her sweetly sentimental expression catches him off-guard.

"You're very good with them," she says quietly. "Thank you."

"You don't have to thank me."

She shrugs. "Not everyone would be as . . . patient. Or charming."

"What can I say? I'm a patient, charming guy."

Annie nods, her smile more fond than amused, triggering an intense reaction in Thom's soul. He wants to tell her that he can do much more for her and the children. So much more than buying them a couple of dinners . . .

But he doesn't dare.

Watching Annie dig into the surf and turf he insisted she order, he tells himself that maybe buying a few dinners will have to be enough.

"Can Thom come in and play, Mommy?"

Annie laughs and shakes her head, shooting a sidelong glance at the man in the driver's seat beside her.

"I think he thinks you're his new best friend," she tells Thom.

"The feeling is mutual," he says so easily that she wants to hug him.

In fact, she's been tempted to hug him all evening, and not just because he's been great with her children, or because he treated three hungry Harlowes to the best meal any of them have had in ages.

Yes, Thom Brannock has a huge heart.

The thing is . . . he's somehow managed to capture Annie's.

And the man is too good to be true. She keeps waiting for him to reveal some fatal flaw, some reason she shouldn't fall in love with him . . .

But you already have your own reasons for that, she reminds herself firmly.

"Please, Mommy?" Milo says from the backseat, where his sister is slumped over, sound asleep.

"It's late, Milo. I think Thom has had his fill of playing for one day," Annie says, though she isn't so sure.

The vibe Thom is sending her way says he wouldn't be opposed to coming in for a while . . . but not to play. At least, not with the children.

He says nothing, just steers along Montauk Highway toward their house, clearly determined to leave the decision up to Annie.

She hedges.

They really should call it a night . . .

But it's been such a wonderful evening she hates to see it end.

First dinner at a casually elegant restaurant in Sag Harbor, then browsing among shops where she pointed out some of her artwork on display. Thom was impressed—at least, he seemed to be. Even after Annie told him that sales had been pretty dismal lately.

"But I'm hoping things will pick up now that the summer people are back," she said with false optimism.

"I bet they will. You're talented, Annie."

He had to say that. At least, that was what she told herself. But she couldn't help feeling a little thrilled at his proclamation. How long had it been since somebody had believed in her?

Before she could remember that Andre used to say things like that, and that Andre used to believe in her, and that it had now been more than a year since his death, Thom was making her laugh and dragging her and the children to a toy store, just to "browse," or so he claimed.

Before they left the store, Thom insisted on buying each of them a kite and promising he'd show them how to fly them. Back in Montauk, they stopped at Fudge 'n Stuff for sundaes—a triple one for Milo, who requested extra sprinkles and two cherries, much to Annie's chagrin and Thom's indulgent amusement. Between the ice cream and a sunset walk along the beach, both kids were so sticky and sandy that Annie cringed when they climbed back into Thom's car.

"Don't worry, everything's washable," he said with a laugh, seeing her face as Trixie left hot fudge fingerprints on the window before rolling it down, and Milo dumped the sand out of his sneakers onto the floor mat.

Through it all, with every kind word he said and every fond gesture he made toward her children, Annie grew more and more captivated.

She can almost convince herself that this is a man who could fit seamlessly into their lives . . . until she remembers that he comes from a world that couldn't be farther removed.

Now, all too soon, Thom is turning into their driveway, steering past hedges that sorely need clipping and violet-and-dandelion-dotted grass that desperately needs mowing and flowerbeds that are choked with weeds.

Home, sweet home.

"Here we are." Thom glances over at Annie, who nods, trying to ignore the unmistakable current sizzling in the air between them.

She looks away, out the window, and murmurs, in an effort to diffuse the tension, "I've got to take care of the yard. It's a mess."

For a moment, there's silence.

Then Thom exclaims, "Violets!"

Annie looks at him. "What?"

"Your lawn is covered in violets." He shakes his head in wonder. "I can't believe I didn't notice that before. They're everywhere."

"Yeah, well, they pop up every June."

"I can't believe it," he says again.

"What can't you believe? That the violets pop up every June, or that I'm too lax to keep my lawn mowed?"

"Just . . . never mind. Wow. Violets." A giddy laugh escapes him.

The sound is contagious enough for Annie to join in, though she has no idea what they're laughing at. As far as she's concerned, it just feels good.

And if it feels good, do it, says the old Annie, the one she thought was lost forever.

"Can Thom come in?" Milo asks again.

"It's late," Annie repeats lamely, knowing that one word from Thom will sway her.

And that if he comes in, they'll end up in each other's arms the second the children are tucked into—

"But look up at the sky. It's still light out," Milo protests.

"It is, but it's late."

"There's no school tomorrow."

"Milo," Annie says in a warning tone.

"Come on, Mom. Daddy would have let us stay up late if it was still light out and there was no school," he informs her, effectively snuffing the electricity sizzling in the front seat. At least, on Annie's end.

"It's time for bed," Annie says briefly, reaching for her door handle as the tires crunch to a stop at the end of the drive.

"But, Mom—"

"No, Milo."

He opens his mouth to protest, and is curtailed by Thom's stern, "Listen to your mom, Milo."

"You said you'd teach me to tie my shoes."

"And I will, the next time we see each other. I promise."

"When will that be? Tomorrow?"

"I have to work for Merlin again tomorrow," Annie says in a clipped tone, her stomach churning with guilt.

For a few hours, she forgot. Everything.

How could she have done that?

How could she have forgotten Andre?

"So what if you have to work, Mom? You don't have to be around."

"Milo!" she says sharply.

"Sorry," he grumbles. "How about Monday, Thom?"

"I have to go back to the city tomorrow night, Batman," Thom says, reaching back to ruffle his hair.

"Back to the city?" echoes Batman, who earlier today growled if anyone dared call him anything other than Green Lantern.

"That's where I live," Thom explains.

"But we're coming to the city!"

"You are?"

Yes. They are. Annie forgot all about Erika's week-old invitation, but obviously, Milo didn't.

"Yup," he says excitedly. "We'll be there on Wednesday to go to the movies. You can come with us!"

Thom looks at Annie, clearly at a loss.

As if Annie has any clue what he should say. Right now, her head is spinning and all she wants is to crawl alone into the bed she used to share with her husband.

"Auntie Erika wants to take you and Trixie to the movies alone, Milo," she manages to say. "Just the three of you."

"What are you doing while they're at the movies, Annie?" Thom asks, resting a gentle hand on her arm.

Suddenly, despite her guilt, despite her urge to be alone, popcorn and HBO don't seem nearly as alluring as . . . other things.

"I'm . . . I'm not sure what I'm doing."

"Why don't I take you to dinner?" Thom suggests.

"I want to go, too," Milo chimes in excitedly from the back seat.

"Milo, relax, nobody's going to dinner," Annie says.

"Why not, Mom?"

"Why not, Annie?"

"Because . . ."

She can't think straight, dammit.

Gazing thoughtfully at her, Thom says, "I'll call you during the week, and we'll talk about it then. Okay?"

With a helpless shrug, she says simply, "Okay."

It seems as though mere minutes have passed since Annie collapsed into bed after an exhausting, unbearably humid evening spent waiting tables at the golden anniversary of Mr. and Mrs. Wilfred Claudius Yates on Sunday evening, another income-netting "favor" for Merlin.

But when she awakens to Trixie's blood-curdling screams, a glance at the illuminated dial on the bedside clock shows that it's already four o'clock Monday morning.

How time flies when you're having fun, Annie thinks, swinging her legs around to the floor.

Fun, in the form of yet another erotic dream about Thom. This one, featuring a romp in a field of violets, was even more sensual than last night's escapade, which rivaled the surfside love scene in *From Here to Eternity*.

Pushing Thom from her thoughts, Annie swiftly makes her way down the dark hall to Trixie's room.

In the glow of the Madeline night-light plugged into a baseboard outlet, she sees her daughter huddled, whimpering, near the foot of her bed.

"It's okay, baby girl, I'm here," Annie croons, taking Trixie in her arms and rocking her the way she did as a newborn.

Annie never minded the wee-hour feedings that are the bane of most new mothers' existence. She enjoyed stealing through the hushed, sleeping household to instantly soothe her little one's wailing; loved having her precious children all to herself for a little while, holding them close and feeling their baby breath soft against her arm.

Sometimes, she'd fall asleep holding them. Then, inevitably, Andre would come looking for her. He'd bring her back to bed and they'd drowsily make love, and Annie would drift off to sleep wrapped in her husband's arms and the knowledge that all was right in her cozy little universe.

How lucky we were then, she silently tells her daughter . . . and her husband, wherever he is.

So lucky, and I knew it all along.

How often, when somebody she knew faced the sudden loss of a loved one, did Annie hear them say that they never appreciated the person while they were alive? That they never stopped to count their blessings?

But I always did. I always knew that what we had was too good to last.

Yes, and she frequently worried that something horrible would happen to take it all away.

So why were you so shocked when it did, Annie?

"Mommy?"

"Hmm?"

"When are you going to marry Thom?"

Annie abruptly stops stroking Trixie's sweat-dampened hair. *"What?"*

"Daddy said you were going to marry Thom and I was wondering when."

"'*Daddy* said'?" Annie's blood runs cold. "Trixie, what are you talking about?"

Trixie yawns deeply, then says, "Daddy was sitting on my bed. He was smiling like in that picture." She points to a framed snapshot Annie placed on her nightstand last fall, when she realized Trixie's memory of her father was fading fast.

"Trixie, maybe you were just looking at the picture and you thought he was really—"

"No," Trixie interrupts stubbornly, "he was here. And he said I was going to have a new daddy and it was Thom."

"Trixie, you know that was just a dream."

"No it wasn't."

Annie sighs. No use arguing with a four-year-old whose imagination is obviously as vivid as her mother's.

"Is that why you woke up screaming?" she asks gently. "Because you thought you saw Daddy?"

Trixie shakes her head rapidly. "I'm not scared of Daddy. And I want you to marry Thom, Mommy. I was screaming because Milo let go of the string on my new pink kite and it flew away. Why does he always have to ruin my stuff?"

Annie sighs. "Trixie, Milo is sound asleep in his bed and your pink kite is downstairs in the closet. And I'm not going to marry Thom, so—"

"But Daddy said that you were. He said Thom was going to be my new daddy on earth because he's stuck up in heaven so he can't take care of me as good as he used to."

"It was just a dream," Annie insists, unable to control the waver in her voice or the tremor in her hand as she resumes stroking Trixie's hair.

"Stop saying that! It was not a dream! He was really here. I saw him."

"All right, sweetie. All right. You really saw him."

"I did."

"Okay."

"You don't believe me!"

"Yes, I do," Annie says softly.

And in that moment, she almost does.

The electric floor fan beside the bed makes a wooshing noise as it arcs toward them, stirring the air with a too-warm breeze.

Trixie yawns again. "He was here."

"Shh . . . I know."

Trixie's body gradually relaxes as Annie holds her close the way she has on countless other restless nights.

Marry Thom?

There's no way.

And yet . . .

No. Lord knows Annie isn't living a fairy tale; Thom isn't a dashing Prince Charming who can zap away her troubles and whisk her off to happily ever after.

No . . .

But he is persistent. Just when she thinks he's gone from her life, he swoops back in to sweep her away like tide does the starfish on the sand.

Yes, she thinks grimly, but sooner or later, the tide always ebbs, and the starfish might find itself beached once again.

It might . . . or it might not.

Sooner or later, Annie reminds herself as she carefully settles her slumbering daughter against the pillows, the starfish might just be carried out to sea, cradled forever in its calming blue depth, never again to be stranded alone on the sand.

Part Two

July

Chapter

13

Opening the door to his sister late Tuesday evening, Thom braces himself for bad news. Susan might live only a few blocks up Park Avenue, but she never drops by unannounced. Especially at this hour.

When the doorman buzzed up to alert Thom to her presence, all he could think was that something horrible must have happened ... something that warrants face-to-face delivery of the news.

"Is it Mother?" he asks, peering anxiously at his sister's face, relieved to note that she hasn't been crying. At least, he doesn't think she has. The unnaturally smooth skin around her eyes is as pale as the rest of her and there are no telltale smudges in her omnipresent mascara and liner.

"Mother?" Susan echoes, incapable of furrowing her brow in the confusion her tone conveys.

"Did something happen to her?"

"No! Mother's fine." She walks past him, her heels clicking across the marble entryway into the living room, where he was in the midst of watching the ten o'clock news. "In fact, I just came from there."

"Southampton?" Thom pads after her in his cashmere slippers and sits beside her on the couch.

"No, she's at the townhouse. Matthew drove her into the city this afternoon." Matthew, of course, is their mother's longtime chauffeur, an elderly Englishman whose patience with the formidable Lillian Merriweather Brannock outweighs his driving skills at this point.

"I thought she was staying out east all week."

"She was planning on it, but I asked her to come home to go with me to a doctor's appointment."

Thom's heart stops. "The cardiologist? Is your heart acting up again?" His mind leapfrogs through a lineup of terrifying scenarios, all of which lead to a chilling destination: his only sibling's deathbed.

"Relax, Thom," Susan says with a chuckle, opening her Chanel handbag and removing an envelope, which she hands to him. "It wasn't the cardiologist, it was my ob-gyn, and I'm fine. Really fine. In fact, I'm ecstatic."

Opening the envelope, he removes what looks like medical X-rays. "Then why . . . oh!" His gaze shifts in quick succession from the white-on-black image in his hand to Susan's twinkling blue eyes to her midsection beneath a sleeveless navy linen dress, where he searches for . . . and finds the slightest telltale bulge.

"Can you believe it? The doctor is ninety-nine percent certain it's a boy. I'm due around Christmas."

He hugs her ferociously. "I'm going to be an uncle?"

"Yup. And I'm going to be a mom. And Wade is going to be a dad. How crazy is that?"

"Not so crazy. You'll be a wonderful mom, and Wade

will be a wonderful dad." He fervently hopes that's the case. Perhaps parenthood will loosen them up, bring some joy into their lives. "I didn't know you were even trying to conceive."

"We weren't, until now. I got pregnant on the first try. You know what Dad always used to say when we were sailing . . ."

"Timing is everything," he says in unison with his sister. "In sailing, in business . . . and obviously, in biology. Oh! I just realized—"

"What?"

"Mother. She's going to be a grandmother. That's absolutely unfathomable."

"You wouldn't think so if you had seen her earlier."

"Don't tell me she's taken up knitting."

"No, but she was pleased about the baby. Quite pleased."

He notes that Susan's expression is as close to an outright grin as it has been in years. "You know, you're actually glowing."

"That's what Wade told me."

"He did?" It's difficult to imagine his stiff brother-in-law saying anything of the sort.

"Yes, and he also said that I'm suddenly snoring like a trucker. I've never snored in my life, and even if I did, he'd never hear me over the racket he makes with his own snoring."

Thom shakes his head at the very idea of his prim sister snoring like a trucker.

"What else did he say?" he asks, then cuts off his own question with, "Wait a second, forget about Wade, what did Mother say? Or should we all be calling her Granny from here on in?"

"That'll be the day. You know Mother. She said congratulations, gave me a perfunctory hug, shook Wade's hand. But I swear I heard her sniffling a little."

"*Mother* cried? With joy?"

"Sniffled with joy. Yes. She came with me to the doctor's office for my sonogram earlier. We saw the baby fluttering, and we heard its little heart beating, and I swear, Thom, she was actually moved by the whole experience."

Maybe, Thom thinks, Lillian Brannock is softening a bit in her old age. Maybe she'll be a more affectionate grandmother than she was a mother. Maybe, if her grandson picks her a bouquet of violets, she'll put them in a vase.

Violets.

Annie.

Annie, who unexpectedly agreed, when he called her from the office this afternoon, to meet him for dinner in Manhattan tomorrow night. So unexpectedly that it's going to be a challenge for Thom to rearrange his already packed schedule to keep their date, but to hell with Saltwater Treasures. That merger isn't looking promising anyway.

But the merger with Annie Harlowe, on the other hand, is looking quite promising.

He's going to see Annie again.

He's going to kiss Annie again.

Annie.

Violets.

"I met someone," he blurts to his sister.

Her smile fades. "Mother told me."

"I take it she isn't thrilled?"

"What do you think?"

Thom shrugs.

"A waitress with two kids? What are you doing, Tommy?"

"Sowing my wild oats," he says grimly. "Isn't that what you called it?"

"I told Mother that you're feeling restless and that she should give you a break and stop pushing you to get married. I told her that it might be good for you to date a few different women before you settle down. Better now than later."

Like Father did.

Susan doesn't say it, and neither does he. But they're both thinking it; he can tell by the look on his sister's face.

"Who did you have in mind?" Thom asks. "Because all the eligible British royals are spoken for, and the Hilton sisters are too young, too nouveau, and much too—"

"Which leaves you with a waitress?"

Thom bristles. "Stop saying it that way, Susan."

"What? Waitress? Isn't that what she is?"

"She's working for a caterer to earn enough money to keep a roof over her children's heads. She's . . . an artist."

"An artist? Even better."

"Why the hell are you being so damned nasty about this? I thought you were on my side."

"I am on your side, and I know what you're going through. I did it too, Tommy, remember?"

"You did what?"

"Rebelled," she says simply. "Only I did it younger. They say girls mature faster than boys. I guess this is your delayed adolescence. But you have to be careful, Tommy. You're a grown man with a lot to lose."

"What do I have to lose?"

"A fortune—and that's at the very least," she says with a shrug.

"She isn't after my money."

"How do you know?"

"Annie isn't a gold digger, Susan. Lord knows I've met enough of them to recognize one when I see one."

"Don't be so sure. Trust me, she doesn't have to have an Academy Award to be a good actress."

"She isn't acting! She's genuine and sweet and down to earth, and she's the best woman I've ever met and I'm lucky she's giving me the time of day!"

That fervent speech is effective in clamping his sister's mouth shut.

"Look, Susan, I'm not going to marry her," he says. "I'm just spending time with her because I enjoy her company, and her kids are a lot of fun."

"Well, pretty soon you'll have a nephew of your own."

"I know, and I can't wait." Thom holds back a sigh. "And I'm sorry for bringing up Annie. I didn't mean to spoil your big news. I'm thrilled for you, Susan. Really. You know that, don't you?"

"I know." She hugs him. "Just like I'll be thrilled with you someday when you find Ms. Right and settle down and have children of your own."

Clearly, there's no doubt in Susan's mind that Annie isn't Ms. Right, nor that her children will never be his own.

But there's a doubt in Thom's mind.

He said that he isn't going to marry her, but did he

mean it? Why is it suddenly all too easy to see himself slipping into Annie's life as easily as he did these cashmere slippers after a long day at the office?

Is he falling in love with her?

Does he dare let that happen?

What if he's wrong about her character?

His heart is telling him that she's sincere, but when it comes to reading the women in his life, he's proven himself illiterate.

Susan . . . Mother . . . Joyce . . . and countless girlfriends before her.

But Annie is different, Thom tells himself, feigning interest as his sister chatters on about baby names and registering for a layette.

He's never felt a yearning this desperate about anything—not even business. He'd trade the pending multibillion dollar deal with Saltwater Treasures in a heartbeat for a chance with Annie.

But . . . a chance for what?

Mergers are your specialty, Brannock.

Yes, *corporate* mergers.

Not . . .

Romantic mergers.

"So which do you like better?"

Susan's voice cuts into his thoughts, startling him back to reality, and baby names.

"I'm sorry . . . can you tell me the choices again?"

Susan sighs. "John Wade Ellington or Wade John Ellington?"

Frankly, Thom doesn't like either of his sister's suggestions.

"How about something more creative?"

"Creative?"

"You know . . . more original."

"More original? Like what?"

"Like . . ." His thoughts flit promptly back to Annie. "I don't know. How about Milo?"

"Milo?" Susan laughs. "You're kidding, right?"

"Actually, I'm serious."

"*Milo?* What kind of name is that? No parent in their right mind would name a baby Milo."

"Forget it," Thom says, resigned to the fact that there are some things his family is, quite simply, incapable of understanding. "It was just a suggestion. Name him John. I think that's perfect."

Annie sits on the front steps with the cordless telephone heavy in her hand, looking up at the stars and listening to thunder rumbling in the distance and the crickets' nightly chorus resonating in the moonlight.

Don't call, she tells herself firmly, as she unsuccessfully attempts to blow her sweat-plastered bangs away from her forehead.

Do not dial that phone.

Carry it back into the house. Now.

But she can't seem to summon the energy to move her hair away from her skin, let alone get up and go into the house.

Summer has arrived with a vengeance, descending over Long Island like a hot, wet towel. The night air is alive with buzzing mosquitoes, dank with the smell of algae that rises from the salt marsh at the low-lying rear of the property.

It's uncomfortable out here, but more so inside, where

the fans stir but fail to cool the steamy night air. At least both children are finally asleep, wearing only their underpants and lying on top of their quilts without even a sheet.

Overnight heat and humidity are more typical of August. It's too early in the season for this oppressive weather.

Annie finally gives up attempting to create a breeze with her breath and finger-rakes the weight of her damp hair away from her scalp.

Hurricane season is going to be brutal this year. That's what Andre always said when summer came too soon, and he was usually right.

Annie's hand comes to rest on the phone once again, her fingers twitching over the buttons.

Don't call, Annie. Didn't you learn your lesson last weekend? If you were going to get through to him, it would have been then, on the anniversary, and you know it.

But her fingers are dialing anyway.

You're not going to prove—or disprove—anything. You know that, don't you?

Annie looks up at the night sky to focus on the brightest star she can find as the phone rings in her ear.

Answer, she wills her husband, wherever he is. *Come on, answer this time. I need you.*

In the distance, she spots a bolt of heat lightning. The next instant, with a sudden burst of sound, the receiver comes to life in her ear.

"Andre? Andre!"

She hears her own name in response, as though somebody is shouting it across a vast chasm.

"You're there! Andre!" Tears stream down her cheeks. "Please, Andre, talk to me."

Static sizzles in her ear, but nothing coherent.

"What am I supposed to do, Andre? Tell me, please . . ." Annie begs. "Do you want me to look for the treasure at Copper Beach? Is that what you're trying to say?"

The line is ridden with atmospheric interference.

Consumed by a longing so extreme that her entire body is clenched in physical pain, Annie wills her husband to come through more clearly.

"Andre? I can't hear you, babe. I know you're trying to tell me something, but I can't hear you."

Grief has taken hold of her, grief and anger. It isn't fair. It isn't fair that this is all she has left of her husband: this disembodied voice she can't even understand.

"Andre, I know there's a reason you're reaching out to me this way. I'm listening so hard . . . please, please try to get it through."

Static.

Yet he's there. She can feel him, all around her, the same as she did the last time.

At least I have this, she tells herself, closing her eyes and imagining that he's here beside her, pretending that his arms are around her, as anger gives way to serenity.

None of it was her imagination.

She tried to convince herself of that because it was easier that way, but she won't make that mistake again.

Somewhere in the back of her mind, Annie realizes that she must note every precious detail to recall later, lest doubt overwhelm her once again.

Details, Annie. Notice the details.

The crickets' chorus seems oddly muffled now, and the smell of the water has been replaced by something else. Something floral, and it takes a moment for her to identify it.

Honeysuckle, Annie realizes, and a shiver goes through her.

The scent of honeysuckle is overwhelming.

Yes, and the night is no longer a warm cloak around her. There isn't a breeze to stir the trees, yet she isn't imagining the change in temperature; the air suddenly feels cool enough to make her wish she had a sweater.

Nor is she imagining the voice on the other end of the phone, or that it belongs to Andre. Maybe she can't hear him clearly enough to decipher his words, but she recognizes the pitch of the voice, recognizes the cadence and inflection.

This is really happening, she tells herself again, opening her eyes. *He's really there, on the line.*

Annie strains to make out what he's saying, decoding brief snatches of conversation. Something about the beach, and love . . .

"I love you, too, Andre. I always will."

" . . . love . . ." The word is more forceful this time, almost vehement, yet buried in an extended, garbled phrase.

"I love you, you know that," Annie says again, even as she senses that that isn't it. That he's trying to tell her something else, something she doesn't already know. Something pressing.

" . . . Trixie . . ."

"Trixie? I know you love her, and Milo, too, Andre. And they love you."

" . . . sorry . . ."

"Sorry? Sorry for what?" Annie asks on a sob. "You couldn't help it, Andre. You were sick."

" . . . know . . ."

"You didn't know, Andre. Of course you didn't know. Don't blame yourself. I don't blame you. I know you didn't want to leave us."

" . . . know!"

That time, the word is clear as the night sky, spoken so sharply Annie's jaw drops.

"You didn't know," she repeats slowly, wondering . . .

Is he saying "know"? Or "no"?

And if it's *no* . . . then what does he mean? *No,* what?

Sensing that his presence is waning, almost as if that one forceful phrase has depleted the fragile energy, Annie says almost frantically, "Andre, tell me, please."

Static. Nothing but static.

And then, so distant that she can barely discern the word, she hears her name again.

" . . . Annie . . ."

"Oh, Andre, no, don't go. Please . . . please, tell me . . ."

" . . . love . . ."

But she can feel him fading into oblivion even before the line goes silent, the receiver beeping twice with its familiar CALL LOST code.

Chapter
14

Craving a glimpse from another angle into Annie's private world, Thom would have preferred to meet her at her friend's apartment on Wednesday night. That way, he could say hello to Milo and Trixie . . . and yes, to Erika Bauer, the woman Annie described as her closest female friend in the world.

But Annie shot down that suggestion as quickly as Thom brought it up, saying that she would meet him at the restaurant.

All right, fine. So where is she?

Thom checks his watch once again, and then the doorway of the small bistro on East Fifty-third Street, wondering if he's being stood up.

What is it about Annie that makes him so insecure?

She matters far more to him than she should. That's what it is.

He's spent the last twelve hours going through the motions at the office when all he could think about was tonight. Basically, he's an insecure adolescent boy in a grown man's custom-made suit.

If Annie doesn't show up tonight, he'll . . . he'll . . .

What? What will you do?

Nothing. Nothing, and you know it.

You'll chalk it up to experience and go back to your life. Back to working hard and playing harder.

If the merger talks fail, you'll make a hostile bid for Saltwater Treasures. Maybe you'll swim with sharks or, or . . .

Or climb Mount Everest.

And sooner or later, you'll find somebody else. You'll forget all about Annie.

Even as he tries to convince himself of that, he knows in his heart that nothing—not even climbing Mount Everest—could possibly be more exhilarating than being with Annie Harlowe.

"You're wearing *that*?"

"What's wrong with this?" Annie looks down at her trim khakis, sandals, and short-sleeved white top, then back up at Erika.

"You can't wear that to a dinner date in Manhattan, that's what."

" 'A,' it isn't a date, and 'B,' it's all I brought to wear," Annie informs her.

"Then you need to shop."

"I don't have time." *Let alone money to squander on "date" clothes.* "I'm late as it is," she adds, checking her watch.

"Then you need to borrow something from me." Erika steps over Milo and Trixie, who are sprawled on the floor playing Old Maid, and heads across the room to her closet. "We're the same size."

"You're a foot taller than me."

"Yes, but we're the same size, width-wise. I have a great dress for you to wear. Brand new, the tags still on."

"Erika—"

"No arguments, Annie. I refuse to let you sabotage this date."

"I just told you, it isn't a—"

"Dinner with an attractive, eligible man is a date, okay, Annie? Call it whatever you want to, but I'm calling it what it is. Here." She thrusts a dress-draped hanger into Annie's hands. "Go change."

What is there to do but obey?

All right, you could have said "no," Annie informs her reflection in the bathroom mirror. *But maybe Erika's right. Maybe you are trying to sabotage this . . . so-called date.*

"My makeup is in the medicine cabinet," Erika calls through the closed door. "Put some on."

"I don't like my face feeling like it's coated in batter, Erika."

"Just lipstick and mascara."

And that's an order.

Annie can't help smiling at how easy it is to imagine Erika barking that unspoken last phrase. She knows her friend thinks she has Annie's best interests at heart. She just refuses to accept that dating anyone—especially the tantalizing Thom Brannock—is definitely not in Annie's best interests.

"There's perfume on the shelf above the sink," Erika calls from the next room. "Put some on."

Annie sighs, shaking her head.

There is, indeed, a row of perfume bottles directly in

front of her. Their fancy labels read like a who's who in
the world of fashion design, aside from one small, partially obscured vial at the back of the shelf. Pulling it out,
Annie sees that it's an essence of honeysuckle aro-
matherapy oil.

All right, that's a little more her speed. She dabs a few
drops on her pulse points, then reluctantly reaches for
Erika's lipstick and mascara, reminding herself that this
still absolutely isn't a date.

"Hi, sorry I'm late," Annie says breathlessly, appearing beside the table so abruptly that if he couldn't smell
her luscious floral perfume, he'd think he might be seeing things.

Thom rises to embrace her, holding on a few seconds
longer and far more fervently than he should in public.
But he can't help it. He seems to be channeling that adolescent boy again.

Holding Annie close, inhaling her scent, he's instantly
transported back to that wondrous encounter on the blanket in her yard.

When he finally, and reluctantly, lets her go, she looks
up at him with a nervous laugh. "Talk about a warm welcome."

"I just . . . I really missed you." He pulls out the chair
opposite his at the small round table and drags it a few
inches closer to his own in the process of seating her.
"And I thought you might not show up, so when you
did . . ." He shrugs and smiles at her, a ridiculously giddy
smile.

"I'm really sorry. We took the train into the city this

afternoon and it was running late." She sits and pulls in her chair, spreads her cloth napkin in her lap.

Her voice is relaxed, but Thom notices that her hands are shaking a bit as she clasps them in front of her on the table.

"The conductor said something about a squirrel chewing through a cable," she chatters on. "Who'd guess one unfortunate little squirrel could be responsible for throwing thousands of people off schedule?"

Who'd guess one little squirrel could have a man like Thom Brannock shaking in his polished Mezlan oxfords?

"I'm just glad you're here." He leans close enough across the table to fill his lungs with her fragrance. "You smell great. What kind of perfume are you wearing?"

She blushes, clears her throat, hesitates.

Then she says, almost as a confession, "It's . . . honeysuckle."

"Honeysuckle," he echoes, wondering why she looks so embarrassed. "I love it. You should wear it all the time."

"I can't."

Not "I don't want to."

Just, "I can't."

Intrigued as much by her odd response as he is charmed by how flustered she obviously is, Thom asks, "What do you mean, you can't?"

"I don't own it, I just borrowed a few drops from my friend." She shrugs helplessly and wrinkles her freckled nose.

Wow. She's absolutely . . . adorable. She's making him want to kiss her. Which he won't do—at least, not here—since he is, after all, a grown man.

Yes, and Annie, bare-legged and bare-toed in flat strappy sandals and a clingy black dress, is a grown woman. An irresistible grown woman.

Blatant adoration isn't your style, Thom reminds himself, forcing himself to take an emotional step back . . . until his eyes collide again with Annie's and he realizes that she's just as drawn to him as he is to her.

Wow.

Thom beams. To hell with being a grown-up. He's a kid who's just been handed a triple hot fudge sundae with extra sprinkles and a cherry. *Two* cherries.

"I'm going to take you shopping after dinner and buy you that perfume," Thom declares, looking around for the waiter to speed things along.

"Take me shopping?" A potential smile seems to be nudging at the corners of Annie's mouth. "So you'd be . . . what? Like Richard Gere treating Julia Roberts to a shopping spree in *Pretty Woman*?"

If memory serves him correctly, Julia Roberts played a hooker with a heart of gold in that movie.

"I never saw *Pretty Woman*, Annie, but—"

"You never saw *Pretty Woman*?"

"Nope. I take it you have?"

"Many times, when I was a kid."

"Well, I guess I led a deprived childhood in more ways than you think, huh?" Thanks to years sequestered at boarding school or with parents who thought Hollywood feature films were frivolous.

"But," he goes on, "I know enough about the movie's plot to tell you that all you have in common with her character is that you happen to be a pretty woman."

The smile bursts past the corners of her mouth to light

her whole face. In Thom's instantly formed opinion, Julia Roberts's hundred-watt grin has nothing on Annie's.

"And from now on," he continues, "you should wear that perfume every day, because I love the way it smells on you."

Just like that, her smile evaporates.

"Thom—"

Uh-oh. The way she says his name, the look on her face . . .

His heart sinks. He knows what she's going to say even before she says it.

What are you, psychic? Haven't you learned never to try to read a woman's mind? Relax.

Okay. Maybe he's wrong, but . . .

"I don't think," Annie says slowly, "that we can have a 'from now on.' "

Nope. He wasn't wrong.

He's psychic. Next, she'll tell him that it's been nice knowing him, say good-bye, and sail off into the skyline alone.

Well, he can't let her go. Not without telling her how he feels about her.

"Listen, Annie, before you say—"

Naturally, the waiter chooses precisely that moment to appear with an obscenely cheery smile, an irritatingly profusive welcome, and a seemingly endless recitation of this evening's specials.

A reduction of this, a puree of that, blah, blah, blah . . .

At last, the waiter winds down his spiel with a friendly, "Can I bring you a cocktail while you peruse the menu?"

Annie orders a glass of the house white zinfandel.

Thom orders an imported forty-year-old single-malt scotch, straight up. If his psychic abilities are to be trusted, a stiff drink is in order.

I don't think we can have a from now on.

Wait a minute.

I don't think?

Not, "We can't" or "we won't"?

Hope springs eternal.

After all, Annie said it herself: Where there's an "I don't think," there's a way.

"Waiters in the restaurants I'm used to don't usually use the word 'peruse,'" Annie feels compelled to comment as soon as theirs makes his exit again.

"No?" With a faraway look in his blue eyes, Thom doesn't even seem to have heard her.

"No. They're more likely to say, 'Do you want to supersize that?'" She laughs.

He doesn't.

She stops.

Hers was forced, anyway.

"Look," she begins, realizing it's impossible to side-step the gaping crater she just dug between them, "I wasn't going to say anything until dinner was over, so that it wouldn't be awkward between us. But now that it's out there . . . I guess I should explain."

"Ya think?" he asks so curtly that for a moment, she assumes he's peeved. But his expression betrays only a wary skepticism.

Wishing the gushing waiter would pop back over with their drinks, Annie says lamely, "It's not that I don't enjoy your company, Thom . . ."

"Is that what we've been doing?" he asks with a salacious bob of his eyebrows. "Enjoying each other's company?"

Annie squirms, looking over her shoulder to see if anybody's eavesdropping, lest they get the wrong idea.

All right, not the wrong idea. The *right* idea. Which doesn't make their relationship anything but wrong, Annie reminds herself firmly.

Because she doesn't want to be the kind of woman who meets her lover for a clandestine dinner in the city.

Not that there's anything particularly clandestine about this dinner. But she can't help feeling almost daring, being here with him. Almost . . .

Like a married woman having an affair?

Erika's voice cuts in wryly, just as it did earlier, in her apartment, when Annie emerged from the bathroom and explained exactly why she had resisted getting all fancied up for her dinner with Thom.

"Whatever you choose to call it is fine with me," he says now, leaning closer across the linen tablecloth, "as long as you don't give me my walking papers without at least explaining your reasoning."

"Your life is so different from mine. I would never be able to deal with any of it."

"What? The city?"

"No, I like the city . . . sometimes. I love the Village, and the museums, and the parks. But your lifestyle isn't about any of that. It's about society, and business, and making money."

"It's more than just that," Thom protests, though he doesn't look entirely certain.

"Well, whatever it is, it's different than mine. And

that's fine. I just can't imagine never having a moment to just . . . *be*."

"So what are you saying? That if I scale back on my business and stop going to charity fund-raisers and move to the Village, and . . . and learn how to just . . . *be* . . . then you'll be willing to—"

"No. It isn't just that! I was just pointing out how my life and yours are worlds apart. There are other things, too."

"What? What else is there?"

"My husband," Annie finds herself saying.

Thom blinks. "Your husband?"

He looks around, almost as though he expects to see a cuckolded spouse glaring from across the room.

"Annie," he says gently, turning back to her, "you *are* widowed . . . aren't you?"

Widowed. Lord, how she hates that description.

"Yes," the Widow Harlowe admits over a lump in her throat, reaching for her glass, wishing it contained something stronger than zinfandel.

"Is it too soon after your husband passed away? Is that it?"

"That's part of it."

"I can wait. We can take things more slowly—"

"No. I don't think time would make any difference in this case, Thom."

"Why not?"

Why, oh why, does she have to explain? Why can't she just say good-bye and turn her back on him?

He'll never understand.

"Why not, Annie?" he presses.

"Because Andre doesn't want me to be with anybody else. Ever. Okay?"

He seems to be letting that sink in for a minute.

Annie braces herself for the accusations that are sure to follow. He'll tell her that she's making excuses. Or that she's lost her mind.

Maybe she has.

"But Annie," Thom tiptoes back into the conversation, "Andre isn't here anymore. And I'm sure he wouldn't want you to live the rest of your life alone . . . not that the rest of your life is what we're talking about, here," he adds hastily, so hastily that she realizes the rest of *his* life is definitely not up for grabs.

It should make matters easier, knowing Thom isn't thinking of their relationship as anything with long-term potential.

So why doesn't it?

Why is she forced to tamp down a wave of regret as she says, "I understand that. But I'm not alone. I have my children. They're always with me."

"They won't be there forever, Annie."

She smiles faintly. "Trixie hasn't even started kindergarten yet. I don't think I'll have empty-nest syndrome for at least a few decades."

"Even so . . . The kids can't fill all your needs."

"No, but . . ."

What makes you think you can?

More importantly . . .

What makes me *think you can?*

Reminding herself that she has no business longing for something that can never be, Annie tells him, "Look, I know you assume that because Andre is . . . gone . . . he has no say in what I do. But . . ." She takes a deep breath, opens her mouth, then realizes what she's on the verge of confiding.

She really has lost her mind if she thinks she can tell him about the phone calls.

"What?" he asks.

"Never mind."

He watches her for a moment.

If he pushes, she tells herself, *I swear I'll get up and leave without looking back. Because I don't owe him anything.*

"Okay," he says unexpectedly. "Let's just have dinner. I'm hungry. Are you hungry?"

She wants to tell him that she isn't. That she hasn't been hungry in a year. That they should just call it a night now.

But, looking into a gaze that's bluer than summer dusk and far more patient than she deserves, she hears herself saying, "Yes, I'm famished, actually."

For food.

For more than food.

But food will have to suffice for now.

Forever, Annie reminds herself firmly.

Chapter
15

And that," Thom says, gesturing at the French doors and beyond, the sweeping view of Central Park in the distance, "is the terrace."

Annie steps closer to the doors, checking out the teak chaises, the table and chairs, the flowering trees in terra-cotta urns. "Don't you ever use it?"

"Sometimes. Why?"

"It just looks kind of . . . untouched."

Thom nods, loosening the knot on his silk tie. "Well, I don't spend a lot of time here."

"But this is your home."

"I work a lot. And weekends, I spend out on the island, so . . ."

"It seems like a waste," Annie murmurs.

"The terrace?"

"The terrace and . . . well, all of it." She waves a hand around at the living room worthy of a magazine spread, the adjacent formal dining room, the marble entry hall. "I mean, it's beautiful. It just doesn't feel . . . lived in."

"Like your place?"

For an instant, she looks offended.

Dammit. How could he go and stick his foot in his mouth, just when they were getting along so well?

Dinner was a pleasant surprise once they got past their rocky start, and so was Annie's acceptance of his spontaneous invitation to come back here for coffee. He didn't dare suggest a nightcap, lest she think he had something more intimate on the agenda.

Coffee sounded safe, both to him and apparently to Annie, so here they are, complete with a bag of pastries they picked up along the way from the bakery around the corner.

And now, just when he assumes he's hurt her pride with his innocently intended comment about the comfortable state of her house, she smiles.

"I guess 'lived in' is a polite way to put it. Another would be 'messy.' Or how about, 'disaster area'?"

"Annie, I told you before, I think your house is great. It has character. Unlike this place."

She opens her mouth to protest, but apparently thinks better of it. "This is beautiful, Thom. I love the decor. You have nice taste. And, um, where did you get that antique spittoon? It's really . . . interesting."

"Annie, thanks, but this isn't my taste, it's the interior decorator's taste," he says with a laugh. "And I have no idea where I got the spittoon."

"You forgot?"

"I never knew. The decorator did everything—all the shopping, the art, the color scheme."

Yeah, right. Color scheme? What color scheme? The whole damned place is monochromatic.

"Oh," is all Annie says, seemingly at a loss for words.

She obviously can't fathom being so busy that you can't even make decisions about your apartment's decor.

Not just busy, Thom concludes after a moment's thought.

Detached.

And that, he realizes with a pang of regret, is almost . . . sad.

Suddenly feeling sorry for himself, he tells Annie, "You know, it's all a little too blah for my taste. I always meant to liven it up with some splashes of color, but I haven't had a chance yet."

"How long have you been living here?"

"Ten years."

"Oh," she says again.

"How about that coffee?" he asks abruptly, sensing that he'd better get them back on common ground.

"Oh, you know what? Maybe I should just—"

"Annie, you have to stay for coffee," he cuts in. "You can't leave me alone with all those pastries because I'll feel obligated to eat them."

She laughs. "All right, but just a quick cup."

"Great. I'll be right back," he says, relieved, heading for the kitchen. He calls over his shoulder, "Make yourself at home," his voice echoing in the marble-tiled, high-ceilinged room.

Make yourself at home?

Yeah, right. *He* never has. In the decade he's lived here, he's never made himself at home. Not really.

But it never bothered him until now. Walking through the dining room and the study on the way to the kitchen, he sees his apartment through Annie's eyes.

It's all he can do not to pluck a few petals from the

fresh flower arrangement in the center of the mahogany table, or muss the perfectly placed cushions on the couch.

In the kitchen, with its glossy black stone countertop and gleaming stainless-steel, restaurant-quality appliances, including a European espresso machine, he debates making her a cappuccino, but only briefly.

Coffee. He promised her plain old coffee, nothing fancy, and coffee is what he should deliver.

As he waits for it to brew, he takes off his suit jacket and tie, draping them over the back of a chair, unfastens his French cuffs and the top few buttons of his dress shirt. After tucking his monogrammed gold cuff links into a drawer, he rolls up his sleeves. There. That's better.

He opens the white paper bag from the bakery and arranges the pastries on the plainest white plate he can find in the cupboard. It's Lenox, but she wouldn't know that unless she turned it over.

It shouldn't matter, Thom tells himself, hunting through the cabinet for mugs instead of porcelain cups. The differences between their lifestyles are the least of the obstacles between them.

So what if ten square feet of his recently re-remodeled kitchen probably cost him more than she paid for her entire house?

That wouldn't matter in the end, as long as . . .

What end? Thom interrupts his own thoughts to ask. *This is the end, buddy. Tonight. Right here. This is all you get.*

No future.

No strings.

"No fair," he whispers aloud, to himself—and to the

ghost of Annie's dead husband, whom he almost expects to see lurking in the shadows beside the Sub-Zero.

If only he could convince Annie that it makes no sense to sacrifice her own happiness out of misguided loyalty to a mere marital memory.

Happiness?

Pretty confident, aren't you, there? Thom asks himself.

Who's to say that he's capable of making Annie any happier than she is on her own—or will be, once her grief subsides?

Honeysuckle perfume and fine china aside, is there anything worthwhile Thom can give her that she doesn't already possess?

A home, a family, a creative career . . . she has all of those things.

What else is there?

The coffeemaker hisses to a halt, none too soon. Another few minutes of musing, and Thom might have convinced himself that Annie needs a new husband—and that Thomas Brannock IV fits the bill.

He fills two cups and sets them on a tray with creamer, sugar, and the pastries. He adds the rose-filled bud vase that's sitting on the counter, courtesy of his weekly fresh floral delivery service. Then he transports the whole thing back to the living room, where he finds Annie surveying a framed row of family photos on the mantel.

Leave it to her to zoom in on the one personal touch in the room.

"So you found my life in pictures." Thom sets the tray on the coffee table and walks over to join her.

"Is this your father?" she asks, holding up a silver frame containing a formal portrait of Thom III.

"That's him. How'd you know?"

"You look just like him."

That might be true, but every time Thom hears it, he holds back a shudder. He might resemble his father physically, but this apple fell miles from the tree in every other way.

Annie sets the photograph carefully back on the mantel and points to another: a recent shot of Thom and Susan arm in arm at a charity ball up in Scarsdale. It appeared in the *Westchester Wag* magazine's society pages, but Thom knows Annie is as likely to have seen that as she is to have spent May Day picking daisies with the Queen of England.

"Who is this in the picture with you?" she asks casually—too casually, to Thom's delight.

It would be fun to prolong the answer, just to enjoy this intriguing hint of a jealous streak, but that wouldn't be fair.

"That's my sister, Susan," he admits.

"Oh! Your sister!"

"Why? Did you think she was a wife I forgot to tell you about?" he asks with a wink.

A wink?

A wife?

Who does he think he is, his father?

Annie's smile fades. "No. I didn't know who she was. I forgot you had a sister."

"Well speaking of Susan, guess what? I'm going to be an uncle," Thom says quickly, sensing that coffee and conversation could change to *"Taxi!"* any second.

"An uncle?"

"Susan's pregnant. She told me last night."

Annie's face lights up. "How exciting! When is she due?"

Nice save, Brannock.

"She's due around the end of the year," he says, leading the way back to the couch.

Annie follows him, sits beside him, and begins spooning sugar into her mug. "Maybe it'll be the city's first New Year's baby. They always get a bunch of great prizes."

"That would be nice." And largely unnecessary, considering that Susan and Wade's son will undoubtedly already be showered with everything money can buy.

"Here," he says, picking up an apple turnover and placing it into her hand. "Try a pastry."

She takes a little bite. "It's good."

"Can I taste?" He leans in, all but forcing her to feed him a bite. "Mmm. Not as good as your molasses cookies, but good."

"Oh, don't remind me. I've got to go home tomorrow and make another twelve dozen of those for a party Merlin's doing this weekend."

"You bake cookies for Merlin?"

"Lately, yes. Why?"

"Did you make those sugar cookie flags for my party?"

"Oh, those . . . yup," she says with a laugh. "I resented you the whole time I was doing all those little frosting stars."

"No wonder . . ."

"No wonder what?"

"I was addicted to those cookies," he tells her, shaking his head in wonder. "There was something about them . . . I just couldn't stop eating them."

"Well, they are pretty rich . . . I use real butter, a lot of it, and always put a few drops of heavy cream in the dough. That's why they're so good."

"It wasn't just that they were good," Thom tells her, knowing he's not making sense. How can he explain that those cookies seemed to have awakened some decadent yearning in his soul? That it isn't just about his sudden sweet tooth, but about something far more meaningful?

He can't explain it. Not without her concluding that he's some kind of New Age freak masquerading as a sensible businessman.

He watches Annie pour a generous splash of cream into her mug, then stir, sip, and add more sugar.

"Not sweet enough?" he asks, amused.

"I like a lot of sugar. Do you always drink yours black?"

He nods.

Annie wrinkles her nose. "How can you stand it?"

"It's good. Really," he insists when she throws him a doubtful glance. "I'm used to it." He sips to punctuate the point and finds himself wondering why his coffee suddenly seems so bitter.

"Well, have you ever tried it with cream and sugar?"

"No."

Annie slides the sugar bowl and creamer toward him. "Go ahead. Live a little."

He hesitates only a moment before adding a heaping spoonful of sugar and liberal dollop of cream to his cup. He stirs, sips . . . smiles.

"Good, isn't it?" Annie smiles back at him. "Life is too short to drink black coffee."

Talk about bittersweet. Coming from her, that comment is enough to bring a lump to Thom's throat.

He puts down his mug and takes Annie's hand.

"Yes, and life is too short," he says meaningfully, "not to grab every opportunity you get for happiness."

"Thom—"

"Shh." He brushes a wisp of hair back from her face and leans closer, taking the cup from her trembling hand and setting it on the table.

"Thom, I told you that we can't—"

"Have *from now on*. I know. But we can at least have *now*, Annie."

He kisses her before she can protest again, and with that kiss, glimpses all that could be between them, if only . . .

If only she could let go of her past.

If only he could see into the future, and know that he isn't going to hurt Annie or the children.

If only he could validate his motives . . . or be guaranteed that he isn't going to turn into his father . . .

"We can have now," Annie breaks off the kiss to whisper. "But that's all. Wouldn't it be easier if I just left, before this goes any—"

"No." He lays a finger against her lips to still them, vainly searching Annie's eyes for the promise of something he knows he'll never see there.

"But—"

"Don't leave, Annie. That wouldn't be easy." He takes her into his arms, lowering her back against the cushions of the couch.

The tantalizing scent of honeysuckle swirls around him, almost seeming to become stronger than it was before.

"Your leaving right now would be torture," he tells her, kissing her lips, her neck, her shoulder. "It would be easier to let this happen, even if we both know that it's just one last time."

"Okay," she whispers, kicking off her sandals and sinking back in his arms.

She laughs as he, too, kicks his shoes with abandon over the arm of the couch, then tilts her head to give him access to the sweet, tender skin at the base of her throat.

He nuzzles her there, and she purrs with pleasure, sparking intense desire within him.

He traces the graceful line of her collarbone with his fingertip, then again with his lips, feeling her quake as his mouth gradually slides across again, and then lower and his fingers expertly ease off her dress, and then her bra.

With a throaty moan she guides his searching mouth to her bared breast, surprising and enthralling him.

This time, there are no sleeping children nearby to worry about, there is no chance of being spotted out in the open. This time it's just Thom and Annie, utterly alone together, utterly captivated by each other.

He lifts himself away just long enough to shed his shirt, trousers, and boxers as Annie wriggles out of her panties. Then he settles his weight against her once again, savoring the exquisite way the length of their bodies fit together, skin to skin, rigid peak to pliant valley.

Holding Annie in his arms, kissing her deeply, endlessly, Thom relishes every sensation: her floral scent, the sweet remnants of cream and sugar on her lips, the low moan of pleasure that escapes her when his fingers slide down over the gentle slope of her hip, and again when they wander brazenly into more intimate territory.

If this one last night together is all they're ever meant to have, he'll memorize everything about it, so that it can last him a lifetime, knowing, even now, that it will never be enough.

A week, a month, a year . . . would any of it sustain him through the remainder of a life without her?

Another moan, higher pitched, slips from Annie's lips as their bodies meld, then move together in effortless rhythm. At last, with a gasp and a shudder, she calls out his name.

He will never tire of hearing her say it; never tire of holding her, kissing her.

She opens her eyes to gaze up at him, radiating intense emotion, and in that instant, Thom glimpses the promise he never expected to see there.

It's fleeting, so fleeting that when her eyelids flutter closed again and she snuggles her face into his shoulder, he isn't entirely certain it was there at all.

But if it really was . . .

Something has clicked into place in his brain.

It's time, he thinks fervently.

Time to grow up, time to give up, time to give in.

Time to recognize that nothing in his life will ever matter without her.

Time to stop fooling himself, and Annie, searching for reasons he might be feeling the way he does—reasons that have nothing to do with love.

Love?

Is that what this is?

Love.

Shaking his head in wonder, Thom feels as though he's been handed a missing puzzle piece, a golden key, a winning ticket.

What can you give her that she doesn't already have?

Willing to embrace the answer to that question at last, Thom impulsively opens his mouth to tell her.

But before he can say it, his name is on her lips once again, only this time, it isn't accompanied by a sigh of pleasure, but one of regret.

"I hate that I have to leave," she says, stretching, trailing her fingers along his bare back. "But I've got to get back to Erica's."

"Stay," he urges, kissing her.

She laughs. "I can't. It's too late."

Too late?

No, Thom wants to tell her. It isn't too late. Thank God, it isn't too late. He might have let her slip away, but now . . .

"Can I see you tomorrow night? Before you go back to the island?"

"We weren't going to see each other again, Thom. Remember?"

"Annie, you know that isn't what you want. It isn't what I want, either."

"I told you," she says, her voice quavering, "I can't get involved with you. My husband—"

"I know." Sensing that it's time to pull back, to let go—if only for now—Thom nods. "It's okay."

Everything has changed, Thom thinks, watching Annie slip back into her clothes. Everything has changed . . . and yet nothing has.

"I'm sorry it has to be this way." Annie presses a kiss on his cheek at the door.

He holds her close. "This isn't good-bye, Annie."

"It has to be, Thom."

"I know that's what you think. I know that's the only way you can do this. But trust me, Annie. This isn't good-bye."

Her only response is one last kiss before she flees into the waiting elevator.

Left alone in his apartment, Thom returns to the couch, sipping his creamy, sugared coffee. It might be lukewarm, but it isn't half bad.

Annie was right.

Life is too short to ever drink black coffee again, he tells himself with a thoughtful smile. And too short to give up Annie Harlowe without a fight.

Chapter
16

Dr. Ronald Leaver's practice happens to be located in the same Midtown suite of offices as Dr. Erika Bauer's practice.

Dr. Ronald Leaver happens to have an opening at eleven o'clock on Thursday morning, precisely the time when Dr. Erika Bauer has an hour to spare in between patients.

Dr. Ronald Leaver also happens to be as willing to spend that hour with Annie as Dr. Erika Bauer is to spend it with Annie's children.

"I know that you said this is one big coincidence, but I so don't believe you," Annie tells Erika, reluctantly delivering Milo and Trixie into her care at five minutes to eleven. "You made the appointment in advance, didn't you? That's why you got me into the city overnight."

Erika shrugs, the plastic beads on the tips of her cornrows swinging jauntily against her shoulders. "Believe what you want, Annie. Tomorrow is a holiday, everything is slow. And anyway, all that counts is that you'll have a chance to talk with Dr. Leaver and maybe find some peace of mind."

"I'll have more peace of mind when I get these two wiggle worms on the train and back home where they belong," Annie says, frazzled from a morning spent wrestling two energetic, question-filled children in and out of a packed diner, two crowded elevators, and four jammed subways.

At least she had very little time during all of that bustling activity to ponder what happened last night with Thom.

Not that she didn't lie awake into the wee hours on Erika's pull-out couch, doing just that.

Try as she might to convince herself that it's over, she can't deny that she feels something for him. Something powerfully mutual, something she felt once before . . .

For Andre.

But back then, she was free to welcome the emotion, embrace it, follow it wherever it might lead.

This time . . .

She isn't free.

"Go talk to Dr. Leaver, Annie," Erika urges, opening a desk drawer and removing paper, pens, scissors, and tape. "He's waiting for you."

"But I'm pretty sure my insurance doesn't cover—"

"Don't worry about that. It's taken care of."

"Did you—"

"He owes me a favor, okay?"

"Erika, I can't let you do this. Just like I can't let you give me that black dress from last night. I'm going to give it back to you the second it's back from the dry cleaner."

"No, you aren't. It looks better on you than it would ever look on me."

"When am I ever even going to have an occasion to wear it again?"

"You don't need an occasion to get dressed up a little."

Annie shakes her head. "It just isn't me."

"The dress?"

"The dress, the makeup, the perfume—"

"That reminds me, you can have that, too."

"What?"

"The perfume. I've never liked Chanel much. It smelled great on you, though."

"I hate to break it to you, but I wasn't wearing the Chanel. I was wearing the honeysuckle."

"What honeysuckle?"

"Your honeysuckle oil."

"What honeysuckle oil?"

"The one in the little vial."

Erika looks perplexed. "I don't have any honeysuckle oil."

"Yes, you do. It was on the shelf. I had it on last night."

"I don't think so," Erika says with a shrug, and glances down at her watch.

Annie frowns. "But—"

"You'd better go, Annie."

"Erika—"

"Better hurry. You're going to be late."

"All right, but . . . you two be good, okay?" Annie warns her children. "Don't drive Auntie Erika crazy, and don't destroy her office."

"They won't destroy anything," Erika says. "We're going to do some artwork."

"I don't know . . ." Annie eyes the materials spread across Erika's desk. "Trixie's only used to safety scissors. Those are so sharp. She might—"

"Go. She'll be fine."

"Why is Mommy going to the doctor?" Annie hears Milo ask worriedly as she steps out of the office. "Is she sick?"

Annie closes the door behind her, then lingers, pressing her ear against it to hear Erika's muffled response.

"No, Mommy's not sick. She's just sad. This is the kind of doctor who helps sad people feel happy again."

Realizing that the receptionist down the hall is watching her eavesdrop, Annie reluctantly moves away from the door.

She takes a deep breath and heads toward Dr. Leaver's office, telling herself that there's nothing he could say or do—nothing anybody can say or do—to make her feel truly happy again.

No. That isn't true.

She's felt happiness since Andre died. When she's with her children, or her friends . . . and last night, with Thom . . .

Happiness isn't the issue.

The issue is that a piece of her heart still belongs to Andre, and that isn't going to change.

She never promised "Till death do us part."

She promised to stay by his side forever.

One love, one lifetime.

Seated at his desk in his corner office with its dazzling view of the East River and the Brooklyn Bridge, Thom makes a third attempt to read the e-mail he just opened.

It's from a colleague, something about abruptly rising stock in a Midwestern financial institution that's been on his radar for quite some time.

Yesterday, this news would have been earth-shattering enough to provoke an immediate response.

Today, the only thing that's earth-shattering for Thom is that he seems to have fallen in love overnight.

And instead of plotting his next business move, here he is, contemplating the odds that Annie Harlowe is still in Manhattan at this hour, or already on a train back to Long Island in the preholiday exodus.

It doesn't make a difference, really—not in the grand scheme of things. But the city without Annie in it suddenly has all the appeal of a week in the desert without water.

First thing tomorrow, he'll head back out to Southampton and win her back.

Yes, and how, exactly, are you going to go about that? an inner voice asks cynically.

I'll just refuse to take "no" for an answer, he decides, with more uncertainty than a man like Thom Brannock is ever accustomed to experiencing.

If he were wise, he'd probably give up the quest and acknowledge the fact that in her overwhelming grief, Annie isn't ready to fall in love again . . . that she might never be ready to fall in love again. That even if she is someday, she might not be capable of loving *him.*

His best move is probably to forget about her and focus on his work.

"Mr. Brannock?"

He looks up to see his longtime secretary, Mavourneen, standing in the doorway. "Yes?"

In the Irish brogue that followed her from Belfast half

a century ago, she says, "Colin Lincoln is on the line about the e-mail he just sent you."

That would be the e-mail Thom has yet to peruse in detail. "Tell him to hold for a minute, please, Mavourneen."

"All right. Do you want me to bring you another cup of coffee?"

"Sure, but this time . . . could you put cream and sugar in it, please?"

If "I've been talking to my dead husband on the telephone" doesn't knock Dr. Ronald Leaver off his leather swivel chair, nothing will.

Now that she's blurted her secret after hemming and hawing through most of the session, Annie rests a knuckle against her mouth and waits for his response, wondering if he's going to refer her to an inpatient mental health facility or a storefront medium down in Murray Hill.

"I see. Do you call him, or does he call you?" the doctor asks, looking about as flustered as a seasoned pediatrician diagnosing the common cold.

"I call him, on his cell phone," Annie confesses, taken aback—and encouraged—by the doctor's apparent lack of skepticism. "I used to do it just to hear his voice on the outgoing message, but then one day, he answered."

Dr. Leaver writes something on his yellow legal pad. "And what did he say?"

"It was hard to hear him."

"But it was his voice? You're sure of that?"

"I'm positive it was his voice," Annie says decidedly, even as she reminds herself that she's also positive she wore Erika's honeysuckle oil last night.

Erika must be mistaken. She probably forgot she owned the stuff.

"So it was his voice, but you couldn't hear him?"

"I couldn't make out exactly what he was saying most of the time. There was a lot of static on the line."

The doctor nods, rubbing his white beard. "What, if anything, were you able to discern?" he asks, watching her patiently through his wire-framed glasses.

"That I needed to take a catering job I had been offered that night. I was planning to turn it down because I didn't want to leave the kids with a sitter. Money's been an issue for us lately, and I've been torn between getting a more stable job and taking care of my kids after what they've been through."

"So you think your husband was reaching out to guide you."

"Do you think that?"

The doctor ignores her question, responding with another of his own. "Under what circumstances do these phone calls tend to take place?"

"Circumstances? You mean . . . ?"

"Time of day, weather conditions, are you alone when they occur?"

"Not always alone in the house," Annie says, thinking back. "The kids are usually around someplace, but never in the room with me."

"Nobody else has heard the voice?"

"No," she says, feeling defensive, "but I know they really happened."

He flashes a reassuring smile. "When did they take place, Annie?"

"The first time it was during the middle of the day, and then it happened at night, so . . ."

"Mm-hm." The doctor scribbles something on his pad. "What else? Has the weather been consistent when you made the calls?"

Annie shakes her head. "It was raining a couple of times, but not the other night. Although . . ." She frowns, remembering something. "There was lightning. Heat lightning."

Dr. Leaver's bushy white eyebrows abruptly chase his receding hairline. "So every time you've made this connection, there's basically been some manner of electro-magnetic atmospheric activity?"

"Do you mean lightning?"

"Yes."

"Yes." Annie's eyes widen. "Are you saying that's why I'm able to get through to Andre? Because of some weird . . . energy thing?"

"Possibly. My research into EVP has shown that—"

"EVP?" Annie interrupts, needing to grasp every possible bit of information she might glean; anything to back up the possibility that Andre is still out there somewhere, looking out for her.

"EVP is 'electronic voice phenomena,' which refers to the deceased communicating with the living via telephone, radio, and television, computers . . ."

Relief courses through Annie. "You mean this is something that happens to other people? I'm not crazy?"

He offers a faint smile. "EVP has been documented since the beginning of technology. I've personally heard a number of recordings of ghost voices actually picked up on audio tape."

"What about phone calls?"

"I've never experienced one myself, but there is extensive research into the phenomenon. The circumstances you've described are fairly typical: the voice of the deceased is usually instantly recognizable, the quality of the connection tends to be poor, and the call usually has some specific purpose, as though the deceased needs to convey some information to the loved one they left behind."

Annie is speechless, nodding with fervent recognition as he touches upon each point.

"The calls also tend to occur at particularly meaningful times," Dr. Leaver goes on. "A birthday, a holiday . . ."

"An anniversary?" Annie asks, her heart pounding.

"A wedding anniversary? Yes, of course."

"No, I mean the anniversary of the person's death?"

"Absolutely. That's very common."

"Andre died a little over a year ago. What about the weather? You said the weather might have had something to do with it?"

"In my own research, I've found a substantial link between electromagnetic activity and EVP."

"So you're a hundred percent positive that it really can happen?"

"'A hundred percent positive'?" he echoes, with an amused shake of his head. "There's very little about which I'm a hundred percent positive, in the field of paranormal research or anything else. But there is substantial evidence to support the theory that the deceased are capable of communicating with the living through various means, yes."

"Various means?"

"According to my research, the deceased can appeal to

different senses to let us know they're there. They can use sight, sound, touch . . . even scent is very common."

"So you believe me?"

"There is also evidence to support the theory that such communication is the product of the bereaved person's subconscious," he goes on without acknowledging her comment.

"You mean, you think I'm imagining the whole thing?"

"I didn't say that, Annie. I'm only telling you that there are no definitive answers. Not yet. I'd like to talk to you about this at length, but I'm afraid we're out of time."

"Already?" Annie is dismayed. Why didn't she jump right into the phone calls at the beginning of the session? Why did she waste so much time worrying about what he was going to think of her?

He flips open an appointment book. "I can see you here next Thursday morning, Annie, at the same time."

Next week?

How can she wait a whole week to figure out what Andre is trying to tell her?

However, she has no choice but to agree, promising that yes, she'll make notes of any other communication she has with the deceased between now and then.

The deceased.

She hates the term as much as any other that has become a part of her life in the past year.

Stepping back out into the corridor, Annie closes the door on Dr. Leaver and the discussion of EVP and immediately reopens the door—at least mentally—on the prospect of Thom Brannock.

Trust me, Annie . . . this isn't good-bye.

Why can't the man take "no" for an answer?

And why, when *she* says "no," doesn't she mean it?

One minute, she was telling him there wasn't room for him in her life; the next, she was lying in his arms.

What's wrong with her?

No wonder Andre is trying desperately to communicate with her from beyond the grave. He's probably trying to warn her to stay away from Thom.

Yes, that seems a bit preposterous . . . but no more preposterous than any of the scientific research Dr. Leaver just told her about.

Her head spinning with possibilities—and impossibilities—Annie strides toward Erika's office, needing to pick up her children and get on the train, back to familiar ground.

Only one thing is certain, she tells herself as she reaches for the knob: She hasn't seen the last of Thom Brannock.

Sooner or later, he's bound to barge back into her life. It's going to take every ounce of strength she possesses to say "no" again . . . and this time, to really mean it . . .

Or . . .

Or what?

Or forget about Andre, forget about what she should do, and follow her heart wherever it leads . . .

Even if it's right into Thom Brannock's arms?

Striding up Third Avenue toward his apartment at the end of an exhausting day, Thom tries to force his thoughts back to the latest report about the Midwestern firm's stock, knowing that the only thing he truly cares about acquiring at the moment is a green-eyed brunette.

If she were a corporation, he'd have a team of

researchers delving into her past, he'd be working around the clock for days, weeks on end, to put together a take-over bid.

But Annie Harlowe isn't a corporation; she's a human being.

A *female* human being, at that.

Still . . .

A challenge is a challenge.

Could it be that he's gone about this . . . this *relationship* thing, with Annie . . . in entirely the wrong way?

Thom might not understand women, but he just so happens to be an expert at mergers and acquisitions.

You don't blatantly go after a company that's been in business for ten days, no matter how successful it promises to be. Nobody knows better than Thom that a potential acquisition must be carefully sized up, thoroughly researched, strategically approached.

Yes, any successful merger is a painstaking process that requires the utmost patience.

Timing, after all, is everything.

All right.

So he won't go chasing out to Long Island tomorrow even though it's a holiday. He won't go this weekend, or this month, or next.

Nothing will have changed by then. He won't be ready, and neither will she.

Never mind that she claims she'll never be ready, that her heart will always belong to her dead husband.

Eventually, she'll get past that.

She has to.

Doesn't she?

Stopping to wait for the light to change, Thom shakes

his head, knowing that in life, as in business, some things are beyond his control.

All he can do now is restrain his own impulses and stay away from Annie for as long as it takes to make his life everything he's always wanted it to be.

Only then can he entertain the notion of sharing the rest of it with Annie.

Still waiting for the light, Thom closes his eyes briefly, wishing he could forget her somehow.

Opening his eyes again, aware that he can't forget her, he finds his gaze falling on a shop on the opposite corner.

A florist shop.

That's odd. He's walked this route between his office and his apartment hundreds of times, and he doesn't remember seeing it before.

Then again, this is Manhattan. Businesses come and go on a daily basis. And it isn't as though he pays much attention to florists.

Plus, the streets are relatively deserted on this night before Independence Day. Everyone who's leaving town has left, those who are still here aren't lingering in the midtown office canyons. Without the usual hustle and bustle on the streets to provide distraction, the florist shop is like a neon beacon.

The light changes.

Thom's feet seem to carry him across the street and into the shop without his permission.

A bell tinkles on the door as it closes behind him. The man behind the counter looks up.

"Can I help you?" he asks.

He looks familiar.

Why?

You've probably seen him around the neighborhood, Thom tells himself. He's familiar the same way the coffee cart guy and the bank teller and the UPS man are familiar.

He notices that the air is filled with a hauntingly familiar scent.

"I need to send a bouquet of flowers," he says, then pauses, waylaid by the intense floral fragrance and the memories it conjures: lying in dew-kissed grass with Annie cradled in his arms.

"What kind of flowers?"

"Honeysuckle," Thom says decisively. That, after all, is what he smells.

"No problem. Is tomorrow okay for delivery?"

"Tomorrow's the Fourth of July."

"Not a problem."

"Really?"

"No. Where's it going?"

Taken aback at the accommodating response, Thom recites Annie's name and address, pausing when he gets to the zip code.

He frowns when he realizes he doesn't know it . . .

Frowns harder when he realizes that the man behind the counter is still writing . . . and has written a five digit zip code after "Montauk, New York."

"I used to live out there," he says by way of explanation, after glancing up to see Thom's incredulous expression. "What do you want to say on the card?"

The card.

Thom hadn't thought of that.

What does he want to say?

Never mind what he *wants* to say.

What does he *have* to say?

For his own good, and Annie's?

"Are the flowers for a special occasion?" the man behind the counter asks.

"A special occasion?" he echoes dumbly.

"Birthday, anniversary . . . ?"

"Oh. No."

"Just a blank card, then?"

"Just a blank card."

He watches the florist reach for a card from the spinner rack, absently noting the scar on his hand as he slides it and a pen across the counter toward Thom.

"Sorry I pushed so hard. If space is what you need, you've got it. I'm here if you ever need me. Sincerely, Thom Brannock."

That's it.

Still standing on the front porch, where she discovered the green tissue-wrapped bouquet just now after a day at the beach with the children, Annie flips the florist's simple card over.

She half expects to find a postscript on the other side, but there's nothing more.

Well, of course there isn't. What more is there to say?

He's done what she asked him to do.

He's given her what she needs.

Space.

Tears stinging her eyes, Annie buries her nose in fragrant honeysuckle blossoms and tells herself that it's for the best.

Part Three

August

Chapter
17

I got through to Andre again last night," Annie tells Dr. Leaver promptly, settling into her usual chair opposite his, depositing her handbag on the floor beside her sandaled feet.

"Over the telephone?"

She nods. "There was a thunderstorm out east, and I decided to try to call him again."

She watches the doctor's face for a reaction, wondering if he considers this a setback.

She's been coming here weekly for over a month now, all through July, and just last session she told him that she really feels as though she's beginning to heal.

"Enough to stop wearing your wedding band?" he had asked her then, a suggestion that made her recoil.

Now, he nods and rubs his chin thoughtfully. "What did Andre say when you spoke to him?"

"He said . . ." She trails off, frowning, watching him. "You don't believe me, do you?"

"Believe you?"

"You don't think I really made contact with Andre."

"What do *you* believe, Annie?"

She lifts her chin and looks him in the eye. "I believe I made contact with Andre."

"And what did he say?"

"There was a lot of static again. I could only pick out a handful of words."

"What were they?"

"My name. 'Love,' 'copper,' and 'sorry.' And 'know.' Or 'no.' "

"And how do you feel about the call?"

"Frustrated. Sad. Angry." She hesitates.

"Clearly, he's trying to convey some kind of message."

"Yes, and I can't figure out what it is."

"What do you think it could possibly be?"

"I have no idea. And it's really bothering me. I feel like everything is so . . . unresolved."

"That's understandable, Annie. When a young person passes on as suddenly as your husband did, the grieving are often left with a feeling of unfinished business."

Unfinished business.

Kind of like her relationship with Thom Brannock.

It's a case that was officially closed when he sent her the flowers last month, but she can't help feeling as though . . .

As though there should have been something more.

A clean break, however, is for the best.

Even if Milo and Trixie still ask about him from time to time.

All right, just about every day.

Which reminds her . . .

"I wanted to talk about the kids," she tells Dr. Leaver. "I'm worried about them."

He nods. "Is Milo still attempting to fly to heaven to see his father?"

"No, it isn't that. It's more that he, um, hasn't been flying to heaven at all this week. It's kind of like he . . . gave up. Or maybe he's forgetting all about Andre."

"Children are remarkably resilient, Annie. Milo is healing."

"But what if he's forgotten?"

"He hasn't forgotten. He's learning to move on. Does he talk about his father?"

"Sometimes."

But not every day.

"Have you told him about the phone calls?"

"No!"

"Why not?"

"Because it would scare him, don't you think?"

"Not necessarily. Not only are children resilient, Annie, but they're open to things adults might not see . . . or might not be willing to see. Bereaved children frequently speak of contact with lost loved ones. It wouldn't be unusual for your son to experience that."

Annie is silent, contemplating that.

"Has Milo ever mentioned having any kind of communication with his father?"

"No."

"What does he say when he talks about your husband these days?"

"He talks about things they used to do, places Andre took him . . . the same kind of things he always said." She smiles. "Oh, and he's mentioned a few times that my husband would be proud of the way my business is picking up."

"That's good news."

Annie nods. "I've got cookie orders coming out of my ears lately, and my seashell sculptures are selling like crazy all of a sudden. In fact, if this keeps up, I think the catering job I have next weekend might be the last one I'll have to take for a while."

"That's wonderful, Annie."

She tells him how it all started: how, according to Devonne Cambridge, a woman with an Irish accent and a large expense account came in around the Fourth of July weekend, bought every one of Annie's shell sculptures on display at the Harborside Emporium, and asked for two dozen more as corporate gifts.

Ever since, Annie has been scrambling to keep up with business.

"It's good for me to be busy, don't you think?" she asks Dr. Leaver.

"Do you think it is?" he volleys back.

"Yes," she says firmly.

Being busy means there's less time to think. About Andre. About Thom.

All too soon, the session has drawn to a close, and Annie finds herself back out on the street. Erika is away on vacation this week, so Annie left the children on Long Island with Merlin and Jonathan.

Walking toward Penn Station, she goes back over all the things she discussed with Dr. Leaver.

Maybe she should have brought up Thom.

But why?

She hasn't spoken of him in the past few weeks. Why should she? He's out of her life now. And anyway, she's seeing Dr. Leaver to help her get over Andre, not Thom.

Her thoughts drift again to the most recent phone call to her late husband, and subsequently, to the doctor's questions about Milo.

No, Milo has never mentioned communicating with his dead father . . .

But Trixie has, Annie recalls suddenly, nearly stopping dead on the bustling city sidewalk.

That night back in June, when she dreamed that Andre was in her room, sitting on her bed and talking to her . . .

I should have told Dr. Leaver about that, Annie realizes, hesitating on the corner opposite his office building.

Maybe she should go back up and tell him.

Just to see what he thinks.

No. Don't do it, Annie.

After all, it was just a dream. And Dr. Leaver would be sure to ask whether Andre conveyed a specific message to Trixie. The parapsychologist is very big on searching for messages.

There is no way Annie can possibly share Trixie's account of the conversation. No, not considering what Trixie said that night about her father.

He said I was going to have a new daddy and it was Thom.

Dr. Leaver would surely chalk that up as a figment of Daddy-deprived daughter's vivid imagination, especially knowing what he does about Trixie's history of night terrors.

Or, embarrassingly, Dr. Leaver might suspect wishful thinking on the part of a lonely, lovelorn widow.

Yes, Trixie's dream is too trivial to mention to Dr. Leaver.

Maybe if there were some other message, or if it had happened again . . .

But there wasn't, it hasn't, and it isn't likely to now that Trixie is sleeping through the nights undisturbed.

Yes, Trixie's night terrors seem to have subsided these past few weeks.

She, like her brother, is gradually healing.

Everybody is healing, Annie thinks sadly, heading on toward the train station, doing her best not to scan the crowded sidewalk for Thom's face.

Everybody but me.

Thom's polished dress shoes make a hollow sound on the scarred hardwood floor as he crosses the empty living room to inspect the ornate marble mantelpiece.

"That was brought over from Europe around the turn of the century," Daisy Kellerman, the real estate agent, informs him after referring to the sheaf of notes in her hand.

"It's beautiful."

"Yes. The *last* century," she amends, as he runs his fingers over the cool marble. "It's over a hundred years old."

Thom nods. "Yeah, I figured." Clearly, little was added to this Village brownstone at the turn of this past century. Located on an uncommonly—for Manhattan—leafy and quiet street, the place is in a state of disrepair.

According to Daisy, a wealthy young couple bought it a decade ago from the estate of its longtime owner, intending to do massive renovations. But before the house could be put back together, their marriage fell apart. The brownstone lay in vacant shambles throughout the messy divorce, part of a complicated property dispute.

One might expect the place to be filled with bad vibes as a result, but, walking from room to room on the first floor and then the second and third floors, Thom is pleasantly surprised that there's no such pall. Maybe that's because the hapless couple never actually moved in. The home's last actual resident was a reportedly sweet elderly widow who was born within these walls, raised a family here, and died here, well into her nineties.

"Well, Mr. Brannock? What do you think?" Daisy asks anxiously, hovering at Thom's elbow as he turns to look out the floor-to-ceiling window facing the back of the house. Two stories below lies an overgrown patch of courtyard, also rare in Manhattan. It's actually large enough for a sandbox, swing set . . . and flowering shrubs.

"I think," he says with a slow grin, "that this place has character," he says with a grin.

"Annie? I thought you were finished with waitressing! What are you doing here?" asks Carlos, one of Merlin's regular helpers, whom Annie has gotten to know quite well this summer.

"This is my last event," Annie says, lifting a heavy tray onto her shoulder. It's loaded with small glass dishes that each contain a single scoop of blueberry sorbet, and she's praying it won't melt between the kitchen and the hostess's distant garden.

"Lucky you." Carlos begins unloading salad plates. "I'm stuck with this gig for the rest of the summer."

"If it weren't for the cookies doing so well, I would be, too," Annie tells him, balancing the tray as she heads for the propped-open French doors.

Carlos nods enthusiastically. "Oh, I heard Merlin got another big batch of cookie orders. Congratulations! You must be thrilled they've taken off. Maybe you'll be the next Mrs. Fields."

"I'll just be happy to pay the rest of my overdue bills." With a smile, Annie slips back out into the midday heat.

As she precariously transports her loaded tray along a winding gravel path, aware of the trickle of sweat building along her forehead, she can't help thinking an evening event would have been a more comfortable swan song. Hustling back and forth around a sprawling estate in the blazing August sun on the most humid day of the year is downright torturous.

What's worse, the guest list for this garden club luncheon consists primarily of elderly females. Call her prejudiced, but Annie's had a hard time warming up to that particular female blue-blood generation. They were bred in an era of pronounced class distinction, and they don't let the help forget it.

At least their male counterparts are friendly. Granted, they're sometimes *too* friendly, but at least they don't treat Annie as if she were invisible. Though many of the same people are present at most of these society events, few of the women bother to acknowledge ever having seen Annie before. Perhaps they haven't, considering the way they seem to look right through her even when she takes their meal orders.

With a pesky bumblebee buzzing dangerously close to her hand and the sweets-laden tray, Annie at last reaches the cluster of white-draped tables in the dappled shade at the rear of the garden. The club's guest horticulturalist is monotonously expounding on some botanical wonder or other.

Setting her tray on a conveniently placed stand, Annie waves the bee away and begins serving the sorbet to the women feigning rapt interest in the speaker.

"Thanks, Annie," whispers white-haired, rosy-cheeked Mrs. Yates, at whose anniversary party Annie was a waitress weeks ago. She is the rare exception, one of the few women in this crowd who bothered to ask—and remember— Annie's name.

"You're welcome, Mrs. Yates."

"It's Louisa, Annie," the woman admonishes in a hushed tone.

Annie smiles and carefully sets a bowl of sorbet before the woman seated next to Mrs. Yates.

"Thank you," she says, looking up with a rather intense expression. "Annie, is it?"

"Yes. You're welcome," Annie says politely.

She can feel the woman's disconcerting gaze on her as she makes her way around the table, handing out blueberry sorbet with her right hand and shooing away the persistent bee with her left.

Nothing like going from one extreme to the other, she thinks, wondering if it's her imagination or if the woman seems to be overly interested in her.

The bee buzzes in again, drawn by the scent of sweet blueberries. Annie swats impatiently at it, inadvertently making contact.

Ouch.

It's all she can do not to scream in pain. She can see the end of the stinger in her rapidly swelling forefinger, but is helpless to remove it. At least, not yet. There's sorbet to be served.

Wincing in pain, she waves her throbbing hand as surreptitiously as she can, not wanting to attract attention. Glancing up, she sees that the older blonde at Mrs. Yates's table is still watching her, more shrewdly, if possible, than before.

An hour later, the party is winding down and the stinger has been removed, thanks to the tube of toothpaste Carlos found in a bathroom cabinet. When Annie protested to his snooping, he shushed her and promised to put it right back after dabbing it on her wound.

"I've never heard of using toothpaste as a drawing salve," Annie comments, rinsing her still swollen finger at the sink in the vast kitchen, which is vacant for the moment. "I've always used mud on bee stings."

"Yeah, well, that can be dangerous. I found out the hard way when I was a kid."

"What do you mean?"

"We were at our neighbor's when a bee flew up my bathing suit and stung me where the sun don't shine," Carlos says with a grin. "My mother ran out to the yard and made mud to put on it, only it wasn't mud."

"What was it?"

"Let's just say she happened to dig in a part of the yard where their Doberman liked to do his duty."

"You mean it was poop?" Annie bursts out laughing.

Carlos joins in—for only a split second. The amusement is erased from his face like chalk from a blackboard, as he gapes at something behind Annie.

She turns to see that the woman who was staring at her

in the garden is now staring from the doorway of the kitchen.

Guests rarely venture into the caterer's staging area during a party. Why is she here? And why now, just as Annie was laughing about poop, of all things?

She can feel her face growing hot as Carlos politely asks the woman, "Can I help you find something?"

"No, thank you. I'd like to have a word with Annie alone, though."

Carlos's dark brows rise in surprise, and he shoots Annie a look, silently asking her if everything's okay.

What is there for her to do but shrug and nod?

What is there for Carlos to do but leave her alone with the oddly intense woman?

"How is your hand?" she asks, crossing to stand beside Annie.

All right. That makes sense. Maybe she saw the sting and she's here out of the goodness of her heart, to make sure Annie's okay.

That would make sense if she struck Annie as a good-hearted, nurturing type. Which she doesn't.

"It's fine, thank you." Annie looks down at her hand, conscious that the woman is doing the same.

"I see that you're married."

Caught off-guard once again, realizing the woman is staring at her wedding band, Annie shakes her head, then manages to say, "No, I'm not. I mean . . . I *was*."

"You're a widow?"

"Yes."

"I'm sorry," the woman says. Her expression remains unchanged, but she sounds as though she means it. "And you have young children?"

"Yes."

"Two?"

Increasingly uncomfortable with this strangely personal line of questioning, Annie merely nods.

"We have quite a bit in common, then, Annie."

Doubting that, Annie echoes, "We do?"

"I'm also a widow with two children. Although, mine are grown now, as they were when they lost their father. I'm grateful for that. Did you have a good marriage?"

Torn between thinking this has gone too far and wondering if this woman is perhaps just a lonely widow like herself, Annie finds herself nodding again.

"And that's why you're still wearing your wedding ring? Because you aren't ready to let go?"

"I . . . I guess so."

"I wore my ring, too," the woman says. "For the first year after he died. And we, unfortunately, did not have a good marriage. But I wore it for all those months, because taking it off sooner seemed wrong. And, maybe, because I was afraid of attracting attention from men if I appeared to be available. I was beautiful when I was younger. Not as beautiful as you are, but quite attractive."

Her words are as oddly void of flattery as they are of narcissism. She's simply stating the facts.

"Did you ever remarry?" she asks, noticing that the woman's ring finger is still bare.

"No. I never did. But not because I was still in love with my husband. Because nobody ever fell in love with me. Has somebody fallen in love with you, Annie?"

Annie's breath catches in her throat. "No," she says, heart pounding, thoughts racing wildly.

"Are you sure?"

"I . . . I don't think you mentioned your name," Annie says quietly, steeling herself for the answer.

"Do you know what it is?"

"I have a good idea."

The woman is silent. Waiting.

"You're Mrs. Brannock, aren't you." It isn't a question.

"And you're Thom's Annie." Neither is that.

But she's wrong. "Mrs. Brannock, I'm sorry, but you have the wrong idea. Your son and I aren't seeing each other."

"But you were?"

Annie nods reluctantly.

"And why did it end?"

Annie fights the urge to laugh. Talk about the million-dollar question.

"It ended," she informs Thom's mother, "because neither of us was interested in a long-term relationship."

Mrs. Brannock seems to be digesting that information. "I see."

Again, her gaze shifts to Annie's now-trembling left hand.

Then the door opens.

The waitstaff comes bustling in, and Mrs. Brannock slips out without another word or a backward glance.

Like mother, like son, Annie can't help thinking, shaken.

Chapter
18

Did you hear the news?"

"What news?" Annie asks Merlin, swatting his hand as he plucks another raisin from the oatmeal cookie dough she's mixing for one of his catered affairs.

"There's a tropical depression churning in the Caribbean that's probably going to turn into a major hurricane and barrel up the coast this week."

The spoon in Annie's hand stops moving. She used to let Merlin's weather forecasts go in one ear and out the other, but not anymore.

It's been the driest summer on record for the Northeast. She glances out the window at her flowerbeds, neglected out of necessity because of the countywide bans on watering.

The impatiens are wilting, the geraniums drooping; even the plentiful weeds look parched in the late August sun.

But a looming storm doesn't just mean a much-needed soaking for Annie's deprived garden.

It could present another long-awaited chance to communicate with Andre.

She's attempted countless calls to her late husband. She managed to get through only that one time last month, on a night when lightning crackled in the air before a rare midsummer storm.

Summoning his official meteorological reporting face and jargon, Merlin informs her, "The storm could become a category four and make landfall here on Saturday, which is just in time to ruin that puppy shower I'm doing for Bitsy Worth. I was going to ask you if you could do twelve dozen sugar cookies in the shape of an Irish wolfhound as a tribute to the guest of honor, but now . . ."

"An Irish wolfhound? Are you sure she's not a Chihuahua or something?"

"A *Chihuahua*?"

"Well, don't you think Bitsy's an odd choice of name for a dog that big?"

Merlin laughs. Hard. "Bitsy is the owner. The dog's name is Dublin."

"Oh! Well, how was I supposed to know?" Annie layers a cookie sheet with parchment paper. "And anyway, Bitsy's an even odder name for a woman."

"Haven't you ever heard of her? Her real name is Bettina Worth, but nobody calls her that."

"Worth? I've never heard of her."

"Well, believe me, she's *worth* billions."

Worth billions.

Why, after two months, does everything anybody says still remind Annie of Thom Brannock?

You'd think she might be over him by now.

You'd think she'd be able to accept the fact that he's gone for good.

You'd think she'd be pleased that, in fact, he respected her wishes and gave her exactly what she wanted.

If space is what you need, you've got it. I'm here if you ever need me.

The terse words still rankle.

Then again, what more was there to say? He had done what she asked him to do. She had no reason to call him, unless . . .

If you ever need me . . .

How many times in the past eight weeks has she been tempted to pick up the phone and dial, not just Andre's cell phone, but Thom's?

The thing is . . . she doesn't *need* him.

Of course not.

She just . . .

Misses him.

The children miss him, too. But not as much as they did at first. They used to ask about him every day, just as they once asked about their daddy.

Not anymore.

A week has gone by since the last time Milo wondered aloud when Thom was going to come and teach him to tie his shoes, and Trixie hasn't brought up the promised kite-flying outing since July.

It's better this way, Annie tells herself, her mantra since she received the flowers back at the beginning of the summer. Better for the children, better for her, better for Thom . . .

"Something tells me you're not thinking about Bitsy

Worth's pregnant Irish wolfhound," Merlin comments, eyeing her with concern as he reaches for another raisin.

She slaps his hand away, harder than she intended.

"Ow! That's some arm you've got there, SweeTART."

"Sorry, Merlin. Just keep your paws out of my cookie dough."

"Technically, it's *my* cookie dough."

"Technically, you're quite the pain in the—"

"Watch it, Annie. Slapping the hand that feeds you is one thing . . . insulting the fabulous human attached to the hand is quite another."

She laughs. "Listen, O Fabulous One . . . I'm grateful for all the work you've thrown my way this summer, but Labor Day is a week away, which means the bulk of your business is about to hightail it back to Fifth Avenue and Central Park South."

"Which is why it's a good thing you're doing so well with your shell art lately," he points out. "Did you finish those fifty paperweights Devonne Cambridge asked you to deliver yesterday?"

"Yes, but she needs a hundred more heart-shaped ones by next week for somebody who wants them as wedding favors."

"A hundred more? Annie, you're going to run yourself ragged."

She shrugs, reluctant to explain that the busier she is, the less time she has to brood about Andre.

Or Thom.

The silver lining in her storm-free summer is that people all over the Hamptons are clamoring for her baked goods and her handicrafts.

Her shell creations have been selling out all over the

Hamptons, more popular than lemon Italian ice in blazing midday sun on Mulberry Street. And Merlin is still getting cookie requests for nearly every affair he caters. Not just any cookies: Annie's homemade cookies.

After all these years of struggling, she has somehow managed to make a name for herself among the island's elite in a single summer season. She hasn't even been forced to take a waitressing job with Merlin since the Fourth of July regatta.

Thank goodness for that, because chances are that sooner or later, she'd run into Thom's mother—or worse yet, Thom himself—at one of the local society events. It's difficult enough to accept that he's nearby every weekend, eating her homemade cookies; she simply can't risk coming face to face with him again.

Now that her unexpectedly profitable summer is waning, she's not exactly rolling in cash, but at least she'll be able to pay the pile of bills that has stacked up on the kitchen counter . . . just as soon as she has a spare moment to actually sit down with them and her checkbook. And she'll also be able to afford long-delayed necessities for the household and the children . . . just as soon as she has a spare moment to actually get out and shop.

First on the list is a new washing machine, along with back-to-school wardrobes for Trixie and Milo. Oh, and more film for the camera, so she can capture their first day. She finally developed the photos that were in there. They were tough to look at, but they brought back happy memories.

Yes, everything has fallen into place for her, financially, at least.

And in another week, the year-rounders will no longer

have to share Montauk with city people, both kids will be riding away on a yellow bus every morning, and Annie will be left in solitude for the first time in . . .

Well, *ever.*

Funny that she, who craved a moment's peace just weeks ago, now finds herself dreading the thought of having an empty house all to herself.

Be careful what you wish for, she thinks ruefully, placing a scoop of cookie dough on the parchment paper and nudging Merlin's raisin-seeking hand away again.

"Hey!" he says suddenly, and grabs her fingers, raising them to examine her hand. "Where's your wedding ring?"

"Don't get excited. I only took it off so that I can mix the dough. It's on the counter."

"Why are you going to put it on again?"

Not *when.*

Why.

Annie doesn't answer, swallowing hard over a painful lump rising in her throat.

Merlin puts an arm around her. "You'll always have him, you know. Even if you're not wearing his ring."

"I know," she says, giving in to tears. "But it's so damned hard . . ."

"You're surviving, Annie. Day by day. You're really doing it all alone."

"Yes," she says softly, sniffling. "I guess I really am. All alone."

"Well, you *are* planning on coming out next weekend, then, aren't you?" Lillian Brannock asks her son over dinner at Le Cirque, on the heels of his announcement that he can't possibly make it to Southampton this weekend.

"I don't think so," Thom tells her, perusing the menu. "I'm really busy right now with the Saltwater Treasures acquisition."

"But it's Labor Day weekend."

"I know, Mother, and I'm sorry. I just don't have the time."

"But you haven't been out all summer," his mother protests. "You've missed every party, every luncheon, every golf tournament, even the July Fourth regatta. People are wondering about you."

"What are they wondering?" he asks, not sure whether he's amused or annoyed.

"Whether you're ill, or carrying on an illicit affair."

"An illicit affair?"

"I tell them you're not involved with anyone at the moment. You aren't . . . are you?" she asks anxiously.

"Not at the moment, no."

How many times is she going to ask him that today? She's obviously been wondering whether he's still involved with Annie, but can't quite bring herself to come right out and ask. Instead, she makes vague inquiries into whether he'll be bringing an escort to this affair or that affair, affairs he has no intention of attending.

Now, apparently, she's moved on to hinting at illicit affairs.

"Oh, and Thom," she says, after they've paused to place their order, "just yesterday Constance Worth asked if you'd be coming to the puppy shower her mother is hosting next weekend for Dublin."

"A *puppy shower?*" *Just when you think you've heard everything . . .*

Thom shakes his head in decidedly amused annoyance.

"Yes, Dublin is expecting a litter in September. In fact, I told Bitsy that I'll take one of the puppies."

"*You're* getting a dog, Mother?" Thom is shocked. Yes, he's noticed that Lillian seems to be mellowing a bit in her old age . . . but he can't imagine her tolerating dog hair on the upholstery of the davenport that once belonged to Mary, Queen of Scots, or paw prints on her new flagstone path imported from the ruins of a seventeenth-century French villa.

"Oh, the puppy isn't for me. It's for the baby."

The baby. Of course. Susan's bundle of joy has been the main topic of many a conversation with his mother this summer. Just last week, she asked Thom for a letter of recommendation on behalf of her unborn grandson, whom she was taking the liberty of preenrolling at the finest private schools in Manhattan.

Thom initially tried to protest that it was a ridiculous proposition, but she presented two pages' worth of wait-listed unborns from Astors to Vanderbilts. He then insisted he was too busy, but Lillian is nothing if not persistent. The next thing he knew, he was putting pen to paper and wholeheartedly vouching for the impeccable character of a fetus.

"Mother," he says wearily now, "a puppy? Don't you think Susan and Wade will have their hands full enough learning how to change diapers and cure colic?"

"There *is* no cure for colic," is his mother's dark reply. "I should know. You had it yourself, and your night nurse tried everything. We finally had to move the nursery up to the top floor so that your fussing wouldn't keep me awake all night. Naturally your father slept like a log," she adds with a disgusted shake of her salon-styled head.

Having heard that tale ad nauseum, Thom does his best to ignore the pang that invariably accompanies the affirmation that it was his night nurse, and not his mother, who attempted to soothe him back to sleep as an infant.

He tells himself that it doesn't mean his mother didn't love him; that it's simply the way things are done in the Brannocks' social circle.

In fact, Susan and Wade have already hired a nanny at Mother's insistence. Nonetheless, Susan swears that she herself will be doing the night feedings, the diaper changing, the potty training—and now, apparently, the puppy training as well.

"Every boy needs a dog," Mother informs Thom, conveniently forgetting that he begged for a pet throughout his childhood and was denied.

"But mother . . . a purebred Irish wolfhound?"

"Absolutely. And getting back to Dublin's shower, as I said, Constance was wondering whether you—"

"I'm sorry, but I really can't make it," Thom cuts in, knowing that his mother would like nothing better than to be planning a baby shower for her only son and the likes of Constance Worth at this time next year.

"It would be so nice if you took her to dinner some night, then."

"Mother—"

"She asks about you every time our paths cross, and I promised her that you'll call. Now that she's back from Paris for good, she's anxious to see her old friends."

Never mind that Constance Worth is hardly one of Thom's old friends.

Constant Comment, as she was known back in boarding school days, is a notoriously narcissistic chatterbox. Considering that Thom would—and actually has— crossed Park Avenue against traffic to avoid her, he certainly isn't about to drive a hundred miles on a holiday weekend to see her.

"I don't have time for my current friends, Mother, let alone 'old friends,'" Thom informs Lillian. "Between everything that's going on at work with this merger, and the house renovation, I've got my hands full."

"That's another thing I wanted to discuss with you," Lillian says.

"The merger?" he asks hopefully.

"The renovation. It isn't too late to change your mind about buying that place."

He sighs. "Mother—"

"It's just that you're going to be so far away, and the neighborhood is dreadful. You'll have to fear for your life every time you set foot on the street."

"Don't be ridiculous. It's a five-minute cab ride from your apartment"—not that Mother would deign to set foot in a yellow cab—"and you know the Village is perfectly safe."

"I'd feel better about it if at least you were going to be in a doorman building on one of the avenues. Why you felt the need to buy a wreck of an old brownstone when you had a lovely, modern penthouse is beyond me."

"I told you, Mother. I was sick of living in an apartment. I wanted a house."

"You *have* a house in Southampton and you don't even go there."

On the verge of filing yet another protest, Thom closes his mouth, knowing it's futile. Mother would never in a million years understand why he's making the move.

In fact, all she knows about is the move. If she had any inkling about what else he's poised to do . . .

But she doesn't. He can't bring himself to break it to her. Not yet. Not until he's actually put his carefully thought-out plan into action.

"I promise I'll come out to Southampton, Mother, just as soon as I have a free weekend."

"Don't bother. The season is over."

Thom takes a long drink of sparkling water, wishing there were something more potent in his glass. Unfortunately, he needs a clear head for the ongoing business negotiations he's been conducting by cell phone for weeks now.

Sometimes he isn't even sure that it's all going to be worth it in the end.

If you win Annie back, it'll be worth it, he reminds himself. *And if not . . .*

At least you'll have been true to yourself, with a life you can live on your own terms.

But he can't help thinking the adventure that lies ahead won't be nearly as satisfying without Annie by his side.

Chapter
19

Walking along the beach beneath a copper-streaked sky at sunset, watching her children wade into the shallow surf nearby, Annie waves Andre's metal detector over the wet, compact sand.

Andre always said that low tide is the best time for treasure hunting. A century ago, the treasure could easily have been buried in this area of beach; it was undoubtedly dry ground back then. Thanks to gradual erosion of the coast, this stretch is now under water a good part of every day.

A hundred years from now, Annie thinks, the remaining strip of dry beach might very likely have washed away. One good storm surge can easily bring the tide line a few inches inland.

Nothing lasts forever.

The sad, familiar refrain runs through her mind less frequently these days. But it certainly is fitting out here, and suits her melancholy mood tonight.

Gazing out at the whitecaps, Annie wonders if the hurricane Merlin mentioned is really going to hit here next weekend. She's experienced her share of fierce coastal storms, but Andre was always here to batten down the hatches.

This time, she and the children will face the gale alone.

Both Merlin and Erika have urged them to come stay, especially if the storm is as dangerous as the National Weather Service is predicting in increasingly dire warnings.

A year ago, Annie might have agreed to leave the house and move to drier, higher ground.

But lately, she's felt almost . . . self-sufficient. It isn't just her improved financial situation. It's the fact that she can make it through most days now without crying, through most nights without awakening in the wee hours, expecting to see Andre's head on the pillow beside hers.

They're all improving, slowly but surely. Milo has given up his daily takeoff and landing attempts, at least for the time being, and somehow taught himself to tie his shoes. Even Trixie's night terrors have been subsiding.

Annie told both Erika and Merlin that, barring a forced evacuation, she and the children are going to ride out the storm at home, where they belong.

What she didn't say, even to Erica, is that she's fervently hoping the weather conditions will finally be right for a cellular connection to her dead husband. It might not work if she tries to reach him from any location other than home. It might not work at all . . .

But she has to try.

"Mommy! I found a starfish!" Trixie calls, bending over in ankle-deep water to examine something at her feet.

"That's great, sweetie," Annie murmurs in a voice that can't possibly carry, her thoughts drifting to Andre.

Funny how one can become accustomed to just about anything . . . even widowhood.

"But I still miss you," Annie whispers, shifting her gaze heavenward. "I miss you so much. I just want to hear your voice again, even if it's one last time."

She wipes her suddenly moist eyes on the shoulder of her T-shirt and looks back over her shoulder so the children won't see her crying.

Her gaze falls on the lone set of footsteps she left on the sand, a stark reminder that she'll walk alone through the rest of her life.

"It's not a starfish, Mom, it's just a rock," Milo shouts, to his sister's immediate protest.

Wearily turning back to see her children arguing over whatever it is that lies on the beach between them, Annie absently swings the metal detector in another sweeping arc.

"Mom, tell her this is just a rock!" Milo is splashing his way toward her, clutching the object in question, with Trixie trailing along behind him.

Suddenly, the metal detector beeps.

Swinging it back again, Annie hears another beep.

She swings the metal detector in an increasingly narrow pendulum to pinpoint the spot. Then she drops to her bare knees and scoops at the sand.

Seeing her, the children hurriedly make their way over.

"What is it, Mommy?"

"Did you find the treasure?"

"I don't know." Annie takes the shovel Milo hastily hands to her and digs deeper.

Her heart is pounding.

The shovel hits something solid.

"Is it a treasure chest?" Trixie is hovering so close beside Annie it's all she can do not to swing her elbow into her as she digs frantically.

"I don't know. It's something big . . ." With Milo's bare-handed assistance, Annie scoops away more and more sand until the buried object takes definite shape.

"What is it?" Milo asks, peering into the hole.

Annie swallows bitter disappointment. "An old tire rim."

"No! That's not fair! I wanted it to be my daddy's treasure!" Trixie wails.

"We all did," Milo says glumly.

Annie hugs her children close. "We'll keep looking," she promises, kicking sand back into the hole. "Maybe someday we'll find it."

And maybe, she can't help thinking, staring at the horizon, the treasure never even existed in the first place.

In the backseat of an air-conditioned black Town Car gliding along East Sixty-first Street, Thom flips his cell phone closed at last and leans his head against the leather seat.

It's been a hell of a long day. Long, but fulfilling.

He boarded the morning's first shuttle to Boston with his CFO, bound for Saltwater Treasures corporate headquarters. The flight was on time, the day-long merger talks couldn't have gone more smoothly, and the return flight actually arrived at La Guardia a few minutes ahead of schedule.

Just now, he had a call from Daisy Kellerman. The latest inspection report on the brownstone is satisfactory, and the closing date will be arranged for early October.

Yes, everything is going according to plan.

In a few months, he'll be ready to step down as chairman of the company his great-grandfather established almost a hundred years ago, in favor of overseeing operations at his latest acquisition.

He'll trade his sterile penthouse for a three-story, nineteenth-century home with crown moldings, plaster walls, working fireplaces, and hardwood floors . . . none of which are in good repair. The whole place needs to be gutted and renovated, but it has character.

Just like Annie's house. Just like Annie herself.

In a few more months, he'll be ready for her . . . and by his calculations, she might be ready to give him another chance. She'll have proven to herself and to the world that she can stand on her own two feet. She'll have survived another season on her own, stronger, and undoubtedly lonelier, than she was when he left.

Thom stretches, yawns, and reaches for his briefcase as the driver pulls to a stop in front of his building's awning. Teddy, the doorman, ruddy-faced from the evening's heat, is on the sidewalk, chatting with a well-heeled, poodle-walking tenant.

After greeting them both, Thom strides through the climate-controlled, carpeted lobby, picks up his mail, and takes the elevator up to the top floor. As usual, the apartment smells of furniture polish and new upholstery, despite the fact that his is several years old.

It just doesn't feel . . . lived in.

He smiles, remembering the look on Annie's face as she said it, trying so hard to be tactful.

God, he misses her. Aches for her.

He yawns again, loosening his tie as he heads for the bedroom, thinking that at least he can see her in his dreams.

Yes, it's corny.

But it's true. He dreams about her almost every night. Usually, she's standing in a blooming meadow, wearing a flowing white dress with a wreath of violets and honeysuckle in her hair. She looks up and sees him, then runs toward him, calling his name.

It isn't a graceful, slow-motion run like in the movies, but a full-out, wholehearted, Annie-style race into his arms.

Thom smiles. Just a few more months, he reminds himself, stopping to check his answering machine.

The light is blinking.

Every time he comes home to find that he has a message, he has a momentary inkling that it might be her.

It never is.

But he doesn't give up hope. If she comes to him first, the waiting game is off. He'll be on his way to Montauk before the end of the message.

He holds his breath as he tosses his keys on the table and presses the button on the answering machine, willing it to be Annie.

But it isn't.

For a moment, as he listens, his body goes motionless in dread.

Then Thom leaps into action, grabbing his keys and racing out the door, praying as he's never prayed before.

*   *   *

"Come on," Annie tells the children, "let's go home. It'll be dark soon. We'll order take-out pizza for dinner."

"Take-out pizza? Cool!"

"Can we have it with pepperoni?"

"Extra toppings are too expensive, Trixie," Milo says with an experienced shake of his head. "Plain cheese is cheaper and it's just as good."

With a pang in her heart, Annie says, "Oh, I don't know. I think it's better with pepperoni."

"Then can we get it that way?"

"Sure," Annie tells Trixie, and smiles as her children exchange jubilant high fives.

Just weeks ago, take-out anything was a forbidden expense. But she can afford to splurge a little, she thinks, gathering up the shovel, the metal detector, the buckets full of shells.

The kids deserve a treat. They're so good, and they've been through so much.

"After dinner, you guys can stay up a while and watch *SpongeBob*," she tells them.

"Can you watch with us again, Mommy?"

"Not this time, Trixie. I have work to do."

"Aw, come on, Mom."

"Sorry, Milo." She kicks a stone with the toe of her sandal and yawns, thinking of the long evening that still lies ahead.

Snuggling with her children on the couch in front of the television is about all she has the energy to do tonight, but Annie has twenty-three more shell paperweights to make for the wedding order that's due the day after tomorrow.

"Oh, look! A firefly!" Trixie says suddenly, looking up.

"Hey, there's another one!" Milo reaches into the air with a cupped hand to catch it.

They head home along the sandy lane through the rapidly falling dusk, the moist air heavy with the scent of brine and somebody's freshly mown grass. Annie leisurely kicks the stone along as she walks, the children scampering in front of her, chasing fireflies and chattering happily about the evening ahead. Their disappointment about the treasure has given way to excitement at the promise of pizza and cartoons.

As Dr. Leaver said, children are remarkably resilient.

"I'll race you to the front steps!" Milo shouts, abruptly breaking into a trot up ahead.

"No fair!" Trixie whines, running after him. "You got a head start!"

Annie follows along at her own pace, kicking the stone and thinking about Thom.

Maybe she should give him a call sometime. Just to say "hello."

But then he might think you need him. He might think you're opening the door to a relationship. He might think you've changed your mind . . .

And she hasn't.

Absolutely not.

Andre was your one true love, she reminds herself determinedly. *Andre didn't want you to fall in love again.*

At least, that's what he said.

But he didn't mean it . . . People say things . . .

Annie shrugs off the echo of Erika's voice, telling herself that Andre did mean it. At the time, he meant it.

But he never suspected he was actually going to die. If he had . . .

With a fierce jab of her sandal, Annie sends the stone skittering along in front of her, and winces. Not just because the tip of her toe painfully made contact with the stone, but because she suddenly finds herself wondering what Andre would have told her if he knew they weren't going to live the rest of their lives together.

What does that matter, Annie? What happened, happened. What was said, was said.

She made a vow, a vow as permanently etched in her heart as it is in the gold of her wedding ring.

But Erika's words suddenly come back to her, just as permanently etched in her memory.

Are you sure you're not just using Andre as an excuse? Some kind of twisted rationalization for your reluctance to get involved with somebody new?

Annie kicks the stone again, so emphatically that it veers off course, vanishing into the grassy scrub brush along the path.

The instant Thom steps out of the elevator and onto a patient floor of Cornell Medical Center, a desolate feeling sweeps through him.

It's just because of the smell, he assures himself, pausing to turn off his cell phone, per the large warning taped on the wall outside the elevator. He tucks it back into his pocket and strides down the tiled corridor beneath dreary fluorescent lights.

All hospitals smell exactly the same: disinfectant, steam-table food, climate-controlled indoor air that has never been stirred by a refreshing cross breeze. He got used to it back in the bleak months when his father was wasting away at Sloan-Kettering.

Now it triggers memories so dispiriting that it's all he can do to propel himself forward.

This is different, he reminds himself. *This isn't Father, and it isn't going to end that way.*

Please, God, don't let it end that way.

If anything happens to Susan . . .

No. She'll be fine. She *has to* be fine.

Yet the message Wade left on Thom's answering machine was uncharacteristically terse. Not frantic, but definitely laced with enough concern to send Thom rushing back down to the street for a cab uptown.

It was long past rush hour, but as they headed east, traffic became snarled due to an accident on the nearby FDR. Finally, in utter frustration, Thom paid the fare and jumped out of the gridlocked cab. He ran the last few blocks on foot, racing along the steamy Upper East Side streets in his jacket and tie.

Now, soaked with sweat and sick with worry, he careens around a corner and expertly sidesteps two orderlies pushing a pregnant patient on a gurney. All three are joyless enough to remind Thom that this isn't the wing of the hospital where radiantly healthy mothers give birth to bouncing full-term babies.

A scrubs-clad female sentry stops him as he passes. "Which patient are you looking for?"

"Susan Brannock."

She consults her clipboard. "I'm afraid—"

In that instant, Thom's heart stops.

"—there's nobody here by that name."

Nobody here.

Oh, God.

Does that mean . . . ?

Oh! By that *name.*

I'm not dead, brother dear; I'm married.

"Ellington!" he blurts in relief. "She's Susan Ellington. I forgot."

The woman offers a brief smile and points him in the right direction.

Moments later, he's walking into a small private room alive with beeping monitors, all of them connected to his wan-looking sister. Mother hovers grimly on one side of the bed, Wade on the other.

"What's going on?" Thom asks, his voice cracking.

"It's her heart." Wade's tone is matter-of-fact, but his face is ravaged with concern.

Her heart. Of course. Thom knew it must be her heart.

He sinks onto the wooden arm of Mother's chair, afraid to touch his sister, who has never looked more frail. Her skin is paler than usual, her eyes red and swollen.

"Is the baby . . . ?" Thom can't bring himself to say it.

"The baby is okay," Susan says quickly. "That's his heart you can hear beating on the monitor."

"What about your heart? What did the doctor say?"

"That continuing the pregnancy could be dangerous," Susan tells him, and adds, mostly to Wade, "but we knew that it would be high risk from the start. We knew this could happen."

Thom hesitates, then asks, "So what are you going to do now?"

"I'm having this baby."

For the first time, Mother speaks up. "Of course you are."

Thom swallows hard. "But what if . . . ?"

His sister's fearful blue gaze meets his own. "You said it yourself, little brother."

"What did I say?"

"The most worthwhile things in life . . ."

He smiles, leans over to take her hand, squeezes it gently. "So this is your version of swimming with sharks, huh?"

"You bet. Think I have it in me?"

"I know you do," Thom tells her.

The children, still panting from their race, are waiting on the steps of Annie's small, cedar-shingled house in the twilight. Delicate white moths flit overhead in the golden lamplight spilling from an upstairs bedroom window.

"Milo left his bedroom light on all day again," Trixie reports, just in case Annie lost her eyesight along the way back from the beach.

Annie, who a month or two ago would have mentally calculated how many pennies' worth of electricity had been wasted, says gently, "It's okay, Milo, just try to remember to turn it off next time you leave the room."

"He keeps it on all day and all night, Mommy."

"I do not! Not all day. And not *all* night."

No, not *all* night. But only because Annie has been stealing in to turn it off after her son is sound asleep.

Though he denied it vehemently the first few times Annie questioned him, she suspects that her superhero son is newly afraid of the dark.

So are a lot of other boys his age, Annie thinks, setting

the buckets and the treasure hunting equipment on the porch. There's no real harm in sleeping with the light on as far as she's concerned. But then, she's no expert in child psychology. Maybe she should run it by Erika, just to be sure.

"Come on," she says, "let's go inside and order that pepperoni pizza."

"Yummy!" Milo leaps to his feet and reaches for the screen door handle.

As it loudly squeaks open, Annie braces for her heart to clench as painfully as it used to.

Strangely, all she feels is a pleasant wisp of memory.
Andre.

The door squeaks shut behind her.

WD-40.

"What's the matter, Mom?" Milo asks after a moment, and she realizes she's been frozen in the entryway; frozen in time, really.

"Nothing, sweetie. I just . . . I have to get something from the basement."

She hurries through the kitchen and opens the door leading to the shallow cellar beneath the house. Descending the ladderlike stairway, she's greeted by cooler air and the musty, earthen scent of the rock walls and dirt floor.

This was Andre's territory; rarely did Annie venture into the spider-populated depths when he was alive, and only out of extreme necessity now that he's gone. Someday, she'll probably have to go through the heaps of fishing gear, the mildewed boxes of discarded household odds and ends.

Someday, she'll probably be ready.

After all, she's managed, over the last month or so, to gradually move his clothes out of the tiny closet in their bedroom. It isn't something she accomplished without guilt, but it's not as though she's tossed them into the garbage. She merely packed the clothes into plastic tubs and stored them in the attic. The closet is so small that it's silly not to claim the extra space.

It doesn't mean that she doesn't love him anymore.

It only means . . .

That he's gone. And he isn't coming back. And it's time to stop pretending that he is.

Wiping tears from her eyes with the back of her hand, Annie makes her way gingerly through the maze of basement clutter toward the far wall.

Andre was such an incredible pack rat, she thinks, shaking her head. He saved everything: old magazines, broken appliances, even the green telephone with a curly cord that used to hang on the wall in the kitchen before they replaced it with a modern cordless one.

On a rickety bookshelf rescued from somebody's curbside trash sit boxes full of tools, rows of nail-filled baby food jars, cans of turpentine and stain.

There are also cans of blue and pink paint from both times they decorated the nursery, the picture-hanging kits they always meant to use to replace the plain nails beneath the hastily hung wedding and baby pictures on the living room walls, the half-finished birdhouse Andre was building with Milo.

Annie's tears are falling more quickly now, blinding her so that she can barely see the packets of flower seeds he never got around to planting last spring, the small footstool he always meant to refinish so the kids could reach the sink in the upstairs bathroom.

Sniffling, she brushes aside cobwebs, moves the paint and then the nails, searching for the small can she knows must be here someplace. It has to be, because he always talked about getting around to it sooner or later.

Life—his life—was just too short.

Annie shrugs her damp cheekbones against her shoulders to dry them. When she looks up again, there it is, right in front of her. She plucks the can from the shelf and carries it back upstairs.

She walks purposefully toward the front door.

"What is that, Mommy?" Milo asks.

She takes a deep breath, exhales shakily. "It's WD-40."

"What's it for?"

"It'll stop the door from making that loud noise every time we open it."

"Why do you want to do that?"

"Because," she says simply, "it's time."

Annie opens the door with one last protesting squeak. She holds it open with her foot and removes the top from the can.

Then, with Milo watching intently, she sprays the aerosol lubricant into the top hinges, then the bottom.

"That stuff stinks," Milo comments.

"I know."

"Does it work?"

"We'll find out."

Annie pulls the door closed.

No squeak.

She pushes it open again.

No squeak.

"It works!" Milo says with delight.

"Yes." She heaves a sigh of relief.

"You're a good fixer, Mom. Daddy's really proud of you."

"Do you think?"

Milo nods vehemently. "I know he is."

"How do you know?"

"Because . . ." Milo hesitates. "I just know. Mom? What are you going to do next? Can you build me a treehouse?"

With a laugh, Annie says, "How about if I order you a pizza instead?"

"With pepperoni, right?"

"With pepperoni," she agrees. Then she tells Milo, "I'll order the pizza in a second, okay? First I have to go do something."

"What? Are you going to fix something else?"

"No, nothing like that," she assures him, heading for the stairs. "I'll be right back."

Alone in her room, Annie crosses over to the dresser, where a carved wooden box holds her meager collection of jewelry. She hesitates only a second before lifting the lid.

First, she unfastens the chain around her neck; the one on which she wears Andre's wedding ring. Then she slips her ring off her finger and tucks it inside along with his, between an outdated velvet choker and a lone silver hoop earring. It was her favorite pair; she kept the single earring just in case she stumbled across its lost partner someday, but that never happened. Now she's certain it never will.

But that doesn't mean she has to get rid of this one. There's nothing wrong with keeping it safely tucked away here with her other things, some more precious than others.

No, there's nothing wrong with finding a way to hold on, maybe just a little longer, even as you're learning to let go.

The traffic has subsided by the time Thom leaves the hospital in the wee hours of the morning. On-duty yellow cabs are plentiful along the avenue, but he decides to walk home through the warm night air.

He needs a chance to clear his head and decompress after the intense day he's endured.

Susan will be hospitalized for at least the immediate future; quite possibly for the remainder of her pregnancy. Touched by his sister's undaunted acceptance of her plight, Thom stayed at her side long after Mother and Wade went home to get some rest.

Only when a sleepy Susan insisted that Thom follow suit did he agree to leave her. But he promised to visit her first thing in the morning, before he heads to the office to update the board of directors on the official status of the Saltwater Treasures acquisition.

After that . . .

He'll be free.

Not forever, not yet . . . but at least for the remainder of the day.

Free to go back home and just *be*. He might sleep, or read a book, or . . .

Or drive out to Montauk for the first time in months.

Okay, where did that thought come from?

He wasn't planning to do that yet.

He's supposed to wait until everything has fallen into place. Until the Saltwater Treasures acquisition is completed, and he's stepped down from the board, and the Village brownstone is his, and he's had a chance to figure out exactly what he wants to say to Annie . . .

Timing, after all, is everything.

He's spent the summer telling himself that every day that passes is bringing him closer to Annie.

Now, having been reminded at the hospital just how precarious life can be, Thom finds himself wondering if instead, every day that passes might be taking him farther away from Annie.

What if she's forgotten him?

What if she's found somebody else?

What if she's sold the house and moved away?

Maybe he should just throw caution to the wind . . .

But if you get this wrong, you might not have another chance, Thom reminds himself, hurrying to cross Park Avenue before the light changes.

What should he do?

Take a risk, or play it safe?

Susan is taking a risk. If it works out, she'll have a baby in her arms in another few months.

If it doesn't . . .

No. Don't think of that.

Safely across the street, Thom continues toward home, telling himself that after a good night's sleep, he's sure to come to his senses and stick with his original plan.

Yes, that's exactly what he should do.

He takes a deep, calming breath . . . and frowns.

The warm air is fragrant with an intoxicating floral scent.

He glances around, half-expecting to find himself standing in front of an all-night Korean grocery, the kind that has buckets of fresh cellophane-wrapped blossoms outdoors.

He sees nothing but a row of apartment buildings, a deserted bus stop, a garbage can.

Not a flower in sight, and yet . . .

Again, he breathes in the distinct perfume, and then, all at once, realizes what it is.

Honeysuckle.

Honeysuckle is wafting all around him, potent and invisible, with no possible source.

You're delirious, he tells himself, hurriedly covering the last block toward his building.

So deliriously tired you're imagining things. You need to get some rest.

But the smell of honeysuckle seems to follow him all the way home, lingering in the air long after he's climbed into bed and fallen into a disappointingly dreamless sleep.

Chapter
20

Out on the screen porch the next afternoon, Annie is gluing the last seashell to the final heart-shaped paperweight when she hears gravel crunching in the driveway. From here, she can't see around to the front of the house, but it isn't hard to guess who the visitor might be.

Merlin, she thinks wearily, turning the shell a fraction of an inch and stepping back to survey its placement. He called this morning in a tizzy over the latest weather report, insisting that she and the kids immediately pack up their belongings and flee the coast.

"Isn't that a little premature?" Annie asked, outwardly amused, inwardly a bit alarmed. "The storm is still a few days away."

Indeed, the sun is shining brightly today and the sky is blue. Only the increasingly rough surf that brought die-hard surfers flocking to Montauk beaches this morning is any indication that a hurricane is brewing.

Now, as Annie puts down her glue gun and rubs her fingers together to remove the sticky residue, she hears a car door slam out front.

Why can't stubborn Merlin just take "no" for an answer? What is he planning to do, manhandle Annie and the children into his car?

Maybe you should just tell him the real reason you're so determined to stay home . . .

But Annie never confided in Merlin about the earlier phone calls. Does she really want to get into all of that now? Does she really want to hear Merlin remind her that she's always had a vivid imagination?

With a sigh, she leaves the screen porch and heads across the lawn to the front of the house.

She'd better waylay Merlin before he can go inside, where Milo and Trixie are watching cartoons, oblivious to the coming storm. All Annie needs is for the drama queen to scare them witless with his perilous weather forecast.

Barefoot, wary of the bumblebees buzzing from dandelion to dandelion in the grass, Annie picks her way past the weed-choked perennial beds along the foundation and the coil of green hose she's forbidden to use because of the drought.

At least hurricane rains will be a reprieve for the garden—and, with luck, from the oppressive dog days of August.

Yes, the storm might be a blessing in disguise.

She'll point out to Merlin that this solid old house has been standing on the coast for a century, has outlasted countless hurricanes and nor'easters, is on relatively high ground. That's what Andre always used to say, reassuringly, when she worried about an approaching gale.

There's no reason to think it won't make it through another storm.

Coming around the corner of the house, Annie stops short.

It isn't Merlin's car in the driveway . . .

And it isn't Merlin she sees striding purposefully up the front steps with a vast bouquet of roses in one hand and a shopping bag in the other.

Speechless, Annie stares at Thom Brannock.

What is he doing here, unannounced, uninvited?

Annie welcomes an immediate flicker of anger, rejects the disconcerting spark of attraction that arrives right along with it.

He has no right to show up out of the blue after months of not bothering with even a phone call.

Never mind that she *asked* him to stay away.

He shouldn't be here.

Ignoring the forbidden stirring deep inside of her, Annie fiercely reminds herself that she doesn't want to see him.

Certainly not now. Her hand flies up to her unkempt hair; her gaze down to her ancient cutoffs and bathing suit top.

No, she doesn't want to see him, not now, not tomorrow, not ever again.

She lifts her head to watch him cross the porch and come to a halt in front of the door. His chest rises sharply beneath his light blue linen shirt as he takes a deep breath. She notices the way his cheeks puff out as he exhales, eyes closed, almost as though he's trying to mentally prepare himself for whatever lies ahead.

In that instant, Annie glimpses an unexpected vulnerability in the man who's always seemed in utmost control.

He's afraid, she thinks, watching in wonder. *He's afraid that I'm going to reject him.*

Still unaware of her presence, Thom nods abruptly, apparently having reached some inner resolution.

Then, taking another deep breath, he lifts his hand to knock on the door.

"Wait!"

Startled by the shout behind him, Thom looks over his shoulder.

Annie.

Annie, sun-bronzed and beautiful, running barefoot through the grass, heedless of bumblebees, pebbles, thorns.

Running toward him, just the way she did in his dreams.

"What are you doing here?" she asks raggedly as he tosses the flowers and presents onto the porch swing and swiftly descends the steps to meet her.

"I had to see you." He welcomes her into his arms, rests his face against her hair.

"But why?" Her voice is muffled in his shoulder as he pulls her closer. "I told you . . ."

"I know what you told me. I know you needed time. And I gave you time, Annie."

"But that wasn't . . ." She pulls back to look up at him, shaking her head. "Nothing has changed, Thom."

She's lying.

He knows it.

He knows it because despite her words, she's wearing the same expression he glimpsed in her eyes that last night they were together. It was fleeting that night, there and then gone . . .

But not anymore.

She's gazing up at him as though she's been waiting for him.

"Everything has changed, Annie," he says gently. "Everything."

He leans toward her until his lips are mere inches from hers. He can hear her breath catch in her throat and then, as he leans closer, escape on a sigh to gently stir the air between them.

"Don't," she murmurs in the last split second before he captures her mouth with his own.

In stark contrast to her vocal protest, she hungrily welcomes his kiss, her hands immediately encircling his neck as she sinks into him.

Only when he realizes that her face is wet with tears does he lift his head abruptly in concern.

"Annie . . ." He brushes the backs of his hands against her cheeks, drying her tears. "I'm sorry."

"No . . . don't be sorry. I've wanted you to come back." A choking sob escapes her . . .

Or so he believes.

Then he sees her expression, her eyes alight with laughter.

"I'm so damned glad you didn't listen to me," she says, clinging to his shirt. "I'm so glad you didn't stay away forever."

"I couldn't. I never meant to." He kisses her mouth, her neck, her throat, feeling her quiver in his arms. "I was always coming back. I was waiting for the right time."

But is this the right time? He was supposed to wait. He

thought he needed more time, that *she* needed more time . . .

"I can't believe this is really happening," Annie says softly, and he banishes his misgivings to the back of his mind, to be dealt with later. Or never.

"It's really happening." He kisses her again.

"I wish we were alone together," she whispers hotly in his ear.

His body taut with desire, Thom pulls back and looks around at the deserted yard. "We *are* alone."

"In broad daylight," she says with a laugh, capturing his hand, swinging it in her own as she pulls him toward the house. "Come on, the kids are inside. They'll be so surprised to see you."

"I brought them presents."

"Oh, no, Thom—"

"Shh. Just small presents. And I brought you these." He hands her the roses. "I wanted it to be honeysuckle, but I couldn't find any. Do you know how hard it is to find blooming honeysuckle in Montauk on short notice?"

"In late August? Impossible?" she asks with a laugh, sniffing the armful of red blooms.

"Oh, I know a florist that has it back in the city, but I didn't have time to stop there. I just wanted to get out here, Annie. To see you. I didn't want to waste another second."

"I'm glad you didn't."

"So am I." He pulls her close again, crushing the roses between them.

It's happened so fast.

Too fast? Annie wonders, fighting a hint of uneasiness.

She turns to watch a beaming Thom, seated at the kitchen table with Trixie cuddled on his knee, applaud whole-heartedly as Milo demonstrates yet again that he can now tie his sneakers.

One minute she and the children were here alone; the next, Thom has slipped into their lives as easily as Milo's shoelaces now slip into a sturdy knot.

Annie turns back to the stove, where she's sautéing onions and peppers and tomatoes in olive oil, creating some kind of concoction to feed the hungry brood at the table.

Thom wanted to take them out to dinner, but Annie insisted on cooking. She isn't sure why she felt the need; it's been so long since she actually prepared a meal.

But it feels good. It feels right. All of it.

Listening to Trixie telling Thom how excited she is to be starting kindergarten next week, Annie reaches past the stack of unpaid bills on the countertop, reminding herself that she has to get to them tomorrow. She grabs the salt and pepper shakers and liberally sprinkles some of each into the pan, then tosses in some fresh oregano sprigs she picked earlier from the overgrown herb garden.

A little of this, a little of that. It's how she always cooked, back when Andre was alive.

Sometimes, her improvised recipes turn out brilliantly, sometimes, disastrously.

You just never know until you taste it.

Annie lifts the wooden spoon to her lips and nibbles a bit of tomato and translucent onion.

"Well? How is it?"

She turns to see Thom watching her, wearing an infatuated expression that sends delicious shivers to her core.

Annie smiles and nods. "I think it's going to be good."

Sitting on the porch swing with Annie nestled into his side, Thom feels as though he's come home at last.

It's amazing how easily things have fallen into place today. He never expected it . . . not really. All the way out here, he told himself that he'd better be prepared for rejection.

Now here he is, with Annie in his arms, just the way he dreamed she would one day be. He's told her all about the house he bought, and the seafood company he's going to oversee.

He hasn't come right out and said it, but she must know that he's done it all for her, that she's going to be a part of his life from now on.

There will be plenty of time for promises. Plenty of time for everything.

But he can't help wondering if maybe, he should have waited, the way he planned.

"What are you thinking about?" Annie asks, lifting her head from his shoulder to look at him in the flickering light of the citronella candle.

"I'm thinking that I'm getting awfully sleepy," he lies, telling himself that it's time to stop worrying, that he did the right thing, coming out here impulsively.

She smiles. "I'm sleepy, too."

"It's a long drive back to Manhattan."

"Especially when you're sleepy."

"Yes," he agrees, with an exaggerated yawn. "I guess I'd better get started."

"I guess," Annie agrees. Then, thoughtfully, she says, "Or . . ."

"Or?"

"Or you could stay."

"Do you have to go?" Annie asks, lifting her head reluctantly from Thom's bare chest, feeling him shift his weight beneath her. "Can't you at least stay until morning?"

"It *is* morning," he says softly, stroking her hair.

Annie shifts her gaze to the bedroom window, where the sky beyond the whirling box fan is bluish-gray with the promise of dawn.

"But you can't go yet. We have a lot to talk about," she tells him, burrowing closer to him beneath the thin sheet that covers them. "You have to tell me more about your new townhouse, and your new company."

"And you have to tell me more about your cookies and your seashell sculptures."

She laughs at the ridiculous juxtaposition of her baking and artwork with his multimillion-dollar real estate and multibillion-dollar business deal.

"There's nothing to tell, other than that my stuff is suddenly selling," she says, and presses a kiss against his bare chest, marveling at how natural it feels to wake up in his arms, here in her bed.

"That's because you're an incredibly talented woman," Thom informs her, and the compliment fills her with pride.

It's too good to be true, she can't help thinking again. All of it. Him being here, her art and cookies selling, his plan to move into a real house and take a less demanding corporate position . . .

She can't help feeling as though the effervescent bubble of happily-ever-after is in danger of bursting at any moment.

It's just because of all you've been through, she reminds herself. *But look how far you've come. Look what you've accomplished on your own.*

She really is a survivor.

Of course she's going to feel a little insecure for a while. But it will wear off. She just has to trust Thom, and believe in him.

"I want to hear about your renovation," she tells him. "Are you really going to take time off from work and do the whole thing yourself?"

"Well, maybe not all of it," he admits. "I was thinking that I'll definitely need some help with the decorating."

"You're going to hire a decorator?"

"No. I thought that since you have such an artistic flair, you might want to help me pick out some paint colors and furniture."

"Me?"

"Sure. I want the place to look homey, like this place."

Annie chuckles. "In that case, I'm sure Milo and Trixie will be glad to come over any time and throw some toys and crumbs around."

They laugh, and kiss, and cuddle until Thom reluctantly rolls away from her to lean up and check the bedside clock.

"I really have to go," he says with a groan. "I've got to be back in Manhattan by eight for a meeting."

"But that's hours away," Annie protests, sitting up to

embrace him from behind. She wraps her arms around his chest and presses her naked breasts against his back, kissing his neck.

"It's going to take me hours to get there in rush hour," he says, then moans softly as she nuzzles his shoulder.

"Come on . . . can't you reschedule the meeting for a little later?"

He shakes his head, then shudders as she allows her fingers to dance lightly down his chest. "No, I can't reschedule. Cut that out, Annie! Do you know what you're doing to me?"

"Yup."

With a groan, he turns toward her and takes her into his arms again, flipping her gently onto her back. "Maybe I can call Mavourneen and have her reschedule the meeting for eight thirty."

And just like that, the bubble bursts . . .

Just as Annie knew it would.

"Mavourneen?"

"Mmm. My secretary." Thom's stubbly cheek grazes her shoulder as he kisses the nape of her neck.

Mavourneen.

Annie bites her lip, her thoughts racing. Maybe she's jumping to conclusions. Maybe she's being ridiculous. Maybe it's her wayward imagination leading her astray once again.

Thom's mouth travels upward to devour hers, but only for a moment.

"What's wrong?" he asks, lifting his head as he senses that she's no longer receptive.

She has to ask. She has to.

"What kind of name is Mavourneen?"

"Irish." He looks puzzled. "Why?"

"I thought so."

Annie rolls away from him abruptly, taking the tangled sheet with her.

"Annie, what's wrong?"

She shakes her head, fumbling with the sheet in her trembling hands, attempting to wrap it around her naked body to shield herself from him.

"I can't believe I didn't figure it out before," she whispers, mostly to herself.

"Figure what out? What are you talking about?"

"It was you. You bought my shell sculptures in Sag Harbor, didn't you!"

He's silent.

It's just as well. She doesn't need an answer.

She knows. "You're the one who's behind all this so-called success I've had. The sculptures, and the cookies . . . What are you doing, paying your rich friends to order stuff so that the poor widow can support her two fatherless children?"

"No, Annie, it isn't like that. I didn't have anything to do with the cookies. I swear."

"I don't believe you. Devonne Cambridge told me that an Irish woman bought all my sculptures and ordered more."

"All right yes, I had Mavourneen go out and buy the shell sculptures. We sent them to the board members and shareholders at Saltwater Treasures after they accepted our preliminary offer. It was a business transaction, Annie. Corporate gifts that happened to be more suitable than anything else I could have bought. I didn't do it out of pity."

Yes, he did.

He manipulated her, thinking she'd never figure it out.

He likes a challenge. He said it himself, back in the beginning. If he wants something he can't have, he goes after it.

She's nothing more to him than one of the billion-dollar companies he so determinedly acquires.

"Annie, please listen to me. I didn't do half of what you think I did. You did it all yourself."

"So you're saying that you had nothing to do with the other orders that have been pouring in for my sculptures?"

He hesitates.

Damn him. Damn him, for thinking he can control her destiny without her ever finding out.

"Maybe I pulled a few strings in the beginning. Maybe I told a few people about them. But I never—"

"Pulled a few strings? You're a goddamned puppeteer, Thom," she hurls on a gut-wrenching sob. "Get out of here."

"Annie—"

"Don't touch me. Get away from me. I can take care of myself."

"I never doubted that. I just wanted to help you."

"I don't need your help. I don't need you. Just go."

"Please don't do this, Annie."

"Go!"

After a moment, she hears the bed creak behind her, feels his weight lifting off the mattress.

She doesn't turn around to see him swiftly pull on the clothes he discarded in the heat of passion mere hours ago, doesn't utter a word of farewell as his footsteps approach the door, then linger.

"You're wrong about me," he says softly. "Yes, I wanted to help you. But I only did it because I'm in love with you, Annie. You and the kids. I love you."

She stiffens.

He *loves* her?

Her and the kids?

She shakes her head, tears streaming down her cheeks.

Tell him, a voice screams inside of her head. *Tell him that you love him, too. Before it's too late! Tell him!*

But she isn't sure. Is she?

Does she really love him?

Is she capable of loving a man who isn't Andre?

"I'm sorry," he whispers.

Tell him, Annie! At least tell him you forgive him!

She opens her mouth.

But he's already going, moving swiftly down the hall, his footsteps pounding down the steps.

Stop him! Before he leaves! Hurry, Annie!

"Thom!" she calls, leaping from the bed, hurrying to the top of the stairs, just in time to watch the screen door close behind him.

She didn't even hear it open.

WD-40.

Outside, his car engine turns over.

Standing in the doorway, wrapped in a sheet, Annie watches him drive away.

Part Four

September

Chapter
21

"Mommy! I'm afraid!"

"It's okay, Trixie," Annie calls, raising her voice above the incessant wind and driving rain. "Get back into the house."

"But I'm scared! The lights keep flickering!"

"I'll be right there. Go!"

Standing in the back porch, Annie watches her daughter scamper back into the kitchen, then gazes again at the view beyond the screens.

The hurricane made landfall early this morning, bringing with it the disarming marine scent of displaced tropical moisture. The sky hangs low beyond sheets of driving rain and violently swaying branches, an ominous shade of charcoal better suited to December twilight than a September Saturday afternoon.

Annie clutches the cordless telephone in the shelter of her open jacket to protect it from the rain that splashes through the screens like buckets of water bailed from a sinking boat.

Just one quick call.

That's all she needs. Just one quick call, just to hear his voice, and then she'll return to huddle with her frightened children until the storm is over.

She says a quick prayer and begins dialing with a trembling finger.

The phone rings once . . . twice . . .

And then the receiver goes dead.

"Mommy!" Milo screams through the window.

"Mommy! The lights went out!"

"It's okay." Annie tosses the useless telephone aside and hurries back inside to her children. "It's just a power failure because of the storm. Mommy's here. Everything's going to be okay."

Standing in the one southern-facing window of his seaside home that isn't covered by plywood, at his insistence, Thom gazes at the towering green-black waves on the Atlantic and worries about Annie.

Did she and the children escape to a shelter before the storm hit?

It's one thing for Thom to remain here in his stone fortress against the advice of the local authorities who came knocking early this morning.

It's quite another for Annie and the children to ride out the storm alone in their little house by the water.

No, the coastal evacuation isn't mandatory. But the authorities at Thom's door warned him in no uncertain terms that it would be risky to stay where he was.

"Don't worry about me, gentlemen," he said calmly. "I've taken successful risks all of my life. In fact, it's what I do for a living."

"Yeah, well, you don't know what you're up against

this time, Mr. Brannock. I'd hate to see your luck run out now."

Thom didn't bother to tell the man that it already has.

"Sing the 'Hakuna Matata' song again, Mommy," Trixie begs, seated on Annie's lap on the couch.

"Again?"

"Please? I'm afraid."

"It's going to be okay, Trixie. I promise." Annie flashes a reassuring smile at her daughter, followed by a worried sidelong glance at the windows overlooking the porch.

Maybe she should have covered them with plywood, the way Andre would have.

Maybe she should have brought the children to Merlin's last night, the way he begged her to when he called.

Maybe she should have done a lot of things differently.

"'Hakuna Matata,'" Trixie urges again, in the plaintive little-girl tone she adapts whenever she's feeling vulnerable.

It's all Annie can do to keep the tremor out of her own voice when she asks, "How about something else this time, sweetie?"

"But 'Hakuna Matata' makes me feel like I'm not worried about the storm."

"I have a better idea. Let's go eat all the sweet stuff in the freezer before it melts."

"Like ice cream?" Trixie asks hopefully.

"Ice cream, Popsicles, that frozen chocolate cake you guys made me buy—"

She breaks off as a savage gust of wind violently shakes the house.

"Is the storm almost over, Mom?" Milo asks, frightened, leaning against Annie's side.

"Almost," she lies.

Outside, there's a thunderous snap and boom as yet another tree limb breaks off and crashes to the ground.

The children cower against her, whimpering.

"Mommy, I don't like this."

"It's going to be okay, Trixie."

"When is Thom coming back?" Milo asks abruptly.

Thom. She knew that topic was bound to come up again sooner or later.

She told the children when they woke up yesterday morning that he'd gone back to the city. Naturally, they wanted to know if he'd be back that evening, and if not then, when? Annie managed to sidestep their questions for the remainder of the day, distracting them with storm preparations like assembling candles, matches, and flashlights on the kitchen counter, putting away the outdoor furniture, filling the sinks and tub with water.

"Why do you want Thom to come back?" Annie asks her son now, pulling him closer against her side as the wind howls around the house.

"Because he's going to be our new dad."

Annie's heart sinks. "Who told you that? Trixie?"

"No. Daddy did."

Speechless, Annie stares at her son.

"He told me that, too," Trixie tells her brother matter-of-factly. "When did he tell you, Milo?"

"One night. In my room. I thought I dreamed him, but he came back again."

"Mommy thought I dreamed him, too. See, Mommy? I told you he was really there," Trixie tells Annie.

Her brain a maelstrom of questions, she settles at last on the least provocative one. "Milo, is that why you've been leaving your light on? Because you're afraid . . . of ghosts?"

"No! There aren't any ghosts. Just Daddy. I'm not afraid of him. I leave the light on so he can find his way down here from heaven. You know . . . like the airport lights up the runway at night so the planes can see where to land."

"Oh, Milo . . ." Annie holds him close. "Why didn't you tell me?"

"Because I didn't think you'd believe me. You didn't believe Trixie."

Bewildered, Annie looks from her son to her daughter, and again at the lifeless telephone across the room.

If only there were a way to reach Andre herself, right now . . .

If only she had another phone, she thinks, remembering that cell phones worked during the blackout a few summers ago, when cordless phones failed. A cell phone, or some other way to—

Annie gasps.

"What, Mommy? What happened?" Trixie squirms as Annie sets her abruptly on her feet and rises from the couch.

"Come with me." She hurriedly grabs a flashlight off the coffee table. "Both of you."

"Where are we going?"

"To the basement," Annie says, herding them toward the kitchen.

"Because of the storm?" Trixie asks. "Like in *The Wizard of Oz*?"

"This isn't a cyclone," Milo scoffs. "It's a hurricane."

"Then how come Mommy's making us go to the basement?"

Annie opens the door and shines the flashlight's beam into the inky depths below.

"Because," she tells her children. "I just remembered something that's down there, and we have to get it right away."

"A boat, so we can paddle away?" Milo asks hopefully.

Annie doesn't answer, just helps her children down the creaky stairs, desperately hoping she'll find what she's looking for.

Why, Thom wonders, staring into the flickering candelabra on the dining room table, didn't he cast aside his foolish pride and drive all the way out to Montauk last night, instead of ending his journey here in Southampton?

It certainly wouldn't have taken him very long. For the first time ever on the Friday before Labor Day, his was practically the lone car on the road leading east from Manhattan. Meanwhile, the westbound Long Island Expressway was clogged from the Hamptons to Queens with islanders fleeing the coming storm.

Thom isn't sure what compelled him to come back out east on a weekend he planned all along to spend in the city. It wasn't as though he had any intention of trying to win Annie back. It's pretty obvious now that his chances of doing that are more dismal than the weekend weather forecast.

Maybe he just wanted to be near her. Just in case the

storm was as fierce as they were predicting. Just in case she needed to be rescued.

He shakes his head, knowing that he's the last person Annie would turn to for help after the scene in her bedroom yesterday morning. If there's anything Annie Harlowe doesn't want, it's to be rescued.

But what about the children? What if they're frightened? What if one of them is sick, or injured?

The coastal roads must be flooded by now. Surely there's no way he can make it out there in this deluge, even if he could think of a good enough reason to try it.

Thom paces back through the shadows to the lone unboarded window facing the water. Looking out over the debris-strewn lawn to the sea, he wonders if the waves can possibly be less ferocious than they were earlier.

That doesn't make sense. The last report he heard before he lost power was that the hurricane's peak intensity is supposed to last at least through tonight.

Still . . .

Is it his imagination, or is the storm subsiding a bit?

Checking his watch, Thom sees that it's barely four o'clock. It can't be over.

No, he thinks, suddenly remembering something, it isn't over.

But this is the eye of the storm . . .

And maybe it's an opportunity to start the journey eastward before the going gets rough all over again.

That is, if he's actually going to go.

Annie. The children. Alone.

What are you, a glutton for punishment? he asks himself, but he doesn't answer his own question, already striding to the door.

*   *   *

"Are you going to call for help if it works, Mommy?" Trixie asks, as Annie drags the cord of the old green wall phone toward the outlet she knows is somewhere on the baseboard beneath the kitchen table.

"I bet you're going to call the Coast Guard," Milo says, holding the flashlight beam steadily above her, just as she instructed.

"Or Thom," Trixie suggests. "You're going to call Thom, right, Mommy?"

Annie stops fumbling for the outlet to ask, "Why would I call him?"

"Because he can come out here in his sailboat and save us."

"That's dumb," Milo says, before Annie can respond. "Sailboats can't go through a hurricane. He'll bring a speedboat."

"He won't bring any boat," Annie tells them tersely, "because he isn't coming."

"Why not, Mommy?"

"Because we don't need to be saved. We're perfectly fine."

She flinches as another tree goes down somewhere outside, reverberating like a gunshot.

"I'm scared," Trixie whimpers. "I need to be saved."

"Don't worry. Mommy will save us," Milo tells her in a reassuring tone that chokes Annie's throat with emotion.

At last, her fingers find the telephone outlet and she pushes the plastic end of the cord into the socket, feeling it click into place.

Then she crawls out from under the table and reaches for the receiver.

"That's a funny looking phone." Trixie twirls the curly green coil around her finger.

Holding her breath, Annie lifts the receiver . . .

And hears a dial tone.

"Sorry to say, but you won't get much farther than a quarter of a mile farther east if you keep going," a slicker-clad, white-mustached local informs Thom, leaning out the window of his westbound pickup truck as he pulls up adjacent to Thom's driver's side window.

"Is the road under water?"

"More than likely, in some low spots. But there's a big tree down across the road right down there, and no way around it."

"I'll get out and walk, then, when I get to it."

"Can't do that. There are live wires all over the place. You'll get yourself electrocuted. You'd better turn around, mister, unless you have a death wish."

"Thanks for the advice, but I think I'll take my chances."

Thom rolls up the window on the yokel's comment about foolhardy city people.

He drives on down the wet road, keeping an eye out for the tree the guy mentioned.

Half a mile has gone by, and then a whole mile, then two, and he still hasn't seen it.

There are branches and trees down all over the place along the sides of the road, and twice he has to maneuver onto the shoulder to avoid hydroplaning through a low spot.

But so far, so good.

Maybe the old guy was lying about the tree, Thom thinks. Or maybe he just imagined it.

Yes, just as Thom is surely imagining that the closer he gets to Montauk, the stronger the scent of honeysuckle seems to permeate the car's interior.

Annie clenches the heavy, old-fashioned telephone receiver tightly against her ear as it rings once . . . twice . . . three times.

Then there's a click, and a high-pitched, three-chord tone, and a voice comes on the line.

A recorded voice.

One that isn't Andre's.

"I'm sorry, the number you have reached has been disconnected. Please check the number and try again."

"What's wrong, Mommy?"

"I dialed it wrong," she tells Trixie, who's lapping ice cream straight from the container on the table between her and Milo.

"Who? The Coast Guard?" Milo asks hopefully, digging his spoon into the carton.

"No, the friend I was trying to reach," Annie says briefly, painstakingly starting to dial again, thinking that it's no wonder she made a mistake. She's used to punching numbers on a touchtone pad, not dragging a plodding rotary dial around.

"Thom?" Trixie asks.

"Hmm?"

"Is Thom the friend you're trying to reach, Mommy?"

"No." Annie sighs, wishing she could snap her fingers and banish the memory of him from all their lives.

"Erika?" Trixie asks.

"No." Annie stretches the cord as far as it will go, dragging the receiver around the corner into the dining room as the line begins to ring again.

"I'm sorry, the number you have reached has been disconnected. Please check the number and try again."

What the—?

Annie dials again, more slowly this time.

The same thing happens.

She dials again.

It happens again.

And then it hits her.

With a cry of dismay, she shifts her gaze back to the kitchen, and the stack of unpaid bills on the counter . . . among them, the long overdue one for Andre's cell phone.

"Nobody's allowed to drive any farther east because of the storm surge," an orange-coated, hooded police officer informs Thom at a roadblock on Sunrise Highway in Montauk. "The tide is coming in and the eye is almost past us."

"But I have to get out there," Thom protests, oblivious to the rain blowing through his open driver's side window.

"Sorry, you'll have to wait until after the storm."

"But I have to get out there," he repeats stoically.

"You live out that way?"

"No."

"Then what? You have a death wish or something?"

"No, I—"

"Look, you go out there, you're taking your life in your hands."

"That's my business, right?"

"Not on my watch, it isn't."

"Look, I was told farther back that I wouldn't get this far because there was a tree down across the road, and there wasn't."

"There are trees down all over the place."

"But there wasn't one across the road."

"Yeah, well, maybe somebody moved it out of the way. All I know is that you're not going any farther from here on out."

"But—"

"Listen, buddy, you need to go back," the cop says tersely. His face is obscured by the shroud of orange hood, but his tone conveys that there's no room for further debate. "Get home before the storm kicks up again."

Thom sighs. There's nothing for him to do but roll up his window and make a U-turn.

He drives west again, watching until the cop turns away. Then he pulls into a deserted parking lot adjacent to the local supermarket and turns off the car.

He can't leave Annie and the kids all alone out there in the storm. There's nothing to do but go the rest of the way on foot, staying away from the main road so the cop won't spot him.

He steps out, locks the car, and turns toward the dunes, wincing as the wind-driven sand and rain pelt him painfully.

It'll be rough going, no doubt about that.

For all he knows, he'll reach Annie only to have her take one look at him and send him right back out into the gale.

But maybe she'll tell you that you can stay, just as she did the other night . . .

Oh, who are you kidding? She told you to get out. She thinks you betrayed her.

Dammit. He gave it everything he had; he took the risk of a lifetime telling her that he loves her and he failed.

Yet here he is, a pathetic, rain-drenched, mud-caked fool.

Look at you. What the hell are you doing?

He's being a superhero, that's what he's doing. Trying to save Annie and the children from the big, bad storm.

Yeah, well, maybe they don't need to be saved.

Maybe they're not even there. Maybe Annie evacuated the children before the storm hit, the way anyone with common sense would do.

"Hey!"

It's the orange-coated cop. He seems to have materialized out of nowhere.

"What the hell are you still doing out here?"

I was wondering the same thing, Thom thinks ruefully. So much for being a hero.

He slowly makes his way toward the policeman, shoulders stooped against the wind.

"Listen, I was just trying to get out there to check on a friend," he tells the officer above the howling storm. "Her name is Harlowe, and she lives alone with two small kids."

"Harlowe? Annie?" Only the policeman's eyes are visible in the gap of his orange hood. They flash with recognition.

"You know her?" Thom asks incredulously, even as he

wonders where he's seen this guy before. His eyes look familiar. Or maybe it's just the expression in them.

"Yeah, I know Annie."

Thom detects a fond note in the guy's voice. Well, what does he expect? To know Annie is to love her. Still, he can't help feeling a spark of jealousy as he asks, "Are you a friend of hers?"

"You could say that. I, uh, knew her husband really well."

"Oh." Thom squints into the stinging rain, deciding he's never seen the guy before, after all. It's just that all cops look alike. Must be the authority thing.

"Listen," he says impatiently, "if you won't let me go out to check on Annie, can you at least have somebody go make sure she's okay?"

"She's okay," the officer says with odd certainty.

"How do you know?"

"One of our guys was out that way just now, and she's fine."

"So she didn't evacuate?"

"Listen, don't worry. That old house of hers is solid. It's on relatively high ground, and it's been standing on the coast for over a century. It's outlasted countless hurricanes and nor'easters."

"I know, but . . ."

"All right, look, I'll check back in with Annie just to be sure."

"You will?"

"Yeah, yeah."

"Are you sure?"

"Yeah, I promise. Now go. It isn't safe for you to be out roaming around in this weather."

Head bowed against the driving gale, Thom retraces his steps toward the car, trying to remember where he might have seen the man before. He seemed familiar.

Maybe he does security for Hamptons parties. A lot of the island cops do.

But he doesn't think that's it. No, it's something else . . .

The nagging curiosity vanishes the moment he's safely inside the car, the door closed to shut out the storm.

He inhales deeply . . . and once again smells the familiar scent of honeysuckle.

Why has the scent of honeysuckle followed him everywhere lately . . . even all the way out here in a storm?

And why, after the old timer's dire warning, did he fail to see a single tree or live wire down across the road?

Thom turns back in the direction toward Annie's house, tempted, torn.

What if those miraculous little events—the smell of honeysuckle, the accessible road—were signs? Signs that he and Annie are meant to be together?

Or maybe, he tells himself glumly, bending his head into the wind, *they were mere figments of your imagination. The old man, the scent of flowers . . . Maybe you want Annie so badly your mind has been playing tricks on you, trying to convince you that it's meant to be.*

And if that's the case—if it's meant to be—then it's going to take another miracle to bring her back to him, because Thom is through taking risks.

*   *   *

The children have fallen asleep at last, despite the hurricane's incessant roar. Seated on the couch with their heads in her lap, Annie strokes their hair and wonders if they're dreaming about their daddy.

Of course those nocturnal visits they both described were merely dreams, Annie tells herself firmly. Milo and Trixie adored their father, yet grew attached to Thom in the short time he was in their lives. It would only be natural that they would fantasize about him becoming their new daddy . . . and that they would feel as though they'd need Andre's approval.

Annie sighs, so filled with longing that she physically aches.

Not for Andre . . .

But for Thom.

Yes, she still misses her husband. She'll always miss him. She'll always wonder what he might have said if he could speak to her again.

But that won't happen now. It can't.

According to the cellular service provider she managed to contact, the account has irrevocably been closed, her connection to Andre's voice permanently severed.

If only . . .

No.

Even if she had been able to reach her husband one last time, she would never have asked him to release her from her vow.

A promise is a promise.

Yet she's filled with regret.

Regret that she'll never know what Andre was so desperately trying to tell her . . .

And that she'll never be free to love Thom Brannock.

Chapter
22

Annie awakens early Monday to sunlight streaming over her bed and the sound of birds chirping merrily outside her closed bedroom window.

Sitting up, she leans over to see that the weekend's deluge has given way to a glistening September morning. Not only that, but as she opens the window and shivers in the cooling breeze, she realizes that summer has given way to a hint of autumn in the air.

She quickly pulls on her clothes and goes downstairs, where she finds Milo and Trixie already dressed and eating dry cereal.

"The TV still doesn't work," Milo informs her gloomily, looking up from a comic book he's read a hundred times.

"And the milk tastes funny so we poured it out."

Annie sighs, knowing she'll need to go through a refrigerator's worth of spoiled food later.

But for now, she wants to go outside to assess the damage.

"Come on," she tells the children, "get your shoes. Let's go for a walk and see what happened in the storm."

Back in the city, Thom decides to visit Susan before he heads over to the office to address the piles of paperwork and e-mail that has accumulated after a weekend spent on Long Island without power.

He heads for the hospital on foot, trying to enjoy the refreshing breeze and the dappled sunlight on his shoulders.

But it's difficult to find pleasure in anything when all you can think about is the fact that you ruined your last chance for happiness.

Why didn't he stick with his original plan?

Why did he have to go barreling out to Long Island last week before he was ready?

At least he steered clear of her on Saturday night, after going through hell and, quite literally, high water, to ensure her safety.

At least he had the sense by then to leave well enough alone.

What's done is done.

Now the only thing you can do is move on and forget her, he tells himself, strolling through his familiar neighborhood toward the hospital.

Focus on your work, and the renovation.

And Susan and the baby.

Maybe he'll stop and pick up the morning papers and some magazines to bring his sister, he thinks, passing a news kiosk. Yes, and perhaps some flowers.

His step quickens as he turns the corner, knowing just where he'll buy them.

*   *   *

"Mommy! The beach!" Milo calls in dismay, skidding to a halt on the branch-strewn path in front of her. "It's almost gone."

"And the trees! Look, Mommy!" Trixie shrieks, pointing at the copper beeches that lie in a tangle of broken boughs.

Annie's stomach turns over.

The trees.

The *tree*.

Their tree, hers and Andre's, the one where he carved their initials on the day he proposed, toppled over in the storm.

She makes her way slowly toward it, feeling almost as though she's staring at the wreckage of a ship washed up on the shore. Splintered wood is everywhere, and rain-trampled, sodden boughs, and the roots that lie in a vertical wall of dirt before a gaping hole.

"No," Annie whispers, kneeling beside the trunk, running her hand along the bark in a fruitless search for the initials.

Over by the base of the fallen tree, Milo lets out a sudden whoop.

"Mom! Come quick! Look!"

Annie glances up, her tear-clouded gaze settling on her son, who is crouched over the hole left where the tree was uprooted.

"Just a second, Milo," she says, needing a moment to regain her composure.

First the cell phone, and now this.

She's lost everything. Every tangible link to her husband. Everything but the children . . .

"But Mom!" Milo calls. "You've got to see this!"

And one day, she'll lose the children, too. They'll grow up and move away and she'll be left here alone.

"What is it?" Trixie comes up beside Milo, and peers over his shoulder into the hole.

"Mommy!" she screams, as only Trixie can. "It's the treasure!"

Annie sighs, stands, picks her way among the fallen limbs to where her children are. She wonders what it will be this time. Another old tire rim? A rusted bike frame? A rock?

Coming to a stop between Milo and Trixie, Annie leans forward, toward the earthen crater . . .

And finds herself gazing at the top of an ancient wooden sea chest.

Stunned, Thom checks the street sign once again, just to make sure he's on the right corner.

This is it, all right.

But there's no florist shop here.

There's nothing but a towering office high-rise and a local bank branch with a lobby ATM he's used countless times in the past.

Frowning, he looks around and spots a familiar street vendor standing nearby, behind a pushcart from which Thom has bought many cups of coffee and morning bagels.

"Excuse me," he says, striding toward the cart.

"Yes? You like coffee today, sir?" the vendor asks, smiling in polite recognition.

"No coffee," Thom says briskly. "I'm just looking for a florist shop. I thought there was one over on that corner?"

"Florist shop? No, no florist shop. Just the bank."

"Are you positive?"

The man nods. "You like coffee?"

"No thanks," Thom says slowly, walking away. "Not today."

He reminds himself that the man could be mistaken. That this is Manhattan. Businesses come and go overnight.

Still . . .

There's not a hint that a florist shop ever existed on this corner.

Yet . . .

Inhaling deeply, Thom is positive that the breeze that stirs the morning air smells faintly of honeysuckle.

With a groan, Annie hauls the sea chest out of the wheelbarrow and plunks it onto the grass in the shade of the honeysuckle hedge at the back of the property.

"Aren't we going to bring it into the house to open it, Mom?" Milo asks, hovering anxiously over their find.

"I don't think I can move it another inch, sweetie," Annie says, collapsing on the ground, panting, mindless of the mud.

"What do you think is in there?" Milo asks, as Trixie does an excited little dance around the chest.

"Treasure!" his sister exclaims. "What else would be in a treasure chest?"

Milo rolls his eyes with the air of a big brother who has little patience for kindergarten logic. "Can we open it, Mom?"

"As soon as I get Daddy's tools from the basement." Annie hoists her weary self to her feet once again and heads for the house.

"Hurry, Mom!" Milo shouts after her.

"I will," she promises, wondering why she isn't as eager as her children are to see what lies inside the chest Andre sought for a lifetime.

Then it hits her.

No matter what it is . . .

Gold doubloons, or a fortune in jewels, or valuable stock worth millions . . .

It won't bring Andre back to her.

All the money in the world can't buy the kind of happiness they shared, once upon a time.

Happiness.

Life is too short not to grab every opportunity you get, Thom told her a few months ago, back in his bland apartment in the city.

Every opportunity . . .

For happiness.

For love.

Annie sighs, reaching for the basement door, remembering how zealously she descended the stairs on Saturday, certain that the telephone Andre saved all those years would allow her to make one last connection.

It wasn't meant to be . . .

But she found the treasure anyway.

Was that the message he was trying to tell her? That it was buried beneath the copper beech tree?

Searching among her dead husband's tools for a crowbar and a hammer, Annie can't help feeling as though there might have been something more.

Something . . .

About Thom?

Annie shakes her head.

She wants to believe that . . .

She really does . . .

As much as she wants to believe that Thom loves her.

"I did a stupid thing."

"You told Mother that we were the ones who dug that hole in her rose garden trying to get to China?"

Thom blinks at his sister. "Huh? Are you feeling all right? That was twenty years ago!"

Susan shrugs. "I have a lot of time to lie here and think. I keep remembering things, okay?"

Well, it's about time. He wonders if she remembered that she used to like sailing and snowball fights.

"So you better not ever tell her about the rose garden, got it? She still thinks Maimie Wilshire's poodle snuck onto our property to bury a bone."

"Hey, I'll never tell. We made a pact, remember?" Thom says with a grin.

"Sealed with spit and blood. You don't get much more official than that. So what's the stupid thing that you did?"

"Do you remember that woman I was seeing after I broke up with Joyce? Her name was Annie?"

"Divorced, three kids?"

"Widowed, two kids."

"Waitress/artist?"

"That's her."

"I remember."

He wonders if Susan's lack of a disapproving expression is due to her lack of mobile facial muscles or the fact that she's come to terms with the fact that her brother is a nonconformist.

"I fell in love with her, Susan."

She nods solemnly. "You're right. That is stupid."

With a wry smile, he says, "That's not the stupid part."

"That depends on how you look at it." Susan shakes her head. "What's the stupid part, according to how *you* look at it?"

He wonders where to begin. "Got an hour?"

She gestures at the row of monitors keeping their short-leashed vigil at her bedside. "Trust me. I've got nothing but time."

"Okay, the thing is, I know you and Mother both think that I fell for her because she's so wrong and I knew everyone would disapprove, and the truth is, maybe I did do that, a little, in the beginning . . . but I'm in love with her, Susan. Really."

"Love and infatuation can feel like the same thing, Tommy."

"This isn't infatuation. And please don't interrupt, okay? Just listen."

She throws up an apologetic hand, the one that isn't attached to the IV tube. "Sorry. I promise, I'm all ears."

"Is that all there is?" Milo asks in dismay, staring at the musty contents of the old trunk, spread carefully on the grass in the sunshine. "Just stupid old clothes?"

Old clothes is right, Annie thinks, setting aside the last pair of woolen breeches, the fragile fabric rotting wherever she touches it.

Yes, just old clothes that belonged to some hapless sailor, and not much of a wardrobe, at that.

Breeches, socks, undergarments . . .

Talk about anticlimactic.

"Yes," Annie tells a scowling Milo, "it looks like that's all there is."

"Are you sure?" Trixie asks, leaning into the chest. "Just check it one more time."

Annie obliges, peering into the mildew-scented depths. "I'm positive, there's nothing else in—"

Oh, yes there is.

Reaching into the trunk, she pulls it out.

"What is it? Doubloons?" Milo asks excitedly.

"Papers," Annie tells him, carefully removing the fragile, ribbon-tied sheaf.

"Maybe it's a map!" he exclaims, reaching.

"Careful, don't touch. The edges are crumbling." Annie skims the spidery handwriting. "It looks like letters."

"ABCs?" asks Trixie, the imminent kindergartner.

"No, love letters," Annie murmurs, reading the first few lines. "I think they're from the sailor to his wife back in England."

"Love letters!" Milo wrinkles his nose.

"That is the stinkiest treasure anybody ever found," Trixie grumbles, trudging off toward the house in disgust, her brother at her heels.

"So now I can't live without her," Thom tells Susan, staring desolately out the window at the uninspiring view of the hospital air shaft. "And even if I move, like I planned, and step down from the board, and start traveling around the world climbing mountains and doing all the things I always said I was going to do . . . None of it will be worthwhile."

Susan remains silent, all ears, just as she promised.

"I want her back," he says desperately. "Hell, I never even had her. I just want her, period. But how am I supposed to compete with a ghost? The only way I stand a chance with her is if her dead husband floats back down to earth and tells her that it's okay to fall in love again. And that's about as likely to happen as Mother is to . . . to marry some Academy-Award–winning actor."

Susan doesn't reply.

Thom winces. "Sorry. I didn't mean that as a dig, I swear. Susan? Sue?"

The room is no longer silent.

He turns around . . . and sees his big sister sound asleep, hands clasped on her rounded belly, mouth wide open, snoring like a trucker.

Annie watches the children disappear into the house, then turns back to the brittle stack of letters in her hand. The first is dated "Twenty-first of April, 1822."

My dearest bride,
Another day has come and gone on the storm-tossed sea
that carries me farther still from my beloved
Annabelle . . .

Annabelle.

Annie smiles. The name is so charming and old-fashioned, far more appealing than plain old *Annie*.

She reads on, carefully turning the painstakingly penned pages, caught up in the sailor's vivid account of shipboard rigors, the promise of making his fortune in

America. He frequently mentions returning home to start the family they'd always dreamed of.

Lying in my bunk last night, I could scarcely sleep for the violent swaying and the overwhelming fear that I might die before e'er I see the winsome face of my beloved Annie.

Annie?
With a startled frown, she goes back to the letter.

If the good Lord should will it that way, please know that I shall always be with you, watching over you from above. And though it breaks my heart to say it, I should be nothing but pleased should you find your way into the arms of another, that you may spend the rest of your earthly days fulfilling your dreams of home and family.

Thom steps out into the bright September sunshine, taking a deep breath, and then another, gulping the fresh air like a drowning man who's just been pulled to shore.

Poor Susan, chained to the hospital bed up there for four long months, he thinks, heading down the sidewalk toward home.

Lucky Susan, who in four short months might just have everything she ever wanted . . .

All because she's accepted the risk of a lifetime.

And what are you doing? Thom asks himself with a sudden flicker of anger.

You've never turned away from a challenge, Brannock.

You've accepted every challenge that ever came along . . . until now.

Until Annie.

Why?

Because the stakes are higher than they've ever been. Because he has so much more to lose . . .

But so much more to gain . . .

If he's willing to take the risk.

With a sob, Annie casts aside the letter.

"That's it, isn't it?" Her voice a ragged whisper, she tilts her face into the sun, closing her moist eyes briefly against the blinding rays. "That's what you were trying to tell me, isn't it?"

Now, believing anything is possible, she listens for an answer from above, or beyond, or wherever it is that her husband's soul has come to rest.

She hears no sound but the crashing surf in the distance, washing over what's left of Copper Beach.

No, the beach won't be there forever.

Nothing lasts forever.

You can stand in the sand in a glorious sunset and wish the waves to stop stealing precious grains with every sweep across the shore, but you can't keep it from happening.

All you can do is feel the warm sand beneath your bare toes while it's still there, and watch the brilliant orange orb sink slowly into the western sky, and know that sooner or later, the darkness will give way to the promise of another brilliant dawn.

Annie opens her eyes and wipes her tears.

"I shall always be with you, watching over you from above."

"Thank you," she says softly.

Then, still clutching the precious letters, she walks toward the house, and the old green telephone that still has a dial tone.

As a child, Thom always dreaded Labor Day, knowing that it heralded an end to carefree days in the sun. The first Monday in September meant it was time to trade sleeping in and sailing for a school dormitory and schedules and homework; Popsicles and flashlight tag for wind chills and early nightfall.

Yes, Labor Day used to mean all the good stuff was over.

But maybe now, he thinks, filling his lungs with the crisp morning air, it can mean that the good stuff is just beginning.

Does he dare take another chance?

Does he dare *not* take it?

Abruptly making his decision, Thom reaches into his pocket for the cell phone he turned off back at the hospital.

He flips it open.

Turns it back on.

He's about to dial the number that he has no business knowing by heart . . .

The number, perhaps, that he has no business ever dialing again . . .

When the phone in his hand rings shrilly.

Startled, Thom glances down at the caller ID box, certain it's somebody from the office.

No.

Wonder of wonders . . .

The number on the digital display is precisely the one he was about to dial.

Trembling with anticipation, he presses TALK . . .

Lifts the receiver to his ear . . .

Somehow manages to say, "Hello?"

There's a pause, so excruciating that he almost believes he imagined the ringing, the number . . .

Everything.

Then, a voice so real it takes his breath away says softly in his ear, "Hello . . . it's me."

Epilogue

Did you ever see anything so precious in all your life?" Thom asks Annie, tilting the blue-blanketed bundle in his arms so that she can get a closer look.

"Only twice before," she tells him with a smile, reaching out to stroke his newborn nephew's red cheek. "It's hard for me to believe Milo and Trixie were ever this small."

Thom shakes his head. "It's even harder for me to believe that my mother actually insisted on taking them to FAO Schwartz this afternoon to pick out anything they want for Christmas."

"She has no idea what she's in for," Annie says worriedly. "Trixie wants a life-sized stuffed jungle animal."

Thom chuckles. "I just had a vision of my mother's chauffeur driving uptown with a giraffe's head sticking through the moon roof."

"Don't laugh . . . that's probably exactly what's going to happen."

"I guess it'll be baptism by fire for Grandmother Brannock, hmm?"

"She isn't officially their grandmother . . . yet," Annie reminds him.

"No . . . she has at least six months to learn the ropes," he says, before heading back into the newborn nursery to return little John Wade Jr. to his mama.

Six months.

Annie smiles contentedly, leaning against the wall to wait for Thom.

Their wedding, of course, will be in June, the month that violets and honeysuckle are in bloom. Thom and Annie are hoping for a simple affair in the yard behind Annie's Montauk house, which they'll be keeping, of course, as a summer residence.

Yes, a simple wedding at home, surrounded by precious loved ones and nature's beauty . . .

Although, if Thom's mother and Merlin get their way, it will be the social event of the season.

Amazingly, the formidably icy Lillian Brannock has warmed up to Annie and her children over the past few months. For whatever reason, Thom says, she let go of her theory that Annie might be a man-hungry gold digger.

Annie never told him about her meeting with his mother in the kitchen that day in August, and apparently, Lillian never mentioned it to Thom, either. Nor did she acknowledge it to Annie. When Thom introduced the two women, she acted as though she'd never seen Annie before.

Rather than being insulted, Annie was relieved.

Lillian Brannock's ultimate stamp of approval on the union came just weeks ago, when she gave Thom an heirloom antique engagement ring to present to Annie. It had been in her family since the turn of the century, and as she put it, "I don't care much for old things, anyway."

But Annie didn't miss the twinkle in the old woman's eye the first time she saw the ring on her future daughter-in-law's finger.

"I told you she'd come around," Thom says frequently, almost as though he can't quite believe it himself.

Materializing from beyond a garland-bedecked door with his overcoat draped over his arm and a blue-ribboned cigar in his hand, he's the picture of the beaming uncle.

"I still can't believe my sister is actually a mother," he says, as he and Annie step onto the elevator. "And old Wade is one proud papa. He's back there handing out cigars to everyone who walks by."

"You sound a little wistful," Annie comments, looking up into Thom's eyes.

"Maybe I wouldn't mind being a proud new papa myself someday," he admits. "I love Milo and Trixie with all my heart . . . you know that. But I wouldn't mind having a few more, if you wouldn't."

"A few?"

"One?"

"Maybe two," Anne concedes, buttoning her coat as they head through the lobby.

"Look, it's already getting dark out."

"How late is it?"

"It's four."

Suddenly, pausing in front of the doors to pull on her gloves, Annie remembers something.

"Today is the winter solstice," she tells Thom. "It's the shortest day of the year."

"And the longest night," he says with a suggestive gleam in his eye. "I wonder if my mother feels like hosting a slumber party for Milo and Trixie."

"I wouldn't push it, Thom," Annie says with a laugh.

"Well, I bet Auntie Erika wouldn't mind a couple of overnight guests."

"Even if they come bearing life-sized giraffes?"

"Why not?" Thom holds the door open for Annie and they step out into the chilly December dusk. "Annie, look! It's snowing!"

She gazes up to see white flakes glistening in the glow of the streetlight.

"Do you think we'll actually have a white Christmas?" she asks in wonder.

"That would be a miracle. I don't remember there being a white Christmas here in I don't know how many years."

"Well, nobody knows better than we do," Annie says softly, tucking her hand snugly into his, "that miracles happen."

Talking of their future, they walk toward home through the swirling snowflakes, leaving two sets of footprints on the white-dusted sidewalk.

About the Author

As a metropolitan New York resident, Wendy Markham spends quite a bit of time on eastern Long Island, where an idyllic August trip to Montauk inspired the charming setting for this novel. Oddly, unlike her heroine's ultra-efficient cell phone, Wendy's cell phone didn't receive a signal in Montauk unless she was standing knee deep out in the Atlantic: wonderful on steamy summer afternoons; not so much on brisk autumn-like nights. Although she thoroughly enjoyed writing about Annie's haunted telephone, the author herself is not a big fan of making phone calls to—nor receiving phone calls from—living, breathing people, much less the dearly departed. Because she has been known to go for days without checking her voice mail, you'll be better off e-mailing her at corsistaub@aol.com. Don't forget to check out her website at www.wendymarkham.com.

More
Wendy Markham!

Please turn this page
for a preview of
Bride Needs Groom
available in paperback
October 2005.

Chapter
1

Champagne?"

Mia Calogera glances up from the open Louis Vuitton carry-on in which she's been fruitlessly searching for an emery board, thanks to the security officer who grimly confiscated her prized sapphire nail file at check-in.

"Would you like some?" A smiling female flight attendant is brandishing an open green bottle and a crystal flute.

All right, probably not crystal. But glass. Definitely glass.

Glass beats the plastic-ware they use back in coach, as Mia recalls from her less privileged past, and she greatly prefers champagne to weak coffee that isn't offered until somewhere over Indiana. Or Illinois. Or one of those Midwestern vowel-starting states that Mia has never seen at a closer proximity than twenty-thousand feet. Which is absolutely fine with her, of course.

"Yes. I'd love some champagne. Thank you." Mia smiles back at the flight attendant, who compliments her on her simple tulle headpiece as she pours the bubbly.

"Where did you get it? I'm getting married next summer and I still haven't found a veil I like."

Mia tells her the name of the Madison Avenue bridal salon where she bought everything from her white satin shoes to the corset that enabled her to effortlessly button the low-cut gown's snug and exquisitely beaded bodice.

"Oh, I've heard of that store. It's outrageously expensive, right?"

"Not necessarily." Not if one is on the verge of inheriting a trust fund worth millions.

"Oh, well . . . Cheers." The flight attendant's modest diamond engagement ring sparkles in the September sunshine streaming in the window as she hands the flute to Mia. "And good luck."

"Thank you," Mia says again, lifting her glass in a toast. "Same to you."

Champagne. Perfect! What else would a bride-to-be sip en route to her wedding?

The flight attendant smiles her way across the aisle to the next passenger, an attractive businessman who's been shooting curious sidelong glances in Mia's direction ever since she boarded.

She's been tempted to say, "What's the matter? Haven't you ever seen a bride before?"

But that would open the door to conversation, and Mia isn't in the mood to spend the next six hours chatting. She'd much rather rehash the incredible series of events that led to her elopement. She still hasn't had much opportunity to absorb it all.

Leaning back in her seat, Mia sips from her flute, swallows, and makes a face. Okay, so it isn't Cristal. But the Cristal will be surely flowing tonight in the bridal suite.

Holding her champagne flute in her right hand, careful not to spill any on her white silk gown, she resumes rummaging in her carry-on with her left: the hand that also happens to have a ragged edge on the fourth manicured fingernail. In other words, her ring finger.

Mia's Sicilian grandmother would probably say that's a bad omen. Nana Mona would undoubtedly tell her granddaughter to get off the plane, jump into a cab back to Manhattan, and forget all about getting married.

Fortunately, Nana Mona isn't here.

Unfortunately, neither is an emery board.

Mia zips her bag closed, takes another sip of champagne, and looks around the first class cabin for a fellow passenger who might have smuggled a nail file on board.

Her gaze collides with the businessman's stare from across the aisle. He reddens and quickly turns away.

So does Mia, who tries to ignore a pang of regret as she glances out the window at the sun-splashed autumn morning. In the past, she'd have found herself fending off advances from a guy like that. Or encouraging them, if she were in the mood.

Men have always been drawn to Mia, and vice versa. But those days are over. Her license to flirt is about to be exchanged for a license to wed.

It isn't that she doesn't *want* to get married, because she does.

Never mind that she is *about to* get married, that in fact she *has to* get married . . .

She *wants to* get married. Really.

It's just that she can't help feeling a little sad about all she's leaving behind.

All?

Come on, Mia.

Well okay, then it's just that she can't quite quell the age-old instinct to engage in a little benign flirtation with every red-blooded male that crosses her path.

But she's quickly discovered that this wedding gown is to red-blooded men as a cross-shaped garlic necklace is to vampires.

So it's probably a good thing she overcame her initial reluctance and opted to wear it on the flight after all. It was Derek's idea. He's meeting her at the airport.

"I'll be the one in the white tuxedo with the yellow rose buttoniere," he said, giving her pause.

Pause because white tuxedos can be tacky, in Mia's opinion, and yellow roses are bad luck, according to Nana Mona.

But Mia quickly pushed her doubts aside. If she believed all of Nana's crazy Sicilian superstitions, she wouldn't be on this plane in the first place. Fridays, according to Nana, are an unlucky day to begin a voyage. Nana would never consider leaving Astoria on a Friday if she couldn't be back well before nightfall, much less embarking on a cross-country journey and married life all in one shot.

But you don't believe that stuff . . .

Do you?

Of course not, Mia retorts to her wishy-washy inner self, lifting her chin stubbornly.

Yellow roses are not bad luck. And on the right person, a white tuxedo might be downright elegant.

Derek is most definitely the right person. As in *Mr. Right* person.

Didn't that sidewalk psychic tell Mia years ago that one day she would marry a man whose name started with a D and ended with a K sound?

"You mean like Dick?" a befuddled teenaged Mia had asked the woman, who nodded.

At the time, the only Dicks with whom Mia was acquainted were AARP card carriers. In her own generation, boys were called Richard and Richie and Rick, but not Dick. Not in the nickname capacity, anyway.

"Maybe you're going to marry a sugar daddy, then," her friend Lenore suggested on the subway back to Queens.

"Yeah, and maybe that psychic couldn't predict the future if it had already happened," Mia retorted.

"Huh?"

"Never mind," Mia muttered, and forgot all about the prophecy until Derek came into her life.

Now here she is, going to the chapel . . .

More specifically, the Chapel of Luv.

The unorthodox spelling probably shouldn't bother her. And it doesn't. Not really. It's just that . . .

Well, she can't help wondering whether this whole thing wouldn't feel a lot more official if she were going to the Chapel of Love.

But Derek made all the arrangements, and she trusts him implicitly. As implicitly as one can trust a future husband whom one has never met.

Yes, Mia trusts Derek, and she trusts her instincts.

This is the right choice.

Never mind that it's her *only* choice.

She's goin' to the chapel and she's gonna get mah-hah-harried . . .

Yes, and just in the nick of time, Mia thinks, smoothing the folds of her long white silk skirt before fastening her seatbelt across her lap.

"Here you go, Mr. Chickalini," the pretty blonde gate attendant drawls, stapling something to his ticket and handing it across the counter. "We're boarding now. In fact, you might want to hurry on over. Takeoff is in a few minutes."

"Too bad," Dom tells her, flashing a flirtatious smile. "If I weren't about to leave town for the weekend I'd ask you for your phone number."

She giggles, her cheeks tinting pink. "Really? Well, if I weren't happily married, I'd definitely give it to you."

Married? She isn't even wearing a ring. Dom checked, out of habit, when he rushed up to the counter, running late as usual.

"Oh, well," he says now. "Can't win 'em all." With an arm swinging, finger-snapping "Darn!" gesture, he strides away from the counter, toward the statuesque, uniformed redhead waiting beside the open jetway. She, too, is married, he notes, following a perfunctory glance at her left hand.

After checking his ticket, tearing off the stub, and handing it back to him, she says, "Have a nice flight, Mr. . . . Chickeno, is it?"

It isn't, but Dom nods, accustomed to the butchered pronunciation of his surname. The redhead pronounces the first syllable *sheik* and invokes poultry with the remainder; the blonde at the counter's southern accent made it even more unintelligible.

Oh, well. Attractive women can get away with quite a bit, as far as Dom is concerned. Even attractive *married* women.

Striding along the jetway with his carry-on over his shoulder, he contemplates the fact that the world—at least, his little corner of it—is primarily populated by married women. And married men.

Married couples. They're everywhere lately, touting wedded bliss as though they're part of some pro-bono campaign for the World Organization of Happily Ever After. How can everyone Dom ever knew be living happily ever after? His older sisters, Nina and Rosalie; his brother, Pete; his best friend, Maggie; his cousins, his neighbors, his college fraternity brothers. Even his kid brother Ralphie just got engaged.

Dom's summer Saturday nights were mainly spent at weddings, engagement parties, bachelor parties, even a couples shower, at which Dom was the only solo attendee. He'd have brought a date, but he was afraid the bridal theme might give an unattached woman ideas.

Hell, mere dinner and a movie tend to give unattached women ideas these days.

It's no wonder that Dom himself is getting ideas. Against his will, of course.

Well, he's going to put a stop to that. Nothing like a decadent weekend in Vegas to remind a red-blooded guy that footloose and fancy-free is the way to go.

Footloose and fancy-free has always been Dom's specialty.

That's why this new advertising sales position for the

MAN cable network is going to be perfect for him. Being an agency executive was far too constrictive. All that time stuck behind a desk, at the client's beck and call . . .

It's a wonder Dom not only lasted as long as he did, but managed an accelerated climb up the corporate ladder. Maggie likes to remind him that only his charm got him up the ranks in account management, and she's right.

Dom's fairly sure that's how he snagged this gloriously high-paying, flexible job at MAN. It certainly didn't hurt that the ad sales director who hired him happens to be a woman. A newly divorced woman who must be partial to dark-haired, dark-eyed men like Dom.

How else could he have beaten all those better qualified, Ivy-League educated, more polished candidates?

The old Chickalini charm. Yes, sir. That's the name of the game in Dom's world, and there's nothing wrong with getting by on that and good looks. No matter what eye-rolling Maggie and his sisters say.

At the door of the plane, Dom comes to a halt as two male flight attendants attempt to wrestle a double baby stroller into submission.

"Press that latch," one is saying.

"No, first we have to turn it upside down," the other retorts.

"Not until after you press the latch."

"Are you sure?"

When neither pressing the latch nor turning the stroller upside down proves effective in collapsing it, both men glance up at Dom.

"Don't look at me," he says with a shrug. "I have no idea how to fold that thing."

Nor is he in any rush to board a flight that contains at least two babies.

Not that Dom has anything against babies.

His world isn't just teeming with married couples; it's crawling with children. He relishes being Uncle Dom, whose pockets are filled with bubble gum and quarters to pull out of tiny ears.

But this morning, he isn't Uncle Dom.

He's a businessman en route to a convention in Sin City after a late night of revelry, and he wouldn't mind a little peace and quiet along the way.

"Try pressing the latch again," one flight attendant urges the other, who obliges.

Naturally, nothing happens.

"Let's leave it here," the latch-happy attendant whispers conspiratorially.

"What about the passenger?"

"What about her? She can buy another one in Vegas."

Dom has been to Vegas enough times to realize it isn't the most kid-friendly destination. He can't help intervening on behalf of the hapless parent who will be forced to man-handle two kids and a mountain of luggage to the hotel after an exhausting cross-country flight.

He steps forward with a gruff, "here, let me take a look," and in two seconds flat has the stroller folded and ready to stow.

"How'd you do that?" asks one of the dumbfounded stewards.

Dom, who isn't quite certain how he did that, shrugs.

"You must have one at home."

"A stroller? Me?" Dom laughs. "Nope."

"You're not a daddy?"

"Nope. I'm not even a hubby . . . and I don't plan to be anytime soon. Or ever." Dom wonders why he finds it necessary to make that clear to two men whom he suspects aren't in the market for wives, either . . . but for vastly different reasons than his.

Lest they have the wrong idea about him, he adapts his most heterosexual stride as he steps at last over the threshold onto the plane.

To the right is coach class, where passengers are jamming themselves into center seats, or struggling to load baggage into overhead bins, or casting wary glances toward the crying babies that seem to be everywhere.

To his left is first class, cordoned off by drawn curtains.

Dom goes left, grateful for the frequent flier mileage upgrade in his hand.

He parts the curtains and is greeted by a welcome hush and a pretty female flight attendant, who pauses with an open bottle of champagne poised in her hand and asks to see his ticket.

"You're right up there in the second row by the window, Mr. Chickalini," she informs him with a blue-eyed gaze that's somehow both sultry and cheerful.

She even comes fairly close to pronouncing his name correctly.

"Perfect. Thank you."

She turns back to the seated couple in front of him, saying over her shoulder, "I'll be out of your way in just a moment so that you can get to your seat."

"Take your time."

He admires the view of her curvy posterior until a

glance at her left hand reveals a diamond engagement ring. Why is he surprised?

And why is he disappointed?

There are plenty of single women in the world. Certainly, there are in Las Vegas. After he checks into the hotel, he'll head right down to the pool and check them out.

Babes in bikinis. Yes, he tells himself firmly, that's just what the doctor ordered after a crazy work week and a traffic-clogged cab ride to insanely busy LaGuardia airport.

Babes in bikinis?

The thing is . . .

Dom is tired.

Not just from work and traffic and endless lines. No, it goes deeper than that.

Try as he might to conjure enthusiasm for a long weekend in Sin City, Dom suddenly isn't entirely certain he has the energy to . . . sin.

He wonders, as he watches the flight attendant's diamond engagement ring twinkling like a beacon in the sunlight, whether maybe it's a sign.

Maybe all of this—the married women, the seeming abundance of gold bands and diamond rings, even the baby stroller—are signs that it's time for Dom to settle down.

After all, he's pushing thirty.

No Chickalini man has ever retained his bachelorhood past his thirtieth birthday. A few have reclaimed it after failed marriages, but nobody in the family ever successfully avoided the altar for a full three decades.

Dom always intended to be the first.

Especially considering the fact that he's never found anybody he can even remotely conceive of spending the rest of his life with.

But now . . .

Now, he can't help wondering whether somebody's trying to tell him something. Somebody upstairs. Somebody with a divine plan.

The Chickalini family is very big on divine plans. And on signs. Especially Dom's grandmother and his sisters.

A dream about somebody you haven't seen in awhile is a sign that you should call them right away because something—good or bad—is going on with them.

An ATM machine that isn't working properly is a sign that you shouldn't be spending the cash you intended to get.

A rained out baseball game is a sign that your team would have lost if they had played.

"But the other team is rained out, too," Dom always pointed out. "And somebody has to win."

Nobody ever had a satisfactory reply to that, because signs, as Dominic's family tends to believe, aren't meant to be questioned. They're meant to be noted, and perhaps heeded as advice or warnings, as the case might be. Signs mean somebody upstairs is trying to tell you something, and you'd better listen.

Dom watches the flight attendant pouring champagne for a pair of cooing, cuddling newlyweds.

How does he know they're newlyweds?

For one thing, they're wearing matching rings and gazing into each other's eyes, something long-married couples rarely do, as far as Dom can tell. For another thing, the flight attendant tells them to enjoy their honey-moon.

Honeymoons, newlyweds, rings . . .

Signs.

You've got marriage on the brain for some reason, that's your problem, Dom scolds himself. *You're getting all worked up over nothing. This is ridiculous.*

He's going to stop looking for meaning in every little coincidence. After all, it's not as though there's a neon billboard flashing *Get Married* in his face, or his dream woman popping up in a wedding gown begging him to say I Do.

Now *that* would be a sign.

Anything less earth-shattering is mere coincidence and not the slightest threat to the unprecedented achievement in Chickalini bachelorhood.

"All set, Mr. Chickalini."

"Thank you." Eager to sit back and relax for the next six hours, Dom at last steps around the flight attendant and down the aisle . . .

Then stops short in front of his designated row.

There, in all her silken white glory, a halo of sunlight beaming through the window to cast her in an actual glow, is the most beautiful woman—the most beautiful *bride*—he's ever seen.

THE EDITOR'S DIARY

Dear Reader,

Like a breath of fresh air, love has a funny way of putting a little extra spring in your step and sparkle in your eyes. And, oh what a difference it is when you've just been through a bad patch. Need a little help keeping your faith in love? Try our two Warner Forever titles this March.

Booklist has called **Wendy Markham's** work "breezy, scrumptious fun" while *Romantic Times BOOKClub* raves it's "wonderfully touching romance with a good sense of humor." Check out her latest, **HELLO, IT'S ME**, and don't forget the tissues! It's been almost a year since Annie Harlowe's beloved husband died, leaving her to raise their two children. But she has a secret: she's been paying his cell phone bills just so she can hear his voice. Yet with funds stretched so tight she fears they'll never dig out of debt, Annie has to face the facts. Her late husband will never answer...until one night when the impossible happens and he does. Thomas Brannock IV has had his life mapped out from birth. But he never counted on Annie, a free-spirited woman with sun-kissed cheeks to blow into his life. When they literally crash into one another, it feels like a heavenly accident. But is an angel with cell phone reception playing matchmaker?

Have you ever worked for something your entire life only to find it just isn't enough? That's exactly how Molly Boudreau from **Susan Crandall's PROMISES TO KEEP** feels. After years of work and sacrifice, she's finally a doctor. But she yearns for a soul-stirring connection and she'll soon find it in her own ER. Molly has befriended a young pregnant woman who refuses to speak of her past. Her only request: that Molly protects the baby from his dangerous father. So when the woman is murdered after giving birth, Molly must keep her promise. Fearing for their safety, she returns home where she passes him off as her son. But before long, Dean Coletta, a reporter with smoldering eyes and probing questions, starts digging for the truth. With each explosive fact he uncovers about Molly and her "son," Dean's desire to protect them grows stronger. But can they build a life together with the secrets of their pasts tearing them apart? *Romantic Times BOOKClub* raves that she "weaves a tale that is both creative and enthralling" so prepare to be dazzled.

To find out more about Warner Forever, these March titles and the authors, visit us at www.warnerforever.com.

With warmest wishes,

Karen Kosztolnyik, Senior Editor

P.S. Next month, check out these two spicy little treats: Sandra Hill delivers more laughter and even more hot Cajun love when a confirmed bachelor looking to escape it all winds up in the middle of a kidnapping plot with a tantalizing celebrity in THE RED-HOT CAJUN: and Julie Anne Long debuts her latest witty and heartfelt tale of a barrister who rescues a feisty pickpocket and passes her off as a lady to win another woman's hand in TO LOVE A THIEF.